Tris

Tris

3. Hide & Go Seek

a novel by
Morgan Bruce

Strategic Book Publishing and Rights Co.

Strategic Book Publishing & Rights Co., LLC
USA | Singapore
www.sbpra.net

For information about special discounts for bulk purchases, please contact Strategic Book Publishing and Rights Co. Special Sales, at bookorder@sbpra.net.

ISBN: 978-1-68235-508-4

TRIS

3. Hide & Go Seek

This novel, as with the seven 'Accidental Angel' books which serve as a prequel to this quadrilogy, is rather obviously, a work of fiction. Although references are made to some localities that exist in England, Scotland, New Zealand and America in the current decade — the time and location in which the story is set — in general, the names, characters and incidents portrayed in it, relating to the main story are totally the work of the author's imagination. This also includes the names of some towns, such as Erinsmuir and Oakton, and also Oakton Middle School and Pinehurst North Middle School. The churches and homeless shelters listed for New York — such as St. Josephs, St. Barnards, St. Peters, etc. — are also total fabrications, to avoid impugning any existing church group within the city. In these regards, any resemblance to actual persons, living or dead, is entirely coincidental.

DEDICATION

This third book of the Tris series – a sequel to the 'Accidental Angel' heptalogy – is, firstly, dedicated to my mother, Ailsa, who delighted in reading the first four books of the 'Accidental Angel' books while on a short sojourn in hospital, but who died, a little unexpectedly, one week after I'd completed the fifth book. I take solace in knowing that she, most likely, has been able to read it, and the final two books of that series, over my shoulder while I have been writing and revising. A second dedication is to my father, Jack, who passed away two years – almost to the exact hour – after my mother. Similarly, he always encouraged me to achieve my best and always led by example as a wonderfully supportive and caring parent for his children, grandchildren and great grandchildren.

Thanks for support in completing this third book of the 'Tris' series, must also go to the rest of my immediate family; most particularly, my two daughters, Tanith and Kerensa, who have given me the encouragement to fulfill a dream of being a writer. A very special thanks must also be given to the late Liz MacDiarmid who was always happy to be a proofreader for all my first drafts ideas... making corrections and suggestions where she felt necessary. A thank you also to Rod McLeay who also acted as a proofreader and sounding board for my ideas and concepts.

And finally, special thanks must go to my younger daughter – Kerensa – who designed and drew the cover image for the series.

Other novels by Morgan Bruce

PRAGUE – 2009

PIECES OF THE PUZZLE - 2015

ALEXEI, ACCIDENTAL ANGEL -'Beginnings' – 2016

ALEXEI, ACCIDENTAL ANGEL - 'Intervention'– 2016

ALEXEI, ACCIDENTAL ANGEL - 'Nemesis' –2017

ALEXEI, ACCIDENTAL ANGEL - 'Brothers' – 2017

ALEXEI, ACCIDENTAL ANGEL - 'Revelation' – 2017

ALEXEI, ACCIDENTAL ANGEL - 'Crowns' – 2018

ALEXEI, ACCIDENTAL ANGEL – 'Dénouement' – 2018

A SKIP IN TIME – 2020

WALTER'S CHILD – 2020

TRIS 1 - 'The Miracle Child' – 2021

TRIS 2 - 'Vipers' Nest' – 2021

TRIS 3 - 'Hide And Seek' – 2021

TRIS 4 - 'Hidden Dangers' – 2022

YOU DON'T ASK WHY!

The 'Tris' series is a sequel to, and a continuation of, the Alexei, Accidental Angel stories… but set twenty years later.

TRIS

Hide and Go Seek

Chapters

PROLOGUE....

'The most beautiful thing we can experience is the mysterious...'
Albert Einstein.

Tris quickly sat up, as a voice seemed to sound in his head; a voice that also seemed to somehow convey a strong sense of desperation. And yet, within it, there also seemed a sense of some inevitability of not being able to succeed. As if the odds of success would eventually be too great!

'Not again,' he thought. Instantly reminded of the prayers that he'd once heard from Matthew Ryan. At the same time, he knew that it wouldn't be the boy whom most of Oakton now believed was dead. After all, he'd just spent over half the afternoon splashing around in the pool playing team-tag with his new friend, along with Carwyn and Finn. Despite the fact that it was still not quite into Spring and the weather was still particularly chilly, the fact that the pool complex was enclosed and heated made it a perfect play area. Glancing at the green fluorescent numbering of his bedside clock he realised that it was 5:37. For a moment, he felt puzzled. Wondering how he could possibly have fallen asleep in his clothes and slept through a whole night. Then, the smell of an evening meal cooking, drifting from the kitchen down to his bedroom, had him realising that it was actually still late afternoon; in fact, not too far off dinnertime. The half-opened book still lying to one side of his pillows, an indication that he'd, somehow, fallen asleep on his bed while reading.

Almost as he felt a slight relief in that fact, the voice was suddenly in his head again. It was still a cry for help, but unlike when Matthew had been in trouble, it seemed different, somehow. Different in that it didn't seem to be directed to him in any specific way. Seeming almost as if he was simply listening in on the private thoughts of a person preoccupied with where they were running, in the hope of getting away from something that they feared. Thoughts that conveyed a sense of being extremely scared of the likelihood of being cornered and recaptured. Also intermingled with the desire for an escape, was a commentary of mixed thoughts. Almost as if whoever was in danger was thinking their moves aloud, perhaps just a means of staying ahead of their pursuers and avoiding capture.

"Dodge left past the big trees…. then keep going down the slope… as fast as you can," the voice he was hearing seemed to say, even as the thoughts accompanying it contained an almost subliminal plea for assistance. "Keep your knees up so it's easier getting through the snow… you can lose them if you just keep going! If you can just get away from the hospital, you'll soon find someone to protect you!"

Taking a gamble that if he kept himself invisible he could always assess the situation and leave, if it turned out to be something that Mykael, or Ithuriel, might feel would be best avoided, he locked in on the cry and made a visualisation. He ended up looking down on an area of snow-covered forest that ended, rather abruptly, at a cliff edge. The edge of the bluff dropped steeply down to a slow-flowing river. A little to his left, and heading in his direction, he could just make out the fleeting images of people; some of them with nets and dogs on leashes, in pursuit of someone running through the forest. A person dressed in a white gown. The person who seemed to be the source of what he was hearing.

Alighting at the edge of the bluff, he quickly hurried through the trees and the snowfall, towards the direction that they seemed to be headed. A moment later, he suddenly emerged into a small clearing. Like the rest of the forest, it was awash with almost knee-deep snow. The other person there, however, was a girl… a girl who appeared, at least to Tris's hasty reckoning, to be of a similar age to himself. More startling, however, was the fact that she also had wings.

Quickly hurrying towards the centre of the clearing; having to almost wade through the deep snowfall, until he was beside her, Tris then made himself visible. The girl immediately staggered away from him in fright. Losing her footing in the process and ending up on her back in the snow; scrambling rapidly backwards as if trying to avoid an unexpected capture. For a moment, there was silence as they both eyed each other. There was something familiar about her face that Tris couldn't quite place. Almost as if they'd met before, or he'd seen her picture somewhere.

"You're like me," the girl then exclaimed in some astonishment. She got quickly to her feet, hastily brushed the snow off her flimsy gown, and then moved a little closer. Tris gave a slight nod.

"So why are you here?" the girl continued, before he had a chance to verbalise a reply, or a question of his own. At the same time, she began to look around, nervously, as the sound of barking dogs could be heard, their pursuit starting to sound rather menacing, as they seemed to be getting ever closer.

"I heard you calling for help. Like, in my mind," Tris began to explain, as the girl suddenly grabbed his hand and began hauling him towards the edge of the clearing. Trying to lead him towards the cover of the trees from where he'd just come, and, perhaps unknowingly, towards the edge of the cliff.

"We've got to keep running," she exclaimed, as Tris seemed unwilling to follow. "They're after me." She paused a moment as she again looked at Tris's wings. "Well, now it'll be both of us. And if they catch us, they'll lock us up in cages so we can't get away."

"Can't you just fly, or 'be'?" Tris queried, moving rather slowly after her. "Or just make yourself invisible?" The girl immediately stopped tugging at his arm. Looking anxiously past him in the direction of the sound of the chasing pack, before focussing her gaze on him once again.

"We can do that?" she queried bemusedly, even as she still seemed to be warily listening to the sound of the pursuit.

"You haven't had anyone to show you how?" Tris responded. The girl shook her head and then reached out for his hand once again.

"They're getting closer," she said, now looking rather alarmed. "Come on! We have to run. We have to try to get to the river so that they'll..."

"Trust me," Tris answered. He quick took hold of her hands and drew her in close. For a moment the girl seemed extremely scared. So much so, that Tris was sure he could feel her heart pounding in her chest as he clasped her tight. Then, the look on her face began to turn to total astonishment as they both faded into opaqueness.

"We're actually invisible to anyone else. It's a trick you'll learn," Tris whispered. Watching, perhaps also just a little nervously, as three large tracker dogs suddenly bounded into the clearing, followed very closely by a group of men with nets and guns.

"Trust me. Stay very still, and don't say a word," Tris whispered, still holding her close in his grasp. Thankful that, as a result of the closeness of their embrace, her right ear was close to his face. "And don't worry, I can get us away from here in an instant, if I need to. I just want to see what's going on."

Staying as motionless as statues, Tris and the girl watched, as the dogs appeared to sniff at the ground around their feet. One of them, it seemed, began to sniff at their clothes. Not that it could actually see anything. As the girl tried to move a little, to get away from it, Tris kept a tight hold of her and quickly made them both intangible.

"Keep very still," he whispered very softly. "Don't worry. No one can touch us, or see us." The girl seemed to relax a little as the dogs suddenly began to circle just a little more widely around them. Sniffing at the surrounding bushes, perhaps trying to pick up the scent of a new trail.

"The damn dogs must've caught the scent of bloody rabbit droppings or a deer, or something," one of the men shouted rather irritatedly. Quickly clipping an extra short lead to the collar of one of the dogs, he began pulling it away from where it, and the others, had been snuffling around a couple of stunted shrubs close to where Tris had emerged into the clearing.

"Which way do you think she went?" the second man hastily asked, slinging his rifle back over his shoulder, grabbing his net and looking around at the ground. The first man pointed down at the path Tris had made in the snow, when he'd first approached the girl.

"It must be this way," the man with the dog on a lead shouted, pulling his dog after him. The other dogs quickly followed. All of them leaping and baying in eagerness, as they seemed to pick up some sort of trail. Tris watched as the dogs headed off into the scrub, followed by the armed men with their nets. Intent on a trail that, he knew, would very soon end with nothing but a cliff edge and empty space.

"What's your name?" he whispered, when it seemed that the trackers had gone.

"Lara," the girl murmured a little nervously. Tris gave a slight nod.

"I'm Tris. If you come with me, I can take you to where you'll be safe," he said brightly. "I live on an island where the idea of angels is quite accepted."

"I'm an angel?" Lara queried, quickly looking totally bemused at the whole idea.

"Of course," Tris replied.

"So I'm not a freak? Or a mutant, or something?"

"Of course not!" laughed Tris rather softly. "And on the island where I live there are quite a lot of us. Not all as young as you and me of course, although they can be if they want. But it's a safe place where no one can hurt you."

"But how do we get there?" Lara asked. She began looking around a little nervously as the sound of dogs barking and the men shouting seemed to grow a little louder once again. They'd obviously found that the trail ended at a cliff edge.

"That's easy," Tris replied. "We just think ourselves home." Shifting his hold on her so that they were now not quite so close, but still face to face, he made a quick visualisation of his bedroom.

***

The slamming of a door, elsewhere in the house, followed by various voices, quickly awakened Rylan from his slumber, and dreams of being high above the earth; almost as if he'd been, somehow, up in the clouds. Instantly alert, he quickly threw off the duvet he'd grabbed for warmth and rolled onto his stomach to face towards the main part of the room. Having retreated to his hiding place under the bed shortly after midday so that there was no likelihood of his being spotted through a window, and after putting the remnants of his meal and its wrapping into the rubbish and the towels he'd used after his shower into the laundry hamper, he wasn't too sure of how long he'd slept. Or whether it was still daytime or now night.

He lay still, hardly daring to breath. Listening carefully as younger voices aired complaints about why they hadn't been able to stay away skiing for just a few more days. The children's higher voices, quickly counterpointed by the father's lower rumblings about the need for him to be at work if they wanted to be able to afford more such fun times in the future. From somewhere else in the house came the soft sound of music, starting up. He recognised the song as being by Benee — the young girl singer from New Zealand who'd taken the charts by storm over the past year or so. Another teenage girl's voice seemed to be singing along to the music.

In contrast to the music, the scattered noise of the conversations, and other goings on in the house, Rylan remained totally silent. Not daring to even move, as he began trying to figure out possible ways to get out of the place without being seen and the likely chances of his having been in the house being discovered before he could make an escape. For a start, he quickly tried to remember everything he'd done since the start of the day. Whether he'd put everything away after his meal, whether he'd turned on any lights anywhere; or possibly left any other telltale signs that would alert the family to there having been someone in their house.

All too soon, it seemed, his thoughts were distracted as he heard footsteps approaching. From his hiding place, he then saw a pair of feet wearing expensive Nike trainers, as a boy entered the room and dropped a large rucksack beside the bed, effectively cutting off half his view; more especially that of the doorway. He felt the bed move a little as the boy sat down on it, rather heavily, and began to remove his shoes.

"Mum, did you take my extra duvet for washing?" the boy suddenly called out. "You know, my favourite one? The one with all the soccer balls on it?" Rylan looked at the duvet that he was clutching, and had been using as a covering; quickly noticing the pattern of goalposts and soccer balls.

"Have you looked for it? Properly?" a woman's voice answered from elsewhere in the house.

"It's not anywhere on my bed," the boy called in response. "Not where it usually is."

"Well, I know I haven't washed it recently, so it must be there somewhere. I'll come and give you a hand to look for it in a few minutes," the woman's voice replied, with just a slight hint of exasperation. "Just as soon as I've figured out what this plastic bag is doing beside the back door."

Rylan immediately tensed. The 'plastic bag' would be the one containing the underwear wrappings and his old clothes! He'd forgotten that he'd left it there as a reminder to take it with him when he left.

"What plastic bag?" the man's voice suddenly interrupted. Rylan heard footsteps heading, almost in haste, towards the kitchen. "I'm sure I put out all the rubbish before we left."

"It's just some old clothes," the woman's voice continued rather more softly. "Good God! They absolutely stink!"

"They look like they belong to a child," the man's voice rumbled. Rylan could hear the rustle of plastic as the clothes were probably shaken from the bag. "But they're certainly not anything that would have belonged to Henry or Arthur. Look, they're covered in… is that paint? Or blood?"

Before Rylan could contemplate further on what the adults might be thinking about the state of his old clothes, he suddenly realised that the duvet had been yanked from his grasp and a pair of blue eyes were looking at him.

"Mum! Dad!" the boy called loudly. He hurriedly scrambled away from the bed towards the far wall of the room, where he remained seated on the floor; his eyes locked on Rylan's.

CHAPTER ONE

A New Home....

In an instant, Tris was back in his bedroom, still holding on tight to Lara. As they stayed clinging together for a moment, he suddenly felt a little shocked in realising that the hand that he had on the girl's back, just a little below her wings, was touching bare skin. Looking quickly down, he realised that the dress he thought she'd been wearing was actually just a hospital smock; a simple 'neck to mid-thigh' covering, that was now hanging half-open at the back. He immediately remembered the embarrassment of having to wear such garments when he'd been hospitalised with a broken arm, when he was eight. As if also suddenly remembering what she was wearing, a little belatedly, Lara hastily reached an arm behind her to clutch the two halves of the gown together to cover the lower part of her back and behind.

"Mum," Tris called, quickly releasing the girl from his grip. "Come quickly. I need your help."

"What's the prob..." Amanda began to ask as, a moment later, she hurried into Tris's room, only to stop short at the sight that greeted her, leaving whatever she had been about to say incomplete.

"Her name's Lara and she's like me," exclaimed Tris excitedly. "She's got wings."

"Well, I can see that," Amanda said, giving the newcomer a warm smile.

"I had to bring her here because she was being chased by some men with dogs and nets," Tris hastily continued. "And... and they also had guns!"

Quickly noting the hospital smock that the girl was wearing, and the fact, by the way the girl had an arm behind her, that it seemed to be partly unfastened at the back, Amanda hastily grabbed the spare blanket that was folded up on the end of Tris's bed and carefully draped it around the girl's shoulders.

"That will keep you warmer and a little better covered," she said softly. "And don't worry, you're completely safe, here." The girl seemed to give her some careful scrutiny, perhaps wondering if this woman, who seemed to be the Tris's mother, also had wings. At the same time, Amanda turned her attention to Tris.

"Send out a thought to Andrew... and to Mykael and Ithuriel," she said hastily. "Tell them that we have a small emergency. Then go and get your dad."

"Already here," a voice said from the doorway, as Joshua arrived. "And I see we've got another special visitor."

"She's just like me," Tris reiterated excitedly. "She's got wings, and..." Any further conversation quickly stalled, as Lara's eyes widened in astonishment at the sight of three further adults suddenly just appearing out of thin air... all of them with wings.

"Hmmm," Mykael mused with a rather warm smile. He quickly glanced towards Tris, giving what seemed an almost resigned shake of his head. "It seems that this time you've brought home a stray angel," he continued with remarkable casualness. His manner so matter-of-fact that it made Tris wonder if his guardian had, somehow, already expected for this to happen.

"At least it makes a pleasant change from the usual," Ithuriel murmured. "Severely beaten children."

"Her name's Lara, and... and she's got wings. Just like me," exclaimed Tris for a third time, and rather unnecessarily seeing as both Mykael and Ithuriel had already made that observation.

"So I see," Mykael replied. Smiling a little in perhaps noting Tris's excitement, he then turned towards Amanda and Joshua.

"Will it be all right if she stays here with you?" he quietly asked. "At least, until we find out a bit more about what's going on with this situation?"

"I don't want to go back to the cage," Lara whispered rather softly, moving just a little closer to Tris. Almost immediately, Tris put an arm around her shoulders, a little protectively. As if to make it obvious that, as far as he was concerned, she should stay... permanently.

"Of course she can stay," Amanda hastily responded. "We can put her in the spare room. She can be here for as long as she needs." In the back of her thoughts was the comment that Mykael had made just a few weeks earlier about the whole situation with Oakton, and the events that had led to the arrest of Matthew Ryan's stepfather, William Daniels, Pastor Isaac and Jessica Scott, not yet being fully dealt with. At the same time, it seemed strange to even think that this find of a girl-angel might, be in any way, connected to those sordid events. Perhaps it wasn't, and this new arrival was merely a coincidence. Not that it really mattered. If the girl-angel needed a place to stay, then she and Joshua would be more than happy to look after her. More so, because she realised, looking at Tris, that to send the girl elsewhere, would very likely upset him even more than when Mykael had insisted that Matthew Ryan had had to return to Oakton.

With an almost weary exhale of breath Mykael gave a subtle glance at his watch. The action appearing to indicate that he and

Ithuriel were urgently needed elsewhere, and that, somehow, it was also somewhere they'd rather not be.

"Unfortunately, we both have other pressing commitments," he eventually said, with a slight sideways tilt of his head, and glancing towards Ithuriel. "And, no doubt, Lara is rather overwhelmed by what has happened, today. Therefore, I think it would be better to leave any further discussion about where she has been and what happens next, until the morning." He leant in a little closer to Lara.

"And don't you worry," he said softly. "There is no way whatsoever that you'll ever be sent back to where you were. You just have a good night's sleep. We'll talk further in the morning."

"So, I can stay here?" Lara asked just a little unsurely. "For good?" The fact that Tris was with her, and no one seemed to be keeping him restrained, caged, or locked up in any way, had already made her start to feel as if this would also be a safe place for her to stay.

"Most likely," Mykael replied. "After all, it's the safest place for you to be," he added as if reading her thoughts.

"It's where all the child angels live," Tris quickly added.

"You mean... you mean, that... that there are more of us?" Lara stammered, almost with a sudden sense of total bewilderment.

"At times," Mykael casually replied. He turned towards Andrew, Joshua and Amanda. "Nine o'clock tomorrow morning be okay for a meeting?" he suggested. Joshua and Amanda both nodded, almost simultaneously. Andrew responded with a casual shrug.

"Okay by me," he murmured.

"I'll pop up to the farm in the morning and get some of Grandma Betty's special shortbread," Tris added excitedly.

"We still have enough from last time you visited," Joshua countered rather calmly. "And some of her fruit cake. I think, for the moment, it would be better for you to just help out here, with Lara."

"I could take her with me," Tris countered. Mykael gave a hasty shake of his head.

"Let's just keep her on the island, for the moment," he softly suggested, in a manner that still strongly implied that Tris should not do otherwise. "I'd venture to suggest that it will be much safer for her to just remain out of sight for a while. Especially if there are people after her." With a nod towards Andrew, Amanda and Joshua, he and Ithuriel then disappeared, once again leaving Lara rather open-mouthed. Amanda immediately took charge and began to delegate tasks.

"Right," she said almost a little brusquely. "Josh, I'll get you to add a little bit to what's on the go for tea, so that there's enough for all of us." She quickly turned to Lara. "You'll be hungry, I take it?" she asked. Lara gave a cautious nod of her head. Appearing just a little perplexed as to how, one moment it had been just after lunch and yet it was evening time where Tris had taken her. As Joshua headed off towards the kitchen, Amanda turned to Tris.

"I'll get you to check out the spare bedroom. Make sure that the heaters are on and that the blinds are drawn for the night and that there's nothing stacked on the bed. When you've done that, you can go and give Andrew a hand. He'll be up at the old house." Tris hastily headed off to check on the spare room.

"And I'll be...?" Andrew asked, leaving the sentence incomplete. Amanda took hold of Lara's hand.

"I'm just going to get Lara through a shower," she said rather abruptly. Perhaps noting that the girl's hair was rather tangled and not too clean. "I need you to go up to see Rowanne and Amy and ask if there would be any of their girls' 'hand-me-downs' that we could make use of. I'm thinking... skirts, tops, jeans, shorts, underwear, socks, shoes, nightwear, etc. In fact, anything that she thinks might be useful and acceptable for a young girl to wear. Give Tris a visualisation when you're there, so that he knows where to find you."

"Won't they be a little bit puzzled about what we want them for?" Andrew queried.

"You can tell them that Tris has brought us another refugee. This time, a little girl," Amanda replied. She sighed softly. "Just try not to mention too much about her having wings, as yet."

When they'd all gone, Amanda quickly threw the spare blanket back onto Tris's bed and led Lara towards the bathroom. Noting, with some slight shock, as she did so, that not only was the gown not capable of being fastened properly at the back, apart from having a couple of overlapping Velcro strips placed lower down, seemingly to enable Lara's wings to be clear of her clothes, but that the girl also appeared to be without proper underwear.

'Where on earth have you been kept? And what's been going on in your young life?' were the questions immediately in her thoughts. Along with the idea of getting a complete medical check arranged to confirm if the girl had been abused in any way. Maybe they'd learn some detail of that, tomorrow, when they had the meeting with Mykael and Ithuriel and were perhaps able to find out more about the girl's past. The thought of her being dressed in such a state and on the run from men with dogs and guns sounded rather chilling.

"Come on," she said brightly, directing Lara into the bathroom. "Let's get you through a nice warm shower."

A few moments later in the bathroom, with Lara having taken off the hospital gown and the paper pants she was wearing, Amanda was pleased to note that, outwardly, the girl showed no signs of bruising, or scrapes, or of having been physically abused.

Nor did she show any visible signs of approaching puberty. At the same time, however, the girl's decided lack of reticence in undressing had her a little just a little bothered. Did it hint of something untoward in her past?

"Do you want to take off your necklace?" Amanda quietly asked, as she turned on the shower. Lara shook her head.

It doesn't come off," she said softly. "There's no catch or anything that I can find to undo it." Amanda gave it a quick scrutiny, finding that, as Lara had just said, there was no visible catch.

"So how long have you been wearing it?" she asked. Lara gave a shrug as she reached out to test the temperature of the shower.

"It was just there when I woke up one morning. You know, like… when I was in the specialist hospital. The military people just told me that it was a special present from the Holts. They were my foster-parents," she hastily added by way of explanation.

***

Arriving back with arms full of clothing, Andrew and Tris placed them onto the bed in the spare bedroom. As Tris made to rush off, Andrew put an arm out to stop him.

"It might be helpful just to sort them out a bit," he suggested, placing the new underwear, that he'd sidetracked to get from a shop in Erinsmuir, carefully to one side where it would be immediately noticeable. With a slightly impatient sigh, Tris began quickly sorting out the jeans, skirts and socks into separate piles, while Andrew moved on to sorting out various tops.

"We really need to find out who the people that she was running away from were," Tris muttered, once he'd got all the socks sorted into matching pairs. "Because they had guns and nets and… and they looked like soldiers."

"Well, all of that can wait until after the meeting tomorrow morning, I'm sure," Andrew quietly suggested. "Then we can probably get more of a rundown of her life. In the meantime, how about we just let your mum get her properly through a shower, first. I'm sure Lara will probably appreciate a bit of one-on-one mothering."

"So what do we do now?" Tris asked, once they'd completed compiling various basic groups of clothes. Aware that Amanda would easily take care of any further sorting, or matching, that was required.

"Well, we could go and give your dad a hand?" Andrew suggested, putting a hand on Tris's left shoulder and guiding him towards the door; perhaps fully understanding Tris's impatience to know more about Lara, and to spend more time with her, because of the loneliness of his own childhood experiences in hospital. At least until, by some accident of fate, he'd been found by Alexei and Tristan and was then adopted by Steve and Evelyn Robertson. Leaving the spare bedroom, they headed towards kitchen. Noting, as they did so, the soft hiss of the shower suddenly cutting off.

The work in the kitchen eventually proved quite minimal. The addition of an extra vegetable or two to what was already cooking, and the setting of an extra place at the dining table, being of almost no consequence. After some moments of impatient waiting, Tris decided that he'd done enough of 'helping' in the kitchen and headed out to see how his latest 'rescue' was getting on. Not that he'd done all that much to help, aside from putting out an extra set of cutlery. Joshua had already got the food sorted, and Andrew had quickly got onto the task of sorting out some hot drinks for everyone.

Having hurried down the hallway, Tris suddenly stopped. Realising that Lara might still be getting dressed, he knocked quietly on the door to the spare bedroom, and then, having heard a quiet 'come in', slowly opened it. He found that Lara was now sitting on the edge of the bed, wrapped up to her shoulders in a very large fluffy towel, while Amanda was using a blow drier to dry, and comb out, her hair. Given the very fair colour that it now appeared to be, it was obvious that it hadn't been properly washed in quite a while.

Almost before he had a chance to make any sort of comment about the change of colour, there was the sound of a knock at the front door. Without breaking from her combing out of Lara's hair, Amanda signalled, with just her eyes, for him to go and see who it was. Tris immediately hurried away to answer the door. Perhaps a little as to be expected, after the request for clothes, it was his aunties and grandmother... Rowanne, Amy, and Evelyn.

"Just thought we'd call in to see if the clothes were okay," Grandma Evelyn said, giving his hair a quick tousle. "And to see who our latest refugee is," she added. Well prepared, from her own experiences with Alexei and Tristan, to a situation of child-angels finding stray children to rescue.

"Lara and Mum are in the spare bedroom,"Tris replied almost a little belatedly, as the three women then hurried past him.

"So, you found someone else needing help?" Carwyn questioned, as he, Victoria, Melanie and Matthew also hurried inside, accompanied by Uncle Ethan. Melanie and Victoria perhaps more than a little curious to know why their 'girls' clothes' were needed. Tris eagerly nodded a reply.

"Her name's Lara," he said excitedly. "And she's just like me. She's got wings." He quickly continued into a brief explanation of how he'd heard her call for help and the fact that men with dogs and guns had been chasing her.

"So she was being kept as a prisoner?" Melanie queried. Not that it was really a question. More a statement of what was clearly self-evident from his description of the rescue. Nevertheless Tris nodded rather earnestly.

"The men with the dogs had little American flags on the front of their uniforms so I think she must have been in some place in America. Like a military base, or something like that," he quickly continued. "She was being kept in a cage." He lowered his voice a little. "And they didn't even let her have proper underwear!"

"So why didn't she just disappear? You know, teleport? Like you sometimes do?" Carwyn queried. Tris gave a slight shrug.

"I don't think she knows how to, yet," Tris replied. "She didn't even know that she could be invisible. Or even make just her wings invisible."

"And so, obviously, the men with dogs were trying to recapture her," Melanie added with a nod. "Now, can we go through and see her?" she then added, with an obvious air of some impatience.

With Tris leading the way, they quickly headed down the hallway and through to the spare bedroom to find that Lara was now dressed in jeans, but still had a towel draped around the upper part of her body. At the same time, Amanda, Rowanne, Amy and Evelyn were discussing how they were to get her upper body covered and yet still allow her to have her wings free. For a moment, Tris was ready to suggest that she could just wander around bare-chested, like he often did, or could perhaps just wear a big floppy jumper or T-shirt. After all, she had no real chest development, as yet.

"Perhaps she could wear a bikini top?" Evelyn suggested. "Or one of those old-fashioned 'boob-tubes, that were popular in… what was it? The seventies, or…" She left the speculation of when that fashion item had come into existence incomplete. "She could always step into it and pull it up rather than trying to fit it down over her wings."

"Or a cardigan or shirt on backwards?" Melanie offered. "Or maybe just a big jumper, or an oversized T-shirt, like Tris used to do." Tris moved a little closer to Lara.

"Can't you just think your wings through your clothes?" he asked in almost a whisper. "Like I do?" He quickly demonstrated the idea. Lara shook her head, keeping the large towel she had around her upper body tightly closed.

"I don't know how," she whispered.

"It's not too difficult," Tris said still rather quietly. "You just think of it happening." Lara gave him a slightly puzzled look.

"Just imagine an image of yourself standing there with your wings showing through the towel," Tris explained encouragingly. "Like, as if you were looking in a mirror but your wings were showing. Only you just do it in your head." For a moment Lara seemed quiet. Then, all of a sudden her wings were visible outside of the towel, as if, somehow, they'd suddenly passed through its weave.

"That's good," Tris exclaimed. "Once you know how easy it is to do, you can wear normal clothes, instead of big, floppy jumpers or clothes on backwards. Or, even worse, one of those horrible hospital smocks, like you were wearing when I first found you." Lara blushed slightly. Perhaps realising that it was probable that Tris may have also noticed that she had almost nothing on beneath it, earlier.

"Have you ever have to wear them?" she asked quietly. Tris nodded.

"But not for my wings," he said. "I was in a hospital before then. Like, long before I got my wings. I had a bit of an accident while trying to skateboard and broke my arm."

"It's sort of awkward how they fall open at the back if they're not fastened properly," Lara said, with a further slightly embarrassed look. "Even when you try to get them correctly done up."

"I was lucky," Tris responded. "I only had those ones for a very short while, 'cause Mum and Dad managed to find some that wrapped right around so that the fastenings were at the front. Although, with one arm in plaster, I still usually needed help to get them fastened properly." Any further conversation between the two of them was quickly cut short as Amanda took Lara's hand.

"Well, now that you know that you'll soon be able to do that," she said with a smile, "we'll just get the boys to head back to the family room while we sort out something temporary for you to wear up top." As the men and boys began to head back to the family room, Carwyn sidled up to Tris.

"She's quite pretty," he said. Tris nodded a reply.

"It'll be good to have a sister," he said with a smile.

"Or a girlfriend," Carwyn teased. "Given that she looks about the same age as you." Tris scowled at him a little. At the same time, he suddenly half-wondered if maybe that was actually part of the plan for his future.

"Anyway, she'll be a special friend to hang around with," he murmured. "Especially now that Matthew seems to spend most of his time with Melanie." Carwyn nodded, and then, after a glance to see that Matthew and Melanie were not within earshot, leant in a little closer to Tris.

"When Andrew first arrived up home, earlier, asking if there were any older clothes that Melanie might not need any more, we were all, sort of, curious as to what was up," he whispered. "I suppose, if it had been a few weeks ago, I'd have thought that maybe Matthew had finally decided to 'bat for the other side'," he continued, still in a whisper. He sighed softly. "Although, now, what with the way he's always hanging around with my sister, with the two of them always holding hands, I doubt that that's likely to happen! I've even caught them kissing!"

Any further comment in that regard was stalled as the bedroom door opened and the female entourage wandered out to join them. Lara was now wearing a large T-shirt, emblazoned with the words 'I was born to be...' with her wings hidden beneath it.

***

Rylan sat with his head lowered. Not sure as to whether he should look at his captors, eye to eye, or remain quiet and subdued, with his eyes carefully averted. Not that he could really call the family sitting around the table with him, his captors, given the way he'd meekly crawled out from his hiding place, when directed to do so. Neither had they seemed all that angry with him, appearing rather more curious as to who he was, and why it was that he'd decided to break into their house and not somewhere else in the street. The two adults had also taken a little time to work out whether he was a boy or a girl, given his long hair and rather androgynous appearance.

The oldest of the children, a girl who went by the name of Marlow, had seemed to immediately decide that he was obviously a boy, despite the length of his hair, given the clothes that he'd chosen. Of the two boys, Thomas in particular, simply seemed chuffed that Rylan had not only chosen his bedroom to hide in, but was also wearing some of his old clothes. Henry just seemed pleased that they might have gained an extra playmate, even if just for a night.

Their mother, Margaret Fulcher, had, nevertheless, insisted that Rylan should remain in the clothes he'd 'borrowed'. Perhaps, Rylan presumed, because none of them wanted to have him stinking out the house by changing back into what he'd arrived in. At least not until it had all been thoroughly washed... and most probably deloused and disinfected! Although, as far as he could figure out, the plastic bag with all his old clothes in it had simply been disposed of. Perhaps in the garbage!

"Now," James Fulcher said just a little sternly, but certainly not with the sense of outrage that Rylan had expected, given his having broken into the house. "Before I think about doing anything as drastic as calling the police, how about you explain yourself to us. Like, why you broke into our house, for a start? And why you're wearing some of Thomas's clothes? And, of course, where you've come from?"

"Please don't call the police," replied Rylan quite softly. Answers to James Fulcher's real questions of 'why?', immediately of far lesser importance as far as he was concerned. "They'll just call my parents and... and then..." Tears started to well in his eyes, at the thought of his mother forcing him to return to the 'special psychiatrist' and his eventually having to, once again, face his father and Pastor Isaac.

"You don't want to be with your parents?" Margaret Fulcher queried with almost a sense of astonishment.

"No," Rylan murmured, shaking his head quite strongly as if to emphasise the point. "They only want to hurt me and… and do bad things to me."

"But why?" Margaret Fulcher questioned. To Rylan, it seemed a quite silly question, because he'd already told them. He then realised that perhaps the woman was asking why he was being hurt, and not why he'd run away.

"Because... be..." Rylan began. He didn't want to really explain about himself. About what everyone at school and at the church thought about him, and the nasty comments to which he'd been subjected for almost a long as he could remember. He gave a slow shake of his head. "Because they hurt me all the time," he quickly said. "And because they sent me to some dumb boot camp where I just got punished all the time with straps, and paddles, and canes, and… and all sorts of things. And Dad... my dad... he just... he...” He lowered his head onto his arms as his eyes welled with tears at remembering the excruciating pain of William Daniels’ abuse of him. Abuse that his mother had simply ignored, almost as if it had never happened.

“Your dad, what?” Margaret Fulcher prompted. “What does he do?” Rylan again shook his head a little. Feeling very reluctant to reveal the worst of what had actually been done to him, to unknown adults. Let alone that their children were also present, and were watching and listening to him. It would simply make them hate him, he felt sure.

“Your dad does what?” Margaret Fulcher softly prompted once again, as she moved to sit beside him. Rylan gave a shrug and stayed silent for a while.

“He hurts me,” he eventually whispered. Perhaps hoping that only the mother, who had now comfortingly draped an arm around his shoulders, would hear and understand what he didn’t want to say out loud. “In... in ways he… in ways… he’s not supposed to,” he stammered. His voice was barely audible. Nevertheless the mother seemed to hear and understand, as she then gave his shoulders a quick squeeze.

“I still think we should call the police,” James Fulcher muttered. “They’ll know what to do. Especially if he has been… you know.” His wife immediately looked up.

“No. Not yet,” she murmured. “Not tonight. Let’s just have something to eat and then get a good night’s sleep. We can decide more about it all in the morning.” She got up and went around to her husband. “After all, it’s not as if he’s really done any damage to the place,” she continued. “It won’t take much to repair that small window pane properly, and I’m sure he just needs a place to sleep and hide out for a day or two. Somewhere out of the cold.

We can see what might be in the papers, or on the radio, or TV, about him over the next few days." She gestured to Rylan, and then reached out a hand towards him. "Come on, we'll just get you sorted out in the guestroom for the night."

Rylan got slowly up from his chair and headed down the hallway after her. In his head, his thoughts were now in a state of intense turmoil. Should he accept the family's offer of a safe bed for the night? Should he let them know that he was some sort of freak? That he had wings? Or simply make a dash for freedom at the earliest opportunity?

Henry and Thomas, who seemed delighted to have the added excitement of a strange boy staying in their house, followed his progress with some enthusiasm. More especially, as they'd already realised that their strange guest was a boy who'd been forced into a situation of having to run away from home, just to be safe. A boy who'd obviously ended up hiding in their house just to be able to have somewhere safe and warm to sleep.

"Are you any good at computer games?" Henry asked with some eagerness.

***

"Okay, now given what has prevailed over the past few hours, what I really want to know, first of all, is who it was who stuffed up? Which of you didn't bother to follow the clearly prescribed procedures regarding Angel-girl?" Lieutenant Colonel Harris McMahon questioned rather scathingly. His gaze seemed to search across the faces of the soldiers of various rank, and other military and hospital personnel, assembled in the room. Almost as if it was the red-spot targeting of a sniper's rifle. "Has anyone worked out who it was who was careless enough to allow Angel-girl the chance to get out of her secure unit? Who it was who left the doors unguarded?" He paused for a moment, still glaring around the room. "Anyone wanting to own up?" he almost snarled. For a good few moments, there was silence, as everyone appeared to glance around at everyone else; perhaps expecting to see a lone hand or two rather tentatively raised.

"The unit on that shift claim that the only time that they entered the room was to take the girl her usual morning snack, Sir," Sergeant Oliver Childers eventually answered. Realising that all the members of that particular unit were, for some reason or another, absent. Perhaps it was simply that their shift had ended more than an hour ago and they'd since headed off home. "And when I checked with them, they were all quite adamant that they'd definitely followed the stated, correct procedures for delivering her meals. That is… only one person is to actually take in the tray, with the other remaining at the door, as per the regulations. The task of the person on the door being to keep the room properly secured while the meal is placed on the table in the room, just in case Angel-girl tries to make a run for it. The third and fourth members of the unit, as per their directives, staying further back to ensure that the doors leading into the secure unit remain guarded and locked so that no one… at least, no one who isn't supposed to know about Angel-girl, is alerted to her presence here. They have all steadfastly assured me that the proper required protocol was carried out exactly as per the established prerequisites, and that the girl was securely contained in her room when they'd completed the whole process and relocked all the doors. A check of the CCTV camera recordings in all the corridors, has confirmed that fact… up to a point."

"What sort of point?" McMahon snapped belligerently, the stern fierceness of his gaze quickly targeting the more junior officer.

"That everything outside the room also proceeded exactly as per the stated procedures, Sir," Sergeant Childers hastily replied, already well aware that any actual views of the 'girl with wings'… conveniently referred to by all the units on duty as 'Angel-girl', were kept totally restricted. That being so that no one, outside of a small and exclusive group of military scientific personnel, a couple of military doctors and the small squad of trusted guards, would know of her existence. "For security reasons, however, and at your own directive, they don't show any views of anything inside the room, because of the risk that the CCTV cameras in that area might accidentally be accessed by persons in other areas of the facility. Such as out at the main desk, or other areas to which the public may have access."

"Well, what do the damn CCTV cameras actually in her room tell us?" Lieutenant Colonel Harris McMahon huffed. In some ways, perhaps hoping for a rather more straightforward admission of a mistake. "The ones that only show through to the special observation room? Have they been checked?"

"They have, and that's what's actually the most puzzling, Sir," Sergeant Childers continued.

"Puzzling? In just what way would they be puzzling?" Lieutenant Colonel Harris McMahon retorted rather sarcastically. "They only have to keep a watch on one little mutant girl inside a locked room! I shouldn't think that that would be too difficult a task!" Sergeant Childers exhaled softly and flickered a glance towards the other members of his squad. Already knowing that what he was about to say was scarcely believable and would, most probably, be met with some manner of derision.

"Well, Sir, when we checked through the restricted CCTV recordings of her room, you see the meal being delivered. After the room is relocked, the girl looks at it, for a moment or two, and then just nibbles at a couple of the biscuits. After that, she wanders over to her bed and then stands on it to look out of the window. She appears to just gaze outside for quite a while, and then slumps down on her bed. Then the CCTV suddenly malfunctions again, much as I mentioned was happening with it last week. When it goes into some sort of over-exposure mode for a moment or two, so that Angel-girl seems to just dissolve into white. Anyway it does that again and then, a moment later, she isn't there. The CCTV just shows an empty room."

"You mean to tell me that, according to what we have on the restricted CCTV surveillance, Angel-girl just magically disappeared into thin air? From a locked room?" Lieutenant Colonel Harris McMahon intoned with some clear sense of annoyance and obvious disbelief. Ignoring the fact that he'd been informed of the strange camera malfunctioning over a week ago, and had chosen to ignore it.

"That's exactly it, Sir," Sergeant Oliver Childers replied. "You can watch it yourself, if you don't believe me. By the time we managed to get the GPS Locater System switched on and working, in order to lock on to her signal, she'd already reached the top of the hill outside the main area of the compound."

"And nobody actually saw her getting there?" Lieutenant Colonel Harris McMahon continued almost mockingly, as if making a sarcastic accusation of incompetence. "Or knows where and how she actually found her way out of a secure compound? No one actually saw a girl with wings sneaking down the corridors and then getting outside and past the fences? Or picked her up on the exterior CCTV surveillance?"

"Seems not, Sir," Sergeant Childers said, with a slight shrug that hid the fact that he felt a little more relieved that the commanding officer in charge of the Angel-girl 'experiment' at least seemed convinced that it wasn't the fault of any one person...

more particularly, himself. "One minute, she was in her room… the next, she wasn't. Once we got the GPS Locater System kicked in and began tracking her, and recovery team was sent out, they were quickly on her trail," he continued. "Admittedly, they hardly needed the dogs. The track she left through the snow was quite clear and easy to follow."

"And you say that you sighted her?" Lieutenant Colonel Harris McMahon demanded, turning to Corporal Austin Merrick, the officer in charge of the dog teams.

"Well, we certainly saw glimpses of the white of her smock, through the trees. As we got closer, she seemed to reach a bit of a clearing, but, then, when we got there, she'd somehow disappeared," he explained a little defensively. "There was some trampled snow, almost like she'd stayed in once place for a few moments, but no other sign of her. The dogs just seemed to circle around for a moment, as if not quite sure where to go. We then noticed some more tracks in the snow and when we got the dogs onto them, they seemed to pick up something, but, unfortunately, that particular trail just petered out rather quickly." What he didn't want to say was that they had almost lost two of the dogs over the edge of a cliff, which was where the trail had eventually led; or that, in his opinion, it was highly likely that the girl had simply been able to fly away. They had spent a fruitless hour or so searching the area at the bottom of the cliff, close to the river, in case she had fallen or jumped. But all they'd found was a foot or more of pristine snow and absolutely no sign that the girl had ever been there.

"So no one can actually tell me how she managed to get herself out of the secure unit? Or where she might have gone to?" Lieutenant Colonel Harris McMahon muttered angrily, before giving an irritated sigh. They were simply statements of fact, more than obvious questions.

"It appears that way, Sir," Sergeant Oliver Childers calmly replied. "It also makes retrieval rather difficult, given that it was also about the time that the GPS tracking just stopped."

"It just stopped?" Lieutenant Colonel Harris McMahon growled rather disbelievingly.

"The signal just suddenly wasn't there, according to what I was told after the dog squads got back," Sergeant Childers quickly explained. "When I went down to communications to check if they were still picking up a signal, they said that it had suddenly made a strange sort of blip and then just cut off." Lieutenant Colonel Harris McMahon gave a slow, rather disbelieving shake of his head. The escape of the most prized, and secret possession ever acquired by the U.S. military, was a complication that he did not really need at this time. Not when he'd hoped to be starting experiments, in the next few weeks, to see if Angel-girl's wings would be strong enough for flight. The large outdoor cage planned for that to take place, was currently under construction. The netting was already secured across the top and sides. It was now just a matter of covering it with screens, in order to ensure that no one without the proper authorization would be able to see what went on inside it. And that there was also no possible way that Angel-girl could simply fly away.

"And you didn't spot the necklace on the ground anywhere?" he snapped, turning to the retrieval team. "Or anything else to indicate that she might have been able to remove it? Or had even worked out its true purpose?

"No, Sir," Corporal Austin Merrick hastily replied, even as he realised that they hadn't at any stage actually looked for such an eventuality. Although, in the circumstances of the chase, the necklace could've quite easily been lost beneath the snow, or simply trampled underfoot. "As I said, it just looked like she'd stood still for a moment and then, somehow, just vanished.

Just like she did from her room." Lieutenant Colonel Harris McMahon gave a slow shake of his head and then sighed in clear exasperation at the unexpected state of affairs.

"Even if she did manage to get it off, somehow, the signal would still be operating," Sergeant Childers quickly added. "After all, the bead containing the signal unit is practically indestructible." Lieutenant Colonel Harris McMahon exhaled noisily.

"I want the GPS Locater currently tuned to the frequency on that necklace to be monitored 'twenty-four seven'," he demanded in an almost stentorian voice. "If, as I was informed, the signal will automatically relay through satellites, then we should be able to track it almost anywhere in the world. So even if she does eventually manage to get it off, it may still give us some clue as to where she has gone. So I want that GPS Locater unit watched! Every minute of every hour! The moment anything comes up, even if it's just the slightest peep, I am to be immediately notified! And I mean immediately! Not at the end of your shift! Not when you've finished off your extra cup of coffee, or your damn lunch! Not when you decide to bother to get around to it! Immediately means immediately! Do you all understand that?" He scowled at those assembled to ensure that they understood his demands. "Getting that freak of nature back under our control is vital for the success of our future plans for a covert surveillance programme! Perhaps more than ever, if she's able to evade foreign security teams as easily as she's escaped from you lot of incompetents!"

***

Skylar blinked as he awoke and then looked cautiously around at his new surroundings. At least as much as he could see of them, given that he was lying on his left side, with his hands securely tied behind his back. He tried moving his feet, quickly realising that they were also securely tied together; bound together at the ankles, with a rope linking them to his wrists so that he was forced to keep his knees bent. There was also a gag, made from some type of ball, it seemed, forced hard into his mouth and tied behind his head, that prevented any chance of him speaking or crying out.

Not that it was the first time he'd awoken, but all the previous times, he'd not only been hogtied and gagged but had also had a cloth bag over his head to prevent him seeing where he was, or who it was who'd kidnapped him. In most of those instances, however, the eventual sharp pain of an injection in his upper arm had usually returned him to a state of oblivion.

Desperate to remain calm, despite the worrying thoughts that rushed through his head, he tried to take in more of his situation. Beside his restraints and the gag, he seemed to be lying on a bare mattress, with no pillow. As for his surroundings, it appeared that he was in a solid concrete room with just one door, that he could see, down in the direction of his feet. The wall closest to his head seemed to be of roughcast concrete; with even the marks of the crude boxing material from when it had been poured still clearly visible beneath a rough coating of grey paint. The ceiling overhead was lined with unpainted plywood and, without turning his head to actually look at it, he sensed by the angle of shadows that there was just a single light bulb, somewhere behind him.

Taking in his own situation a little further, besides being hog-tied and gagged, he was still wearing his jeans, for which he felt thankful, and his shoes and socks, but was now bare-chested. The shirt and jacket he'd been wearing to keep out the chill of the morning while doing his newspaper deliveries were gone. But how long ago that had been… how many hours, days, perhaps even weeks, he had no idea.

Unfortunately, nothing of what had happened in that time made too much sense. His last proper, definite memory was of getting off his bike and approaching a car to answer a request for directions, before he was roughly bundled into the back of the car by a man he hadn't seen approaching. After that, everything had gone black. At the same time, he could also vaguely sense having been in other places. Such as in the back of another car, with a cloth soaked in some chemical over his mouth. Then possibly in a truck, then in an upstairs room at another house, then in another truck. And then there were also the injections, which after rendering him comatose for a while, also seemed to make him feel extremely fatigued. He shook his head a little to try to clear the fog in his thoughts and ease the ache in his jaw caused by the pulling of the gag.

"About bloody time you woke up!" a gruff voice suddenly muttered. Even though his head still throbbed, Skylar was immediately on alert, his attention quickly drawn to the fact that he was obviously not alone. That there was someone — it had sounded like a man — somewhere behind him.

Rolling awkwardly onto his back, with his knees pulled up and his arms awkwardly pinned behind his back, Skylar suddenly winced as his left shoulder hurt. Looking down towards where the pain had seemed to come from, he noticed a small, strange-looking tattoo etched onto his upper arm just a little below his shoulder. From what he could see of it, it looked like a capital 'N' inside a circle.

"It'll stop hurting in a day or so," muttered the man, without bothering to get up from where he was seated. It was obvious that he'd realised that Skylar was wondering about the mark. "It's just to let you, and anyone else, know that you are now my property."

"What do you mean?" Skylar tried to say, as he returned his attention to the man; the gag making the words a meaningless jumble of muted sounds. Nevertheless, the man seemed to somehow sense the gist of his question simply from the frightened look in his eyes.

"What it means," he drawled, "is that, from now on, I own you! Totally! You're mine to do with whatever I like!"

Skylar's thoughts immediately began to conjure up the worst possible nightmares of abuse. The man, yet again, seemed to notice his shocked reaction and understand what he was thinking.

"Don't worry," he said with a smirk. "You haven't had anything bad happen to you. At least not yet! You'll be safe from that for a little while, no doubt... at least until the right event comes along. Maybe some special function that I can make use of as a means to get you initiated. And also get paid a real good price for giving some client the chance of doing so. Innocent kids are worth a great deal more than those who already know the ropes, and know what to expect, so to speak." He laughed a little at the suggestion. "Or I can simply wait and see what I get offered for you at auction," he eventually continued. "With you having a reasonably close resemblance to one of those kids from that dumb Stranger Things series on Netflix, I'm pretty sure I'll end up with a really good offer from some rich pervert who wants to 'own' a celebrity, so to speak. There's always good money to be made in supplying kids who look similar to young celebrities, to those who want their own private fantasy playthings. I certainly got damned good money for the two young Justin Bieber lookalikes I acquired a couple of years ago."

He got up from the chair on which he'd been sitting and wandered over to Skylar, producing a sharp hunting knife as he did so. Skylar immediately cringed away from him. At least as much as he could, given his hogtied state.

"Don't panic!" the man muttered rather bluntly, before Skylar could start trying to scream for help. A rather futile action, admittedly, given the gag tightly fastened into his mouth. "I'm just going to cut your ties." He knelt beside Skylar and rolled him back onto his left side. Putting the knife to the ropes, he then paused before cutting. "If you can behave yourself and keep your mouth shut, I'll cut you loose and remove the gag," he said abruptly. "Try to escape, or make too much noise, and I'll get really annoyed. Then, after I've finished dealing with you, you can bet your little boots that the very least of your problems will be the rough edge of my belt on your little arse, and you not being able to sit down too comfortably for a good few days. Understand?" Skylar nodded and then stayed very still, as the man cut through the ropes. Not wanting to aggravate his captor in any way, or risk moving in a manner that might just make the man slip with the knife. Even when his feet and wrists had been untied, he remained still. Waiting until the man had then untied and removed the gag, before he tried properly stretching out his legs. They tingled and ached a little, from being restrained and kept in one position for so long, and his mouth suddenly felt as dry and gritty as the bottom of a birdcage.

"There's a bottle of water by my chair you can have and I'll send down something for you to eat in about an hour," the man said getting to his feet. He then gestured towards the far wall with the knife, before slipping it back into its sheath. "If you need to go, there's a bucket over by the far wall, covered with a board, and a roll of paper," he continued. "I suggest you use it sparingly, because I don't need you stinking the place out." With his hands free, Skylar began rubbing at the numb feeling in each of his wrists from where they'd been tied, trying to ease a bit of life back into them. He then quickly felt in his jeans pocket for his house key.

"If you're looking for this, I have it," the man said as he fumbled in his top shirt pocket momentarily and then tossed a key up into the air and caught it, before sticking it back in his pocket. "I'll just keep it as a little souvenir. You certainly won't be needing it any more. There's no way you'll ever be going back home to your darling mommy."

"Are you working for my dad?" Skylar nervously asked. Suddenly wondering if he was simply the victim of a custody kidnapping. At the same time, that seemed a little unlikely, given that his dad had always been totally against any ideas of tattooing… even for himself. The man seemed to laugh a little.

"What's eventually planned you, I very much doubt your daddy would approve of," he then sneered. "But then, he's not around to do anything about it, is he?" He paused a moment and then gave a slight laugh. "Don't you worry, we watched you for long enough to know that it was just you and you mother living in that scungy little trailer."

"So how long are you going to keep me here?" Rylan nervously asked, as he pondered on what the man had said and what might eventually be planned for him. More than a little warily, he shuffled to the far end of the mattress so that his back was against the wall. The man looked around the room, and then shrugged.

"If you mean, in here, it'll just be for tonight," he said casually. "Tomorrow, I'll be taking you to another of the holding houses, where some of the other children are waiting. At that stage, I'll do a proper inspection of you, along with some other new recruits that we've recently acquired. As for the future... well, now that you're mine, that's for me to decide. If a good offer gets made for you, once you're made available, then you'll probably be sold, straight out. If other clients happen to like you on a 'one-off' basis, you could be with me for a quite a while. After that, well, who's to know? Although, in the long run, no matter what eventuates, it might just be a bit dangerous for whoever ends up owning you to just let you go free, if you catch my drift!" He followed the comment with a very obvious throat-slitting gesture, before returning his knife to its sheath. He then turned and headed towards the door. "My name's Vittorio," he added, pausing for a moment in the open doorway. "And from now on, you just realise that you always do exactly as I say! Immediately, and without any argument or complaint! Not unless you really do want to suffer!" He paused for a moment, perhaps to let his words sink in, before adding a final comment. "So, given that I quite like to hear little boys screaming in pain, more especially if it's me doing the hurting, I suggest that, while you're down here, you just be a very quiet little mouse and don't do anything at all to upset me!"

As the door eventually slammed shut and Skylar listened to the man's footsteps heading up what seemed to be a flight of stairs, his eyes began to well with tears and, despite all his efforts to be brave, he began to cry. If he'd thought it was bad enough being considered as a 'whitey, trailer-trash outcast' at his new school, what now beckoned for his future could only be regarded as a total nightmare.

CHAPTER TWO

Decisions Made....

Amanda quickly set out four bowls of porridge, topping each uncooked mixture with a handful of chopped nuts and diced dried fruit, before placing them ready for the microwave. Not that she needed reminding of the need to prepare an extra bowl for their newcomer. Tris had been awake from sparrow-fart it seemed, eager to spend more time with his new companion. He's also reminded her, more than once, that Mykael, Ithuriel and Andrew would be arriving a little later in the morning to discuss the circumstances of the girl's rescue. From their evening discussions, they at least now knew that Lara was the same age as Tris... eleven.

As she added a little extra soymilk to each of the breakfast mixtures, from the rest of the house she could hear a strange mix of sounds. Soft beeps, and other extraneous noises, from Joshua's computer, the hiss of water from Lara's shower, and a cascade of notes from Tris's piano practice, as he worked his way through Bach's Chromatic Fantasia and Fugue. In her thoughts, she again wondered if Tris's finding Lara had been what Mykael had meant when he'd commented that the concern with Pastor Isaac and Oakton might not yet be finished with.

At the same time, the fact that Tris had found Lara near to a military installation hidden in a mountainous area where there was still a heavy snowfall late into the spring season — a place obviously far removed from the flat lands surrounding Wichita, and all the intrigues that had occurred in Oakton — made it hard to see any obvious correlation between the two events. Even as she pondered on possible connections, the sudden cessation of muted hissing in the pipes had her realising that Lara had completed her shower. Quickly placing the four bowls into the microwave, she set it for five minutes, instead of the usual three and a half, given that there was one extra bowl to cook.

"Do you need a hand with anything," Joshua suddenly asked, startling her a little out of her meandering thoughts. Amanda nodded, even as she continued to watch the bowls revolving in the microwave.

"We could probably do with some hot drinks," she suggested. "Maybe you could put on the kettle while I get out some mugs." For the next few minutes, accompanied by the dull whirring of the microwave, they got the rest of the breakfast prepared. By the time the microwave had impatiently chirped its completion, the kettle had finished boiling and Joshua was starting to pour hot water into mugs to make instant coffee for himself and Amanda, and hot chocolate drinks for Tris and Lara. Almost abruptly, as if by some sudden realisation that breakfast was ready, the music from the piano room suddenly stopped, almost mid-phrase.

"It'll be on the table in a few minutes," Amanda called towards the hallway, hoping that both children would hear. In the back of her thoughts was also a small fear. A worry of whether Tris might change in his feelings towards her and Joshua, now that he had someone of his own 'kind'— for want of a better description — to be with.

"It was really nice being able to take my time having a shower," Lara enthused as she hurried into the kitchen ahead of Tris, and then waited to be directed to a place to sit. Perhaps not wanting to usurp someone else's usual place at the table. "At the military place, I always rushed through having a wash or a shower as quickly as I could, because it just seemed really creepy."

"Creepy?" Amanda immediately questioned. Lara nodded.

"Yeah," she replied, looking a little cautiously towards Tris and Joshua. "Because the bathroom was just this little room off the main room that I was kept in. It had big mirrors on two of the walls, so I always used to worry that they might be some type of one-way glass and that there would be people on the other side watching me. I used to try to cover the mirrors up with towels, when there were enough spare for that purpose. Which there usually weren't!"

"You should probably mention that to Mykael when he arrives," Amanda quietly suggested. "But for now, get yourself seated and have your breakfast before it gets cold." She casually indicated for Lara to take the place beside Tris that she'd occupied the previous night, placing the first bowl of porridge into the place in front of her, and another where Tris was also in the process of being seated, before heading back to the kitchen for her own and Joshua's breakfasts.

***

Mykael sat quietly sipping his coffee as he waited for Lara and Tris to finish fussing around and get seated. What he needed to know, for 'starters', was where Lara had come from, beyond the mere fact that Tris had rescued her from armed men in semi-military uniforms, with a pack of tracking dogs, on some snow-covered mountain. There had to be a past beyond that. A time when she'd lived a more normal life. More especially as it was most unlikely that she would have been born in a military hospital.

"Okay," he said, once he had their undivided attention. "I've got a fairly good idea of how the actual rescue came about, from what you told me last night. What I now need to know is where you were held, how you were being treated and, perhaps more importantly, who you were living with before you arrived at the military hospital, or research centre, or whatever sort of place it was?"

"I suppose it would be best if I started from when I was first adopted," Lara suggested a little cautiously. "Especially as I don't remember too much before then. Like when I was really little. You know, like maybe three or four." Mykael quickly nodded. It seemed as good an idea as any.

"Well, just do that then. Just explain to us what happened after you were adopted," he replied. Lara nodded and then took a few deep breaths.

"I can remember that, at first, I was in an orphanage. It was in Boston, I think. But then, when I was almost six, I was adopted by Rex and Abigail," she began. "They lived in Fitchburg, Massachusetts, so that's where I went to live. I was pretty upset about it, at first, because they only wanted a girl, which meant that I got separated from my twin. He ended up being adopted by some other people who lived in Holyoke, which was about fifty miles away."

"So you have a twin brother?" Mykael quickly questioned, even though the answer seemed quite obvious from what Lara had just said. From his point of view, however, that item of information immediately raised a further red flag. If there was a boy who was a twin to Lara, he might also have the same attributes. Nevertheless, the 'twins' issue could be looked into at some later stage, so he quickly indicated for Lara to continue. Lara nodded in response to his question and continued with her explanation.

"I'm older by about fifteen minutes, and, at some stage, I think I remember being told that he'd spent quite a bit of time in intensive care. Like, about five or six months, or maybe more, 'cause they didn't think he'd survive, at first. I do know he spent a lot of time in hospital, even after that." She paused and sighed rather softly. "I suppose we probably had real parents at some stage, but all I can really remember is us eventually being in the orphanage together, up until we were almost six. That's when we were both first adopted. And then, for a while, after we both got adopted out, we still used to see each other on occasions. You know, like about once a month. Rex and Abigail would either drive down to Holyoke, or the people who'd adopted Lawrence would come up to Fitchburg. But then, after a couple of years, they suddenly moved somewhere out West, and so we weren't able to meet up anymore." She gave a small sigh, as if a little sad at that loss of contact. "Anyway," she then continued, "just after I'd turned ten… and a half, I think, I started getting back pains and noticed that I had two funny little ridges between my shoulder blades. The Holts took me to our usual doctor, but he didn't know what to make of it. He poked at them a bit and said that he could arrange to get X-rays done, but then, because the ridges didn't seem to be causing me too much discomfort and they would've had to pay for them to be done privately, Rex and Abigail decided that they'd just wait and see what happened, rather than have the cost going against their medical insurance."

"So Rex and Abigail were the Holts?" Mykael questioned. Perhaps already noting that the girl had not, so far, generally referred to them as her 'parents'. Lara quickly nodded and then continued her story.

"Anyway, one night, quite a few weeks later, I suddenly ended up bleeding from my back, where the bumps had been, and found that I had these small wings. Like, I just woke up one morning and there was all this blood on the back my nightgown and on my sheets and they… like, the wings, were just 'there'… only quite little. The Holts were a bit freaked out by it, but they eventually decided to take me to our usual doctor to try to find out what was going on. This time, however, instead of mentioning X-rays, he told the Holts that he would think about calling in a specialist. So, because they weren't hurting me, or anything like that, we just went home. Anyway, a short while later, the doctor rang us and told us to come down to his surgery at ten o'clock the next day, because the specialist would meet us there. Which he did! Only, when he arrived, he had on what looked like a military uniform, which I thought seemed a bit strange. You know, like, for a doctor for children to be in a military uniform."

"So what happened then?" Mykael quickly prompted.

Well, before I knew it, he took my parents aside and spoke to them for a while and then called for an ambulance to take me to what he said was a specialist hospital. Only it took ages to get there, and then it turned out to be more like a prison. Mainly because, once I was there, I was separated from Rex and Abigail and taken to what I eventually found was called a single containment ward. They had a guard on the door and I wasn't allowed to leave my room at any time, unless I had an armed escort. And even then, I wasn't ever allowed to go outside or anything. It was almost as if they didn't really want anyone else to know that I was there. You know, like, apart from the doctors who examined me, and the military people, and some other specialists."

"And what happened to the Holts?" Mykael asked rather quietly. Lara gave a slight shrug.

"When I was taken to the ward, I thought that they'd be able to come down to be with me, but I never saw them again," Lara replied. "Although I heard, about a week later, that they got paid quite a lot of money for me. Like, for them to give me up. Only, I don't think I was supposed to know that."

"So what happened to you in the time when you were in this specialist hospital?" Mykael encouraged. Lara looked down at the floor for a moment, and then towards Amanda. Quickly sensing that the girl wanted some moral support, for what might be awkward to repeat, Amanda moved quickly to sit next to her, taking a hold of Lara's left hand. At the same time, subtly indicating to Joshua that it might be better if Tris was not there for the moment. With Tris looking a little puzzled, Joshua gently ushered him out to the kitchen, on the pretext of preparing more hot drinks for everyone. In the small silence that followed, Lara seemed to brush away the start of tears.

"It was awful," she finally whispered. "They took away all my clothes. Like, everything, except my underwear, and gave me one of those horrible hospital gowns to wear. The first day I was there, I ended up spending the rest of the day in that one room and wasn't allowed out. Not for any reason. And then, the next day, the doctors came back and said that I had to be given a very thorough medical examination so that they could try to find out what was wrong with me. They took me to a room that looked like an operating theatre. Like, it had all these really bright lights suspended over a low table in the centre. Then they made me take off the gown, and even my underwear, and get up on the table so that they could check me over. And I don't just mean my wings and how they came out of my back, I mean... 'everywhere'." She glanced downwards and seemed to blush a little with embarrassment. "It was just like I was some weird new animal that they'd found," she then continued rather softly. "It felt really horrible to have them looking at me like that. And then, after they'd given me some disposable underwear made from some sort of paper, they started taking blood tests and photographs and X-rays and even some funny scan things. That was in another room, where I had to lay flat and keep very still on this narrow bed while it rolled me through this big tube thing, which kept making funny little beeping noises. They also listened to my heart and put all these little sticker things with leads attached all over my chest to get some sort of reading of it. They also kept checking my blood pressure, and taking blood samples and stuff... and doing all sorts of other silly little tests. It seemed to take hours and hours, but was also very embarrassing because they were all fully dressed and had white coats on while I was just... like, almost naked."

"And what happened after that?" Amanda quickly asked, perhaps wanting to get through the sordid details before Tris and Joshua arrived back. Perhaps, also, pre-empting the question Mykael was about to ask. Lara gave a slight shrug and sighed softly even as she cuddled a little closer to Amanda.

"Eventually, they took me back to my room. Only, as I said, it felt more like a jail cell. I used to call it the 'cage', which they didn't seem to like very much. When I got there, one of the nurses gave me another new gown to wear. After that, there would be a new one waiting for me, just inside the door of my room each morning when I woke up, along with another pair of the funny paper pants. You know, like I was wearing when I got here. But that was all I ever had. It was really embarrassing having to wander around all of the time in gowns that didn't fasten properly at the back and pants that almost seemed to be made out of tissue paper."

"And was that the end of the examinations?" Mykael quietly queried. In a way, it was what he'd expected from the scientific side of the military. Once they had a specimen for study in their grasp, any rules of proper, moral behaviour quite often went out the window, so to speak. Nothing mattered beyond the end result of whatever studies they had planned. As far as they'd have been concerned, the girl may as well have been just another lab-rat. Lara quickly shook her head.

"No. They used to take my blood pressure each morning, before they brought my breakfast, and the same would happen at night. Like, before they brought my dinner. They did blood tests every Monday and I was also re-examined about every five days or so. Only, nothing quite as bad as the first time, even though I'd often end up half-naked when they checked my wings. Most of the time, they'd just measure them… like, my wings, and check my height and weight and ask me whether I thought I'd be able to fly anytime soon."

"And did they tell you what was eventually going to happen to you?" Mykael continued. Lara gave a shrug.

"They didn't say it outright, but I think that they were just waiting for me to be able to fly, so they could start training me for spying missions or something. I think they also wanted to know when I'd be old enough to have a baby," she murmured, looking away with some sense of embarrassment. "I'm not exactly sure, but, sometimes, like, when they were doing the medical examinations and I used to hear some of the military people asking about how close the doctors thought I might be to puberty."

Any further conversation, regarding that particular matter, was suddenly cut short by a loud knocking at the door. Before anyone else could move, it seemed, Tris had hurried through to answer it. A little to his surprise, not only was it Peter McCormack, whom he already knew had been asked to come over to give Lara a quick medical check-over, but also his Grandma Evelyn, Aunt Rowanne and Aunt Amy, as well as all the children from the big house.

"We're the official welcoming committee," Carwyn announced with an air of almost unbridled enthusiasm. "We've come to check on how your new sister is getting on," he added as they all quickly followed Peter McCormack inside.

"My sister?" Tris half-croaked in response to the older boy's teasing.

"Well, as I said yesterday, she can either be that, or your new girlfriend," Carwyn retorted with the hint of a laugh. Tris seemed to look away, even as he blushed slightly, which immediately gave the other children the idea that that was perhaps how he viewed Lara. Or how he hoped to view her.

"She's just..." Tris began, and then stopped. Not sure of what answer to give. By the time he'd ushered all the children into the family room, Amanda was already leading Lara off to her bedroom for a medical check-up… even as Ithuriel and Andrew also arrived.

***

With the sound of music drifting down the hallway from the music room, where it appeared that Melanie and Tris were giving an impromptu concert of their next exam pieces and a couple of duets for their next village concert, all of the adults, including Peter McCormack, Amanda, Mykael, Andrew, Ithuriel, Rowanne, Amy, Evelyn and Joshua, had settled into the family room to discuss Lara's future. For a moment or two, no one seemed all that sure of how to start the discussion. Everyone, it seemed, looking to someone else, to start the ball rolling.

"Well, she appears to be in fairly good health, and it also doesn't appear that she's been abused in any way," Peter McCormack eventually murmured rather softly. "Although, I was actually quite pleased that Amanda was present the whole time, given how compliant the girl was to being examined. That, in itself, struck me as slightly unusual, given most children's reluctance to disrobe for almost any medical situation. In a way, I'd almost have to say that it was something that she was quite used to; something that indicates that such examinations were possibly a fairly regular occurrence."

"From what she's already told us, you'd be quite correct in that assumption," Mykael replied, giving a rather knowing nod of his head.

"The bigger question is, what happens next?" Andrew asked, glancing around at all those assembled.

"Well, she's stays here, obviously," Amanda immediately replied. "Joshua and I are certainly quite happy to have her staying on, and I think Tris is already enjoying her company because..."

"That's not quite what we meant," Mykael quickly interjected. "And yes, I am totally in agreement that Lara should stay here. More especially if it does not create any sort of a problem for you, and you're quite happy to have her stay. What we do need to discover, however, is who this military group who had her imprisoned might be, and if they are likely to continue to be a threat to her in the foreseeable future." He paused a moment, and then looked briefly towards Andrew and Ithuriel. "We just get the feeling that, whoever this military group may be, they will not be wanting to let someone, or something, as valuable as Lara be taken from them too easily, if you catch my drift… and most certainly not if they were beginning to be aware of even just a fraction of her abilities. A person who can be invisible and teleport would be an invaluable asset to their needs in the world of espionage and military surveillance."

"But she's just a little girl?" Evelyn protested. "Even if she does have wings."

"That she may be," replied Mykael. "But a little girl with a very special purpose, as far as certain military minds would be concerned, if they ever realised her true potential. The same way in which they'd have viewed any of your boys and, I dare say, Tris, if they ever got hold of him. Which is why they will have 'bought off' her parents, to get them out of the scene, obviously. Well, foster-parents to be more correct."

"So what do we do about it?" Amanda questioned. Mykael gave a nonchalant shrug of his shoulders.

"For the moment, nothing," he stated rather firmly. "I'll start some investigations into the matter in the next day or so. In the meantime, however, I think it would be best that Lara remains fully confined to the island." He paused for a moment as if rethinking that idea through. "Although if Tris is adamant that he wants to take her elsewhere, such as the farm, then it might be best if Andrew also tags along as a chaperone. Just in case there are any unexpected problems."

"Okay by me," Andrew replied, giving a casual shrug of his shoulders. "I'm always up for tasting a bit of Grandma Betty's home baking." They listened for a moment, to the sounds of happy laughter coming from the piano room.

"Judging by the sound of that, I doubt that there'll be any problems with her staying here," Amanda said with a slight laugh.

***

Angela Jeffries sat on the edge of Skylar's bed, clutching the all-in-one outfit that he still sometimes wore to bed when it was particularly cold. Admittedly it was getting just a bit small for him, but he still seemed to find some comfort in wearing it. She held it to her face and breathed in the faint aroma that was her son, as her eyes flooded with tears. Wondering where he was, and if he was even still alive? Would there be a knock on the door sometime today... or tomorrow... or perhaps later in the week… or the next week… or month… or whatever, for the police to inform her that they'd found the body of a child and could she…?

She quickly dispatched that notion from her thoughts and wiped at her eyes. It didn't help to sit and think of worst-case scenarios. Skylar had to still be alive, somewhere… and perhaps just lost. Although the fact that the police still seemed to regard his disappearance as a 'runaway situation' made absolutely no sense at all, to her way of thinking. There was nowhere that he could go to, as far as she knew. And it wasn't as if he'd even given any indication of being unhappy with being without his father, even if he was having some difficulties with settling into his new school, and living in the cramped confines of a trailer.

To be honest, he'd never been that close to his father; especially not with Todd being away from home so much of the time, and with the strict religious discipline that he imposed on Skylar when he was around. Always insisting that Skylar had to attend morning and evening services with him at the New Christian Mission every Sunday, despite her protests that Skylar should be able to decide for himself which church he wished to attend. Not allowing him to see his school friends on weekends and then forcing him to attend the church boot camp for a weekend of corrective discipline the one time he did over-step the mark, so to speak; an experience that had eventually turned out to be nothing short of a sustained, vicious assault on the boy.

She wondered whether Todd had felt any remorse, for the brutality that had been enacted upon Skylar, when the news of Pastor Isaac's arrest as a serial paedophile had made the news, along with the revelation that the 'discipline training' aspects of the church camp had simply been a source of child-porn videos. Recordings that had even included Skylar being severely brutalised, according to the police officer who'd come to interview them a couple of weeks after the Pastor's arrest; having tracked them down through school enrolment records. In the light of which, she'd immediately wondered if she should have enrolled him at Pinehurst North Middle School under her maiden name, just in case his name ever become public in the process of a trial. It was always easy to be wise in retrospect, of course. Thankfully, with guilty pleas from Pastor Isaac and his accomplices, there had been no need for Skylar to have to return to Wichita to testify.

At the same time, it also seemed unlikely that Todd would've had kidnapped Skylar. As far as she knew, Todd had no idea of where they were now living. Not unless the police had informed him of their likely whereabouts, in their efforts to track down Skylar. She'd certainly left no forwarding address when they'd vacated their rented house in Oakton, and she'd had no phone contact from Todd since the evening that he'd stormed out. Not even for him to offer to pay something towards Skylar's school expenses.

But then again, she mused, if Skylar had just decided to run away, why would that be now? Just when they appeared to be getting settled? And if for any reason he had just decided to run away, why had he not taken any extra clothes, or a backpack for his personal belongings? And why on Earth would he not take his bike? That aspect of his disappearance made absolutely no sense whatsoever. Why would he have just abandoned it in the middle of his delivery schedule; left it at the side of the road, along with his bag of newspapers, for the police to find and return?

The only logical answer had to be that he'd been abducted off the street, and whomever it was who'd grabbed him wasn't worried about a bike. Perhaps even hoping that someone else would find it and take it. Thoughts of other high-profile boy abduction mysteries that had been in the news in the past few years, were immediately in her thoughts… Johnny Gosch, Eugene Martin, Jacob Wetterling, Danny Eberle, Steven Stayner. Names that were just the tip of the iceberg as far as abductions and disappearances of young boys was concerned. Notable for the fact that none of them had been children who'd had any reason whatsoever to run away from home, despite the continued obstinacy of some police authorities to want to still regard them as just 'runaways'. Some of those children, similar to what appeared to have happened with Skylar, had also been abducted while doing a morning newspaper route.

With a sigh and a further wipe at her tears, she placed the 'all-in-one' suit back on the end of the bed, where Skylar had left it, and headed for the bathroom to fix her make-up. Her place of work had quite understood the situation and had given her time off, with basic pay, when Skylar had first gone missing. She'd spent a week working with the police and using her savings to have posters printed with a picture of Skylar, asking for information as to his whereabouts. She'd then spent the next few days posting them around Orange, and its surrounding districts, but also understood that she couldn't rely on the generosity of her employers lasting for too long. Lucy's would expect her back behind the counter, now that it seemed the immediate search for Skylar appeared to have reached a dead end. Whoever had taken him had certainly been careful enough to not leave any trace of their actions.

***

Tris hurried into the family room with Lara in tow. After a couple of days of foul weather, during which time they'd remained basically house-bound, apart from a number of visits up to the big house, the weather was fine, if still just a touch chilly. Nevertheless, that time had not been wasted, with Lara now reasonably practiced in thinking her wings through her clothing, so that she could dress more normally.

"Mum," he asked eagerly, coming to a rather abrupt halt in front of Amanda, while still holding tight to Lara's hand. "With it being sunny, do you think it would be okay if I take Amanda down to the church? I think Andrew will be down there and I want to ask him if he could start teaching Lara how to fly and 'be'." Amanda looked up, made a brief sideways cant of her head, and then smiled and gave a slight shake of her head in some amusement at the eagerness evident in his face.

"Please," Tris pleaded, appearing to take her actions as possibly being a negative response.

"Of course," replied Amanda. She leant forward to ensure that she had his complete attention. "Just as long as you don't go anywhere else. More especially, off the island, without letting Andrew know, so that he can go with you," she added a little sternly. "As Mykael has told you must happen. And, if you do, it would also be nice to let me, and your dad, know where you're headed. Understood?"

Tris quickly nodded, and then, still holding tight to Lara's hand, simply disappeared. Amanda looked at where they'd been standing for a moment. Tris had seemed so happy, over the last few days, with having a companion angel to be with. The only issue might be whether he would eventually regard Lara as simply a sister, or perhaps as something more. Still, given how young they both were, if it was the latter, that was a concern for some future time. Quite a few years into the future, she quietly hoped.

***

"Where are we?" Lara exclaimed, looking around the interior of the church. "This place is..." She left the statement unfinished. Perhaps feeling unable to fully describe the impressions in her head. The place had an incredible serenity, and yet also a sense of age and strength, along with its aura of almost austere beauty.

"It's the island's church," Tris murmured. "It's a really special place for us angels." He glanced around. Realising, a little to his disappointment, that Andrew was not there. For a moment, Tris wondered whether to send out a thought to him, but then decided not to. While it would be important to have Andrew instruct Lara for any activity as dangerous as flying lessons, he felt sure that learning to 'be' would not entail any great risk. Especially if he used the same methods for Lara as Andrew had done with him.

"Why?" Lara questioned, as Tris began to lead her up to the front. Stepping up onto the sanctuary so that they were standing right in front of the altar and facing the large wooden cross that dominated the end wall.

"Because it's our safe place," Tris replied in hushed tones. "A special place where no one can hurt us. Not even bad angels."

"Bad angels?'" Lara echoed, her expression seeming to convey the idea that the idea of bad angels did not make too much sense.

"Not all angels like to do good things," Tris hastily explained. "Some of them like to make people do bad things, or even try to hurt good angels. Mykael calls them 'turned' angels. The church is our safe place 'cause it's where we are completely... well, safe from being hurt by them."

"So has it always been like this," Lara whispered, noting the soft, faint echo of her voice in the stillness. Tris gave a quick shake of his head.

"It was actually destroyed over a thousand years ago," he whispered in reply, almost as if not wanting to speak too loudly in such a special place. "When three angel children were killed inside it. If you look carefully at the cross you can even see the marks left from when two of them, Gofraidh and Aerynn, were nailed to it. You know, like... crucified!" Lara gave a slight shudder at the thought and, once having discerned the nail marks in the wood of the cross, glanced down at her own hands.

"So how did the third angel die?" she quietly asked. Perhaps hoping that it wasn't an equally gruesome death.

"Conlaodh was only about eight or nine and he'd simply had a very bad asthma attack," Tris replied. "It was while they were having his funeral that the island was attacked by slave traders. When they left, they took away a lot of the children and then set the church on fire."

"So how did it end up like this?" Lara queried. "Like, all proper again?"

"That was when the big miracle happened," Tris quickly continued. "Evidently, two of Andrew's older brothers, who had already become angels, had to complete some strange prophecy about restoring some weird crown things to the three angel-children who'd died, and had then been hidden away in the crypt under the church before it was destroyed over a thousand years ago. After Alexei and Tristan found the crypt and the skeletons, they also found out that there was a prophecy written on the big stone cross that's now out by the gardens. It was about how three special crowns that had been stolen by the Viking invaders and were now lost somewhere in a cave, had to be returned. What was really weird was they had dreams about all of what had happened... like, the angels being killed, the church being destroyed and where the crowns had been lost. Anyway, after finding the crowns and also having to battle against some bad angels, they placed the crowns on the skeletons of the three angel children and they all came back to life, along with another boy who'd been buried down there about a year earlier… who also became an angel. And while they were all down in the crypt doing that, the whole church just rose out of the ground somehow, and became as it is now." He glanced around the interior of the church. "Without all the lighting and heating and the modern organ, of course."

"So that meant that there were..." Lara did a quick count in her head ... six angels?" Tris nodded.

"And then seven, when Uncle Andrew also became an angel." Tris quickly explained. "Now, to get onto why I really brought you here, I'm going to teach you to how to 'be'. Which is really just like teleporting."

"Like how you rescued me and how we came here?" Lara eagerly queried.

"Exactly," Tris said, giving a nod of his head. "And it's real easy, once you get the hang of it, and understand how it all works." He took a hold of Lara's arm to get her to take a step back from the altar, but, at the same time, indicating for her to stay looking at the cross.

"Now, shut your eyes and visualise exactly what you see in front of you. Just as if it's a picture in your mind," he instructed. After a moment, Lara nodded to indicate that she'd done as he'd asked. Seeming to trust him implicitly.

"You got it? Exactly?" Tris asked. Lara nodded yet again. "Okay," Tris continued. "Now, open your eyes and follow me." He quickly led her outside and had her stand facing the sea, with her back to the church.

"Now, shut your eyes and visualise the exact view you had in your head a moment ago," he instructed. "You know, of the altar and the cross on the wall." Tris waited a moment. "You got it?" he asked. Lara nodded. Tris gave a soft sigh. "Now, just think of yourself as being there. Like, just imagine that you are standing exactly where you were standing a couple of minutes ago."

An instant later Lara vanished. Tris ran back to the church, hoping that his instructions had worked. Almost colliding with Lara as she was running up the central aisle to come back to him.

"I did it," exclaimed Lara excitedly, as Tris held her at arm's length. Quietly getting his thoughts under control, and understanding, in some way, how Andrew must have felt in re-teaching him that same skill just a few months earlier.

"Now we have to practise that," he said rather matter-of-factly, trying not to show too much excitement. "So go outside somewhere and do it again." Lara quickly did as he'd asked and a moment later, reappeared in front of the altar.

Tris had her repeat the process two more times, just to be sure and then sat her down on the front pew.

"This is the first place we learn to 'be' to," he quickly explained. "Once you get good at it, we can start to add other places by learning new visualisations. Like, outside the front door at home and in the back of the barn for when we visit the farm."

"What about indoors at other places?" Lara quickly asked. "Like when you took me home that first time?"

"That just takes a bit more practice," Tris replied. "So once you've get good at doing bigger places, like here, we then start to add more places and start coupling it with more skills. Like learning to be invisible and how to make your wings invisible."

"Can we start that now?" asked Lara eagerly. Tris gave a slight shrug.

"I suppose so," he murmured.

They spent the next thirty minutes or so with Lara concentrating on trying to make her wings invisible and intangible. As Tris had found, Lara soon realised that it required real concentration at first, but started to get just a little easier with practice and effort. Eventually, when he sensed that Lara was getting a little tired, Tris called an end to the session.

"We can do some more at home, tonight," he suggested. "That way, we can try playing games of some sort, while you also try to keep your wings invisible. It takes some effort, at first, until it eventually becomes almost automatic. I used to practice doing it while playing the piano."

As if taking his final comment as a spur for action, he wandered over to the church organ, turned it on, and began playing through a Bach Prelude and Fugue – the No. 6 in D minor from Book 1 of the '48'. For a while Lara just listened, nodding her head in time to the lilting triplet patterns of the Prelude and then the slightly more strident quaver entries of Fugue.

"I was just wondering," Lara suddenly asked, when he seemed to have finished the two items. "If Andrew still lives here, like, on the island, what's happened to all the other angels?"

"They sometimes visit," Tris casually replied, running his hand nonchalantly across the nearest manual in a gentle downward glissando, before reaching across to switch off the organ. "There are actually rooms still set aside for them up in the big house. But Mykael says that they are often very busy doing other tasks. More especially, with all of the problems that are currently going on in the Syria, Iraq, and Afghanistan, and places like that. Although they all turned up when we last had a big party. That was when we welcomed Matthew and his mother to the island. And because adult angels can change how they look, they all reverted back into their child forms to play football with us. Even Mykael and Ithuriel. It was really neat, and also a bit confusing."

"Why?" Lara asked. Immediately intrigued by the idea that there could be many angel children, but also wondering why it would be confusing to Tris.

"Well, the odd thing about it is that quite a few of them are twins, which makes it a bit difficult to know which is which. Especially when they revert to their child forms. But it's weird because you have, like, one angel child from a thousand years ago and one from now… like, modern. But they still look identical. Andrew explained to me that it was because of some weird anomaly in the way in which they were reincarnated. So, Alexei and Gofraidh are, like, identical, even 'though they were born a thousand years apart. And so are Tristan and Aerynn, and also Taylor and Conlaodh. It's kind of spooky when you see them all together and think about that."

"I'm a twin," murmured Lara almost a little sadly. "Although I don't know where Lawrence is now, or what's happened to him. I haven't seen him since we were about seven… or eight?"

"Lawrence?" Tris queried.

"Yeah, he's my twin," Lara explained. "Like I mentioned the other day. Only we're not properly identical, obviously, 'cause he's a boy. But we do look quite a bit alike."

"So how did you get separated?" Tris immediately asked. In a way, it seemed strange to him that an adoption agency would ever contemplate splitting up children who were twins. Lara gave a soft sigh and shook her head.

"As I explained to Mykael, I think it was because the Holts only wanted a girl. So they just took me, and left him behind for someone else to adopt. When they eventually changed their minds about it, mainly because I was so upset at leaving him, they found out that another family had already adopted him. So they… like the Holts and the other people, tried to arrange it that we would see each other every few weeks. Like, for a playdate. It was a bit weird, but I managed to see him quite a few times. But then his family suddenly moved away. The Holts simply told me that Lawrence's dad had got work in another state, but they never said where."

***

Rylan huddled down into the warmth of his bed and shut his eyes. Even 'though he was comfortable and safe, his thoughts still raced. Everything in his life, over the last few days, had moved so fast. At times, almost too fast, it seemed.

Since leaving the old, abandoned car he'd been using as a temporary shelter, mainly because the front seats had been taken over by a couple of older street kids, he'd spent two uncomfortable nights under the cardboard behind the dumpster. Admittedly, the street kids had offered to share the car with him, but because it was obvious that were always high on glue and other drugs, he'd felt it would be better to be well away from any chance of being coerced into the same habits. Or to leave himself open to abuse. Eventually finding that the cardboard he used to hide under had been collected for recycling, and with no idea of where else to go, other than the daunting prospect of simply wandering the streets, he'd headed into an area of slightly better class housing, with the hope that he might find a place that was temporarily vacant. Or a house that might have a garden shed, or lean-to, out back, that he could use as a temporary shelter.

With the weather suddenly taking a turn for the worst, however, he'd eventually taken the risky step of breaking into a house, in order to get out of the freezing cold, find something to eat and a safe place to sleep for even just one night. Ironically, as a result of being discovered by the family that lived there, he was now safe, clean and cosily tucked up in a proper bed. Living in a place that was as far removed from his life on the streets, and what he'd last experienced as home life, as he could imagine. Far from what he could ever remember, if he was to be brutally honest.

It appeared that the home he was now a part of clearly regarded children as rather special. A home that saw the enforcement of parental discipline as simply being grounded to your bedroom for an afternoon, evening, or even a day; with no access to a computer, according to what Henry and Thomas had told him, when he'd asked. There had certainly been no mention of paddles inscribed with religious quotations, or leather straps, or belts, or canes. Or, worse still, having visits to the basement for special talks, which usually went a great deal further than any acceptable father and son interaction.

The Fulchers, it appeared, had decided to take pity on him. Perhaps more particularly, Margaret Fulcher, who seemed very concerned at the mere idea that a child of his age should ever being out, alone, on the streets in such freezing weather. When James Fulcher had reiterated the idea of calling the police, she'd had quietly taken her husband aside and whispered a few words to him. While Rylan hadn't been able to hear exactly what had been said, by the looks that had been passed his way during their conversation, he felt sure that mention had been made about his home-life, and of the abuse that he'd suffered. Whatever decision had eventually been made, James Fulcher had simply nodded and acquiesced to his wife's judgment. Nothing more had been said, since then, about involving the police in the matter; at least not in his presence.

During that first evening he'd been there, after being shown to the guest room, and told that it would be his bedroom while he was with them, he'd spent a good hour playing computer games with Thomas and Henry, until they'd all been called to an impromptu evening meal of Domino's pizzas. It had all seemed so much as he imagined would be a normal family interaction; a circumstance far removed from anything he could previously remember. At the same time, he presumed that Margaret and James Fulcher had, most likely, further discussed what to do about him. The next day, however, James Fulcher had simply headed off to work. Which, as he'd explained to his children the previous night, was necessary for their chances to go on holiday.

With no police intervention, Rylan had simply spent the day at home with the rest of the family... Mrs. Fulcher, Marlow, Thomas and Henry.

At one stage, Margaret Fulcher had taken him quietly aside and, while well out of the hearing of her children, had asked him to explain the details of his past to her in more explicit detail. While he'd not bothered to mention too much about the 'problems' regarding his sexuality, she had still been quite astonished and had seemed greatly shocked at the extent of the abuse that he'd suffered at the church camp and in the basement. As a result, she also seemed to have completely understood his reluctance to go out shopping with them, later in the day, for fear of being recognised. Eventually deciding to leave him at home, in the care of Marlow, while she took Thomas and Henry with her.

The older girl, while perhaps regarding him as a little too young to be a true close friend, seemed rather nonchalant about his presence, however. Seeming not too put out by having to babysit, just as long as he didn't interrupt her while she was texting her friends. As he'd sat watching the television, with the sound turned down to a very low level, he'd wondered if she'd made any mention of him to them.

He'd felt his spirits lift, however, when Margaret Fulcher had arrived back with some new underwear for him, as well as a couple of T-shirts and a new pair of jeans, having taken his sizing from the fact that he fitted the clothes he'd borrowed from Thomas reasonably well. Nevertheless, the next two days had also been just a little nerve-wracking. Even with the fact that he'd been able spend most of his time with Henry and Thomas and had almost been treated as if he was a permanent member of the family, there was always the quiet worry in the back of his thoughts that, at some stage, the police suddenly might arrive to collect him. Either because the Fulchers felt that he really needed to be in the care of social welfare, or had simply thought better of looking after him. More especially, given that there was no legality to their 'unofficial adoption' of him, for want of a better description.

Turning onto his side, perhaps in the knowledge that it was highly unlikely that anything of that nature would happen at night, he snuggled down under the duvet and further into the warmth of the bed. Taking care, at the same time, not to catch his wings in any way beneath the long T-shirt that he was wearing as nighttime attire. They were growing rather rapidly, by almost an inch or two each day, it appeared. But he'd so far managed to keep them hidden under the T-shirt and a bulky jumper of Thomas's that he'd borrowed. How long it would be until they became too big to hide, he wasn't sure. In truth, he had no idea of how fast they'd grow, or how big they might eventually get. It wasn't as if there were any books that he could read, or sites that he could go to on the Internet, to find out about it. At the same time, he wondered what having them actually made him. Was he an angel? Or was he simply some unexpected, mutant freak of nature? Something that would mean that he'd ultimately become an object of curiosity and perhaps ridicule; as had happened for so much of his school life? Or something very special that would have people in awe of him?

With a sigh, he closed his eyes and tried to will himself to sleep, trying to ignore the questions that continued to impose themselves on his thoughts. The bed was warm and cosy, and if he had any worries, they could at least wait until morning.

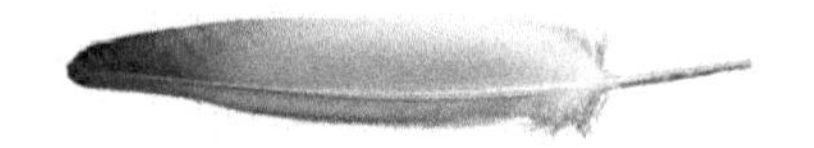

CHAPTER THREE

Military Action....

"So, have we managed to get anything at all from that damn GPS Locator System?" demanded Lieutenant Colonel Harris McMahon scathingly, as soon as the junior officers had acknowledged his presence by standing to attention and saluting. "Such as some new signal that just might tell us where Angel-girl is currently hiding?"

"Not a ping, Sir," Private Bradford Sullivan quickly replied, indicating with a sweep of his hand towards the array of the monitoring equipment he'd been seated in front of. "At least, for the moment."

"For the moment?" Lieutenant Colonel Harris McMahon queried rather tersely. "So, we have had something?"

"There was just a hint of a signal briefly picked up just a few moments after the time she first went missing," Private Sullivan quickly explained. Lieutenant Colonel Harris McMahon wandered over to where the soldier was now seated. Then stood beside him, peering at the screen, as if expecting it to suddenly burst into action.

"So what has happened to it? And where is it now?" he impatiently demanded. Private Sullivan seemed to cringe a little. It didn't pay to get offside with the Lieutenant Colonel; especially when he was actively engaged in some pursuit. Whether it be the simple tracking of an enemy, as in the case of a military exercise, or, as in this case, a mutant child. Not that there'd ever been any other mutant children for them to track.

"We have absolutely no idea, Sir," Sergeant Oliver Childers hastily interrupted. "Although, when it occurred, just after she'd first disappeared, the blip suddenly became very faint. Almost as if it suddenly seemed to be coming from quite some considerable distance."

"Just how big a distance are we talking about?" Lieutenant Colonel Harris McMahon muttered, turning to face the officer he'd left in charge of the tracking. Sergeant Childers briefly cocked his head to one side; the subtle gesture seeming to indicate some sense of his not being all that certain about that particular item of information.

"Given how faint it was, Sir, I'd almost be tempted to suggest it was perhaps somewhere on the other side of the Atlantic," he cautiously offered. "Or at least at some comparable distance." Harris McMahon scowled in his direction. What he was hearing did not make for too much sense. Not unless the girl was capable of flying such vast distances at impossible speeds.

"So what you're actually suggesting is that, somehow Angel-girl was suddenly able to travel several thousand miles? And do it at considerable speed? Like Mach 4, or better?" he queried in some clear manner of disbelief.

"Well, as I said, it was there quite clearly when she first absconded, and when we had the men and dogs chasing her," Sergeant Childers quickly explained. "I made sure that we had the tracking system activated almost as soon as we knew she was missing. But, then, it just faded," he hastily continued, hoping to show that he'd been efficient in undertaking his part in the search. "The very last activation we got was just a brief blip shortly before the local search was ended."

"I was under the impression that this expensive array of tracking equipment was supposed to be the very latest technology. With the ability to work continuously, and be able to pick up a signal from anywhere on the damn planet!" Lieutenant Colonel Harris McMahon almost barked rather sarcastically. "And that the actual GPS beacon, the necklace, was virtually indestructible!"

"I doubt that Angel-girl will have figured out its purpose, Sir, given that she believes that it was a special present from her parents. In which case she'd have no reason to want to be rid of it. So it should still be capable of being picked up by any of our satellites," Sergeant Childers commented. "Unless she's at the bottom of a coal mine!"

"So now you're suggesting that she might be hiding underground, somewhere?" Harris McMahon retorted mockingly, yet with some growing sense of irritation. "Like, in a cave?" Sergeant Childers glanced towards the tracking screens; his action, in some ways, just a means of avoiding his superior's stern gaze for a moment or two. Also just a little flabbergasted that his senior officer could somehow decide to interpret a common figure of speech as being an actual reality.

"Not necessarily, Sir," he flustered. "It could be that…"

"So she could be dead?" Lieutenant Colonel Harris McMahon interrupted.

"Not necessarily, Sir," Sergeant Childers cautiously reiterated. "But that being so, even if she was, we'd still be getting a signal of some sort."

"And so now we're getting...?" Harris McMahon snapped. Sergeant Childers gave a slight shrug and again glanced towards the tracking screens.

"Nada! Zilch! Absolutely nothing!" he murmured.

"Do you think she could have figured out a way to stop it working?" Harris McMahon suggested, moving closer to the screens and peering over the shoulders of the junior officers tasked with monitoring them. An action that immediately seemed to make them all a little nervous.

"I'd think that'd be most unlikely, Sir," Sergeant Childers quietly replied. "As I said a moment ago, given that there's nothing on it to indicate that it's actually sending out any form of signal, I doubt she'd ever realise its true purpose. And even if she did work out that we were tracking her, and did find a way to remove it, it would still be sending out a signal that we should pick up. Its internal batteries are guaranteed to keep a charge for at least five years or more."

"And you're absolutely certain that she wouldn't have any reason to suspect we would be able to track her by means of the necklace?" Lieutenant Colonel Harris McMahon questioned.

"Well, she didn't seem to find it all that strange that she simply woke up wearing it," Sergeant Childers said, giving an almost insignificant shrug of his shoulders. "When Doctor Stafford told her that it was a special gift from her parents, she actually seemed rather delighted; even if she was still a bit upset that they didn't hand it to her themselves, and that they seemed to have abandoned her." Lieutenant Colonel Harris McMahon exhaled noisily, and looked back at the silent sweeping of the tracking equipment.

"Speaking of her parents," he eventually continued rather abruptly. "Have we got anybody checking to see if they've heard anything from her?"

"I had that done almost straight away, Sir," Sergeant Childers replied, looking towards another of the officers. "Lieutenant Carver reported that they totally denied any knowledge whatsoever of what had happened."

"And they seemed believable?" Lieutenant Colonel Harris McMahon asked, briefly glancing towards Lieutenant Joseph Carver.

"It would seem that way. Not unless they're extremely good actors," Sergeant Childers countered. "To be honest, it seemed as if they were totally surprised that she'd gone missing. But we've still got them under discreet surveillance. Just in case they do have her hidden away, somewhere."

"Did they mention anything further about her twin?" Lieutenant Colonel Harris McMahon asked rather bluntly. "You know, that other kid that they mentioned, when they first brought the girl to us? Lawrence something or other?" Lieutenant Joe Carver gave a slow shake of his head.

"No. Not at all, Sir," he replied. "Our conversation with them was mainly to do with Lara and, as I said, they certainly did seem rather surprised that she'd absconded."

"So there was no indication, at all, that they regretted giving her up?" Lieutenant Colonel Harris McMahon queried. Lieutenant Joseph Carver responded with almost what seemed to be a rather wearisome shrug.

"Not that they mentioned, Sir," he replied, before making a brief sideways cant of his head. "Well, not that I could perceive, at any rate. In fact, as far as I could tell, they seemed to be rather enjoying their newfound wealth. A brand new EV SUV in the driveway and a seventy inch TV in the lounge made that fairly obvious."

"And that also needs to be kept secret." Lieutenant Colonel Harris McMahon suggested, with a subtle tap of a forefinger to the side of his nose. "Kept on a 'talk directly to me if you need to know' basis." He paused, sighed and looked around at the other officers present. "We certainly don't need it becoming common knowledge that we were willing to buy a child from its parents. No matter how much of a freak it might be!"

"I think we're all well aware of the need for total secrecy, Sir," Sergeant Childers quickly affirmed, glancing around at the other personnel present. "We certainly don't need to have any unnecessary X-men panic amongst the public." Harris McMahon sighed a little resignedly and gave a weary shake of his head. The idea of X-men was just a far-fetched movie fantasy as far as he was concerned. Angel-girl was also most likely just some genetic freak, regardless of any suggested religious connotations that might be inherent in her name.

"Getting back to the original adoptions, does anyone have any idea where the girl's twin might now be living? Like, have we managed to find out who it was who ended up adopting him, and where he was taken?" he finally asked. There was a general shaking of heads. "Well, what about the Holts?" he quickly continued. "Have we managed to get any more specific details about their adoption of the girl? Such as, who arranged it and what agency they dealt with? After all, it would seem logical that both children would've originally been together at the same orphanage." There was again a general shaking of heads. Harris McMahon sighed with a sense of exasperation. "What puzzles me a little," he eventually conceded, "is that the Holts would surely have known, right from the start, that Angel-girl had a twin brother, and possibly looked at adopting him, as well. The question is, therefore, why didn't they?"

"They made absolutely no mention of it, when I called on them, Sir," Lieutenant Joseph Carver replied. "Apart from reiterating what they told us when we first acquired the girl. You know, that when they first applied to adopt Lara, they only wanted one child. And that while they knew that she was a twin, they simply decided to just take Lara. Which, I must admit, also seems pretty strange, to my way of thinking. You know, that they would even contemplate splitting up twins when there were probably a good number of other children they could have chosen. However, it simply seems that, when they left with

Lara, the brother was still up for adoption. As they told us right from the start, when they enquired, a week or so later, about the possibility of also adopting him, they found that the boy had already been placed with another family. They did try..."

"Just get onto the original adoption agency, wherever it may be," Lieutenant Colonel Harris McMahon irritatedly interrupted. As far as he was concerned, the Holt's were most probably a dead end in regard to locating either of the children. "Even if you do have to go back to the Holts and put a little extra pressure on them to find out just who it was they dealt with! I want to find out exactly who the brother was adopted out to and, more importantly, where the hell he is now!"

"You think that finding him might lead us to the girl?" Sergeant Childers queried.

"It's possible, but I doubt it!" Lieutenant Colonel Harris McMahon snapped, and then sighed quite noisily. "But, you never know, with them being twins, we may just find that the boy has the same attributes as his sister."

"And if we do manage to find him?" Sergeant Childers continued.

"Offer the parents whatever they want, in the way of a cash incentive, to let us take care of him," McMahon directed. "Whether it looks like he has wings or not! Given what the girl is, even if he hasn't got wings, he may just have other attributes that we can make use of."

"And if they don't want to give him up?"

"There are always ways of making sure we get what we want!" Lieutenant Colonel Harris McMahon muttered. "But let's not get to talking about those sort of dealings just yet. Just get a squad out there and start searching. Use your military authority to get into whatever information sources you need. You know, adoption records, school records, medical records, and that sort of thing; whatever you think might be useful as a way to find him. If necessary, say it's a matter of national security. Given the current paranoia over terrorist threats, that reasoning shouldn't seem too far-fetched."

***

"Will it be okay for me to take Lara up to the farm?" Tris asked a little cautiously. "You know, to meet Granddad Roger and Grandma Betty, and for me to teach Lara how to 'be' to there?"

"Have you checked that Andrew is free to go with you?" Amanda countered. "Do remember that Mykael has asked you not to leave the island with her, unless you are chaperoned."

"But I was only going to take her there for a little while," Tris softly pleaded. "Just so she can learn about 'be'ing to the barn," he added. Seeming just a little embarrassed that he would need to be chaperoned just to take Lara to the farm.

"Well, if you're not happy with those conditions, I suggest you talk it through with Mykael," Amanda suggested calmly, but still with some hint of severity. Not really wanting to be putting a damper of Tris's enthusiasm, but also wary of his getting caught up, once again, in something that might lead him into danger. "But keep it in mind that he doesn't usually make such restrictions lightly. I do get the feeling that he sees something far more important than we realise behind your finding Lara. Maybe he senses some danger in what is taking place that we might not yet be aware of."

Tris nodded a little resignedly, and then was quiet for a few moments.

"Andrew said that he can go with us, but not right away," he eventually murmured. "He said that we should give him a bit of time to get a few things finished up at the big house." Again, he was quiet for a few moments. "I think he'd actually prefer to go tomorrow morning," he finally muttered a little resignedly.

"Well, you do need to fit in with him," Amanda said quietly. "It would also give you time to check that there's not likely to be anyone else up at the farm who could pose a problem. Such as your dad's parents!" Tris nodded, and began to head down towards the music room.

"Can we mind talk with each other?" Lara asked with some surprise as she trailed after him. Tris gave a slight shrug.

"I think we can with other angels," he murmured. "Like, ones that we know, if they're not too far away."

"But how?" Lara asked.

"You just try to think a message to them," Tris replied. "It's a bit like saying a prayer, but directing it to who you want to hear it."

"So I can let you know what I'm thinking?" Lara asked. Tris nodded and then was silent for a moment, before giving a slightly embarrassed laugh. Perhaps not really wanting to be thought of as 'cute'.

***

Skylar cautiously opened his eyes. His head throbbed from the after-effects of whatever it was that had been used to render him unconscious for yet another trip. Apart from a vague sense of being in something that was moving, the last thing he could properly remember was being in the strange basement room and then being given a glass of orange juice and told to drink it all down, quickly.

He was now lying on a different mattress. Albeit, one just as dirty and worn as the previous one. Above him, a single bulb, in the centre of what once again looked like the underside of a house, cast a dim light around another room with solid concrete walls. Like with his previous prison, there also seemed to be only one door. A solid construction made of some metal. Steel, he presumed. But if there was one major difference, at least he wasn't hog-tied and gagged.

"Where am I?" he mused almost to himself.

"Hell!" a voice quietly answered. With a start, Skylar rolled over and realised that there were two other boys present. One sitting on another mattress, the other curled up under a blanket.

"What?" he queried, perhaps half in curiosity, half in surprise.

"Well, we may as well be," the quiet voice, which belonged to a dark-haired boy of a similar age to himself, replied rather resignedly.

"Who are you?" Skylar quickly queried, as he sat up. "And where are we?"

"I'm Riley, and this..." He pointed to the other boy lying, seemingly asleep, on a mattress beside him, "is Cooper. We've been here about a week." Skylar quickly noted that, like himself, the two boys were both shirtless, dressed in only jeans and trainers and had the same tattoo mark on their left shoulder. Riley looked fairly athletic with a slightly elfin face, while Cooper, even while asleep, almost looked like he could be model material, given the length of his eyelashes and his almost carefully shaped eyebrows. Not that he looked effeminate, just… well… Skylar wasn't too sure quite what to think.

"So where are we?" he questioned once again.

"In a basement under a house, miles from civilisation, it seems," Riley murmured. "So there's absolutely no point in yelling for help. Not unless you want to get your butt beaten to a flippin' pulp!" Skylar nodded. It seemed clear that the same threat had been issued for all of them.

"Are we the only ones here?" he asked, looking around the room and seeing several more mattresses. Riley gave a quick shake of his head.

"There were about five or six other boys when me and Cooper first arrived," he said quietly. "Some of them were quite a bit older. But they got taken away… like, upstairs somewhere, a few days ago, and haven't come back yet." He gave a casual shrug and pointed towards the far wall. "There are also a couple of girls in another room on the other side of that wall. I think they're also like us. You know, captives."

"What for?" Skylar queried. Riley gave a dispirited shake of his head.

"You don't want to know," he murmured.

"Why?" Skylar asked almost without thinking.

"Because it's obviously very painful and it involves beatings and… and, you know…" Riley muttered, looking towards the door.

"Know what?" Skylar queried, even as, in his thoughts, he was beginning to realise what Riley was implying. Before Riley had a chance to answer, however, there was the heavy thump of boots on stairs, somewhere outside the door. As it opened, another slightly built boy, of perhaps twelve or thirteen and dressed in only his underwear, was shoved roughly through the doorway, so that he tripped and sprawled face first onto one of the vacant mattresses nearest to the door. Riley immediately shuffled backwards so that his back was hard against the wall. Cooper remained asleep. Taking a cue from Riley, Skylar also moved back against the wall. His instinct once again telling him that this man was serious trouble and hoping that he wouldn't be dragged upstairs for a beating… or whatever else was likely to happen.

"And the next time you try taking off, you'll get more than just a good leathering!" the man snarled. "I have other particularly nasty ways of hurting little boys who cross me!" He threw a pair of jeans onto the floor beside where the boy was now scrambling towards the wall. For the moment, the boy made no move to get his clothing, but remained curled up in a ball with his face hidden. The back of his thighs and part of his lower back clearly marked with vivid welts from a beating with a belt of some type. It was also reasonably obvious that the area beneath his underwear would be similarly marked… most probably to a far greater degree.

"Next time, anyone else upstairs who wants to hurt you will also get to have a little fun!" the man sneered. He then turned and glowered around the room, quickly spotting Skylar. "You're awake!" he muttered, in a statement of the obvious. Skylar nodded.

"Well, just take a lesson from what you see. As I told you the other day, you're my property to do with what I like. As you can see, any trying to run away will be met with severe punishment." He glanced at Riley and Cooper and then came closer. "Just be thankful that you three are currently part of a special order I'm building up for a special private event that's coming up in a couple of months; with wealthy clients who want a sense of 'innocence' in their entertainment, and are quite prepared to pay up large for it… if you get my drift! Otherwise you'd have already been put to far more profitable uses than just sitting down here on your assets." He turned and headed for the door. "Sleep tight," he said mockingly, as he slammed the door. Skylar immediately heard the sound of a padlock being clicked into place.

Riley gestured towards where the older boy, now that his tormentor had gone, began to struggle back into his jeans, wincing with pain as he did so.

"That's Peter," Riley whispered. "He gets taken out quite regularly."

"Where to?" Skylar asked. Riley shrugged.

"Private parties, and such," he whispered. "He's part of the 'entertainment', so to speak. That's what'll eventually happen to all of us, I suppose." As he spoke, Cooper groaned slightly and seemed to whimper a little in his sleep.

"He and Peter tried to escape a couple of days ago," Riley whispered. "The local sheriff brought them back here last night." He gestured towards Cooper. "He got a beating too, but not anything like what's probably happened to Peter. Mainly because, as Vittorio just said, he's got something special lined up for some of us."

"Special?" Skylar queried, looking at Cooper. "Like what?" In some ways, he already had a fair idea of what was implied and, even having endured three days of beatings at the church boot camp, knew that it would be far worse. Riley shrugged in response.

"It certainly won't be anything to enjoy, going by what some of the other boys have told me," he murmured.

***

Having told Lara to count to ten before doing her visualisation, Tris waited anxiously to one side of the sanctuary. An instant later, Lara appeared; first of all with her gaze focussed up at the cross, before turning towards Tris. She hurried over and grabbed his hands.

"I did it," she exclaimed. "All the way from my bedroom."

"As you'll realise, distance is not really a problem," Tris replied. "It's accuracy and knowing whether other people will be where you want to be."

"So you don't end up landing on top of someone?" Lara queried. Tris shrugged.

"I suppose so," he murmured. To be honest, it wasn't something that he'd thought about all that much. In the act of 'be'ing, it just seemed that they were able to arrive where they wanted, without worrying about complications such as who might already be there. "Anyway," he quickly continued, "while we're here, and seeing as we can't go to the farm until tomorrow, I may as well explain a bit more about this place. Such as how it was realised that it was a very special place, and Uncle Alexei and Uncle Tristan eventually finding out that there were bodies down in the crypt."

"Is that who you were named after?" Lara cautiously queried. "Like, Tris for Tristan and Alexei for your middle name?" Tris blushed a little and nodded.

"Mum and Dad, who were actually my Godparents when I was born, named me. I didn't find out where they got the names from until I came to live here... like, permanently. Up until then, I wasn't really sure where the names came from." He also didn't want to mention that at school in Glasgow the bullies had quickly branded him with a nickname of 'Sissy Trissy'.

"So what happened to your real parents?" Lara continued.

"They died in a plane crash," Tris softly replied. "Somehow, I managed to be the only person to survive. That's why I used to be called the miracle child."

"And then you came to live here?" Lara queried. Tris nodded.

"And that's when I started to get my wings." He glanced around. "Anyway, let me show you the crypt. I can tell you all about where the bodies were and show you what happened with Uncle Taylor's coffin."

They hurried across to the doorway to the side room, where Tris stopped just a little abruptly. Grabbing a torch from a shelf just inside the doorway, he then pointed back to the cross.

"Remember I told you that you could still see the marks where two boy-angels were crucified," he exclaimed. "Well, as

I may have mentioned, they were called Gofraidh and Aerynn and they were in the church for a special funeral service, because their younger brother, Conlaodh, had just died. After the Vikings killed the two older boys, Huydhran, who was the priest at that time, hid all three bodies in the crypt to stop the Vikings from realising what they were and stealing them as curiosities. According to Uncle Andrew, even when dead, their bodies would've been worth a lot to some people. Like, as curiosities. Anyway, quite a while before Uncle Alexei and Uncle Tristan started having dreams about what had happened all those years ago, and well before anyone even knew about the crypt, one of the boys who lived on the island also died, after breaking his neck while trying to use a hang-glider that was too big for him to control.

"So you think that he wanted to be like your uncles?" Lara queried, as she followed Tris into the side room and down the steps leading into the crypt. "Like, he wanted to fly?" Tris nodded as he flicked on the torch

"According to Granddad Steve, Taylor was absolutely obsessed with the idea of trying to fly. He used to follow Alexei almost everywhere. Anyway, after he died, he wanted to be out near the church, so they buried him right beside the old ruins. When the crypt was discovered, Ithuriel moved Taylor's coffin into it, so that it would be safe. Well, more safe than if it was just buried beside the church ruins, because it was a bit too close to the old churchyard and everyone wasn't too sure if some historical research group might eventually start doing some excavation of that area."

"So when did the church end up being like it is now?" Lara quickly asked as she looked around the torch-lit crypt. Tris gave a quick shrug of his shoulders as he cast the torchlight around the room, before focussing it on the larger of the stone slabs.

"When Andrew was about our age, I think," he murmured. "Or maybe just a bit younger. Like, sort of nine or ten. Which means it must now be almost twenty years ago. Anyway, that's where the three bodies were placed. Only, by the time Alexei and Tristan found them, they were just skeletons, obviously."

"And the coffin was…?" Lara asked. Tris quickly used the torch to show the smaller stone slab, to one side of which were stacked some pieces of wood that were quite clearly the remnants of a small coffin.

"Ithuriel evidently moved Taylor's coffin from out beyond the ruins to there," he said almost in a whisper. Almost as if to speak too loud about all that had happened would somehow be wrong.

"So how did the church eventually get rebuilt?" Lara asked. Tris went back over to the steps and sat down, quickly indicating for Lara to sit beside him.

"That was quite a long process," he said quietly. "From what Mum and Dad have told me, it all began when Alexei and Tristan found some Viking relics in a cave up near the farm. The one we're going to tomorrow."

"Is the cave still there?" Lara asked with some excitement. Tris shook his head.

"No. There's just a big waterfall tumbling down the cliffs that comes from the stream that used to run into the cave system; at least until it collapsed and started flooding." He didn't bother to mention that the waterfall was now named after him. Feeling that that would've seemed a bit like boasting and, anyway, his memory of how that had all come about was still a little vague. Apart from knowing that it involved a time when he'd done some very bad things.

"Anyway, to cut a long story short," he hastily continued. "When Alexei and Tristan brought a couple of the relics back home… like, a cup and a cross, they started having weird dreams about what had happened on the island, and in the church, over a thousand years ago. Like, back when Gofraidh, Aerynn and Conlaodh were originally living on the island. Eventually, that led to them having a dream about a big stone cross… the one that's now outside the church, which had some weird prophecy or something on it about returning some crowns to the three boys who had died all those years ago, to make something right."

"And so they found the crowns, obviously," Lara interjected. Tris nodded.

"They had dreams that told them that they were in the cave. Then they got trapped in the cave by a rock-fall, and had to be rescued, from a bad angel," he continued.

"So after they'd got the crowns, what happened then?" Lara quickly asked.

"That's when all this happened," Tris replied, gesturing at their surroundings. "Even 'though the bad angels tried to stop them, they managed to put the crowns back with the skeletons. As soon as they'd done that, and as I said the other day, the three skeletons came back to life, as well as Taylor. Having the help of the extra four child-angels allowed them to defeat the bad angels, but what was also amazing was that all the ruins somehow just arose out of the ground to become the church as it is now. Uncle Andrew says that it was just like one of those controlled building demolitions in reverse. Like, everything… the stones, the bits of timber, the pews and everything… even the cross, just came up out of the ground up and settled into place. Just as if they'd never been destroyed."

"So that meant that, with Andrew, there were seven child-angels," Lara said, in a statement of the obvious. "Which is obviously why this place is called Seven Angels Island."

"At least until I came along," Tris added."

"So you're the eighth and I must be the ninth," Lara added, with a look of delight.

"If we don't count Mykael and Ithuriel," Tris murmured, as he got up and started up the stairs. "And they don't tend to be here all that much, apart from when I have a problem." Leaving the crypt and church, they wandered out to stand looking out to sea.

"When do you think I could start learning to fly?" Lara asked as she watched the gulls circling and wheeling a small way out from the cliffs. Tris exhaled softly.

"I'll need to check that with Andrew or Mykael," he quietly replied. In some ways, it was more that he was nervous about starting that teaching process on his own. "But I know something we could do to help you for when you do," he quickly added.

"What?" Lara questioned.

"Swimming," Tris eagerly replied. "Mykael says that swimming helps build your chest strength, which makes it easier to fly. More especially if you then think of yourself as being a light as a feather. Like, that you don't weigh anything at all."

"The military hospital place I was kept at didn't think I weighed enough as it was," Lara murmured with a look of surprise. "They used to try to get me to eat these huge meals, and were always trying to give me extra vitamins and stuff to make me grow faster. Not that I used to take all of them. A lot of times, I'd just keep them in my mouth and then spit them down the plughole in the bathroom washbasin when I hoped they weren't looking. Like, I'd pretend to be washing my face, or brushing my teeth, and would bend down close to the basin so that they wouldn't see the pills because of the flannel."

"But all us angel-children weigh much less than we should," Tris explained. "That's one of the first things that Peter McCormack noted about me."

"Who?" Lara queried.

"That's the doctor who checked you over when you first arrived," Tris replied. "He used to look after all my uncles, as well. According to Uncle Andrew, that was because one day Uncle Tristan got shot by some nutter who wanted to try to prove that there were children with wings."

"But that's what we are, in a way," Lara murmured.

"I know," Tris replied. "But that still didn't give him the right to try to kill one of us." He took a hold of Lara's hands. "Come on. Let's head to the swimming pool. If I can't start you flying, yet, you can at least start swimming to build up some chest strength." With a quick visualisation, they were suddenly inside the pool complex.

"But I haven't got anything to wear for swimming," Lara belatedly whispered, as they looked across to where Carwyn, Melanie, Finn and Victoria were sitting. Tris looked at her for a moment, then hurried over to where the other children were sitting. A moment or two later Melanie hurried over towards where Lara was waiting.

"Come on," she said almost eagerly. "You're about the same size as me, so you'll probably fit into one of my swimsuits." Taking a hold of Lara's left hand, Melanie quickly led Lara through the side doors of the pool complex and across to the main house.

As Tris watched them leave, Carwyn sidled up to him.

"So what is it?" he teased. "Is she still just your adopted sister? Or your girlfriend?"

"Umm, I'm not..." Tris began, even as he blushed a little. "I just want to see if she can swim."

"You mean you just want to see her in a bikini," Carwyn laughed, teasingly. "After all, she is quite pretty." Tris blushed even further.

"Sw... swimming practice will... will make it easier for her to fly," he half- stammered, a little self-consciously.

***

Rylan put his head back and let the warmth of the shower rinse through his hair. Feeling the foam from the conditioner wash from his shoulders, over his wings and down his back. His week with the Fulchers had, so far, been a joy. Especially when compared with his time of hiding out on the streets and being forced to sleep under piles of discarded cardboard, or in abandoned cars. To then being awakened every hour, it seemed, by some dark figure or other, rattling futilely at the car's door handles. Always worried that they might just smash the glass to gain entry, or set fire to the car out of frustration, not realising that he was inside.

Even just the mere fact that he'd been able to have a shower whenever he wanted, and a change of underwear every day, made his life far more enjoyable. More particularly because the water was gas-heated, so there was no time limit on the 'boys' bathroom'. James, Margaret and Marlow having separate bathrooms upstairs — an en suite, and a separate small 'girls' bathroom — meant that the downstairs facility that he'd used the first night he'd broken into the house was just for the boys. Taking the removable showerhead from its socket, he quickly used it to rinse the last of the conditioner from his hair, and any remaining soap, from under his arms, before moving down to the more intimate areas of his body and then down his legs. Almost automatically spreading his wings out a little as he then let the water also cascade over his shoulders and down to where his wings emerged from his back. As he finally stood upright, replaced the showerhead in its socket and simply let the water continue to surge down his back to his legs, even as he fluttered his wings a little, he heard a slight noise behind him and quickly realised that he'd forgotten to lock the bathroom door.

"Sorry to interrupt, but Mom was just wanting to know if..." The rest of Henry's comment about what Rylan might like for lunch, was cut short as he gazed at the image of his new friend through the glass of the shower. With having quickly turned his back towards the door to hide his more intimate parts from view, Rylan had failed to realise that the boy would clearly see his wings through the glass walls of the shower.

"Mom, I think you should see this," Henry called, as he remained standing in the doorway to the bathroom with the door half open; his eyes now wide with amazement, at the sight of a boy with wings. "I think you'd better come, quick! It's Rylan! He's... he's... an..." His gaze not leaving the sight in front of him, even as Rylan quickly shut off the shower and then hastily reached for a fresh towel to cover his nakedness.

By the time Rylan had got a towel wrapped firmly around his waist, and was reaching for a second towel to wrap around his hair and shoulders, Margaret Fulcher was already at the bathroom door. Perhaps she was worried that he might have fallen and been injured in some way, or that he still had the visible marks of some recent abuse. Like Henry, and now also Thomas and Marlow, who, drawn by the sound of a commotion, had arrived to find out what was wrong, for a moment or two, they simply stared. With Marlow and Mrs Fulcher's arrival, Rylan felt thankful that he'd at least managed to cover his private bits from their sight. His wings... now that was another matter altogether.

Quickly taking control, Margaret Fulcher hastily ushered the other children out of the bathroom and then shut the door. Coming closer to Rylan, she sat herself, just a little tentatively, on the edge of the bath and beckoned the boy towards her. Until he was close enough for to reach out and take a hold of his hands.

"I'm sorry," Rylan murmured as his eyes welled a little with tears. "I should have told you before. You know, about my having..." He lapsed into silence. Wondering what she was thinking of him. Did she think he was an angel? Or would she see him as just some horrible half-human mutant freak?

Margaret Fulcher gave a quick shake of her head. For a moment, she just continued to stare at him, as he simply stood, facing her. His tears now running freely down his cheeks. Eventually, taking the matter in hand, she got to her feet, grabbed yet another towel, and gave his hair a quick, but thorough, rub to stop the water dripping from it onto the floor, almost as if it was the most natural thing in the world to towel this remarkable boy's hair dry.

"Are you an angel?" she eventually asked, casually tossing the towel in the direction of the laundry basket. It was the thought that had first entered her head on seeing him as he was, and noting how beautiful he looked, even as a boy. A thought prompted by a remembering of the final scenes of a film she'd watched at church a few months ago… 'I Am Gabriel'. Rylan gave a quick shrug and then a somewhat tentative shake of his head, fully knowing that she was referring to his having wings.

"I don't know," he murmured. "They just started growing… a short while ago."

***

Having allowed Rylan to go to his room to get dressed, Margaret Fulcher and her three children sat in the family room awaiting his arrival. All thoughts about what they might have for lunch now temporarily put aside in the light of what they'd just seen.

"Do you think he's an angel?" Thomas quietly asked. "Like, you know, from heaven or something?"

"I don't know," his mother softly replied, giving a small shake of her head "And, to be honest, I don't think he even knows that, himself."

"Maybe he's a mutant," Henry offered excitedly. "You know, like in the X-Men movies?"

"That's just made-up stuff," Marlow countered, with almost an air of derision at the stupidity of her younger brother's suggestion. "From comic books and films. This is something..." Whatever else she was about to say was cut short as Rylan appeared in the doorway. Now dressed in jeans and a large T-shirt.

"I don't know what I am," he murmured, making it rather obvious that he'd at least overheard the last part of their discussion. "They just started growing a few weeks ago, I think. I'm not sure exactly when, apart from the fact that it was when I was still living out on the streets. I only really noticed them when I was first here." He took the place at the table that had clearly been left for him. Not wanting to mention that the reason he didn't know exactly when his wings had emerged was simply because he hadn't had the opportunity to wash or change his clothes for all the time he'd been on the streets. For a while there was silence, as everyone seemed a little unsure of what to say next.

"Did your parents have them?" Margaret Fulcher eventually asked. Rylan gave a strong shake of his head. Given his parents' brutality towards him, even the mere idea that either of them might have vague links to being angels seemed just a sordid travesty of some kind. At any rate, William and Molly Daniels were only his foster parents, the people who'd adopted him just a few days after his sister had left the orphanage. He couldn't remember anything at all about his true parents.

"No," he murmured. "And I don't know of anyone else who has."There was a further period of silence as they all just watched each other. Rylan could sense that the other children wanted to see his wings, but were not quite sure whether or not to ask. In the end, he shrugged, then took his T-shirt off and indicated for them to come closer.

Almost immediately, Marlow, Henry and Thomas were crowded around him. Rather tentatively touching his wings and pressing very gently at where they emerged from his back. Almost as if taking extra care not to risk damaging them in any way. All the while, their mother just watched him.

"Can you fly?" Henry asked rather eagerly. Rylan gave a slight shrug.

"I don't know," he murmured. He tried to look over his left shoulder to see his wings and then shook his head. "I don't think they'll be big enough, yet."

"But they're getting bigger?" questioned Marlow. Rylan nodded.

"Slowly," he murmured, again trying to look over his left shoulder. "And quite a bit since they first emerged."

"Emerged?" Marlow echoed. Again Rylan nodded.

"At first, they were just these funny little ridge things that used to ache a bit. But then, as I said, the first night I was here, I found that they'd already burst through the skin. I don't quite know even when that was, 'cause I didn't get too much chance to wash when I was out on the streets. But that was why my old T-shirt had all that blood on it and all my clothes were so stinky." He wondered, for a brief moment, where all his old clothes were. What had happened to them? Whether they'd still be stashed in a rubbish bin somewhere, or already on their way to become part of some landfill?

"I think I remember seeing something on YouTube about a little boy who was an angel appearing in a church somewhere near Wichita," Marlow suddenly announced, as she finally resumed her seat on the other side of the table. "Was that you?"

Rylan gave a quick shake of his head. For the moment, at least, not wanting to admit that he had any connection at all with Wichita, but also puzzled as to how such a story might have originated.

"It was just a short while ago, in fact," Marlow enthusiastically continued. "At a place just south of Wichita called Oakton, if I remember right. I can get my laptop and look it up if you'd like?"

Rylan half-nodded. While he still didn't want to admit that he'd ever been in Oakton, or knew anyone there, he was now even more curious to know why Oakton might have been singled out for such a visitation.

Marlow hurried away and returned a few moments later with her Apple laptop. Having watched her quickly typing in 'boy' and 'angel' as search factors for Google, Rylan was surprised to find that there were several responses referring to the appearance of child-angels; a few of them purporting to link to videos on YouTube. Most seemed to date back to almost two decades earlier, and to a diverse range of countries such as England, Scotland, Australia and New Zealand, but second on the list was a reference to a video of a supposed more recent appearance in Oakton, Wichita. Marlow quickly located it and set it playing.

After a moment or two of watching, it became obviously that there was not going to be any actual video, or even clear pictures, of an angel, beyond the showing of a blurred photograph. A picture taken on a cell phone, that was purported to be the image of a child-angel who had appeared in a local church. Having immediately recognised the exterior of the building as being one of the places where he'd been abused, Rylan watched, with growing interest, as a person who was obviously a regional television reporter for some television channel, gave the background story to the claimed angel sighting and then turned to talk to a teenage girl who had been at the church service.

According to April Morrison, who'd taken the blurred picture with her phone, the angel had suddenly appeared at the front of a church in front of the altar. Supposedly to explain the mysterious disappearance of a young local boy named Matthew Ryan. This had evidently occurred at the same time as the leader of the church, Pastor Isaac Scott, had been arrested on child pornography charges; a man who, it was claimed, had also been the last person to be seen with the boy, when he was alive.

The reporter then continued to explain the situation a little further. Stating that the pastor's two accomplices had also been arrested at a church boot camp, which the police now claimed to be the main source of the illegal pornographic material; most of which was recordings of children being severely disciplined in various nasty ways.

Even as the video ended, Rylan still felt uncertain. He certainly remembered Matthew Ryan from school and quietly wondered just what had happened to him. Especially as the video quite clearly seemed to suggest that he was dead. He also remembered that, like himself, Matthew had sometimes been accused of being a bit effeminate by the pig-headed 'jocks' at their middle school. Particularly because of his resemblance to the boy who'd been in the TV series 'Touch'. An autistic boy obsessed with numbers who didn't speak. Perhaps, he realised, he'd also been subjected to a week at the boot camp and, somehow, had not survived. At the same time, the mention of the pastor's two accomplices being arrested, quite likely meant that his father was now in custody. Not that he could be too sure of that fact, given that no names, beyond Pastor Isaac Scott, had been mentioned, and he had no idea of where his parents now were. Perhaps, if his father had been arrested, his mother was still living in the apartment that they'd rented in New York, but he wasn't going to risk attempting to find out.

"I really think we need to talk to Father McGeehan about you," Margaret Fulcher suddenly suggested, her comment bluntly interrupting his train of thought. Not that he was likely to let on that he knew anything at all about Oakton, or anything of what was claimed in the YouTube video about the church and Pastor Isaac.

"Down at St. Josephs," Margaret Fulcher continued. For a moment Rylan was a little taken aback. In some ways, he had hoped that the Fulchers would simply want to keep his having wings a secret.

"Is that a church?" he asked a little hesitantly.

"Of course," replied Margaret Fulcher with some enthusiasm. "And Father McGeehan has been with our church for over twenty-five years. He baptized Marlow, Thomas and Henry when each of them was born. I'm sure he'd love to meet you, and talk with you."

"What does he do in the church?" Rylan asked just a little tentatively.

"Well, he gives sermons and things," Margaret Fulcher replied. "And he also hears confessions and does baptisms and marriages and things like that."

"Does he punish children?" Rylan queried. "You know, like, by hitting them if they've been bad, or...?" He quickly left the question incomplete. Not wanting to mention the reason why he'd been punished, in case the Fulchers thought badly of him.

"I shouldn't think so," Margaret replied, looking just a little astonished that he should even ask such a question. "He might scold children who have behaved very badly, but as for any punishments, I very much doubt it." To her thinking, the idea of old Father McGeehan giving any child even a reprimand, other than just a stern word or two, seemed almost nonsensical.

"Is Father McGeehan like a pastor?" Rylan asked a little cautiously. Margaret Fulcher inclined her head sideways for a moment.

"I suppose so," she quietly replied. "I mean, they're all supposedly a 'Man of God', in some way or another. It's really just that sometimes they use different names for what they are. It all depends on what church they belong to. Some of them are called ministers, others are deacons, or pastors, or fathers, or… whatever." Rylan was quiet for a while. Much as he was happy being with the Fulchers, he certainly did not want to have anything to do with a church, or any 'Man of God'. Not after what he'd suffered the last time he'd been taken to a church.

"How about we pop down to talk to him sometime tomorrow morning?" suggested Margaret Fulcher rather brightly. "We can all go, if you like. With it being a weekday, I doubt Father McGeehan will be all that busy. Not like if it was a Sunday, and he had a sermon to give and confessions to hear.

***

Skylar stood as still as possible, with his hands clasped behind his head, as instructed. Not wanting to move, for fear of the suffering the severe punishment that was always promised for any slight act of disobedience. Especially after seeing the results of what had been dealt out to Cooper and, more especially Peter, a few days earlier.

He watched, without making it too obvious that he was doing so, as Vittorio and Angelo continued loading the photographs they had just taken of him onto a laptop computer. He felt a little embarrassed that he was still dressed in what seemed just like underwear. But, then again, Riley, Cooper, Maia and Persia were all similarly attired. Each of them wearing just a pair of very skimpy white briefs that seemed more like swimming attire, and the new necklaces they'd each been given, which stated their name and age on a series of beads. All of them remained bare-chested, even accounting for the fact that both Maia and Persia were girls. Not that either of them they had any chest development to speak of and with their short pixie-cut hair could've easily passed as rather androgynous-looking boys. Nevertheless, the five of them, as the Network's latest 'acquisitions', had just had their 'preliminary inspection', as Vittorio so casually described the process.

The first detail of that 'inspection', of course, had been the really embarrassing part of what they had endured over the past hour, in that it had involved a quite lengthy and detailed physical examination. A process that had started from when they'd first been ordered to strip off completely and put on what Vittorio called their 'display wear', to now; as they stood as still as possible, in just the white briefs, with their hands clasped behind their head. All the while, fearing that to show the slightest act of disobedience or flinching might very likely result in severe punishment.

During that time Vittorio and Angelo had probed and poked at their bodies and even looked at their most intimate areas. Carefully measuring and making note of all their various body features. Such as how tall they were and how much they weighed. The particulars of which were then carefully entered into some form of computer record. Details that also included their eye colour, the colour and length of their hair, their general physique and other details almost too embarrassing to even contemplate regarding their development into puberty… or lack of it.

Their physical examinations had then been followed by a series of photographs being taken of each of them. A few being of just their face, front and side... a little in the manner of police arrest photos. Most, however, were full-length shots... front, side and back. Thankfully, there had been no full nudity. Each of them had at least been wearing their briefs, while they'd stood with their hands clasped behind their head, for the photos. Which, according to Vittorio, was to... 'just keep a little something in surprise' for possible clients.

All the information and photos, it appeared, would eventually become part of the Network's encrypted connection to the dark web. Thereby enabling prospective customers to chose whichever particular child — boy or girl — that they might want; either for temporary use or, more likely, given the way Vittorio had explained things, as full-time 'playthings' for people who had enough money to pay for others to provide for their nasty, illegal predilections.

Without wanting to seem as if he was staring, Skylar quickly noted that like himself, all the other children were also only about five foot in height and were, similarly, of a rather slender build; although, not so much so that any of them could be classified as skinny, or malnourished. Likewise, none of them even had what could be callously called a 'puppy-fat' physique. In a way, it seemed obvious that Vittorio and his 'helpers' were clearly not interested in kidnapping children who might be a little 'chubby', or 'over-weight'.

From what he'd also gleaned from overhearing the men's conversation, Vittorio had seemed rather pleased about Skylar's close resemblance to one of the major boy stars in the first series of the TV series Stranger Things... thc one called Mike Wheeler. That factor, Vittorio reckoned, would be his most likely attraction when he was put up for auction.

While the stunning dark-blue of Cooper's eyes, especially the way that the darkness and length of eyelashes almost seemed to emphasise that fact, would prove to be his major selling point. For Riley, it was evidently his elfin face and the general tautness of his muscular body. A physique honed by his having been recently selected for an Under 12 regional representative soccer team and the four practice sessions, plus two games a week, that that status required. For both Maia and Persia, it was also their quite elfin features that would prove to be their major selling point, a factor in some ways emphasised by their short pixie hairstyles.

Now that the marks from Cooper's recent beating had faded somewhat, all of them also seemed to have rather pale skin. Nor did any of them show any signs of growing body hair, apart from what was already on their heads. That particular aspect of their appearance had also seemed to please Vittorio to some considerable degree, more especially given that, from what Skylar had also managed to glean from the man's casual conversations with Angelo, they would be worth a great deal more at auction if they were not yet into puberty.

"Well, it looks like you might all just have to be kept on hold for a little while longer yet," Vittorio suddenly announced with a smirk, as he looked up from the computer. "We'll make good money from all of you, eventually, but for the moment, I still need to get at least a couple more boys for the special event. There's one boy we've acquired, who's likely to be added in a couple of days, if he fits with what we're looking for. But we're still keeping an eye out for fresh talent, so to speak, so don't think that I won't change my mind and get rid of any of you, straight away, if we manage to find a more suitable-looking boy or girl. Or if any of you decide to cause me problems in any way. Understand?" The five children all hastily nodded in response;

all of them anxious to avoid suffering a little 'reminder' session from Vittorio's belt, or the prospect of being 'sent out' for a bit of 'experience'.

"We could always try passing off Noah, as an innocent?" Angelo quietly suggested. Vittorio gave a nonchalant shrug. "After all, he's good-looking and has also got the sort slender physique that our clients tend to like. He's only been out on one private gig, so far, and that didn't turn out to be anything all that much, beyond a bit of touching, given how much Judge Peterson had had to drink."

"He's a possibility," Vittorio murmured and then nodded. "As with these five, we'll just keep him a little restricted in the meantime and see what else turns up in the way of new acquisitions. If it turns out that he's not required for the special show, I'll still be able to get good money for him, once we put him out for the more regular type of booking. There's already quite a bit of interest in him showing up on the net."

"So how many are we going to need for the special event?" Angelo queried.

"Most likely about five or six boys and the same in girls," Vittorio muttered. "Six would be better, of course. Although we could probably take along a few extras to auction off, as well, such as Peter... and Noah, if he's not required as an 'innocent'. Given that there'll probably be a good number of clients with money... both in person and via computer link, we should be able to do pretty well out of it." He sighed softly and glanced towards the five children standing to attention. "And as for these five, considering how young they look, even if they do the special event, it might just be worthwhile hanging onto a couple of them for a year or two, at the least. Anyway, just get all that stuff encrypted and onto the web, so that our clients can see what's in the pipeline, for upcoming auctions."

He suddenly got to his feet and moved towards where the five children were still standing, not daring to move. The hurriedness of the action almost giving the impression that he'd only just remembered that they were still present.

"Okay you lot!" he snarled. "All of you... back downstairs! Get yourselves washed and dressed, and make use of the bathroom if you need it. We'll be heading out in about an hour, to pick up another new kid, and to also look into a couple of other possibilities we might try to acquire in the next week or so."

Well aware that to 'acquire' in Vittorio's terms usually meant an 'abduction' of some sort, the children quickly headed downstairs to their respective rooms... boys to one room, girls to the other. Pleased to be away from the discomforting gaze of their captors, yet knowing that 'heading out' meant that they'd, most likely, end up being be hogtied, gagged and chained to the metal bar in the back of a truck.

***

Margaret Fulcher hurried down to the kitchen where her children were already getting their breakfasts prepared. On checking the guest room, she'd been surprised to find that Rylan's bed looked as if it had hardly been slept in.

"Have any of you seen Rylan this morning?" she hurriedly asked, as she clasped the note she'd found on his pillow in her right hand. She paused a moment, as if waiting for each of the children to respond. "It looks like he might have run away."

"But why?" Thomas quickly asked, as Henry and Marlow each gave a shake of their head. "He told me, yesterday morning, that he really liked being here?"

"Well, it looks like my mention of taking him to meet Father McGeehan has scared him off," his mother softly replied. She exhaled softly and gave a slow shake of her head. "It turns out that the last time he went to a church he was treated very badly. At least judging by what this says." Having placed the note on the table, somewhat pleased that, for her children, it also provided a reasonable explanation of Rylan's past, she then reached for her cell phone to ring James Fulcher. Thomas, Henry and Marlow all quickly gathered around the note to read what it said.

Dear Mr and Mrs Fulcher, and Thomas and Henry and Marlow.

Please don't be angry that I have run away. I do not want to go to a church because they are very scary places. The church man that you mentioned may be a nice man, and a Man of God, but I was also told by my father that Pastor Isaac was a special Man of God, but all he did was hurt me real bad.

When my father took me to the church, Pastor Isaac made me take off all my clothes. Then he beat me with a strap until I was bleeding and couldn't sit down properly. Then he made me stand at the front of the church, in front of everyone, while he said all these horrible things about me. Afterwards, my dad took me to a special church camp where Pastor Isaac gave me more beatings and hurt me in some other horrible ways I do not want to mention. I am scared to have that happen again.

I hope that Thomas will not be angry with me for taking his old backpack and coat, but I needed something to put my clothes into, and to hide my wings.

Thank you for looking after me. I liked being in your house. I will try to pay you back for the nice things you gave me.

Rylan

PS. Please don't tell the police about me because I don't want to ever have to go back to my mom and dad.

"I just can't really fathom why he would want to run away?" Margaret Fulcher mused softly, as she waited for her call to be answered. "I know the note says that that Pastor Isaac hurt him, but I only wanted him to meet with Father McGeehan. Surely he wouldn't be scared of such a kind and loving 'Man of God' as Father McGeehan?"

"I think the note suggests otherwise," Marlow countered a tad cynically.

"But if he is an angel, why would any person involved in the church ever want to hurt him?" replied her mother, as the number she'd dialed switched her to an answering service. She promptly switched off her phone and came back over to the table. "He must be in a meeting," she mused to herself.

"We can't know how every person will react to seeing someone like Rylan," Marlow replied.

"But Father McGeehan would only want to help him," Margaret Fulcher continued. "And if he is telling us the truth about this horrible Pastor Isaac, why on Earth would such a man, if he truly professes to be a Christian, ever want to treat him so horrendously?"

"I think he might be gay!" Marlow murmured.

"Don't be silly. He's an angel! He can't possibly be gay," her mother countered a little bluntly.

"He does look a bit like a girl," Thomas suggested. "You know... like, with his long hair."

"That doesn't mean he's gay," Margaret Fulcher contradicted. "And anyway, he wouldn't be if he's an angel."

"How can we be sure of that?" suggested Marlow with a rather nonchalant shrug. "Have any of us ever met an angel? Like, before Rylan?" For a moment, there was simply silence. The whole idea of meeting angels, and then to have one stay in their house, even if he was just a young boy, still seemed in some ways, quite unbelievable.

"He did say that he'd only just had his wings start to grow," Thomas quietly suggested. "Maybe all that bad stuff was before he became an angel? Like, you know, before those bad people really knew what he was?"

"Hey, wasn't Pastor Isaac the name of that man the police arrested?" asked Henry, quickly turning towards his sister. "You know, like, in that YouTube video you showed us yesterday?" Marlow was thoughtful for a moment or two, and then nodded.

"I think you're right," she murmured.

"So he must have been the same Pastor Isaac who beat Rylan," suggested Thomas. "Probably because he..."

"I just think that he was a little mixed up," Marlow softly interrupted as she got up from the table. "And got taken advantage of by some very nasty people." She sighed, softly. "I just hope he stays safe. Wherever he is."

CHAPTER FOUR

Exposure....

"So, are you two ready to go, yet?" Andrew asked, raising one eyebrow and giving them a slightly cheeky grin as he wandered into the kitchen area. Tris and Lara immediately looked up from where they were seated, side-by-side at the breakfast bar, just finishing off their breakfasts.

"You want to leave, now?" Tris queried, getting hastily up from where he'd been seated and quickly wiping the back of his hand across his mouth to remove the faint remnants of a chocolate milk moustache.

"Well, it is already after nine, and I really do have some other things to do this afternoon," Andrew replied, briefly cocking his head a little to one side. "So it would be good for us to get going reasonably early."

"More like you just want to test taste some more of Grandma Betty's baking," quipped Tris a little cheekily. Lara watched and listened to the exchange with some bemusement. At the same time, quickly finishing off the last remnants of her porridge. Almost before she had finished the last mouthful, however, Tris had grabbed her bowl, as well as his own, and rushed it out to the dishwasher. That done, he rushed off down the hallway to clean his teeth. Having finished swallowing her last mouthful of porridge, Lara downed the last of her chocolate milk and hurried off to do likewise.

"Are you planning to be long?" Amanda asked as the sound of happy chatter emanated from the children's bathroom, as the main bathroom had now been designated.

"An hour or two at the most," Andrew replied. "I do have some other work I want to do out at the church, a bit later on. It's mainly just some cleaning and polishing and there are a few things I need to sort out down in the crypt. It's nothing major, but I do need to get it done. I actually thought I might try and inveigle those two into helping me."

"Helping with what?" Tris asked as he emerged from the hallway, followed closely by Lara. Understandably, they'd seemed almost inseparable over the last few days, apart from when they were in the bathroom or asleep.

"I need to sort out a few things in the crypt, later on," Andrew quickly replied. Not bothering to mention the cleaning and polishing, which he felt sure would not be quite so readily accepted. "If you two would like to give a hand, it would also be a good opportunity for you and me to explain to Lara about the miracles that happened there. We can even make it a bit of a picnic lunch, if you like?"

For a moment, Tris wondered whether to say anything about what he'd already told Lara, but then decided it would be better not to do so, perhaps for fear of stealing Andrew's thunder, so to speak. Anyway, there was so much extra knowledge that Andrew had of the church and its origins that he felt sure that he would also be just as keen to hear whatever Andrew had to tell them.

"I'll get something prepared for your lunch while you're away," Amanda suggested. "It'll save you having to bother anyone up at the big house." In the back of her thoughts was the idea of ensuring that they would all have a healthy lunch, rather than just making do by snaffling a few packets of crisps and some snack bars, along with some biscuits and cans of drink to take with them.

***

"Where… where are we?" Lara asked, looking around at the interior of the barn with some puzzlement. Perhaps, given she'd been told that they were going to a farm, expecting to arrive in open fields, but quickly noting that the tractors and other farming equipment that you would expect to find in such a place, were rather carefully arrayed around where they were standing.

"It's my grandparent's farm," Tris quickly explained. "Well, great-grandparents to be more correct, but I just call them Grandma Betty and Granddad Roger. They won't mind if you do the same. You'll also meet Mischa and Zhenya. They help to look after the farm. They were two Russian children that my grandparents adopted, years ago. Like, long before I was even born. Granddad originally set aside this area of the barn for my uncles to 'be' to when they came to the farm, but we all still use it, because sometimes the weather's a bit too cold, or wet, to just 'be' to the top of the hill. Or if there's heaps of snow, or we need to check on who else might be visiting. Like, people who don't know what we are. That's why it's important that we learn to always keep our wings invisible when we arrive at various places."

Well, we'd all better go in and say 'hello'," Andrew quickly advised, indicating towards the doors. "Before we start any practice with 'be'ing." With Tris quickly taking the lead, and holding tightly onto Lara's hand, they headed out of the barn and across to the main house.

"So who have we got here?" Grandma Betty gently enquired, as Tris hurried through to the conservatory, where his grandparents were having a morning tea break.

"This is Lara," replied Tris with keen enthusiasm. "And she's like me... an angel."

"Well, you've certainly arrived at a much better hour of the morning than the last time you brought a girl for a visit," Granddad Roger teased, at the same time rolling his eyes a little. "And at least this one's not comatose." Lara immediately looked rather puzzled and moved close to Tris.

"What other girl?" she whispered. Tris immediately looked mildly embarrassed, even as he gave a shrug of his shoulders.

"I'll explain it all later," he hastily murmured as he leant in close.

"Tris wants to have Lara practise 'be'ing to the barn," Andrew quickly explained, before either of the grandparents could ask the reason for the visit. "Lara's just beginning to learn her basic angel skills. Mykael has suggested that Tris should teach her, with me acting as the supervisor."

"Well, I'm sure that all of that could wait until you've had a warm drink and some shortbread," Grandma Betty announced, in a manner which implied that that was what would happen next... come hell or high water.

***

"Hey, we've got something!" Private Bradford Sullivan suddenly announced. As one of the special squad assigned to track down Angel-girl, he was more than four hours into yet another eight-hour shift of just watching a screen on which nothing of any significance had happened for more than a week.

"Like what?" Sergeant Oliver Childers queried, hurrying over from where he'd been busy at his computer.

"Angel-girl's locator signal," Private Sullivan replied, quickly pointing to the screen. "We're suddenly getting a very faint response."

"But, from where?" Oliver Childers questioned, trying to figure out the co-ordinates that were now starting to be displayed. "It's certainly doesn't seem to be anywhere local." He sighed, noted down some numbers on a pad, and then began trying to work out grid references on the large world map that was displayed under a clear glass covering on a nearby table.

"So where is it coming from?" Private Sullivan asked, turning around in his seat to look to where Sergeant Oliver Childers was marking positions on the glass.

"It almost appears to be somewhere out over the Atlantic," Sergeant Childers murmured, mainly to himself. "At least, that's how it seems." He looked back towards the screen. Noting that the numbers displayed were changing a little unexpectedly. "It's almost as if it's jumping around a bit," he continued, shaking his head a little. "Like one minute it was off the west coast of Scotland, the next it was sort of to the east. Somewhere just south of the Orkneys, or maybe just somewhere on the northern coast of Scotland. The variances could just be atmospheric echoing."

"You think I should I send for Harassment?" Private Bradford Sullivan asked as he began to reach for the internal phone, taking the risk of using the superior officer's nickname when he obviously wasn't present to overhear it. Sergeant Oliver Childers nodded as he smiled. Lieutenant Colonel Harris McMahon could quite often be a major pain in the butt… hence the nickname! More especially with the way he always expected that everyone else should immediately drop whatever it was they were doing just to see to his personal demands. Still, Oliver Childers mused, it wasn't good to encourage junior officers to show disrespect in such a way; not with the trouble Lieutenant Colonel Harris McMahon could eventually send their way.

"Put a call out for him. He won't be too far away, given how keen he is to find the girl," he murmured. He then wandered over to stand directly behind the junior officer. "I'd also be a bit careful with the use of his nickname," he whispered. "Especially in front of your superiors. Not unless you want to find yourself re-assigned to piloting garbage scows in the Philippines for the next ten years. I've heard he can be pretty ruthless with people who upset him." Private Bradford nodded, in acknowledgement of the subtle reprimand, even as he dialed Lieutenant Colonel Harris McMahon's personal number. A few minutes after his call, the Lieutenant Colonel hurried into the room.

"Have you figured out where she's hiding, or where she disappeared to, yet?" he demanded rather curtly, coming over to stand directly behind where Private Bradford Sullivan was hurriedly writing down the latest satellite co-ordinates for the signal.

"Not exactly, Sir," Sergeant Childers replied. "Given that we've only just managed to get this new signal, we're still trying to get a better triangulation on her position from the satellites."

"Well, that shouldn't be too difficult, should it? Not with the help of all this expensive new technology?" the Lieutenant Colonel snapped a little irritatedly, glancing around the room at the various dials and screens. "Exactly what have you got, so far?"

"Well, Sir, at the moment, she seems to be settling somewhere near the northern coast of Scotland," Sergeant Childers explained, pointing to the map co-ordinates. He gave a slight shake of his head, as the readout of the co-ordinates seemed to flicker for a few moments. "She's on the other side of the Atlantic, at least."

"If she's got that far, perhaps she's finally learnt how to fly," Lieutenant Colonel Harris McMahon muttered a little bluntly and with a hint of irritated sarcasm.

"It's still a long way," Sergeant Childers murmured. "Especially if there's nowhere she could have rested up on the way." Lieutenant Colonel Harris McMahon sighed impatiently.

"Well, maybe she went North, first" he suggested rather tersely. "And headed up through Canada, Newfoundland, Greenland, Iceland and so on. There's certainly been more than enough time for her to accomplish such a trek, if she did it in stages." Sergeant Childers gave a slight shrug.

"It's still a long way, Sir. And, by all rights, we should have been able to pick up the signal from her GPS locator the whole way. Certainly much earlier than this, if that was the case," he offered in quiet response, perhaps also not wanting to appear too argumentative. After all, just how Angel-girl had managed to get to the other side of the Atlantic was in many ways immaterial. All that really mattered was that they had now located her. From this point in time, it would just be a matter of arranging for her recapture. "Admittedly, the signal just appeared out of nowhere. Almost as if it was just suddenly turned on," he added. Lieutenant Colonel Harris McMahon seemed to ignore his comments, appearing to be deep in thought.

"We'll need to get on to the Navy," he suddenly announced. "If she's close to the coast of Scotland, we'll need to find out if they've got anything afloat somewhere near to that area!"

"And what do we tell them to look for?" questioned Sergeant Childers. "We can't make it seem as if we're sending them on some wild goose chase, and I doubt they'd be too interested in just tracking down one little girl. Even if she is what she is. Especially if we don't want to reveal the fact that she's special." Colonel Harris McMahon appeared, for a further moment or two, to once again be deep in thought.

"For the moment, just tell them that we have an important 'package' that needs to be retrieved," he suddenly announced. "And that the locator beacon attached to it has given us a signal from just off the coast of Scotland."

"What if they want more detail?" Sergeant Childers continued. "So that they know what they're supposed to be looking for."

"Just tell them that it's a piece of equipment related to something from a satellite, or... or... a weather balloon. Yes, that's it. Tell them it's a highly specialized data unit from a weather balloon! And that the balloon was unexpectedly blown a long way off course by jet stream winds, so that when the 'equipment' came down by parachute, as scheduled, it was a long way from where it was expected to be. Just tell them that it's an extremely high security device that needs to be kept secret from the Russians and that any more information will have to be on a 'need to know' basis, directly from me.

"I'll try and get these co-ordinates a little bit more accurately noted, and then..." Sergeant Childers began. Whatever else he was about to suggest, was hastily cut short by Harris McMahon.

"Leave all that to Sullivan," he snapped. "I need you to get onto to the Navy, pronto. As I said, find out what ships they might have anywhere near the area. Anything that could assist with a..." He paused a moment. "Better still, when you contact them, tell them that I'll be arranging to get there myself, to personally take charge of the retrieval. And then arrange for us to get there by helicopter... or jet, or whatever else might be available at short notice. We need to get out to whatever ship is nearest." He gave a small shiver. "By damn submarine, if necessary! Not that I like being in those damn tubes, but Angel-girl is far too important to our future infiltration and surveillance plans against the Russians and the Iranians to just let her slip through our fingers." With an exasperated shake of his head at knowing that there'd obviously be a delay in getting it all organised, he glanced around towards the screen.

"Your job," he snapped at Private Sullivan, "will be to get us the best and most accurate co-ordinates you possibly can.

Whatever you can manage within the next hour. And relay them on to me as soon as you've done so. And then, when I'm on my way, I'll expect to receive regular updates; even if it means you having to watch that damn screen twenty-four seven, personally! Understand!" Private Sullivan hastily nodded a response. Harris McMahon then turned back to where Sergeant Childers was already putting a call through to the US navy.

"And, when you've finished with contacting the Navy, get on with getting some local transport arranged. Like, yesterday! We'll want to be on our way within the hour! If you encounter any problems, tell them to get in contact with Chief Admiral Calvin Ainscourt at the Pentagon. I'll contact him immediately and tell him it's a matter of the most absolute highest priority. With top-level urgency and complete secrecy from all media. The damn press-monkeys will have a field day disrupting our plans, if they get even a slight hint of any of our arrangements to do with Angel-girl."

***

Skylar shook his head a little as he opened his eyes and then looked about. It seemed strange for him to have simply been asleep of his own volition while travelling, given that, for all his previous trips he'd been in a semi-drugged state. Then again, the truck he was now in appeared to have been specifically designed for transporting groups of captured children around from place to place.

It took a moment for him to once again adjust his vision to the rather dim light in the interior of the room he was in. Or, more correctly, what was, essentially a small, soundproofed, totally secret compartment constructed inside the back of a large truck and carefully hidden behind a false façade of metal drums.

As he'd seen when he and the other children had first been escorted to the garage where the truck had been housed, the rear portion of the truck's interior had been fashioned to give the appearance of being a full load of waste oil destined for recycling. Even the door to the hidden compartment, hidden behind two, double-stacked rows of fifty-five gallon drums filled with foam — so that when tapped they appeared to be full, and yet were light enough to easily move — was disguised as a two drums of waste oil stacked one on top of the other. They were, however, also cut in half lengthwise so that on the interior side, the side facing into the secret compartment, they were flat.

The compartment itself had, on the far end wall opposite the hidden door that backed onto the cab of the truck, one low wattage light bulb and a single small speaker. The interior of the room contained several old mattresses on the floor for them to lie on and a metal bar about three to four inches off the floor, running down the centre of the room.

He'd only been dozing slightly and, almost as ridiculous as it now seemed, imagining that he was at home. It took only seconds for him to realise that he was still a captive and lying in the back of the truck, along with the seven other special 'innocent' children, according to Vittorio. Persia, Maia, Riley, Cooper and Noah… as well as Luka and Martyn, the two new boys who'd been added to the group at their last stop. Peter was missing, having been sent away… 'out on loan' according to Angelo. But he would, evidently, rejoin them at some later stage. Ostensibly, so that he could possibly be auctioned off, as well.

They were travelling east, it seemed, en route to meet up with some other children. Mainly the remainder of the girls who, like him and the others in the truck, had also been kidnapped and were now the 'property' of the Network. Most of them, according to Vittorio, were also 'new' abductions who would eventually end up being part of the 'special event'. Something that Skylar was not looking forward to in any way whatsoever, given what he'd been told would eventually happen to them. Not that he could do much about that particular situation at the moment. Not that any of them could.

He only knew the new boys' names from when the truck had stopped for a while, miles from civilisation, it seemed. There, they'd been untied, taken from the truck and forced into the cellar room of an old farmhouse in the middle of vast fields of fallow land. At that stage, they'd been given a basic meal to eat of corn soup, followed by cold sausages and slices of buttered bread, and had been sternly encouraged to visit the toilet; given that they still had a quite considerable distance to travel, once they set off again.

That was when Luka and Martyn had been added to their group. From what Luka had told them, Skylar quickly realised that Luka, like himself, he'd also been snatched off the street while doing a morning paper route, while Martyn had simply been grabbed on his way home from soccer practice. In fact, all of them, it seemed, had been abducted off the street in some roughly similar manner. Almost as if each of them had been watched for quite some while, to deduce when an instant could arise for a possible abduction, without raising immediate suspicion, or the likelihood of someone attempting to intervene.

For Riley, as for Martyn, it had been on a darkened street while on his way home from a soccer practice. Noah had simply been waylaid while on the way to his local shops to pick up some milk for his mother. The subterfuge to get him off the street being of a man requiring help with an injured dog just a little way down a side alley near to the shop. Maia had been simply walking her dog in the park, while Persia had been snatched while on her way to a dentist appointment; one of the few times she was not under the direct control of one of the elders. Of all of them, Cooper's case was the one that was slightly different. He'd been picked up, when a man claiming to be a friend of his stepfather — he had even known the secret password that had to be given — had met up with him straight after school. Giving Cooper the excuse that, because his young stepbrother had had to be admitted to hospital with appendicitis, he would need to meet his parents there, as there would be nobody waiting at home and his parents didn't know how long they'd be at the hospital. It had quickly turned out to be a lie. The moment he'd climbed into the back of the man's car, he'd been quickly handcuffed, gagged, had a cloth bag placed over his head and then been forced to lie on the floor so that he could not be seen, or see where it was he was being taken.

As Skylar looked around at the other children, he noticed that, like himself, they were all wearing a necklace with their name and age spelt out in beads, and also had the same tattoo etched into their upper arm, just below the shoulder. He fully understood, of course, that it marked them all as being the property of the Network.

Peter had told him that all the boys were tattooed just below the left shoulder, while the girls had a similar tattoo on the right. The purpose of that difference evidently being so that Vittorio and his helpers could quickly tell the boys from the girls. Given that, unless they were fully naked, some of the boys, especially those like Noah, who had almost shoulder-length hair, tended to look rather like girls, and similarly, a good many of the younger girls, more especially those with shorter hair, and little chest development, like Maia, could quite easily pass for rather androgynous-looking boys.

For most of their travelling time, however, they were still kept hog-tied. Their feet bound together at the ankles, and hands tied tightly behind their backs. With short ropes attached between the fastenings for their feet and hands to prevent them from standing up. They were also chained, by their ankles, to the metal bar in the centre of the room. For some of their travelling, Skylar now presumed it must be for when they were travelling through more populated areas, they were also gagged. Usually by having a small ball of some type firmly placed in their mouths, and held in place by a strap going behind their head; ostensibly, he figured, to prevent them calling for help.

At any rate, put quite simply, their chances of escape were certainly not all that great. Even on the off-chance that they somehow managed to get out of their restraints, they were still inside what amounted to being a fully enclosed, soundproofed, locked box, for however long any journey would take.

As the truck suddenly seemed to make a rather tight turn, the centrifugal force resulted in Skylar rolling against the boy chained up beside him… Riley. Like himself, Riley was eleven-years-old, and a late developer, which Vittorio had already suggested would very likely mean that they might eventually be asked to 'perform together', at the auction. Vittorio had similarly designated Luka and Cooper, who were both twelve, even if they didn't quite look it, as another likely 'special' pairing given that they were of the same height and of a similar build.

Some of things that Vittorio had suggested that the 'pairs' might end up doing to each other, Skylar did not like to think about. In fact none of them did. But even that depravity still seemed better than what they'd been told would most likely happen to them once they'd been auctioned off, or were made available for 'rent'.

Like Riley and Luka, and indeed almost all the other captive children he came across, he wondered if his parents, particularly his mother, was still looking for him. If she would have any idea at all of the depravities to which it seemed likely he would eventually be subjected. Or would she even realise that he was still alive, and not lying dead in some water-filled ditch beside a rural back road, or buried in a shallow grave somewhere out in the wilderness beyond the city limits of where they were living.

Admittedly, Cooper didn't seem to have the same 'family' worries. In the whole time of his captivity, he'd made absolutely no reference to the idea of going home, given that he seemed totally convinced, by the simple fact that his abductors knew the secret password that had to be provided, that his stepfather had simply wanted him gone.

As he'd explained to Skylar, his real father had taken off well before he'd been born and then, after his mother remarried, meaning he had a stepfather, his mother had died in a car accident. His stepfather's marriage to another woman from a broken marriage, so that he suddenly had two much younger siblings, had also meant that he'd quickly become an outsider; a child not biologically connected to either of his stepparents. To put it more bluntly, he'd simply become 'surplus to requirements' as far as the family unit was concerned, and so had been 'sold off' to the Network.

Some of them, as Vittorio had bluntly informed them, might eventually be destined to a teenage life of simply being shuttled around the whole of the United States as occasional special playthings for the rich and famous. People of high status who had a predilection for abusing children, but also had enough financial clout to have others provide for their perverted needs, rather than risk being caught openly 'grooming' or 'abducting' a child. Others of them might also, at times, have a use in helping set up noteworthy people for blackmail possibilities. Simply by arranging to have them captured on film in compromising situations with an underage child.

For most of the children, however, it seemed that they were simply destined be sold on at the earliest opportunity for considerable sums of money, in order to become semi-permanent slaves for whomever offered the most at auction. What happened when they grew beyond their teenage years, and were no longer a saleable 'item', was anybody's guess. Vittorio had already hinted, more than once, that when they got too old to be saleable, they might very likely end up being the targets for a special 'turkey shoot'. Being allowed to escape into the wooded grounds of an enclosed private estate close to the Canadian border and then hunted down like wild animals.

Whether Vittorio had simply been trying to frighten them into submission, or whether it might be a reality, was moot. Although, given what they might eventually be able to divulge about what some important people got up to — in particular, the sordid details of child abuse — it didn't seem all that likely that they'd just be told that their services were no longer required, and then be allowed 'go free', as it were.

As the truck appeared to pick up speed on a straight stretch of highway, and the hum of the tyres on the roadway created a constant droning sound that seemed to be lulling the other boys into sleep, Skylar mused back on all the 'what ifs' that, over the last few weeks, had seemed to dominate his thinking.

What if he hadn't bothered to sneak out that night to hang out with Randy Kelleher in order to prove that he wasn't a 'wimp-out'? What if he hadn't been picked up by the Oakton Police for hanging out around the back of the Mall after midnight and taken home? What if it had all happened when Dad had still been 'on the road' with his work and it had only been Mom who'd been woken by the Police? It was likely that she would've probably just ticked him off, expressing her intense disappointment in his actions, and then grounded him for a few days… perhaps even for a few weeks!

And that simply created another 'what if' in his thoughts. As it turned out, his dad had been home for a couple of days and had taken his breaking curfew far more seriously. So much so that, at first, Skylar had been scared that he'd end up on the receiving end of his dad's belt. Instead, it had been decided that he should be sent to Pastor Isaac's church boot camp for a weekend, to supposedly 'straighten him out'. The aim being that a dose of strict military-style discipline for a couple days, might serve to curb his misbehaviour before it got too serious. And that circumstances simply created even more questions and 'what ifs'.

Was it likely that his dad really had no idea of what went on at the camp? Had he had any idea of the less then wholesome activities that were also enacted? Sadistic abuse that went well beyond the semi-military physical exertions that were always promoted as being beneficial for instilling a sense of self-discipline and self-worth, during the times Pastor Isaac was extolling the virtues of the camps? And if that was the case, and his dad had really known what went on at the camps, why would he still have sent him there?

And then there were all the extra 'what if's' that had accumulated since then. Those that had happened as a direct result of the excruciatingly two days that he'd spent at the camp. Starting with forced physical exercises and then punishment when he didn't complete them in time, it had been over thirty-six hours of sheer torture, during which he'd been reduced to a state of complete physical exhaustion and had had his bare backside beaten so many times with paddles, leather straps, and other similar punishment devices, that he'd ended up cut and bleeding!

Such as… what if he'd taken the time to rinse out his underwear when he'd arrived back from the camp and then put it directly into the washing machine, rather than just dumping it in his bedroom hamper? What if his mum hadn't found the bloodstains on his underpants? What if he hadn't been taken into her bedroom so that she could check him over? And, of course, what if she hadn't then seen the severe damage that the Pastor, and those other men, had willfully inflicted on him? In particular, the way the skin on his bottom had been left cut, bruised, and bleeding!

The resulting argument later that night, with him as an unwilling observer, as his parents had tried to apportion the blame on each other, and then onto him, had eventually resulted in his parents separating. His father complaining, at first, that he'd only sent Skylar to the camp to 'straighten him out' and teach him 'right from wrong', and that if his mother wanted to molly-coddle him for the rest of his life then she was making a rod for her own back when he became a delinquent. His mother, conversely, complaining that 'sheer uncouth brutality' wasn't the answer to any of the problems that Skylar might present, given that he'd never been a willfully disobedient child, and that if Todd had been a proper father, and been around more often to lend proper support and guidance, instead of always being 'on the road', then perhaps the situation of Skylar's sneaking out might not have arisen in the first place!

In the end it all came back to one simple issue. If he hadn't decided to sneak out, just to prove that he wasn't a 'wimp-out', then he'd probably still be safely tucked up in his own bed, back in Oakton. His only worry then being whether he'd properly completed his homework. Or, perhaps more correctly, had at least completed it well enough to avoid being put in detention. And thinking of that situation only left more of the 'what ifs'.

What if his dad hadn't left, making it impossible for his mother to keep up the rental payments on their apartment? What if he'd simply refused to leave his school, and his friends, just so that he and his mother could move to Texas? While it was, as she put it, a chance for them to start a new life well away from the past, it had still left him totally isolated; ostracized and bullied for being a trashy 'trailer-park kid'! And that was a situation that simply led to even more 'what ifs'.

Like, what if he hadn't decided to take on an early morning paper delivery route, so that he could buy a new cellphone and perhaps garner enough extra money to maybe help his mother send him to a better school? More especially with his mother's new waitressing job paying so little as a basic wage, relying on tips to earn enough to make ends meet, as it were. And even while doing those papers, what if he'd been a little more aware of stranger danger and hadn't moved so close to the blue car with darkened windows?

Still, there didn't seem much that he could do about it now, it seemed. His being kidnapped, he'd soon come to understand, was part of a well-planned operation that targeted 'special' children. His particular classification as 'special', simply being because of his small, quite slender build, his general good looks, and striking similarity to a recent child television celebrity, and what someone had supposedly seen of him on some video that had been made. Not that he had any real idea of what that video might be, although he did have a fair suspicion that it was possibly linked to his time at the church boot camp. All of the punishments inflicted upon him had certainly been filmed… much to his intense embarrassment.

***

"Ready to do another length?" Tris asked, as he and Lara rested for a moment at one end of the pool. After a second visit to the farm with Andrew, they'd decided to spend some time being 'sociable' with the other children. Tris not wanting to have it seem as if he no longer needed their company, now that he had a sister who, like himself, also had wings. "It all helps for when you start flying," he quietly added, aware that the other children were also in the pool and perhaps not wanting them to be jealous of them having such an ability, by flaunting it in front of them. It was bad enough that they could 'be' wherever they wanted, without rubbing it in, as it were. For that same reason, Tris had, of late, also kept the use of his telekinetic abilities to a minimum when around the other children. Making the salt and pepper shakers move to his hands when having meals at home might just be harmless fun; but doing things such as making his towel jump from a chair into his hands every time he got out of the pool now seemed too much like 'showing off', even if Lara found it amusing.

"Race you to the other end," Lara suddenly announced as she quickly set off for the other end of the pool. Tris watched her go for a moment before setting off after her. He didn't really want to make each length a race, or always ensure that he would win. It was better that the sense of competition was simply to ensure that Lara was putting in enough effort to guarantee that she was building up good chest strength.

A moment or two later, he touched the far end of the pool just a second or two after Lara, and quickly turned a somersault in the water.

"Do you think Andrew will let you start teaching me to fly?" Lara asked as he resurfaced. Tris gave a slight shrug.

"Maybe," he said. "We can go and ask him, if you like. Like, once we've got dressed."

"Yes," Lara said eagerly as she visualised herself out of the water and standing at the side of the pool, then picked up her towel and began hurrying over to the girls' changing rooms. Tris swam slowly to the side of the pool as he watched her go. As he clambered out, Carwyn came over to stand beside him.

"She looks good in Melanie's old orange bikini," Carwyn half-whispered. Tris nodded.

"Have you asked her if she wants to be your girlfriend yet?" Carwyn queried. Tris gave a non-committal shrug of his shoulders. Given his and Lara's young age, it seemed to him a bit presumptuous for him to be wondering about them being boyfriend and girlfriend. Perhaps that might come later.

"Not yet," he replied, watching as Lara went into the girls' changing rooms. "But at least I think she likes me."

***

"I think we've got company," said Lara suddenly, as Tris continued to lead her along the edge of the cliffs up at the farm. It was their third visit to the farm over the last couple of days and, with the weather being gloriously fine, it had been a chance for Tris to finally show her Lake Robertson and the new waterfall that tumbled down the cliffs. Andrew, for the moment, was in the barn giving Mischa a hand with repairing the gearbox of the smaller tractor. He'd decided that the two children would be reasonably safe on their own for a short while, provided that they didn't leave the confines of the farm.

Lara quickly pointed out to sea, where Tris suddenly realised that there were a couple of small U.S. navy frigates, to judge by their flags. Some distance further out, an aircraft carrier also seemed to be waiting, and watching. The two frigates seemed to have anchored in the shallower water, because heading from them were several amphibious landing vehicles. Each of the landing vehicles appeared to contain a number of marines and items of sundry equipment, including a couple of small jeeps.

I think it's the military," whispered Lara, as Tris stopped them a short way from where the cliff dropped almost straight down to the surging water. They'd not got too close to the edge, at any stage, for fear of further collapses, even 'though it would have been easy enough for them to both simply 'be' to safety. "The same people who held me captive. They must have tracked me here, somehow." Tris nodded as they quickly made themselves invisible, just in case anyone was scanning the cliffs with binoculars. While it was possible that it could just be a normal military exercise, there was no point in taking chances. They hastily visualised themselves back in the barn.

"What's the rush?" Andrew half-laughed, seeing the anxious looks on their faces as he peered up at them from the floor beside the tractor.

"It looks like that military lot might have tracked Lara down, somehow," Tris blurted. "There's a couple of warships and a carrier anchored out to sea and some amphibious vehicles are already heading for that beach area a bit further down the coast." Andrew immediately scrambled to his feet.

"It could be just some unrelated military exercise," he said, echoing Tris's earlier thoughts. "But, still, there's no point in taking any chances. You two get back to the island now," he ordered. "I'll hang around and keep an eye on things, up here."

"What about Grandma Betty and Granddad Roger?" Tris queried a little cautiously. "Will they be okay?"

"If that lot out there are after Lara, they'll not be bothered with your grandparents," Andrew said, giving an amused shake of his head. "You just go and tell them that you have to leave in a hurry, and then go home. I'll meet you back there, a little later on. When I'm sure that everything is settled, here."The two children hurried off to the farmhouse.

"Are you two ready for..." Grandma Betty began. Tris quickly interrupted her.

"Sorry Grandma, but we've got to go. Right now," he exclaimed. "There are some military people heading for the beach from some warships. We think they might be after Lara."

"Landing on the beach down the road?" Grandma Betty queried a little bluntly. Quickly understanding the situation from what she'd previously been told about Lara's rescue. Tris quickly nodded.

"It looks like it," he replied. "Andrew wants us to go back to the island right away. If they, like, that military lot do come to the farm, you won't say anything about us being here... will you?"

"Do I look like I'm soft in the head, or something?" Grandma Betty retorted, with a smile and slow shake of her head. "Of course I wouldn't say anything about you and Lara. Now, you two just make sure you get back home, safe and sound. And I'd suggest you also let Mykael know what's going on. Immediately!"

Having given his grandmother a quick kiss on the cheek, Tris took hold of Lara's hand and made a visualisation of his bedroom and was instantly there. He hurried out to the family room where he knew Amanda and Joshua would most likely be.

"It looks like the military might have tracked Lara down," he exclaimed as he hurried over to where Joshua was working on the school's math's programmes for the next term. "Some warships turned up on the coast just out from the farm and there were people coming ashore when we left!"

"Is Andrew still there?" Joshua asked. Tris hastily nodded.

"He's going to keep a watch on what happens," he added. "Grandma Betty also said that we should also get hold of Mykael to help sort out what's going on."

***

"What's the problem?" Lieutenant Colonel Harris McMahon suddenly barked. Perhaps sensing a change in the earnestness with which the men on board the frigate had been tracking the GPS signal.

"It's just winked out again, Sir," Sergeant Childers responded. "Like, the signal. One moment it was there, and the next... nothing, nada, zilch. Just like it did the other day."

"Then double-check it!" Harris McMahon demanded. He slammed his fist down on the desk in front of him rather angrily. "When we're this close, we can't afford stupid little slip-ups!" He sighed with some sense of exasperation and then turned rather abruptly. "Are you absolutely sure it's not just some stupid equipment malfunction?" he barked. Sergeant Childers hastily rechecked the equipment. Quickly feeling reassured that it was all working just as it should.

"There's still nothing, Sir," he eventually replied. "And everything appears to be operating properly."

"Well, keep looking!" Harris McMahon commanded irritatedly. "There's no way the GPS mechanism we've got on Angel-girl can just turn itself on and off of its own volition. It's not designed for that to ever happen."

"But, there's absolutely nothing, Sir," Sergeant Childers cautiously responded, keen not to bear the full brunt of the senior officer's sense of irritation. "Not even a faint echo!" Harris McMahon gave a weary shake of his head, as he slowly counted to ten to get his temper under control, and then exhaled rather noisily. Trying, at the same time, to think through his various options. His keen anticipation of having the girl with wings back under his control seemed suddenly thwarted. He did not like such frustrations!

"Sir, should we get the Captain to tell the amphibians to return?" Sergeant Childers queried a little warily. In some ways, half expecting a rather torrid outburst from Harris McMahon. To his surprise, the senior officer simply gave a slow shake of his head.

"Not yet," he eventually murmured. "Let's just see if they can find out something that might give us a clue to her whereabouts." He rubbed at his chin for a moment, and then nodded. "In fact, get hold of the captain, immediately, and tell him that you and I also need to go ashore, immediately. If that GPS signal reappears again, I want to be right on top of it."

"Technically, we don't actually have clearance to do that, Sir," Sergeant Childers reminded him. "In fact, even the amphibians already on their way don't have anything in the way of official clearance to go ashore."

"You let me worry about what's officially legal or not," responded Harris McMahon rather bluntly, not too happy at having his attempt to recapture Lara seemingly thwarted at the last minute. "If we can find the girl and get her quickly back on board, without attracting too much attention, we can always fob the British off with some addle-headed story about tracking a boatload of terrorists, and then having to take offensive action when they tried to sneak ashore to evade us. And us not having time to wait around for official notification, or clearance, or some such damn nonsense!"

CHAPTER FIVE

An Illegal Invasion....

It wasn't all that hard to hear the sound of the 'secret military invasion'... for want of a better description. The motor noise and other associated sounds of a number of landing craft alighting on the beach, even if they couldn't actually be seen from the farm, carried easily enough on the chill breeze. As did the sounds of men shouting out orders regarding the setting up of tents and other sundry temporary accommodation necessities. The excessive revving of motors, as the vehicles they'd brought with them were taken down the ramps and then powered through the surf and up onto the beach also did little to keep the operation a secret.

"So much for a stealthy, undercover operation," Grandma Betty mused aloud as she stood on the front porch beside Granddad Roger, listening to the racket echoing up from the beach.

"Just as long as they aren't on our bloody property," Granddad Roger murmured in reply. Giving a slow nod of his head as he did so.

"You think that Tris and Andrew are right?" Grandma Betty quietly continued. "That all the kerfuffle of that lot down on the beach is them trying to track down the girl?"

"Can't think of any other reason for them to be coming ashore here," Granddad Roger replied. "If it was all part of some official military exercise, then I'm damn sure that we would have been notified of it weeks ago. Along with all the other hoo-hah that usually accompanies that sort of bombastic procedure. And there aren't any other warships out there to show that it's any sort of joint exercise. Certainly none of ours."

"So you think that they might be here illegally?" Mischa queried. Granddad Roger gave a further nod of his head. There had been a time many years previously, when Mischa and Zhenya were still just young children rescued from danger by Gofraidh and Aerynn, that the mere thought of any official action, military or otherwise, in the local area had had them all rather wary of the possibility of officialdom in Russia, for some obscure reason, wanting to claim them back. The present situation with regard to Lara now seemed an echo of those fears.

"They most likely think that they can sneak ashore, grab what they're after, and be gone before anyone is any the wiser," Granddad Roger muttered. "Mind you, according to my father, for all the extra assistance they gave us during the war, the Americans were never were any good at doing things quietly," he added as the sound of a motor vehicle approaching the farm became rather obvious. "Or being all that accurate with bombing runs."

A moment or two later, a small jeep came into view and with some excessive revving of its engine, turned into the start of the farm's driveway. For a while, they all simply watched as it made its slow but noisy progress up the winding, unsealed drive. Eventually, Granddad Roger began moving off the porch to effectively block its path, with Mischa close beside him for support.

"That's as far as you go," he said authoritatively, putting a hand up and then stepping out to block the driveway, so that the vehicle was forced to a halt. They then watched, just a little warily, as the senior officer in the passenger seat got out and came forward to meet him.

"Hi, I'm Lieutenant Colonel Harris McMahon," the man announced rather gruffly. "United States Military. Sorry to be intruding upon your day, but we're just trying to track down some missing equipment. It's sort of linked to um… a... stray... um... a weather balloon that's gone off course."

"And you seem to think that it might have ended up on this farm?" Granddad Roger queried a little bluntly, quickly judging the mention of a weather balloon to be a probable fabrication. Fully aware that nothing of that nature had either appeared over, or landed anywhere on, the farm in the past two days or more.

"Well, according to our tracking signals, that appears to be where it has probably come down," Lieutenant Colonel Harris McMahon replied. "It's an important item of military intelligence that we do urgently need to recover."

"Well, I also have some questions," Granddad Roger responded rather determinedly. "First of all, I would like to ask why you feel you have the right to trespass on private property? And, secondly, given that you're obviously not British, to somehow decide that you have permission to come ashore in a foreign country without official approval? There has certainly been no public notification to say that there was to be any sort of international military exercise taking place in this area. And, even if there was to be such a bombastic nonsense occurring, it certainly would not include anyone having any access to my farm, or any other private property in this area! Regardless of whatever military force that they might claim to be a part of!" Lieutenant Colonel Harris McMahon seemed immediately a little taken aback.

"Look, we're dreadfully sorry for the intrusion," he said rather more politely. "But, as I said, we're just trying to be locate an item of military equipment that seems to have alighted somewhere in this area."

"So what is this object?" Granddad Roger questioned. "Given that you feel that it might just be somewhere near, or even on, our property? Given that you mention it 'alighting', I take it that it's some sort of new flying device? Some sort of means of spying on us Scots, perhaps?"

"I'm afraid I'm not at liberty to divulge that sort of information," Harris McMahon replied quite stiffly. He quickly lowered his voice a little as if trying to make it seem as if everything was top secret and that he was doing them a favour by even making mention of it. "It's fully classified. In fact, it's so off limits that I'm not, yet, at liberty to divulge anything that might lead to an understanding of the exact nature of this piece of 'equipment'. I'm sure you understand such a situation. You know, what with inter-governmental security concerns and all that."

"So how do you know that it's even here?" retorted Granddad Roger quite bluntly. Harris McMahon sighed and gave a quick nod of his head.

"It has a special GPS tracking device attached to it, that gives off a continuous signal," Harris McMahon quickly explained.

"So it gives off a continuous signal, does it?" Granddad Roger echoed rather loudly. Not that it was anything more than a rhetorical question. Yet again, Harris McMahon gave a quick nod of his head.

"As I said, it has GPS tracking unit attached to it. Just like you would probably have in your cell phone," he explained. "So that its position can easily be triangulated from various satellite relays."

"But this one must be on a rather special frequency, of course," Granddad Roger countered, in a careful effort to gain a little more information. "After all, you certainly wouldn't want its special signal to be getting mixed up with all the local phone frequencies, I'd hazard. Or have it interfering with local radio transmissions."

"No, most certainly not." Harris McMahon replied just a little officiously. "As you've suggested, it has its own special frequency. One that's exclusive to the U.S. military." Granddad Roger gave a slight sigh and nodded his head, knowingly.

"You do realise, of course, that if it has crashed on private property, particularly ours, you would need permission of the owner to enter onto that property and remove anything from it, regardless of to whom it belonged," he suggested rather casually. "And that the owner of the property would certainly have first option on its salvage; just the same as if it was an abandoned boat found at sea. More particularly, when you would be trespassing onto private property in a country over which you have absolutely no jurisdiction. You have to remember that this is Scotland, and part of the United Kingdom. It's certainly not any part of the bloody U.S. of A.!"

"It's not an object that's actually all that salvageable!" Lieutenant Colonel Harris McMahon hastily flustered. "Certainly not something in the nature of an actual satellite mechanism that would have some monetary value as salvage. It just has a GPS tracking unit on it so that we can keep track of where it goes."

"So are you implying that this missing unit is actually capable of independent movement?" Granddad Roger intimated, avoiding making it too obvious that he knew that the 'object' referred to was actually a child. He put an arm out as Grandma Betty came down off the porch to join them.

"Well, normally it is kept within a secure unit," Harris McMahon bluntly replied. "But, somehow, it managed to evade our normal methods of keeping it protected."

"Perhaps it didn't want to be kept in a bloody cage!" Grandma Betty muttered rather bluntly. "If you excuse my French!"

"I didn't mention anything about a cage?" replied Harris McMahon a little quizzically.

"Well, what else would you call a secure unit?" Grandma Betty retorted. "A box? A locked room designed to keep whatever's in it from getting out?" She paused a moment, then gave a slight shake of her head. "You also mentioned that 'it' supposedly evaded your methods of keeping it secure," she added. "Which, to most ways of thinking, would tend to suggest that 'it' is not only capable of independent movement, but also thought! And that 'it' also didn't want to be kept in a secure unit in the first place!"

"Look, all I am really at liberty to say is that we detected a signal from it, in this immediate area..." Harris McMahon began. Now starting to wonder if the total secrecy that he'd hoped for had already been breached, somehow.

"So you think that 'detecting a signal' somehow means that it gives you the right to illegally invade private property in another country?" Grandma Betty interjected. Despite her relatively diminutive stature, she took an immediate pace forward, almost threateningly. "I think you should all just get back into your little tin boats and scuttle off back to your battleships and go play your silly little war games somewhere else. And get proper permission to come ashore! Before we notify the War Office and the newspapers!"

Lieutenant Colonel Harris McMahon took a couple of hasty steps backwards. Perhaps a little taken aback by the elderly woman's angry outburst. He sighed, shook his head, and returned to the jeep. Quickly realising that to get into a prolonged confrontation with the local inhabitants of the region would only create an opportunity for the local media to become involved in the situation. And in some ways, any interest or intervention by any media was the very last thing he needed; given that it could easily then be picked up by the major news factions. Before getting into the passenger's seat, he turned for a moment by the door.

"If it's okay with you, we'll be setting up a provisional base down on the beach," he said stiffly. "I'm sure that, given that it is public land, we are at least allowed to camp there, temporarily."

"Suit yourselves," Grandma Betty snapped. "Just remember that temporary access to a public beach does not give you any authority at all to have access to our private property. Not at any time of day, or night!"

***

"I suppose we should ring through to Steve and let him know what's going on," Granddad Roger sighed, once the jeep was out of sight and they'd headed back inside. Much as the military group was not actually trying to sneak onto their property, they all still felt a little uncomfortable at having their presence, nearby. More especially when it seemed likely that they'd come ashore without the knowledge of the British Government. They also felt a little worried about Tris and Lara. Especially about what might happen if they returned to the farm. Given the unsettled nature of the situation, it might also be pertinent to suggest that the two angel children remain grounded to the island, temporarily.

"Well, if you do, be careful what you say," Grandma Betty warned. "I wouldn't put it past that lot down there to try bugging our phone wires, given that they seem to think that their precious lost item is definitely somewhere on our property."

Almost before either of them could reach for the phone however, it began a shrill clamour. Grandma Betty quickly picked it up.

"Hi," Steve Robertson immediately said. "Just a quick call to see how you are."

"We're okay," Grandma Betty replied. "Just keeping a weather eye on things."

"Did the boxes of doughnuts arrive as expected?" Steve queried. For a moment, Grandma Betty felt puzzled at the reference.

"Doughnuts?" she queried.

"Yes," Steve replied with a slight laugh. "Those funny little American treats you love so much."

"Oh, those!" Grandma Betty exclaimed. Realising that her son must already have some knowledge of the military's arrival, most likely from Tris, she quickly understood the hidden intent behind the slightly obtuse question. "Yes, a good lot of them. At least two or three boxes full, in fact," she replied with a sigh. "But we'll work out what to do with them, eventually. Perhaps have them for a picnic down on the beach. Anyway, how are things at your end?"

"Pretty much okay," Steve replied a little guardedly. "Amanda and Joshua were very pleased that Tris arrived back quite safely from his recent trip and that he was also able to bring his new toy with him."

"That's good to hear," Grandma Betty casually continued. "I always worry when that boy has to travel to places on his own. And that new toy that he recently acquired, does it still have that extra special attachment? You know, so that it doesn't get lost all the time?" Steve was quiet for a moment, perhaps trying to work out the meaning of the reference.

"I'll pop down and check that out with him," he eventually replied. "If there is a problem, I'm sure Mykael and Andrew will soon be able to solve it."

"That would be good. And the sooner the better I'd suggest. Perhaps Tris should keep it safely stored at home, if he doesn't want to lose it," Grandma Betty advised.

"So what else has been happening up that way?" Steve casually asked. Quickly understanding the reference to keeping both Tris and Lara on the island for the time being, but also realising that if anyone was listening in, then they'd certainly expect the unwarranted beach invasion to be mentioned. "Anything particularly exciting or untoward?

"Well, would you believe it, we had a bloody invasion," Grandma Betty answered, appearing to quickly pick up on his intentions. "Some military group have parked two bloody great warships just off the coast, if you pardon my French. And a bloody great aircraft carrier as well! Then they sent some of those funny little amphibious craft things in to land on the beach, with a bunch of soldiers. They're supposedly looking for some top-secret item from a weather balloon that they think might be on our property. They've been tracking it by some sort of special GPS signal, or something, so they say. It's all to do with the weather balloon having gone astray, according to the officer in charge. Of course, your father made it quite clear that they were not to enter our property without the appropriate permission. So, at the moment, they're camped down on the beach. You know, that little bay that you go past on the way up to the farm, where hardly anybody ever swims because the water's always too darn cold."

"You should get Mischa to set up a camera," Steve casually suggested. "Just to let you know if they do try to come onto the farm without permission."

"That sounds like a good idea," Grandma Betty replied. "But honestly, all that fuss over one silly little weather balloon with some special GPS attachment. You think that they'd just inform the local police, or something, that it needed to be retrieved, instead of sending a fleet of battleships and mounting a sneaky little invasion!"

***

Rylan hastily looked up from where he was seated on the sidewalk, with his back against a wall to one side of the entry to the McDonalds, as a gruff voice suddenly asked for his name. Quickly realising that, with his being distracted with trying to sort out what he could actually buy with the little money he had left in his pockets, he'd not seen the police officer's approach.

"Um... Chris. Christopher Makin." he lied. Conveniently remembering the name of a boy who had been in his class two years previously. A cute boy for whom he once thought he'd felt some attraction. Not that he'd ever made that situation too obvious in any way.

"And why aren't you in school?" the policeman asked rather bluntly. He leant in a little closer so that his considerable bulk almost seemed to be towering over Rylan in a rather intimidating manner.

"I... I'm... on my way to a dentist appointment," Rylan flustered, as he scrambled to his feet and quickly pointed back down the street, in the vague hope that there might just be some form of dental practice somewhere in that direction. Hoping, at the same time, that the rather dishevelled state of his clothes, from sleeping under piles of cardboard behind a dumpster for the previous two nights, wasn't too obvious. "I was at school earlier, but I'm supposed to make my own way there. Like, to the dentist. And then meet up with my mom, afterwards."

The police officer scanned the street in both directions, almost as if trying to figure out which of the buildings was likely to be the office of a dentist, or perhaps even the possible location of a school that he did not already know of. Given the nature of the district, neither option seemed all that likely. And, to the officer, the boy's unkempt appearance still seemed to purvey an air of his being truant, or perhaps even a runaway of some type; or just unnecessarily nervous, to say the least.

"What's the name of your dentist?" he suddenly asked. Rylan shook his head a little, trying to think of a likely name… a name that would at least seem believable.

"Um... Mr... Mr Reynolds. Doctor Carl Reynolds," Rylan fudged. Feeling sure that the officer would have no way of realising that Carl Reynolds was actually the name of his last home-room teacher back in Oakton. It seemed extremely unlikely. Given that Carl Reynolds had, on more than one occasion, proudly told the class that he'd lived in Wichita his whole life, and had at one stage even been a pupil at Oakton Middle School, sitting in the same desks as they were. At the same time, he wondered if the officer even truly believed that his name was Chris Makin. Something in the way in which he was being scrutinised gave him the feeling that that was also just a little unlikely.

"So what school are you enrolled at?" the officer suddenly barked, as he seemed to fumble for a moment or two with the handcuffs hanging from his belt. "What direction is it from here?"

"I'm... I'm... I'm homeschooled," Rylan quickly blurted. Realising, almost as he spoke, that he'd previously mentioned that he'd been on his way from school to visit the dentist. He hoped that the officer might not notice his slight 'faux-pas'. Or if he did, presume that his earlier reference had been to a homeschooling situation. He briefly glanced up and down the street, trying to spot a means of escape, even as, for a moment or two, the police officer simply eyed him a little suspiciously. Glancing about, Rylan quickly realised that the interaction between himself and the officer, already seemed to be attracting the curiosity of patrons inside the fast-food joint, as well as the casual attention of the pedestrians hurrying by. Some of them possibly seeing him as just another 'truant' caught up in a police swoop; others, more than likely, simply wondering if he was being questioned about some recent petty crime, such as shoplifting.

"How about you just stand over there by the wall for a moment, while I check out a few details of what you're telling me," the officer suddenly instructed, pointing towards where Rylan had previously been seated. His manner already seeming to suggest that he wasn't really into believing a good deal of what he was being told. Rylan felt a slight sense of relief, in that the officer had not already handcuffed him, or forced him to get into the back of the squad car. Perhaps that was simply an oversight. Or maybe the officer was being a little wary that, if he did handcuff a child going about his legitimate business, it might result in quite serious repercussions if the boy's parents decided to lodge a complaint. After all, the kid had certainly not committed any crime just by sitting outside a McDonalds, even if he did look a bit scruffy.

As the police officer wandered back over to his squad car, said something to the officer behind the wheel, and then reached through the open passenger's side window to make the call, Rylan saw his opportunity. Even with the officer still watching him, as he spoke into his radio, Rylan suddenly took off. Hoping to make a dash through the crowd that had gathered, and use his small size to get out of sight within them.

Dodging his way through the sidewalk traffic, making quick apologies as he did so, he sprinted as fast as he could. Almost immediately hearing the steady thump, thump, thump of the officer's feet coming closer in pursuit, as he weaved this way and that around the oncoming pedestrians. Henry Fulcher's borrowed backpack bouncing from side to side against his back as he dodged his way along the crowded sidewalk. While most of those he dodged past just seemed surprised, and a little offended, by his bustling actions, a few tried to reach out to grab him in half-hearted attempts to halt his progress; actions that he was easily able to avoid.

Just as he thought he might've got clean away, a hand suddenly clutched at the backpack, stalling his progress a little. Quickly realising, with a glance over his shoulder, that it was the police officer, a little reluctantly, Rylan quickly dipped his shoulders to one side and then the other. In the process, allowing the backpack to slide from his shoulders. The action seemed to slow the man's progress. So much so, that the man actually stumbled a little over the bag. His hands reaching out towards the ground to stop himself sprawling to his knees; his sudden faltering steps quickly allowing Rylan the chance to gain just a little ground.

Turning into a small alleyway, hoping that it would lead to an area with more pedestrians, Rylan was suddenly confronted by a tall wooden fence that effectively blocked his way. He paused for a moment, feeling trapped. Hearing the steady thump of the policeman's feet getting closer once again, before quickly noticing that a couple of the planks had been busted off at the bottom left-hand side of the wall, creating a small opening. Anxious to escape, he sprinted to the fence, and dived headfirst for the gap. Just managing to wriggle the top part of his body through it before a hand grabbed at his left ankle. In desperation he kicked out with his right foot in almost a stamping motion and was relieved to hear an angry curse as his shoe make contact with the police officer's hand; the impact being hard enough to make the man release his grip.

Scrambling to his feet on the other side of the fence, Rylan looked hastily around for somewhere to hide. Even as he hoped that the police officer wouldn't suddenly clamber over the fence, he was already realising that he'd need to get well off the streets for the rest of the day. After all, it would only require the other officer in the car to have made a call back to the local precinct, for every police officer in New York to have a rough description of what he looked like, and where he'd last been seen, and so be on the lookout for him.

Hurrying further down the alleyway, towards the next major street, a slightly open door to his left immediately beckoned as a means of hiding. He slipped inside it a little cautiously and closed it behind him, hastily ensuring that it was locked. Looking around, he was surprised to find that, rather than being confronted with puzzled looks from people working there, he was in a building that appeared completely deserted. From its shop-like appearance, it had perhaps been, at some earlier time, some type of major retail outlet, but now all that was left were rows and rows of empty shelving.

Eventually finding, quite near to one of the walls, what seemed to be an old shop counter of some kind, he scurried behind it. In doing so, discovering that there was a small alcove beneath it, just to one side of a set of movable drawers. He quickly crawled into the alcove and then manoeuvred the set of drawers so that they looked like being a permanent feature of the counter, before pulling the hood of Henry's jacket over his head and sitting with his back against the wall and his knees drawn up close to his chest. Hoping that, even if the police officer had looked over the fence and seen him go through the door and the place did end up being searched, with all the shelves to work around no one would actually bother to come around to the far side of the counter. Or if they did, give the space behind it nothing more than just a cursory glance, assuming that the drawers were fixed in place.

***

Rylan listened carefully, and then, hearing nothing to be wary of — no sound that indicated that anyone else might be nearby

— carefully emerged from his hiding place. It had started to go dark outside, and his joints twinged from the sudden burst of movement. In his worry about a possible police search for him, he'd spent most of the afternoon huddled away in his hiding place, hardly daring to move. Just listening to the sounds filtering into the building from the streets outside and hoping that nothing of it was any part of a search for him. Normal city sounds that, nevertheless, had frequently included police and ambulance sirens. And now, even though his stomach was rumbling with hunger, he desperately needed to find a toilet.

Moving quietly in the evening gloom, in case there were people elsewhere in the building — not that he'd heard or seen any sign of them — he made his way towards what he guessed must have once been the main entrance. It was securely bolted and barred. Beyond the large, graffiti-daubed windows and doors there was some form of tall, mesh fencing, to prevent anyone from entering from the street.

To his left a small side door opened out into a smaller foyer that seemed to also have a separate entrance onto the street. Like the main building, there was a mesh fence outside the doors. Not that it seemed to have been all that effective given the amount of food debris, wine bottles and other unmentionable items that littered the floor close to the main doors. And, of course, there was the obvious fact that the side door that he'd first snuck through had been left open at some earlier time.

In this smaller foyer, there seemed to be a long corridor leading off towards what he presumed was further rooms, some stairs and a bank of elevators for access to the upper floors. Not that any of the lifts appeared to be working, given that the buttons to summon them had been smashed in, and one elevator had open doors that gaped down to the blackness of a basement level.

Still feeling an urgent need to at least relieve his bladder, he headed down the corridor in search of a bathroom. Eventually finding a men's bathroom, he was quietly surprised to find that the water was still turned on, although the filthy state of the room, coupled with the smell of stale urine, certainly didn't make it an inviting place to use. He hurriedly exited and found the 'ladies' bathroom a little further down the hallway. With there being more individual cubicles, he was pleased to find one that was just a little cleaner, although it was still badly daubed with obscene graffiti. It surprised him a little that women would write those sorts of obscenities. Granted that, with the building no longer in use, he supposed that they could have been written by anyone.

Having relieved more than just his bladder, by squatting a little awkwardly to try to avoid actually touching the toilet seat, and pleased to find that there was actually still some toilet paper available and that the flush system still worked, he washed his hands afterwards. That done, he dried his hands on the sides of his jacket and then quickly pulled back the hood, and looked at himself in the large mirror that extended the full length of the wall above the washbasins. His face didn't look too grubby, but his hair and clothes certainly looked like they needed a wash. He supposed that was simply a consequence of where he'd spent the last few nights. As his stomach rumbled, yet again, he sighed and set off in search of something to eat and a place to bed down for the night.

Within the ground floor of the building, it proved to be a fruitless search, apart from finding out that he was not alone. In one of the smaller rooms on the left side of the building, not too far from the entrance, he found obvious signs that people were living there... or at least sleeping there at night. Perhaps, he judged by the long strips of fluorescent lights suspended from the ceiling, the room had once been an office of some type. Not that any of the lights appeared to be in working condition.

As he moved cautiously into the room and looked down at the scattering of threadbare blankets, grubby pillows, food wrappers, liquor bottles, and other detritus, and tried to figure out just when the room had last been occupied, a rustling sound suddenly disturbed him. Turning quickly, he was unexpectedly confronted by a rather stooped and bearded man, holding two battered-looking plastic bags, standing just a little way inside the doorway.

"What in hell are you doing here?" the man growled as they stared at each other for a good few moments. "This ain't no place for no damn street kids! So git!"

"I'm just..." Rylan began, and then quickly lapsed into silence. There seemed no point in arguing the case.

"We don't need no bloody street kids, or runaways bringing the law down on us," the man rumbled, his voice sounding harsh... most probably from the after-effects of years of smoking and hard liquor. "Find yourself somewhere else to bloody hide!" he continued. Hobbling over to a scruffy pile of blankets and putting down the bags, he waved his hands to indicate towards the door. "Go on, git outta here!"

Hastily dodging past the man, Rylan quickly scurried away, back in the direction of the foyer. Noticing, when he reached the main doors, that the lock on them had been broken, and that beyond them there was a small gap in the mesh fencing. For a moment, he stayed still, close to the doors giving access to the street. Trying to decide whether to head out, and risk being spotted by the police or social welfare officials, or to simply conduct a further exploration of the building in search of a new hiding place. After all, he'd already been able to hide behind the counter for almost a full day without disturbing anyone.

Quickly realising that it would be better not to take the risk of being seen outside… at least not when it was likely that there might still be a search going on for him, and also wanting to be well away from the homeless people in case he was at risk from them, he made a decision to head upstairs. Realising at the same time, a little ironically, that he was similarly 'homeless'. Still, it seemed safer, for the moment, for him to remain on his own. Given his vulnerability and inexperience with regard to life on the streets, the fewer people knew where he was, he surmised, the better.

Taking little time in surveying the first three or four levels, simply because the rooms there already appeared to have been cleaned out of anything useful, or had been simply trashed and grafittied, he quickly continued on to higher levels until, eventually, on the sixth floor he found a room that was not only still lockable, but also contained a large couch that hadn't been totally trashed and looked big enough for him to sleep on.

A hurried check of the switches by the door soon confirmed that, like elsewhere in the building, there was no electricity. His search, however, did unearth a couple of tins of food, albeit without labels, hidden away in the very back of a cupboard in what had once been a rather small kitchen area. Given that there was also a bathroom and a working toilet, both of which were in a reasonably clean condition, especially when compared with what he'd found downstairs, he realised that the rooms on the upper floors had most probably been converted into some sort of studio apartments at some earlier time. The one he was now in even had a balcony with a view out over the street.

For a moment, he casually wondered why the room was in such good condition, compared with what he'd previously encountered, and then surmised that, with the elevators not working, perhaps most of the other occupants of the building simply couldn't be bothered with climbing the stairs to the sixth floor each night. With a slight nod at that understanding, he realised that that might also mean that there would be more 'booty' to be found in other rooms on the same floor. Perhaps some more food, or money, or extra clothing... and hopefully, some candles.

Within twenty minutes, he'd completed his rough search and, while he'd found no more food that was of any use, apart from a rather mouldy loaf of bread and a damp half-packet of very stale biscuits, he had managed to find a couple of coarse blankets that he could use for extra warmth and three cushions for use as make-shift pillows. All the time, he wondered what the people downstairs would be thinking of him being in their building. That was, of course, if they even realised that he was still there. And, more importantly, whether he'd be safe from them.

As he threw the blankets and cushions onto the couch, his stomach suddenly rumbled. Instantly reminding him of his not having eaten for over a day. Once he'd locked the door, he began a search through the kitchen drawers for something to open the cans. Eventually finding what he needed in the fourth of the drawers.

Grabbing the nearest can, he wondered, for a moment, what it might contain. At the same time, he felt hungry enough to even eat dog food, if that turned out to be what the tin contained. He carefully opened it and was quietly relieved, and also delighted, to find that it contained circles of pineapple. He quickly ate a few of them and then decided to leave the rest for later. Perhaps he'd eat them in the morning.

Afterwards, he lay back on the couch. Pondering on his situation and his next likely move. On one hand, he could possibly go back to the Fulchers and persuade them not to take him to any church. That would mean, of course, also explaining about what had happened to Henry's backpack and all the clothes that they'd bought for him. The police, no doubt, would already be examining the backpack and its contents for clues to his identity. He tried to remember whether there had been a name inside the backpack or on any of the clothing, but couldn't be sure either way. Nevertheless, that also created a further problem. If the backpack had been named, then the police might already be waiting for him at the Fulchers.

***

"Alright you lazy lot. On your feet! Now!" Miguel Sicario bellowed. The eighteen children lounging around on old mattresses in the large basement room scrambled quickly to their feet. Knowing that to be too tardy might result in a receiving a little extra painful incentive from the horse whip Miguel had attached on a loop around his right wrist, as a reminder for them to be quickly obedient. While Vittorio and Angelo could be harsh if they did anything wrong, Miguel was quite often straight-out cruel and the one who seemed the most likely to want to take them upstairs for a bit of extra 'fun'!

"We've got some assignments to sort out," he said bluntly. "Some of you have even got a nice little party to attend," he smirked. "Tonight!" A slight murmur, and also a sense of alarm, immediately spread through the children.

"Don't worry, they won't be needing all of you," Miguel continued rather casually. "Probably just about six to eight of you will be all that's required for tonight. Vittorio will make the final choice after he's checked you over. And as you already know, he's also made it quite clear that he wants to develop a group of ten to twelve totally innocent boys and girls for some special function that's in the pipeline; one that'll be worth a great deal of money to us. In fact, more than triple the usual payments, so it's going to take total priority for the next few weeks. They'll be requiring just five or six girls and a similar number of boys, but the proviso is that they must be 'totally innocent', so that, once they've been sold at auction, the clients can have a bit of fun 'breaking them in', so to speak. And I'm sure you can understand what is meant by 'totally innocent' and 'breaking them in'." He slowly scanned the room. Seeing the looks of horror evident as they children realised what was being described. "So, for the moment," he then continued, "and until we organise a more definite date for that particular function, for the children who're selected, anything more than just a bit of light touching by the clientele at any engagement, is strictly 'off limits'. Understand?" The children all hastily nodded. "And just to make you feel a little safer, until we have the big auction, you will be issued with the same 'display wear' you wore at your inspection, when you go out. Understand?" Once again, all the children nodded, feeling some sense of relief, in that they would at least have some covering, even if it did resemble just the briefest of beachwear.

"Can you tell us which of us have been selected?" Cooper Stanford cautiously asked. "Just so we know not to allow anyone to go too far with...?" he nervously added. In response to the dark look he got from Miguel, he left his query incomplete. Perhaps merely out of a reluctance to actually mention what he suspected would eventually happen to them, but also not wanting to find himself on the receiving end of immediate punishment. For quite a while there was silence as all the children nervously cast surreptitious glances his way. All of them noting the way Miguel almost eagerly fingered the thin strap attaching the horse whip to his wrist, and maybe expecting Cooper to be given a severe thrashing; as usually happened if you spoke out of turn, or offered questions that were not asked for.

"Well, given that you're one of the boys who at the moment is still an 'innocent', for want of a better description, you'll be pleased to know that you're definitely one of the boys being considered, at present," Miguel replied with almost a smiling sneer. "Unless you piss me, or any of the others, off, so that we decide to get rid of you a little early. Understand?" He waited until Cooper had nervously nodded a reply and backed away a little. "The other boys at present on the short list are Luka, Riley and Skylar… and maybe Martyn, if he hasn't been auctioned off by then. As you realise, that means we are possibly short of a boy, or two, for what we need for the special event, so we'll hope to acquire at least two new recruits to add to that list, as most of the older boys here, and the few we have at the other house in Nevada, are all a bit too experienced for what the special engagement requires. So those that I've named, make sure that you keep yourselves well clear of any danger, tonight. As I said a moment ago, a bit of light touching is okay, but you're mainly just 'eye-candy' for the 'pervs'. So anything else is totally off limits." He sighed and shuffled the papers that he had in his left hand to reveal another list.

"And just so you know, the girls currently on the list are Natasha, Jessamine, Persia, Rochelle, Maia and Camille. Although, that might change considerably between now and the date when you'll actually be needed, depending on whatever new stock we manage to acquire. Nevertheless, the same will apply for you as I've said for the boys. Don't let anyone get too close, unless we tell you otherwise. And all you girls are lucky. You won't be required at all tonight." He turned back towards the boys. "The client just wants a few good-looking boys to act as special 'waiters', at some private function. Although I dare say that a few of the guests present at tonight's little gathering might also be keen to possibly acquire some of you at the next auction."

He glanced around at the whole gathering and then focussed his gaze back on the eleven boys assembled on the left-hand side of the room.

"Now, in addition to the five 'vestal virgins'..." he sneered, "tonight's little group of entertainers will also include James, Peter, and Noah. That makes a total of eight for Vittorio to check over." He again glanced around the room. "So, if I didn't mention your name as being required, you're to just wait down here, for the moment. Angelo has another little 'assignment' for some of you in two days time, in Denver. That group will probably also include some of the girls from the Nevada holding house, and it will very likely also include an auction, for those of you that we want to move on to permanent placements a little earlier. Vittorio will get you organised a bit later, and you'll be transported later tonight." He paused a moment to let his instructions be fully understood and then moved over to the doorway and opened it.

"Okay," he continued. "The eight boys that I mention earlier, you can head up to the showers and get yourselves properly cleaned up. Once you've finished, leave all your dirty clothes and towels in the baskets in the washroom, and head through to the main office. Vittorio will check each of you over before you're given your 'display wear'. After all, the Network does have standards to keep, with regard to the cleanliness of our merchandise. For this particular assignment, you'll also be dressed as Roman slaves, so Vittorio will also fit you out in your costumes just before we're ready to leave. As I said earlier, you will simply be acting as waiters for the finger foods at some Roman style toga-party, so it'll be essentially a 'no touching' assignment, with you playing the part of child slaves. Just keep in mind however that, as I previously mentioned, you will also be on view for possible purchase by auction at some later stage, so you may be photographed. We also expect you to be on your very best behaviour, even if you are asked to linger a moment for a closer inspection. Otherwise, you know the consequences. Now, get going!"

"Wow, we actually get to wear some actual clothes!" Noah murmured to Skylar, Cooper, Riley and Luka, as they hastily followed James, Peter, and Martyn towards the shower room. Perhaps remembering back to his last 'assignment', when each member of a group of six boys and four girls had had to perform a musical striptease routine for their 'guests', that ended up with their only covering being their 'display wear'. Clothing that left only a little to the imagination in that it resembled just the lower half of a girl's bikini. Luckily, it had also been a 'look, but don't touch' occasion, which, although embarrassing, wasn't anywhere near as bad as when the guests' hands were allowed to roam rather freely, or, as Peter had warned them, guests were allowed to take them away to other rooms for far less enjoyable interaction.

"Depends what the costumes are like," Skylar murmured. He half-remembered once seeing a film that had been set in the days of the Roman Empire. From what he could recall, the important adults were swathed in robes of considerable size, while the 'slaves'... and more especially the younger child-slaves, seemed to wear a very short style of dress that looped over just one shoulder and barely reached their thighs.

He also understood the meaning of 'consequences'. The thrashing that Cooper had received after misbehaving during their last transportation had left the boy unable to sit comfortably, or even walk without wincing, for almost two full days. Still, as Noah had also told them, Cooper had got off very lightly, compared with what could have happened to him if he hadn't been lucky enough to be one of the children that Vittorio had decided would be kept 'innocent'.

***

The abrupt, loud knock on the door instantly startled Rylan into wakefulness. With no power, the room he'd found as a temporary bolthole was only dimly illuminated with the light through the window from outside. The lights from the street below, that spread a glow across the ceiling, coupled with the 'off and on' reflection of various patterns of light from a few flashing neon signs. He threw back the thin, coarse blankets he was using as covering and tiptoed quietly over to the door.

"Hey, kid... are you in there?" a voice whispered rather gruffly. For a moment, Rylan stayed very still. Almost not daring to breath. A moment later, the knocking was repeated before the man spoke again.

"Hey, kid, if you're in there, it's George. I'm one of the men from downstairs. I've got some food for you and a couple of candles."

"How do I know you won't hurt me?" asked Rylan very softly, automatically putting his hand onto the lock.

"I'm not into hurting kids," the man replied. "Whatever you are. I just wanted to check that you were okay. After all, we don't get too many kids in this place." Rylan thought for a moment. A candle and some extra food would come in handy. He cautiously began to open the door. A little to his surprise, the man was standing, quite unthreateningly, against the far wall of the corridor, appearing to be making no attempt to push his way into the room. In his left hand he held a half-loaf of bread. In his right, a box of matches and a couple of large candles. One of which was lit.

"May I come in?" he asked, without bothering to move. Rylan shrugged, then nodded and indicated for the man to enter. Stepping to one side to let him walk past, Rylan left the door open, just in case he needed to make a hurried exit. He then watched from close to the doorway as the man put the unlit candle and box of matches onto the bench, along with the half-loaf of bread, and then, having grabbed a saucer from one of the cupboards, dripped some wax onto it and set the lit candle standing on its own, before glancing around the room.

"Well, Rebel, you do seem to have got yourself nicely set up," he said, giving a bit of a laugh as he looked at the makeshift bed of cushions and blankets. "And reasonably safe, I'd suggest. It took ages for me to work out just where you were. It was only because old Alf mentioned that he'd definitely seen you heading upstairs, and was pretty sure that he hadn't seen you come back down, that anyone would have known that you were here." Rylan nodded and tentatively moved a little closer.

"Why did you call me Rebel?" he questioned, his face reflecting a considerable degree of puzzlement. George seemed to give a further slight laugh.

"Because that's what old Alf called you," he said. "Well, at first, he actually called you 'Rebel Rebel'. Like, with the name twice." Rylan still looked a little mystified.

"Why?' he eventually asked. George gave a shrug, as he sat down on the couch and then indicated for Rylan to be seated as well.

"I won't hurt you, I promise," he murmured. "I had three kids of my own, once… leastwise until my wife decided to head back to Croatia. So hurting kids is definitely not my thing." Rylan moved to sit at the furthest end of the couch; half seated on an armrest and still well away from his visitor. Still tense, and ready to bolt at the slightest sense of danger. After all, a good many other adults in his past had not always kept their promises.

"Alf's a long time David Bowie fan," George quickly explained. "He decided that you looked androgynous enough for him to be a bit confused as to what you were, if you catch my drift. It made him think of the song... 'Rebel Rebel'." Rylan shook his head a little, as if still unable to comprehend any meaning in the name. Once again, George seemed to laugh a little; it came out as a rumbling, gruff sound.

The opening lines of the song are what got him," he said, and then quickly sang the lines in a rough, rasping voice.

"You've got your mother in a whirl. She's not sure if you're a boy or a girl...."

Rylan still looked rather puzzled, even as much as he understood the obvious reference to his rather androgynous appearance.

"They're the opening lines to old Alf's favourite Bowie song... 'Rebel, Rebel', and he thought of it because, as I said, he wasn't quite sure what you were. Like... whether you were a boy or a girl." George hastily explained, after singing the lines and seeing Rylan's continued bewilderment. "He seemed to think the name was appropriate for you. I think he found it rather amusing."

"I'm a boy," Rylan muttered a little bluntly, as he fully picked up on the reference. George nodded.

"Okay," he said quite casually. "Now that we've got that little matter sorted, how about you tell me your real name and why you're hiding out on the streets, instead of being safely tucked up in bed at home? And don't you worry your little head. I ain't about to go running off to the police or Social Welfare about you. I'm just curious, that's all. And I certainly don't want to see you getting hurt." Rylan looked at his hands for a moment, and then at the loaf of bread and the flickering flame of the candle.

"My name's Rylan," he finally said rather resignedly. "And I ran away from home so that I wouldn't get punished all the time."

For the next ten minutes, George listened attentively as Rylan detailed his beatings and abuse at the hands of his father and Pastor Isaac. Of his being brought to New York to see a psychiatrist and the way Edward J. Stanford's leering at him, while photographing him, had made him feel extremely uncomfortable and had led to his decision to run away from his parents. Of how he had ended up sleeping under piles of cardboard and stealing food from dumpsters, until his unexpected encounter with a policeman that had resulted in him hiding out in this particular building. He didn't bother to mention the Fulchers, because that would've seemed out of place and would've ultimately raised the question of... 'If you'd found a nice, safe place to stay, why on Earth did you decide to leave?' He also wasn't going to reveal to this stranger, or in fact to anyone, that he had wings, even if they were still growing at a quite surprising rate.

When he eventually ran out of words, George sat looking at him for a moment.

"At your age, it's not really safe for you to be living on the streets on your own," he finally said just a little resignedly. "Still, I can understand why you left home. And, to put it bluntly, you certainly wouldn't be the first kid to do so for those very same reasons." He reached out a hand, patted Rylan tentatively on the shoulder and then looked about the room. "At the same time, I think it would be best that you stay up here, for the time being. Someplace where you can keep a door locked. While most of the regulars downstairs won't want to hurt you in any way… not even Alf, for all his grouchiness, I can't always vouch for some that sometimes turn up for a night or two; especially some of the crack-heads. There's some of them wouldn't care what you were… boy or girl, if you catch my drift. Especially if they wanted a bit of action or thought that they could make use of you to get a bit of money for their habit." He paused a moment as if waiting for Rylan to make some response. When the boy didn't, he continued.

"Now, I'll try to keep an eye out for you to see that you're safe. Like, I've brought you some bread for tonight. But you'll also need to work out ways of getting some for yourself, because one or two of them downstairs are just a bit worried that you might bring the cops down on them simply by being here. Especially if your parents get the police involved in a search for you. Now, if you keep out of sight, I doubt any of the regulars downstairs will hassle you in any way, but if they do, you just tell them that George has given you his word of protection. Okay?" Rylan quickly nodded, finding some sense of relief in realising that he had some sort of 'friend' in the man.

"One or two last things, before I go," George added, as he got to his feet. "As I said a moment ago, keep your door locked when you're in here, and stay totally off the streets at night. You'll be far too vulnerable a target for the type of lowlifes that can tend to be out in these areas after dusk. And, given your age, you can bet your sweet little boots the police will simply arrest you the minute they see you. Finally, the best bet for food, if you've got no money, is a couple of dumpsters behind a café a block south of here. They tend to close at about three-thirty each afternoon and quite often the food that can't be saved for another day, or that nobody wants to take home, gets thrown into the dumpsters about four to four-thirty. If you're quick, you can get some good stuff before the rats get into it... both animal and human." Rylan nodded. He'd already discovered the world of dumpster diving for food. But it was nice to know that George bothered enough to tell him where it was best to go. Perhaps they might even go together, sometimes.

"Thank you for the candles and the bread," he murmured as he followed George to the door. The man nodded and pulled his coat a little tighter.

"I also suggest that you blow out your candle before you go to bed," he advised rather nonchalantly. "Not only will it make it last longer, but, while this place is most likely due for demolition sometime in the next six months or so, there's no sense in needlessly starting a fire. Not if it might get you trapped up here." He stopped in the doorway and tapped the door. "Lock this as soon as I've gone," he continued softly. "If you keep quiet, no one will know where you are. Even if they do make the effort to clump their way up six flights of stairs." He reached out and tousled Rylan's hair with a grubby hand. "Keep safe, kid!"

Rylan watched him head away towards the stairs and then closed and locked the door. While he was still homeless, in the true sense of the word, and on his own, and would have much preferred to still be with the Fulchers, with George's offer of friendship, he at least didn't feel quite so alone. Crossing back over to the bench, he grabbed the bread and tore off a hunk, perhaps just as a way of showing George that he appreciated the gift. Then, having chewed and swallowed it, using a bit of the pineapple juice to give it some moisture, he blew out the candle and snuggled himself back under his blankets on the couch.

CHAPTER SIX

A Cunning Device....

"Okay, let's get things underway," Steve Robertson said as Mykael, Ithuriel and Andrew were suddenly present. He looked to where Lara was still keeping close to Tris; following him almost like a shadow it seemed. "It appears, from what I've been told, that our little newcomer is being electronically tracked, somehow. According to Granddad Roger and Grandma Betty, it'll be some form of GPS locator that's hidden on her person. At least that's what the American officer in charge intimated when he came ashore. What we obviously need to do is to find it and then find a way to deactivate it. And we can only do that once we know how it's actually hidden on her person."

"Would it be something that they might have planted under her skin?" Amanda quickly asked. "You know, like in all the sci-fi movies when they want to keep track of people? Like Ender Wiggin had on the back of his neck at the start of the movie 'Ender's Game'?" Admittedly, having seen the girl through a shower and subtly checked her over for possible signs of abuse, when Tris had first brought her home, she'd not noticed anything untoward. At least, not anything such as a small scar, that might have indicated the presence of a concealed GPS transmitter. Neither had Peter McCormack noticed anything untoward when he'd examined her.

"Like how they tag animals in the wild?" Carwyn eagerly added.

"Or cats and dogs, so that they can be identified if they get lost?" Melanie offered. "You know, like how they stick some little capsule thing under their skin, usually at the back of their neck."

"It's a possibility, but let's just try to figure out if it's actually a bit more obvious than that, first," Mykael softly suggested, displaying a slightly amused smile. They all turned to look at Lara, perhaps still wondering if some device had been medically implanted somewhere on her person. Mykael immediately beckoned for her to come over to stand in front of him.

"Do you know if the military people who had you held captive, ever planted anything under your skin," he asked. "Some sort of small capsule or disc? It would most likely have entailed some small bit of surgery." Lara gave a quick shake of her head.

"I don't think they ever did?" she said softly. "I mean, even if they'd put me out to do it, I'm sure that I would still have noticed something when I woke up. You know, like, a bit of soreness, somewhere, or a scar, or something not quite right." Mykael nodded and looked at her for a moment.

"Well, did they give you anything special to wear, after you arrived at the military base? Aside from the hospital smocks?" Lara gave a quick shake of her head. That had been something she'd hated. Having just a hospital smock that was open at the back to cover herself… even if there was a fresh one provided each morning, along with the paper underwear. It was almost as if they'd somehow classified her as being non-human and therefore decided that she did not require such basic niceties as proper clothes. Mykael looked her up and down for a moment or two. Perhaps trying to remember back to how she looked when he'd first set eyes on her.

"Well, what about your necklace?" he eventually continued. "Do you actually know where it came from?" Lara responded with a slight flex of her shoulders. The fingers of her right hand immediately coming up to her neck to finger the loop of brightly coloured beads.

"It was a present from my foster parents," she softly replied.

"And when did they give it to you?" Mykael queried. In some ways, he was already starting to feel sure that the necklace would be the likely culprit. More especially, as he already knew that it couldn't be unfastened.

"Well, it was after they left me at the first hospital place," Lara hastily replied. "The people there… like, the military people who were looking after me, they just said that they'd left it for me."

"So the Holts didn't actually give it to you?" Mykael quickly asked. "Like, you didn't actually have them put it on you, themselves?"

"No," replied Lara softly, a little nervously. She still felt a little in awe of Mykael and Ithuriel; especially with them being senior guardians. "That's just what I was told when I woke up and noticed I was wearing it. As I just said, the people at the hospital place just said that my mom and dad had had to leave in bit of a hurry and that they'd wanted to give me something as a special parting gift. It's a bit weird, though, because, as I told Aman... I mean Mum, when I first got here, I can't actually take it off. I tried to at first… like, when I first wanted to have a shower at the hospital. But it didn't seem to have a catch or any sort of fastening that I could find. One of the nurses who was looking after me at the time eventually said that I should just leave it on, and that the shower probably wouldn't hurt it." For Mykael, the comment that the 'shower probably wouldn't hurt it' simply appeared to back up his theory that the necklace would be the culprit… the source of the signal. Even as he nodded his head, Steve Robertson moved closer to Lara and started to examine the necklace more closely.

She's right," he said, after moving the necklace gently around her neck to give it careful scrutiny. "There isn't any sort of catch on it. At least nothing that seems all that obvious. Not unless one of the beads has some secret mechanism."

"There has to be," Amanda countered. "If they were able to put it on her, it must be possible to take it off."

"It could be super-glued, in some way," Tris offered.

"Well, if it is the tracking device… which, by the way we're all thinking, does seem rather likely, then we do need to find a way to remove it," Andrew suggested. He turned towards Joshua. "Have you got any bolt-cutters in the garage?"

"They won't be necessary," countered Mykael with a rather wry smile. "Removing it is easily done." He looked towards Ithuriel and seemed to exchange a quick thought. "Well, technically, not quite so easily," he added with a casual shrug.

Beckoning for Lara to come closer, which she did just a little tentatively, he gently took her two hands in his left hand and then placed them on the end of the fingers of his right hand, so that her fingers pointed towards his palm. He then crouched down until he was almost kneeling; an action that meant that his arm was reaching up almost to the level of his head.

"Now lean forward, so that your head is over your hands and keep very still," he instructed. Lara, still a little puzzled by his actions, quickly did as he had asked.

Mykael gave a nod towards Ithuriel, and then, with a slight wave of his other hand, Lara suddenly vanished, to be replaced by a brilliantly coloured butterfly, resting lightly on the fingers of his right hand. The necklace quickly dropped from the air where Lara's neck had been; passing easily around the butterfly, and in the process, neatly encircling Mykael's upraised fingers until it was left dangling on his arm, almost at his elbow. An instant later, the delicate winged insect, was suddenly transformed back into a young girl with her fingers still lightly touching Mykael's. As Lara stepped back and shook her head, appearing rather bewildered by whatever had just taken place, Mykael got to his feet, slipping the necklace off his arm as he did so.

"Now it can be examined a little more easily," he said with a slightly cheeky smile.

"Show off," Ithuriel murmured, rolling his eyes and then giving a slow shake of his head.

"We can change people... in... into other creatures? Just like that?" exclaimed Tris rather eagerly. While he'd briefly wondered why Mykael hadn't just thought of telling Lara to 'be', while also thinking of herself as not wearing the necklace, his thoughts were now already awash with a myriad of possibilities of transformation. Particularly, of who could be changed into what! Mykael gave a slight shake of his head, before changing it into a single, slightly sideways, nod.

"A few of us can," he replied. "It's a very advanced skill. One that you'd be unlikely to master for quite a long time, I'm afraid."

"But, it was so neat!" Tris gushed. "I really would like to learn. Then I could…"

"Learning to change your own appearance will be far more important for you as a first stage of such a skill," Mykael suggested, interrupting his flow of words. "And, to be honest, you're not quite ready to do even that, as yet." Noting that Tris suddenly seemed just a little deflated by what he perhaps perceived as a slight reprimand, Mykael reached over tousle his hair. "I know you have been through a phase of having a changed appearance, in order to bring down some bad people. But remember that that particular change was created and protected by Ithuriel and me. As such a young angel, making such changes yourself can leave you quite vulnerable to bad outside influences. And I suggest that you also have a quiet talk to Andrew, one day, about the lessons he had in changing his appearance," he murmured rather softly. "It does take quite some effort." He glanced across at Andrew. "And can sometimes get you into quite serious trouble."

"But we can make people take on other shapes?" queried Tris, earnestly. "Like, butterflies? And…" Mykael sighed softly.

"Well, I could have just visualised her elsewhere without it, or turned her into a snake, or a fly, or any type of insect at all," he murmured. "But a butterfly did seem so much more appropriate for such a beautiful young angel." He glanced down at the necklace that he now held in his right hand. "More importantly, however, the next thing is to get this little beauty looked at by someone who can puzzle out its mysteries," he murmured.

"It might be pertinent to put it in this," Steve Robertson suggested, proffering a small metal box. "I had a few of these shielded boxes made quite a few years ago to preventing my phone from being accessed when I was off the island. It was around that time when there was all that kerfuffle over newspapers hacking into the phones of royalty and celebrities to get news scoops. It should prevent that military lot from picking up its signal when it's off the island."

"Good thinking," Mykael replied, giving a quick nod of his head. "While we'll eventually need to let them know where it is, it'll be better if they can't track it until we're ready to put counter-plans into action."

***

"When do you think I could start learning to fly?" Lara asked as she sat beside Tris, on the grass beside the church, just looking out to sea. Tris quickly got to her his feet and beckoned for her to do the same. He then walked behind her and gave her wings some scrutiny.

"They look just as big as mine were when Andrew started teaching me," he murmured. "We can ask him later today, if you like? Maybe we could start tomorrow, or the day after."

"That'd be neat," Lara said quietly, taking his hand in hers. "We could then go flying together, all around the island."

"As long as we stay on the seaward side, or go somewhere isolated," Tris replied. "Uncle Andrew told me that when all his brothers were here and they were just children, they always had to be a bit careful about being seen from the village. Most of the people over there don't know anything about us. You know... like, with there being angels on the island, and there's always the chance they might spot something unusual and decide to check it out with binoculars."

"We could always go up to the farm," Lara suggested. "There's never anyone around that area for miles, from what you've told me."

"Apart from that military lot!" Tris muttered a little bluntly.

"So that means that we can't go there?" Lara queried disappointedly. "Not for any reason?" While Mykael had, after having Colin Watters arrange to have the necklace checked over, confirmed that it had been the source of a GPS signal, he had stressed that there was no guarantee that the military would not still be searching for her.

"Well, it would be best not to," Tris murmured. "Not for a couple of days at least. But after that, it should be okay, because Granddad Steve rang some lot in Edinburgh to tell them about an unknown military group landing on the coast. He purposely didn't say that they were American, but did say that it did seem a bit suspicious because there had been no notification to any of the local people of any joint military exercises planned for the area. He also dropped the hint that he thought that they might be drug traffickers."

"Yeah, but that still doesn't mean that I can go back to the farm," Lara muttered rather dejectedly. A sure indication that she'd enjoyed her visits there with Tris. "Especially if that military group is anywhere close by. As Mykael said, they'll probably still be looking for me."

"But not if they can't track you," Tris quickly explained. "Not now that you don't have your necklace."

"But they know where I was. Or at least where I was when they last picked up the signal from the necklace and… and they also know what I look like," Lara repined. "And that means, I'll always have to be on the lookout for them."

"Not when you're on the island, or with me," Tris replied, giving her hand a quick squeeze. "And it doesn't matter if they see you, anyway. Not now that you can 'be'. You can always just disappear, if they ever try to grab you. You just don't let them ever get too close."

"Why?" Lara queried.

"So that they can't use some drug on you, or try to hit you with a tranquiliser dart, or something," Tris hastily explained.

"A tranquiliser dart?" Lara hastily echoed.

"Well, we can't do much when we're out to it, evidently," Tris explained. "Cause obviously we can't 'be', or make ourselves invisible, when we're drugged."

"So what would happen if they did get me?" Lara anxiously queried.

"Well, if you weren't able to 'be' out from wherever they had you, Andrew would simply find you and bring you back to the island," Tris replied. "That's one of his special skills. Like, all of us angels have some special skills that tend to be a little bit more advanced than usual. Mine looks like it might be telekinesis. You know, the ability to make things move without touching them."

"Like what you did with the salt and pepper shakers, the other night?" Lara queried. Tris blushed a little.

"I didn't think you'd noticed that," he muttered. He looked away for a moment and then gave a casual shrug. "Anyway, Andrew's special skill seems to be locating angels. According to Mykael he was able to do it even before he became an angel himself. It started when he was in hospital. After the Robertsons adopted him 'cause he was an orphan, and he came to live on the island, he even helped save Alexei and Tristan when they got trapped in a cave up near the farm. Sort of where the waterfall now is. Evidently, some bad angel had trapped them in a cave when they were trying to find the crowns I told you about the other day, and no one knew if they were even still alive because of a cave-in the bad angel had created. When Mykael bought Andrew to the farm, he could sense that they were still alive and even that there was a bad angel there and some demons. And that, as I said, was all before he even became an angel."

"So he could find me?" Lara murmured. "No matter what that military lot did?"

"If he's had contact with you, he'll find you," Tris proudly retorted. "Almost anywhere in the world!"

"I'd still prefer not to be captured," Lara responded.

"Well, Mykael has your necklace with the GPS being worked on," Tris suggested. "So I'm sure that he'll figure out some way of making it so that that military lot will just decide that it's a waste of time even searching for you."

***

Skylar, Noah, Luka, Riley, Martyn and Cooper sat side-by-side on the mattress in the back of the truck, with their backs to the wall. Camille, Persia, Jessamine, Maia and Natasha were similarly situated on another mattress with their backs against the opposite wall. While for once they weren't hog-tied and gagged, they were still cuffed and chained by their ankles to the central bar. Nevertheless, they were all quite tired; still feeling rather dirty and embarrassed from what they'd been forced to do for the 'entertainment'. Luka's eyes were also still reddened from crying, after the extra 'special punishment' he'd received.

Not that tonight had been in any way abusive... just totally embarrassing. After all, having to parade and do a striptease dance, in time to music, in front of a bunch of strange men, and a few women, half hidden by the subdued lighting at the back of the room and the glare of the six spotlights focussed on the small raised area that had served as a stage, was not what most eleven or twelve-year-olds would ever envisage as being normal 'entertainment'. Thankfully, that had been the full extent of their actions for the night. They hadn't had to strip off completely, or even stay in just their 'display wear' afterwards, and then wander out into the audience, so there had been no touching of any type to endure. Although, a little to their bemusement, Luka's punishment had been for being too quick to strip, and, as far as Vittorio was concerned, for not having enough 'tease' in his actions.

Skylar quietly nudged Cooper with his elbow as the truck swayed a little in its progress.

"That was just so embarrassing," he murmured. Cooper nodded in agreement.

"It was still far better than what I've sometimes endured," Noah whispered. "I'd rather do just a basic striptease like that any day, than have..." He didn't bother to complete the sentence, as the truck seemed to brake rather suddenly and veer slightly to the right. Immediately, a voice crackled from a speaker mounted on the wall at the cab end of the hidden room.

"Any noise from anyone and you're all dead meat," Reggie Vargas snarled. "It looks like it's just a routine traffic stop checking for drunk drivers, so you lot all just sit tight on your little assets. I also suggest you keep totally silent, if you know what's good for you." For a minute or so, they all stayed quiet.

"We could still shout out," Jessamine eventually suggested. "The cops wouldn't care what threats he's made to us. Not if they get us out of here."

"The problem is that, even if they do arrest Reggie and we get taken to a police station, as soon as Vittorio gets to hear of it, he'll just get his friends in the FBI to get us back," Noah sighed. "And then you know what'll happen. To all of us!"

"A thrashing?" Natasha murmured. Not that it was really a question.

"That! And worse!" Noah retorted softly. "You ask Peter just how nasty things can get, if Vittorio's really pissed off with you. You most likely won't be able sit comfortably for about a week. And it won't just be from the sting of his belt and your ending up with a badly bruised bottom!"

"Even just calling out will probably get us all thrashed," Maia murmured. "Regardless of whether the police hear us, or not."

"So, we do nothing?" Jessamine queried. Noah cocked his head briefly to one side.

"It's a risk," he murmured, at the same time giving a non-committal flex of his shoulders. Before they could make any definite decision about a course of action, however, the truck suddenly lurched forward, rapidly gaining speed as it did so; the traffic stop obviously having been passed without any hassle.

"That was good little mice," Reggie announced over the speaker. "It's best for you when you do as you're told. It's also good that you're starting to learn that attempting to escape is futile. Now, I suggest you all settle down for a nice little sleep. We've still got quite a way to go before we get to the next holding house."

***

After a hurried glance behind him, to see if he was still being followed, Rylan scurried down the alleyway and scrambled behind the dumpster at the back of the appliance store. It was a just few yards away from the café dumpster he'd begun frequenting, usually in the late afternoons, to scavenge for food that was going to waste. He quickly curled himself up in a ball, under the few stray sheets of cardboard that had slipped over the top of the severely overloaded dumpster. Most of it simply being old boxes that had once enclosed large, flat-screen televisions, but were now collapsed down into semi-flat panels, ready for collection and recycling. He quickly lay still, hoping that he was totally hidden from sight. Trying to quieten the raggedness of his breathing, the thumping of his heart in his chest, and ensure that he was as small and inconspicuous as possible. Desperately hoping that he'd remain unnoticed by the group of teenage boys who'd begun tailing him for the last ten minutes or so. From the comments and catcalls they'd been making, he had a fair idea what they wanted from him, even if they hadn't yet realised he was a boy. And if it came to that, given what they were after and the way they acted, if they thought that he might be gay, it possibly wouldn't make any difference.

"It's a cul-de-sac. The bitch has got to be hiding around here somewhere," he heard a voice shout. Rylan curled himself up tighter. Still desperately trying to silence the thumping of his heart and even the sound of his almost silent breathing.

"I don't think we should risk..." That was another voice. It was quickly cut short.

"She's homeless. She's on the streets," the first voice interrupted. "So who's really gonna care what we do to the bitch. It's probably what she'll end up doing anyway, once TakerZ or Carlos gets a hold of her!" There was further subdued muttering as the search continued. Some of the boys appearing keenly intent on finding the homeless 'girl', and using her for a bit of fun; the others seeming just a little reluctant to get themselves involved in what could very likely result in prosecution for a criminal offence and jail time, if they were caught.

Rylan heard their footsteps come closer and then the lid of the dumpster being lifted and the rough shifting of the cardboard that was inside it. The lid suddenly slammed down again. There was quiet for a moment, and then the voices, again. This time they seemed much quieter, almost as if his pursuers were moving away... or were perhaps just whispering.

'Maybe they're leaving,' Rylan thought nervously. At the same time, half-wondering why he'd even risked wandering out onto the streets so late at night. Especially after the warnings George had given him about the area, and knowing that he'd still be safely hidden away in his room on the sixth floor of the derelict building — the place where he'd spent the last four nights — if only if he'd heeded the old man's advice and only gone out in the late afternoon to get food.

During the daytime, the other squatters on the lower floors didn't bother him, or appear to take any interest in his presence. Admittedly, a good many of them, he felt, were usually too 'stoned' or 'spaced out' to notice him, or to even know what might be going on around them. In those circumstances, perhaps they also preferred to remain on the lower floors to have easier escape routes if, for some unexpected reason, the police arrived.

Or perhaps, as he'd first surmised, and George had hinted, they weren't going to bother to negotiate six flights of stairs just to discover where some grubby-looking kid might be hiding out.

The sudden movement of the cardboard, as it was lifted off where he was hidden, instantly brought him back to the present. A moment later, a hand quickly grabbed his left ankle and began hauling him backwards out of his hiding place. Rylan kicked out frantically with his right foot in an attempt to break the hold on his ankle.

"Told you she'd be hiding somewhere," announced the first voice rather smugly. "She might be young, but it'll be better than paying for it from any of those disease-ridden 'ho's' out there on the streets!"

As he was pulled into the open, the back of his jacket scraping on the surface of the alleyway, and almost resigning himself to being severely abused — with the hope that the group of youths wouldn't be too brutal, and might at least not simply beat him or kill him when they realised that he was a boy — he thought of his safe place on the sixth floor. Even as he writhed and struggled to get free, in his thoughts, he pictured the place where he now most desperately wanted to be. Visualising the dark safety of the room as it looked from in front of the window, when illuminated by just the meagre light of one candle. Seeing, in his mind, the row of cupboards, the kitchen sink and the taps that still provided fresh water, along the wall to his left; the doorway into the corridor directly opposite; and, on the right, the door to the bathroom just beyond the couch that served as a makeshift bed.

In an instant, it seemed, he was suddenly there. Still in the grip of the boy who'd grabbed him, but now lying on the floor beneath the window. Rylan watched in amazement, as the teenage boy's eyes seemed to slowly roll back in his head.

Almost simultaneously, he released his grip on Rylan's ankle and slowly collapsed, like the controlled demolition of a tower, from his semi-crouched position, onto the floor... almost as if he'd suddenly been tranquillised. Rylan hastily scrambled away from him to the relative safety of the far side of the room... the side nearest the door. For a while, he simply sat there, with his back against the door, breathing heavily. Waiting to see if the boy would wake from what now appeared to be a deep sleep and ready to run downstairs to George.

At the same time, he wondered what had just happened. How it was that he'd managed to somehow just disappear from one place and then magically reappear in another. He shook his head at the impossibility of it all. It was something he'd really need to think about, even if just to reassure himself that it wasn't all just some fantastic nightmare. At the moment, however, other matters were far more pressing. The most urgent being how he could get his comatose antagonist out of his special hiding place, before he woke up and grabbed him again.

After a moment or two of simply watching, still ready to flee to find George if that proved necessary, with the boy still remaining motionless, Rylan moved cautiously closer to the seemingly 'out for the count' teenager and gingerly checked his pulse and breathing. They seemed quite normal. It almost appeared as if the boy was simply fast asleep.

Quickly feeling a little more emboldened, he carefully checked the teenager's pockets. The pockets of the jeans revealed nothing more than a rather nasty-looking flick knife. In the left pocket of the jacket, however, he found a cell phone and, in the right, a wallet. He quickly hid them in one of the cupboards above the sink on the far side of the room, and then, for a moment, stood looking down at the comatose teenager while trying to decide what to do next.

If he wanted to keep his 'safe' place as his own, he knew he'd need to get rid of the interloper. That would mean finding a way to move him to some other place. To somewhere where someone else would eventually find him. Or where he would eventually wake up of his own accord. Some place where, even if he was somehow able to work out what had happened to him, he'd still not know where he'd been. An idea eventually came to him.

Grabbing the teenager by the hands, Rylan began slowly dragging him across the linoleum floor towards the door. Even though the boy wasn't too solidly built, with being 'out to it' he was still a dead weight, and it took almost all of Rylan's strength to move him. Nevertheless, over the next fifteen minutes or so, all the time fearful that the rough movement would awaken the teenager, Rylan manoeuvred him from the room and out into the corridor and then down six flights of stairs to the ground floor of the building. The boy's head bumping a little on each step as he was dragged down each flight. At the bottom of the final set of stairs, Rylan paused and listened to check who was around. Cautious about not being seen by any of the building's usual residents — a factor helped by the knowledge that by nighttime most of them would now be well beyond caring of what went on around them — Rylan eventually left the teenager sprawled just outside the doors of what once was the main entry to the building.

Given that his 'safe place' was at least a block away from where he'd first been grabbed, he hoped that his assailant, when he awoke, might not realise that he'd, at some stage, been on a higher floor of the building. As he was about to close the doors once again, however, he was suddenly startled by a voice almost directly behind him.

"What you got there, kid?" the man asked. Rylan quickly recognised the voice, and felt an immediate sense of relief in realising that it was only George.

"He tried to attack me," Rylan murmured. He wasn't going to explain too much about his being out at night and how he'd ended up back in his hideout. He still felt a degree of confusion about that whole matter. "I managed to hit him with a bottle," he added, glancing towards some of the empty wine bottles that were lying around. He fervently hoped George wouldn't want to get too hung up on minor details. Such as, how he'd actually managed to subdue a teenage boy who was certainly much bigger, and a great deal more strongly built, than he was.

"Let's just put him outside the fence," George said quietly, as he nodded his head. Seeming prepared to accept Rylan's version of events, even as improbable as they might appear. "That way, the police will eventually spot him and arrange to have him carted off. With any luck, they'll just think he's off his head on drugs or something and they won't give us any hassle."

Between them, over the next few minutes, they managed to manoeuvre the teenage boy through the small gap in the wire fencing and out onto the footpath.

"That should do it!" George exclaimed as they eventually rolled the boy up against the barricade so that he was to one side of the sidewalk and people could still pass by. "The police will just think he collapsed here." Clapping his hands together in a sideways motion, as if wiping his hands of the matter, he then ushered Rylan back through the gap in the fence and into the foyer. He then reached into his overcoat pocket and handed Rylan a couple of slightly stale sticky buns. "Here, take these with you up to your room," he murmured, reaching out to tousle Rylan's hair almost affectionately. "And, next time, remember to take heed of my good advice. Don't go roaming anywhere out there at night! It's far too dangerous for a boy like you." Rylan quickly nodded in response, at the same time wondering at George's reference to a 'boy like you'. Did it mean that George realised what he was? Or was it just an allusion to his young age and supposed innocence?

"How about you just head back up to your room," George quietly suggested as he walked Rylan back towards the stairs. "And lock your door," he added. "I'll keep an eye on things down here, and answer any questions the police might ask. You just get yourself safe." Feeling a strong sense of relief in how things had worked out, and the help he'd got from the old man, Rylan quickly headed upstairs. Nevertheless, even the mere thought of the danger he'd just avoided, and how badly it might have worked out for him, had been a little too close for comfort. Even if he had been able to escape by means he still didn't understand.

Returning to the safety of his room on the sixth floor, and heedful of George's advice, Rylan carefully shut the door and locked it. After a moment or two of thought, he retrieved the wallet and the cellphone from the cupboard. At first, he ignored the sound of the phone, which began alternating between sounding out an annoying little rap tune and uttering a singular chime numerous times, and turned his attention to the wallet.

It contained three credit cards, a driver's licence, a small notebook in which were listed several phone numbers, and a little over a hundred dollars in cash. The driver's licence indicated that the teenager's name was Xavier J. Hernandez, and that he was eighteen… almost nineteen. Rylan quickly dumped the credit cards and the driver's licence back into the cupboard and slipped the wallet, now containing just the cash, into the pocket of his jeans. Making sure, first of all, that it contained nothing at all that might identify its original owner. Returning his attention to the notebook, he quickly browsed through it, noting that it just seemed to contain phone numbers prefixed with various initials.

The back page of the book, however, had three sets of initials – MC, V, AE – each of which was followed by a four-digit code.

He puzzled over them for a moment, before it dawned on him. The four-digit codes were probably for each of the credit cards. 'MC' being MasterCard, 'V' most likely for VISA and 'AE' for American Express. Going back to the cupboard, he quickly grabbed the cards. In his thoughts was the possibility of using them to get extra cash. Then, after looking at the cards for a moment, he quickly abandoned the idea. Using them would simply bring him into the range of CCTV cameras. And, nowadays, there were always CCTV cameras at money machines. That wasn't a risk he could afford to take... at least, not unless he was really desperate.

With a slight sigh of resignation, he quickly threw the cards back into the cupboard, along with the notebook, and picked up the cellphone. Almost as he sat down on the couch, it gave a further soft chime to indicate yet another text message. He quickly read it... **'WRU?'**

Rylan smiled and quickly typed... **'Cen Pk N. CYT'** – then pushed 'send'. Less than a minute later, a fairly predictable... **'WTF?'** appeared on the screen. Followed almost immediately by... **'WTF hapnd?'**

With a smile at the thought of the sense of bewilderment the group of teenage boys would now be experiencing, Rylan sent a happy face emogi and a further **'CYT'** and then switched off the phone. Opening the back of it, he removed both the sim card and battery, before tossing all three items into the cupboard. There seemed no point in leaving it active and perhaps traceable.

With time on his hands, he began to eat one of the sticky buns while he thought, once again, about what had happened earlier. In some ways, no matter how he looked at it, it still didn't make any logical sense. One minute he'd been down in an alley, being dragged out from behind a dumpster by his left ankle; the next he'd been in this room with his assailant collapsing into a faint. What had happened in between had to be impossible.

With a sigh, he finished off half of the second bun, then collapsed onto his makeshift couch-bed and cuddled up under his two blankets in an attempt to ward off the increasing cold. As he rubbed at his arms for extra warmth, he suddenly realised that he should have kept the teenager's socks and jacket for extra warmth. For a moment or two, he wondered about going down to get them; but then changed his mind. He'd survived the last few nights in his 'safe' place without extra clothing. And he had blankets, so could survive yet one more. And with money in his pocket, he could easily buy himself something warmer in the morning… even if it was just something that was secondhand, to save money. He could also afford a decent breakfast.

***

Suddenly disturbed by an unexpected loud noise from elsewhere in the building, Rylan was quickly awake. From somewhere outside, he could hear police sirens. Although, at first, it seemed that they were quite a few blocks away. So, for a while, he simply remained curled up on the couch under his coverings and ignored them. As it seemed, did everybody else. There were always sirens, at all hours of night, in New York. It was certainly a far cry from Oakton, where the sound of a siren late at night was still a rare enough event to have families looking out their front windows, and wandering out into the street in their nightwear and dressing gowns to find out what was happening.

When the sirens seemed to suddenly be getting closer, he took a little more notice. Out of curiosity, he got up off the couch and moved closer to the door leading out onto the balcony that looked down into the street. Having carefully checked that there was no one in any windows opposite who might spot him, he opened the door and looked cautiously down towards the sidewalk at the front of the building.

Less than a minute later, the road below became a hive of activity, as, with the arrival of the police and then an ambulance, the buildings all around were illuminated in the strobe-like glare of their lights. The two police cars and the ambulance were parked, at rather crazy angles, at the front of the building, and a small crowd of late night wanderers had begun to gather to watch the events unfold. As he watched, the back of the ambulance opened and a gurney was wheeled towards the front of the building, Not that he could see too much of what was directly below him, given the overhang of the balconies below. At the same time, he noticed a couple of the regular downstairs inhabitants, somewhere beyond the back of the throng, quietly sneaking off in various directions. George was not amongst them. He hurriedly glanced around to check that the door to his hideout was properly locked. Locked doors might detour the police from investigating too thoroughly on the higher floors… if they bothered at all.

Almost too quickly, it seemed, the gurney reappeared, carrying his assailant, and was lifted into the back of the ambulance. Rylan crouched down and moved forward just far enough to get a slightly better view down to the street. In the chill night air, the voices from below seemed to drift up to him... albeit, not necessarily all that clearly. Nevertheless, the words 'stoner' and 'crackhead' seemed to give him the understanding that the police viewed the teenager's comatose state as most probably being a result of the use of recreational drugs. Rylan also hoped that it would also mean that they wouldn't be too worried about making any search of the building. He just hoped that it was also likely that the teenager's missing cellphone and wallet would, likewise, eventually be viewed as an opportunist theft, by either the ground floor squatters, or perhaps just by someone passing by. That would be, of course, only when Xavier J. Hernandez came to and realised that they were missing.

CHAPTER SEVEN

Spying, and Other Unusual Pursuits....

Mykael, Andrew and Tris, carefully alighted on the deck of the frigate in a state of invisibility. The one to which the first amphibian, with Lieutenant Colonel Harris McMahon on board, had eventually returned, now that the military encampment on the beach was in the process of being abandoned. It seemed logical, somehow, that it would also be the boat acting as temporary headquarters for the military group that was searching for Lara.

Their objective was mainly to find out a little more about the GPS signal. In particular, its frequency and likely range. For that reason, on reaching the boat, Mykael had removed the necklace from the metal box that shielded its signal. Now, they carefully followed the senior officer, as he made his way through the various corridors of the warship's interior. Taking care, as they did so, to avoid knocking into anyone, or do anything that might somehow indicate their presence, even if they could not be seen. Eventually emerging into a control room of some sort, they were not all that surprised to find that the room was a hive of extreme activity, given the fact the necklace was now broadcasting its signal. As a result, the GPS tracking system was pinging very loudly and clearly, causing a good deal of serious consternation amongst those gathered around the electronic equipment.

"It's back, but I still can't figure out why it just suddenly disappears?" one of the junior officers complained. "We were to be able to locate it quite easily when it first seemed to be somewhere about that farm. But then, the first time it started, after about an hour or so, it suddenly just seemed to cut out. It's done that three of four times over the last few days. It's almost as if it's being turned on and off, somehow."

"So where is it now? Lieutenant Colonel Harris McMahon demanded, looking about at all the attention focussed on the screens. "I presume from all the activity in here that you've picked it up again?"

"It actually appears to right be here, Sir. In fact, somewhere on board the ship," the junior officer replied almost a little anxiously. "From what I'm getting it's almost as if it's in this room, if not somewhere quite nearby." For a moment or two, Lieutenant Colonel Harris McMahon seemed rather stunned. Then he reached for a microphone and hastily gave an order for the ship to be searched, top to bottom.

The three angels watched with some sense of amusement as men began to hurry from the room to join their shipmates in carrying out the search order. Many of them it appeared, perhaps just anxious to be well away from Harris McMahon if, or when, the search eventually failed to turn up anything of note. As most of the men departed, the three angels moved towards the far end of the room; positioning themselves well away from where the three officers who'd remained were now peering intently at one of the screens.

"Just wait here a moment," Mykael whispered. Still in a state of invisibility, he headed over to where the officers were standing and began watching their interactions. Almost just out of curiosity, Andrew and Tris began looking around where they were standing, and suddenly noticed that the noticeboard on the wall behind them had a series of pictures of Lara.

Most of them appeared to have been taken at the medical facility, to judge by the background. While there were a few that showed her face while dressed in a hospital smock, most of the images showed her back and various stages of her wing development. The majority of them, thankfully, just views of her upper back, but it still seemed that she'd most probably been close to being naked when most of them were taken; especially as a few of them were full-length shots that, from the lack of shadowing on her hospital smock, somehow gave the impression that she might not be wearing anything underneath. Mykael returned a moment later.

"I have the frequency that the necklace is operating on," he whispered. "So now we can start to properly sabotage their efforts." Andrew and Tris pointed out the photographs. Mykael seemed to nod and instantly there was silence. The regular pinging of the GPS tracking equipment was suddenly absent and the three officers seemed like waxwork dummies.

"Just grab anything that you think relates to Lara," Mykael instructed, as he began grabbing the pictures from the wall with very little finesse. "Folders, pictures, videos, anything at all. If some of it is unrelated, that'll be too bad. We just don't need to leave them with anything that might relate to Lara."

Moments later, with each of them carrying an armload of folders and pictures, and even a laptop computer, they returned to the family room of the Rankin's house.

Well, we have had some success," Mykael said as Joshua, Amanda and Lara hurried over to them. "We now know the frequency of the GPS, and we also managed to grab what we could see of the material they had relating to Lara."

"Why do you think that they were saying it kept cutting out?" queried Tris, as he dumped the folders he was holding onto the low central table. "You know, like, how they could find Lara at the farm, but not elsewhere?"

"That'll most likely be because of the frequency blocking that Steve Robertson has set up for the island," Joshua quickly explained. "Years ago, when there was a problem about various newspaper reporters using electronic interception devices to listen in on private cell phone conversations in order to dig up dirt on various celebrities and politicians, he had special equipment installed that automatically codifies any connections with the island and re-routes them through a set-up over on the mainland. Any attempts to track conversations or signals coming from the island are automatically blocked by an electronic barrier, unless they are routed through the coding which Steve has had installed for all cell phones and other such devices in use on the island. That's why most of the children on the island don't have cell phones. Not that you really have any need of them."

"Which also means the GPS tracking system is also automatically blocked from locating the signal from the necklace when it's on the island," Andrew added. "So, if Lara had gone over to the village, when she was still wearing it, it would have been immediately picked up. Which it was, of course, when we all went to the farm."

"I think that the next move should be to also check out the supposed medical facility that she was kept in," Mykael suddenly announced. "Given the material we found on the ship, I'd suggest that there is likely to be a great deal more to be confiscated from there, as well."

"Can we come too," Tris eagerly asked, indicating himself and Lara. Mykael nodded rather thoughtfully.

"Provided you do as you're told, I don't see it as a problem," he murmured. "It actually might be important for Lara to be there, anyway, so that we know where to go within the place. Just remember, however, that you will be under Andrew's care for that time. So whatever he decides for you, is what will happen! With no questions asked! And no arguments or complaints! Understood?" Both Tris and Lara nodded rather eagerly.

***

Rylan lay back on his makeshift bed, thinking through the details of his nasty confrontation with the group of teenagers and of what had happened afterwards, as the morning sun gradually made the room a little lighter, warmer and more welcoming. Out of fright over his narrow escape from danger, he hadn't left the room for two whole days. Perhaps just in case others of the group of teenagers finally worked out where the police had found Xavier J. Hernandez.

The detail that most puzzled him, however, was how he'd managed to get himself back to his hiding place so weirdly. He couldn't think of a word to properly describe the action. It had almost been akin to what he'd seen on episodes of Star Trek when various members of the crew had been sent down to a planet's surface and needed to return to the USS Enterprise. "Beam me up' came instantly to mind.

Instantly wide awake at the implications of what that sort of ability could mean, and figuring that it might probably related to his having wings, he hurriedly devoured some of the half-loaf of bread George had given him the previous afternoon, while he thought out how to test the ability. A few moments later, he wandered out into the hallway outside his room and over to the top of the stairway. He tried to remember what he'd done the previous time; trying to visualise the room as he'd just left it. For a while, nothing happened, but then, just when he was beginning to feel like giving up, he visualised exactly the same view he'd made on that night and was instantly back in his hideout. With a feeling of elation, he repeated the process several times until he was sure that he had it right.

A little cautiously, he then crept down to a lower floor and tried again. Immediately, he found himself back in his hideout on the sixth floor. The same occurred when he went down to the foyer. Merely thinking of the particular view of the room he'd first thought of, and imagining being there, was all that was required for it to happen. It didn't take too much further experimenting to discover that he could even change the view he'd first imagined, to one from somewhere else in the room.

Despite the excitement of realising that he had a rather special ability, however, he began to realise that, as with his wings, it would be better for him to keep it all a secret. If people saw him just disappearing into thin air, it would simply draw extra attention to what he was able to do, and increase the likelihood of a special police search being set up to find him.

At least, he quickly surmised, it would make it easier for him to be able to get food. While there still was a reasonable amount of money in the wallet he now had, there was always the risk of his being seen by the police, or anyone else who might question his presence, when he was out on the streets. With this new ability, it would be possible for him to disappear simply by getting somewhere out of sight and then thinking of 'home'. As his stomach rumbled a little, he decided that it was possibly time to put his new ability to a proper test.

***

Fifteen minutes later, after a cautious walk through the streets, during which time he'd kept ducking into the shelter of doorways and alleyways to avoid being seen, Rylan stood outside the McDonalds where the police officer had accosted him about a week or so, earlier. He'd avoided, of course, going anywhere near to the alleyway where Xavier J. Hernandez and his mates had waylaid him. Even with his new ability and the fact that it was the middle of the morning, there seemed no sense in tempting fate. Taking out the wallet, he headed inside and ordered a Big Mac Combo after, first of all, checking that the bathrooms were open for use.

Once seated in a booth with his order, he ate a few of the chips and cautiously watched the other customers. One group of teenagers seemed to be regarding him with some casual interest. Although, at a second glance, he quickly realised that it was probably just his nervousness that had him imagining that they might be a possible threat, simply as a result of his frightening experience with Xavier J. Hernandez. At the same time, the simple fact that they were reasonably close to where he was seated didn't make him feel too comfortable. Perhaps it was just because there were quite a few of them and he was so obviously on his own. Suddenly anxious to test his new ability and also keen to be away from the gaze of the teenagers, he picked up his drink and the paper bag containing the cardboard container with the remainder of his chips and his Big Mac and headed towards the bathrooms.

An instant later, he was back in his sixth-floor hideout; drink and paper bag still in hand. If anyone at the McDonalds wondered about his taking his meal into the bathrooms and then not returning, he wasn't too worried. All he cared about was that his new ability would be invaluable in keeping him safe. At the same time, he felt even more determined to not get caught out by using it too obviously. In other words, no simply disappearing when he was around other people. A bit like with Superman changing into his costume, it would be best for him to find places to hide in order to make a 'jump'.

***

"Okay," Vittorio announced, as he carefully eyed the group of six boys who'd been selected for this particular 'entertainment' session; a 'display' that was, in essence, nothing short of being a prelude to an eventual slave market. "This is mainly another chance for some buyers to assess you before the upcoming auction. They have been told that anything beyond just a bit light touching is totally off limits as a part of tonight's programme, so nothing too bad should take place while you are out doing your serving duties. So I expect you to be on your best behaviour." He glanced around at the six boys, who all shuffled a little nervously. "Not unless you want extra special treatment at the end of the evening!"

Skylar glanced at Cooper, who shuffled his feet a little nervously. He'd suffered an extra special treatment at their last 'entertainment' session, as a result of spilling a plate of finger food onto a guest. Cooper had tried to claim that it was an accident; that he'd simply been surprised when the man had suddenly tried to reach under his loincloth costume to touch him rather intimately. Regardless of who had been at fault, it had been Cooper who'd eventually had to suffer the embarrassment of being given three hard strokes of the paddle, in front of all the guests, at the end of the night.

Not that such extra treatment had been entirely unexpected. According to Noah, even on most of the 'only light touching' entertainment engagements, there would quite often be at least one person who'd get extra treatment with the paddle… sometimes even two or three. In some ways, from what he'd noticed, it almost appeared as if such punishments were actually a scheduled part of the programme. No matter how often Vittorio tried to claim that such treatment had simply been for some particular disobedience. At the same time, unlike the paddles that were used at Pinehurst North Middle School that had numerous holes to create patterns of circular bruises, Vittorio seemed happy to use a plain, flat paddle so that there wasn't too much bruising. Perhaps that was simply because he didn't want his merchandise to be too marked.

Glancing down at himself, and at the other boys, Skylar quickly realised that tonight's 'display wear' costumes, seemed a little smaller than what they usually wore. And, on their previous two outings, they had either a loincloth or the roman slave 'dresses', over top of their display attire. Their clothing for this display, however, appeared to simply consist of what seemed like the bottom half of an extremely skimpy girls' bikini, with just small, elastic sections at the sides and small triangles of cloth at the front and back. In some ways, being quite similar to the briefest Speedos he'd seen boys wearing in swim competitions; apart from the fact that the back panel didn't cover as much of their behinds as seemed appropriate for competition wear. And unlike their usual white briefs, for each of them, the new 'display wear' was of a different colour. Skylar's was bright yellow.

Trying to remember that what he was wearing was just normal beach wear in some parts of the world, Skylar steeled himself to just concentrate on the aim of getting through what was about to happen, without giving Vittorio a reason to be angry with him. As a distraction, he carefully fingered the necklace of nine beads that he'd been given when he'd first been 'inspected'. The other five boys all had similar necklaces.

"Now," Vittorio quickly intoned, as the boys hastily formed a line just outside the entrance to the room, where at least a dozen or more men were seated in a rather more dimly lit area of the room. "We'll be working to the usual routine. Each of you will parade, one at a time when I give the signal, across to the left side of where the guests are seated and then walk slowly across in front of them to the right, before returning the middle of the room. Do not rush! Allow them plenty of time to appraise you." He paused a moment as if to ensure that they'd all understood that last instruction, before continuing. "When you get to the middle, you will turn to stand with your back to the guests so they can appraise you from behind. After silently counting slowly to ten, you will then turn, take a three steps back, and then stand facing the guests in the proper 'display position'. Do I need to remind you that that means standing straight, with your legs slightly apart, looking directly forward, and with your hands firmly clasped behind your head! Understand?" The boys quickly nodded. They had been taught the proper 'display positions' as part of their earliest training. Vittorio again gave them a stern glare.

"No boy is to start on his parade, however, until I give the signal. And that won't be until the previous boy has completed his routine and taken up his position at the front on the right side of the room," he continued. "The guests will want some time to assess each of you individually. After all, you may eventually become their personal property, depending on how much they're willing to pay for you when it comes time for the auction." Skylar shuddered at that prospect and knew that the other boys also dreaded such a fate. His thoughts were quickly distracted as he felt Vittorio's hand touch him on his shoulder.

"Skylar... you can go first!" the man commanded.

Not wanting to be chosen for extra 'special' treatment, Skylar stepped quickly out into the main room; the glare of two or three spotlights half-blinding him as he did so. He started walking quickly to his left and then, remembering Vittorio's instructions, hastily slowed to a rather more leisurely pace as he paraded in front of the men. Almost feeling the intensity of their scrutiny as he did so, and thankful that he had at least some covering of his more intimate areas. Something that Vittorio had stressed was important at these preliminary functions, in that it added a little mystery to their appearance.

Reaching the far side of the small room, he turned and slowly headed to the right before returning to stand at the front of the room; firstly turning his back to the 'guests' and silently counting to ten, before turning face-on, taking three steps back, and quickly assuming the 'display position'… as Vittorio had instructed. Noting, as he did so, that Luka was the next to join the 'parade'.

A short time later, when all six boys were in place and in 'position' at the front of the room, Vittorio sauntered out to stand to one side of the boys. Taking up a position next to Skylar.

"Well," he began, as he scanned the guests. "While we do, as you know, cater for all interests — in other words both boys and girls — tonight you see in front of you six new items of the 'boy' merchandise we can provide. As always, of course, for a fee." He then gestured along the line of boys. "As you will note, in this case they are all rather excellent examples of American boyhood, having been especially selected to meet the particular desires of our most valued clientele... such as yourselves." He gave a small laugh, as the assembled gathering murmured approval and also laughed a little. Vittorio briefly indicated towards the six boys.

"This current selection has been carefully acquired, with an emphasis on their good looks, their fine, graceful physique and also their general docility." He again gestured with a hand towards the six boys. "All of them, you must admit, are very pleasing on the eye. The sort of boys you could certainly enjoy having around you as objects of desire." He looked towards the boys, all standing on display and then made a quick raise of his eyebrows, as he, yet again, gestured towards them. "And, as you can clearly see, we don't do obese or overweight. Not even mildly chubby." He gave slight laugh as he shook his head a little. "After all, which of you would really want to snuggle up to a big, smelly, overweight kid with a big fat butt and floppy love-handles, when you could have something as delightfully well-proportioned and pure as what you now see before you?" His comment was greeted with a subtle murmur of agreement and some mild laughter from the darker confines of the room.

"I thought you'd see it that way," Vittorio replied with a quick grin and a slightly conspiratorial raise of his eyebrows. He then indicated for each of the boys to do another slow turn before moving to the back of the stage.

"For the rest of tonight's entertainment, the boys will be serving you with the variety of finger foods that have been made available," he eventually continued. "This will also be a chance for you to peruse the merchandise a little more closely; perhaps with a desire for future purchase at our upcoming auction. They will be obedient to what you ask, particularly if you wish for them to linger for closer scrutiny, but I must stress that this is a time for perusal only, so there is to be no touching. These boys are, as yet, totally off-limits for any more serious action. With all of them still being quite 'innocent', if you catch my drift." There was a sudden general murmur of increased interest throughout the assembled guests. Vittorio nodded, with a smirk on his face before continuing.

"Well, I did say they were new; only recently acquired and not yet fully aware of your specific needs. If you feel, however, that any of them might be of special interest to you, in the near future, then, as I said, it's likely that at least some of them will be available for bidding at our next auction. Early bids of course, will also be accepted on-line as per usual, via our encrypted website. And in that regard, as you may have already noted, given your particular tastes and your usual keen interest in what the Network can provide, each of the boys has a necklace indicating his name and current age. That being so that you can identity any of them that you might like to acquire. Keep in mind, however, that unblemished merchandise of such excellent quality certainly does not come cheap. So peruse them well, and then make sure to get your bids in early when these little puppies do come up for auction, as I'm sure that they will prove extremely popular with a most of our clientele. You will of course be notified, via the usual encrypted website, of where and when the actual auction will take place. Especially if you want to be there, in person, to collect any purchase that you may make. And I do remind you that tonight there will be no roaming hands. Let's just keep what's hidden from you as a delightful surprise, if, as I said a moment ago, you decided to purchase one of these delightful little puppies"

At a nod from Vittorio, the six boys headed, in a rather orderly fashion towards a side room where the plates of food had already been set up. Knowing that their being 'serving boys' was merely a ruse to cover what was essentially a meat market; a chance for this particular gathering of nastily perverted rich men to make decisions over which boys they might like to own.

***

Skylar tried to get comfortable on the thin mattress, as the truck in which they were hidden began to make its way away from the palatial residence where he, Cooper, Luka, Martyn, Riley and Noah had been the subjects of vile scrutiny for almost an hour. Not that he had any idea of where the place actually was, who owned it, or the name of any of the adults present — many of whom had worn masks — apart from Vittorio and Angelo. Although, from the gist of some the comments he'd overheard, Skylar was sure that the owner of the premises held a position of some considerable political rank in society. An elevation amongst his peers, that purported to portray a very normal existence of his being a happily married man and a loving father to two teenage daughters. A 'standing' in society that would come quickly crashing to earth if by some chance his particularly perverted preference for young boys was ever to become public knowledge.

At the same time, as Noah had whispered while they were being directed back to the truck, all of them had been lucky that it was just a 'display session', as Vittorio had designated it to be. A chance for a few favoured of the Network's clientele to view a small selection of the merchandise being offered for future acquirement; either as a brief rental for a few days enjoyment, or as a permanent purchase by auction.

Nevertheless, Skylar's bottom still stung from the three strokes of the paddle he'd received at the end of the night as part of the 'extra' entertainment. Not that he'd necessarily been caught doing anything wrong; at least not that he could think of. Nor had he been the only one subject to that humiliation. It seemed that Vittorio had simply decided that all six of them should receive a 'paddling' as a part of an extra entertainment session for the clientele. He wondered if that decision might even have been at the request of some of the guests; perhaps because some pervert had simply wanted to gauge how each of them would react to stern physical discipline. It certainly wasn't beyond the realms of possibility that Vittorio would quite happily accede to such a request, if it meant the likelihood of an extra 'donation'.

He also felt dirty. Feeling as if he desperately needed to wash away every tactile memory of the engagement. While it was supposedly a 'no touching' function, it had seemed that, over the time that he'd been on display, he'd lost count of the number of times that groping hands and sweaty fingers had surreptitiously reached out to stroke his skin as he'd walked amongst the 'guests'. Hands and fingers that, on occasions, had also tried to surreptitiously touch his 'display wear' in some attempt to discover more about the hidden areas of his body. Afterwards, eliciting exclamations about the softness of his skin and the fact that his body seemed completely smooth, and hairless, apart from what was on his head.

And then, of course, there were also the more vulgar comments and suggestions that had come from many of the guests. Nasty asides murmured to each other concerning what they would like to do to some of the boys as soon as they were able to purchase their services. Venting their crude, perverted desires to each other almost as if the children they were viewing were incapable of overhearing. Perhaps even because they knew full well that the boys would, most likely, overhear what was suggested. Regardless of whether there was any purposeful intent, or not, nothing of what was insinuated by the guests had made for very pleasant hearing. If he'd ever been at a loss to understand just what Vittorio had planned for them, he knew now of the full range of depravities that probably awaited him and his companions once they'd been sold!

The final humiliation of the night, of course, had been the extra entertainment session. His having to assume the 'position' — standing, legs a strict two feet apart, hands clasped behind his head — while Vittorio reddened his barely-clad behind with three strokes from a wooden paddle. All the time knowing that to move from the 'position' would result in the punishment being restarted.

Consequently, while he'd only just managed to get through his three allotted strokes without releasing his hands, Martyn, Luka and Cooper had received a total of four strokes each, Riley had suffered five, while Noah had barely endured a vicious eight; all their extra strokes being a result of removing their hands from the clasped position before they'd been instructed to do so.

"We still got off lightly," Noah whispered, seeming to understand that, while their punishments had been painful — his particularly so, given how many extra strokes he'd received — they hadn't actually been forced to be totally naked, or suffered any other depravity beyond their punishment.

"It still doesn't make me feel any better, with knowing what will eventually happen to us," Skylar replied. Noah nodded and then winced a little as he shifted position.

"Peter says that you eventually get used to it," he murmured, and then sighed rather resignedly. "But somehow I doubt it!"

"I just pray that I'll get rescued before any of that happens," Skylar murmured in reply.

"I did a lot of that as well, when I first got kidnapped," Noah murmured in reply. "Not that it's done me much good!"

***

Lara looked a little nervously around at Tris and Andrew. It was her first flying lesson and she still felt a little unsure as to whether her wings would be strong enough to support her. She'd also found it a little strange that Tris had insisted that she should wear bike pants and a tight halter-top.

"You have to remember to think light," Tris reminded her. "Just imagine that you're like a single thistledown blown on the wind," he added, remembering what Andrew had told him. "If you do that, everything will just happen."

"But what if I don't know how to make my wings move properly?" Lara cautiously asked. Tris simply shrugged.

"Trust me," he said. "As long as you think of yourself as being lighter than a feather, then everything will just be automatic. Just like with how you breathe. You don't have to even think about doing it; it just happens. It's the same when you try to fly. Somehow, you just do the right thing. It'll just sort of happen automatically."

"Well, if you're ready, we may as well get started," Andrew murmured, taking hold of Lara's left hand. Tris took a hold of her right. A moment later they were high in the air above the church.

"Let your wings spread," Andrew hastily instructed. Still keeping a tight grip on the hands holding hers, Lara did as instructed.

"And think light. Like, imagine that you're weightless," Tris reiterated. Lara nodded, and then seemed to smile a little.

"Now, when Tris and I let go of your hands, just keep your wings spread and try to glide slowly towards the ground," Andrew instructed. "But don't angle yourself down too much, otherwise you'll go too fast. And don't worry. If at any time you think you're not in control, just 'be' to where we were standing outside the church, and we'll start again."

Lara nodded and released her grip. For a moment, she looked rather fearful, even as Tris angled below her. Then, seeming to realise that she was gliding without effort, she began to smile.

"Just keep gliding," Andrew instructed, from beside her. "Try to make it a slow spiral downwards. And when you get close to the ground, be ready to take some quick steps forward so that you don't fall over."

"You can always practise your landings by jumping off the roof of the church," Tris shouted, perhaps remembering back to his own lessons. "As you get better at flying, you find you can sort of backstroke with your wings a bit as you land, to slow your progress."

Lara nodded, as she angled into a spiral turn. Tris and Andrew paralleling her movements, beside and below. Eventually, she stumbled into a slightly rough landing. Reaching out at the last minute to grab a hold of Tris, who'd followed her down rather closely, to stop herself from falling over.

"That was really good," Andrew enthused. "Now what you need to do is practise it over and over."

"What about takeoffs?" Lara quickly asked. "Do we always just 'be' into the air?" Andrew gave a nonchalant flex of his shoulders.

"It's the easiest way, when you're just starting," he explained. He then gestured towards the edge of the bluff beyond the church. "Or you can also start by just leaping forward from high places like cliffs," he added. "Once you get more chest strength, however, you can just leap into the air and your wings will do the rest; as long as you always remember to think light."

"And so that's why you've got me doing all that swimming?" Lara cautiously asked, turning to Tris, and perhaps imagining a continuing regime of strict physical exercise.

"That's why I've been pushing you," Tris quickly answered, before Andrew could start to suggest something similar. "That's also one of the reasons why I always work really hard at my swimming lessons with Mr Martin. It helps with flying."

"You'll also find that most of us angels end up being very good at doing butterfly," Andrew added, giving her a slightly cheeky smile. "Mainly because we get some help from our wings, even if we make them invisible; which is cheating a bit, I suppose. But then, if no one else ever knows..." He left the statement incomplete, the remainder seeming obvious.

"So," Tris questioned, giving Lara an almost cheeky grin. "You ready to try again?" Lara nodded a little tentatively. Tris took her hand and, instantly, they were once again high above the church.

"We'll just do it over and over until you get the hang of it," Tris enthused, letting go of her hand. For an instant, Lara seemed to panic. Then her wings automatically spread to their full extent and she began a second slow glide.

"Try to follow me," Tris called as he angled slightly below her and began a slow spiral to the left. In the process using the updrafts from the cliffs to actually gain further height.

"We're going up?" Lara queried, as her wings seemed to give a couple of extra stokes to match Tris's movements.

"It's because of the way the winds are deflected up by the cliffs,"Tris shouted in reply. "It works the same way for sea birds."

"Are we going to do more landings?" Lara asked. Tris nodded a reply.

"When we get down from this flight, you can do some practising from the church roof," he shouted, as he launched into a shallow dive, that Lara quickly imitated. A few minutes later, they landed, side-by-side, beside the church.

"That looked pretty good," Andrew exclaimed. "Now it'll be just a matter of practice, practice, practice." Lara nodded.

"Why did I have to wear bike pants and this?" she queried, pulling a little at the shoulder straps of the tight-fitting halter-top. Both Tris and Andrew grinned a little.

"Because loose clothing, like jeans and loose shorts can slip down off your hips when you go into a dive," Andrew laughed. "We didn't want you to end up suddenly finding your pants slipping down around your ankles." Lara nodded, giving a slightly embarrassed smile. While she'd got used to being almost naked in front of all the doctors at the military hospital — mainly because there was little she could do to prevent it — she, for some reason, felt rather more reticent about the prospect being half-naked in front of Tris and Andrew.

"Thank you for that," she whispered. Tris gave a casual shrug of his shoulders and grinned.

"Uncle Andrew told me that Uncle Tristan once ended up stark naked when Alexei first started teaching him to fly," he laughed. "Evidently, he ignored what Alexei had suggested and decided to just wear surf shorts and boxers, not realising just how strong the wind can get when you go into any sort of dive. That's why, right from the start, Andrew always made me wear speedos for my flying lessons. Which I still like to do! If I'm wearing jeans, I always have a good, tight-fitting belt, just to be sure."

"I think that was what all my brothers were waiting for, when I had my first flight," Andrew laughed. "I think they were starting to think of it as some form of amusing initiation for all those doing their first flight. Well, amusing for them and embarrassing for whomever it was who was trying to fly for the first time, I suppose. Luckily, Alexei made sure that I had long-legged speedos to wear. Which, as you can see, is what Tris wears. When you get older, it becomes less of a problem because you have more control over your appearance." To Lara's sudden astonishment, he quickly morphed into a young boy of about eleven or twelve years of age.

"When I was teaching Tris, we'd often fly together, like this," he said with a smile. "It just made it more fun, and less like teacher and pupil. Now, let's see you do a few landings from the church roof."

***

"Okay," Mykael said with a slight sigh. "As I suggested the other day, I think our next plan of action should be to get rid of any further material that might be out there that relates to Lara. Particularly anything that might be on file at the medical facility." He looked around at the small gathering of adults and angels assembled in the Rankins' family room. "I'm mainly thinking along the lines of anything at all in the way of videos, photographs, and X-rays, as well as any sort of documentation and medical records."

"What about the necklace?" Tris queried. Mykael gave a slight shake of his head, which seemed to emphasise his mild sense of exasperation.

"We'll deal with that in due time," he replied. "After all, its signal can't be picked up while it's on the island, and now that we know its broadcast frequency, I've got Colin Watters working on a little side-project that will make it almost impossible for it to be easily tracked when we dispose of it."

"Why not just destroy it?" Tris suggested. Mykael gave a slight nod.

"I had thought about that," he murmured. "But then realised that doing so might only result in that military group continuing to focus their efforts to find Lara on the area near to the farm, which is where they last picked up her GPS signal. What I have in mind will leave its signal intact, but extremely difficult to trace."

"So what are you going to do with it?" Lara asked.

"If Colin Watters can get his contacts to create what's needed, we'll soon have a good half dozen, or more, little devices capable of producing exactly the same GPS signal. Devices that we will then distribute in various ways that will be difficult to track down." He paused a moment, as if expecting a question. "Anyway, let's get this current little expedition under way, before we worry too much about the necklace." He turned to Lara and Tris. "What I now need from you is some sort of visualisation of where you first met up with each other."

In an instant it seemed, they had vanished from the room and were standing in deep snow in a small clearing in a forest. The air was remarkably chilly with it being only about seven in the morning.

"Perhaps we should have left home later in the afternoon. Maybe even almost tea time, to take into account the time difference," Andrew quietly mused as he reached out to give Lara a feeling of warmth. Mykael appeared to ignore his slight protest.

"Okay, so this was where Tris found you?" the senior guardian asked, looking around the clearing. Lara gave a quick nod of her head.

"I was running down from the top of the hill," Lara said, pointing towards the trees covering the slope. "Like, before I got to here. I mean, at first I was just trying to figure out where to go, and still puzzling over how I'd even got out of the hospital. Then I realised that they'd sent a search party out after me, and that they had dogs. So, I started running, and sort of praying for help. And then I reached this clearing. I stopped for a moment, trying to decide whether to keep running, or give myself up, and then, all of a sudden, Tris was there."

"And do you know how you ended up on top of the hill?" Mykael asked. Lara gave a further slight shrug.

"Not really," she replied. "I... I was just suddenly there. I mean, it was like... one minute I was in my cage, looking out the window at the hill. I mean... it wasn't that it was anything special. It was just a hill I could see in the distance. But anywhere seemed better than being locked up in a cage. Anyway, one minute I was looking at the hill and wondering what it would be like to stand on top of it, and then, the next minute, just after I'd slumped back down on my bed, I was just there. Lying in the cold snow, right where I had been looking. As I just said, at the time, I didn't know how I got there!"

"It's called 'be'ing," Mykael explained. "And, as you now realise, from what Tris has taught you, it's an ability we all have for getting from one place to another. You must have just thought of yourself as being at the top of the hill and so... you were there. When you get more practiced at it, you can also 'be' by taking a visualisation from another angel. That's how we all came here now, and how Tris was able to find you and bring you to the island. Now, what we need to know is where you were before you got to the mountain, and before Tris found you."

"Do I have to go back there?" Lara asked a little tentatively.

"Well, the whole purpose of why we are here, is to find out where you were kept prisoner," Mykael responded rather calmly. "But don't worry. There's absolutely no way the people there can ever catch you and keep you captive again. Not in any way. Not when you're with me. In fact, they won't even be able to see us. Or know that we're there."

"You mean we'll be like I was when Tris found me and he held me close so that the people hunting me couldn't see us?" asked Lara, still just a little tentatively.

"Exactly," Mykael replied. "Now, as for us getting there, we don't really need to go back to the top of the hill. If you just try to remember what the place was like where you were being kept captive, I'll be able to take us there and we can look it over."

"Can I come too?" Tris hastily enquired. Perhaps worrying that Mykael might suggest that he and Lara immediately return to the island.

"You may as well," Mykael replied. "Just keep close, and invisible, and help Lara to stay invisible. Maybe hold her hand. If it looks like there might be any sort of a problem, be prepared for you both to go straight back home and let me deal with the situation." Tris quickly nodded an understanding of Mykael's directions.

"Now, where do you think this medical facility is from here?" Mykael asked, turning to Lara. She pointed along the ridge.

"I think it's over that way," she replied a little nervously. "Down the other side of the ridge. But it's surrounded by fences, and there are guards with dogs, and alarms and stuff like that."

"We can bypass all that," Mykael hastily informed her. "All I need is a good visualisation of where you were kept locked up."

"So what do I do to give you that visualisation?" Lara asked a little anxiously. Mykael took hold of her hand.

"Just do what Tris did to get us here. Try to imagine an image of the room that you were in," he said gently. "Just imagine that you are standing in it by trying to picture it in your head. The same as Tris has had you doing with the church and in the back of the barn up at the farm," he added with a smile. "Then, I'll get a visualisation of it from your thoughts."

Lara quickly shut her eyes. It wasn't all that hard to visualise the room in which she'd been held captive, given that it had been more like a prison cell than a hospital ward, and had been her 'home' for quite some months. A place where there'd been many locked doors requiring electronic pass cards, and security guards in every corridor. The Holts had not even been allowed to come down to her room when she was being 'settled in' and had never come to visit. Quite why such visits were not permitted, she wasn't too sure, although she was also certain that she'd heard one of the nurses mention to a colleague that the Holts had been paid a substantial sum of money to 'forget' about their adopted, mutant daughter.

"They probably didn't deserve to have you anyway," Mykael suddenly murmured, as if reading her thoughts, as well as making a visualisation. Lara gave a slight shrug. In a reserved way, her adoptive parents had always been kind enough, especially before her wings had emerged, but perhaps Mykael was right in what he'd mentioned a couple of days ago. That she might have been better off with a family that would also have adopted her brother.

"It's almost like a prison cell," Tris suddenly exclaimed, as he and Andrew also picked up on the visualisation.

"Okay," Mykael said, with a sigh. "Hold hands, so we keep close together, and let's go. Tris and Lara, remember to stay invisible!"

An instant later, they were in a small room. In a way, Tris had been right. It did resemble a quite upmarket prison cell. More like something you might encounter in one of the more generally rehabilitative facilities in Northern Europe, rather that the quite punitive American cellblock systems. The 'cell' being more akin to a room in a private living facility, such as a high-class boarding school, than any sort of 'containment' lockup. Apart from the fact that, the main access door was securely deadlocked from the outside and could not be opened from within.

Inside the room itself, there was a small bed to one side of a set of drawers, a bookshelf with a small collection of books and a table and chair. A small alcove, not viewable from the doorway, led off the main room to an area that contained separate toilet and showering facilities. As Lara had mentioned just after she'd first been rescued, two of the walls of that area were floor to ceiling mirrors. The door that presumably led into the corridor contained a small viewing window. On the opposite side of the room, covered on the outside with a fine steel mesh, there was a slightly larger window high up above the bed, which gave a view of the outside. In particular, of the hilltop that led down to the forest area where they'd just been standing.

On the side of the room opposite the table and next to the bathroom alcove, there was also a large mirror that seemed to reach almost from floor to ceiling. It looked very much like the sort of mirrors that you might find in a dance studio. Not that any of them was reflected in it at present.

"I'm pretty sure that there were people behind that, too" Lara murmured, glancing towards the large mirror. "Because when I was very quiet, I often used to hear faint talking, and it always seemed to be from behind the mirror."

"Cameras," Tris suddenly whispered, pointing towards the ceiling. Mykael looked up at them. A second later, the red lights that showed they were operating, winked out.

"And if we crash a few more, let's just see what sort of reaction we get," he murmured. Within ten seconds, warning sirens began to wail.

'Emergency. Unrecognised security breach. Lock down in five minutes...' a mechanical voice suddenly intoned. ***'Please move immediately to your designated assembly point.'*** A few seconds later, as the sirens continued to wail, the warning was reiterated. ***'Emergency. Unrecognised security breach. Lock down in four minutes and fifty seconds. Please move immediately to your designated assembly point.'***

"Well, that certainly seems to have stirred things up a little," muttered Mykael, with a brief upward flex of his eyebrows and a rather cheeky smile. "So maybe we can take a good look around, while they're all distracted with running around after imaginary bogeymen."

Keeping hold of Lara's hand and reaching for Tris, Mykael looked towards the door. A second later they were all standing in a long corridor that seemed to stretch in both directions. Further along from where they were standing, men in white coats were hurrying towards some large doors. In the other direction, soldiers were starting to conduct an armed sweep of each of the rooms that led off the corridor. Moving, almost methodically, from room to room, with weapons poised and at the ready for firing.

"Let's get out of their way and do a little 'sweeping' of our own," Mykael said casually. Leading them through an open door right next to Lara's cell, they immediately found themselves in an observation room. Much as Mykael had surmised, and Lara had suspected, the large mirror was in fact one-way glass, and a means of observing whatever was taking place in the 'cell' that had been her 'home'. A little further over, and set back a little around an alcove, there were two other windows. From what they showed it didn't take a genius to realise that they were the other side of the 'mirrors' that gave a view into the bathroom.

"So they were watching me all the time? Even when I was washing myself, or going to the toilet?" Lara murmured, appearing somewhat embarrassed at the thought of that happening. Not that they were really questions requiring answers.

"Most probably. But that's just part of the way it is with science," responded Mykael, with a softly resigned sigh. "Particularly where the military are concerned. Contain, provoke and then observe!"

"Provoke?" Tris queried.

"Well, in Lara's case it was most probably just seeing how she reacted to certain aspects of her confinement," Mykael replied.

"I lost count of the number of times they x-rayed me," Lara murmured. A quick glance around the room also showed that X-rays were not the only photographic records taken. Some of the photos on view had obviously been taken when Lara had been in the bathroom.

"I think it might be a good idea for us to 'acquire' all of this," Mykael said quickly reaching out to confiscate some of the more 'explicit' views of the girl, before she became too embarrassed with them being pinned up for all and sundry to see. An instant later, Ithuriel appeared along with several other angels, including

Alexei, Gofraidh, Aerynn and the rest of the brothers; all of them in a state of invisibility and visible only as vague outlines.

"We need to remove every bit of information pertaining to Lara," Mykael instructed. "All photographs, X-rays, notes, medical records, video films, DVDs, etc. All of it can go back to the room I use on the island. We can sort through it at some later time, and then destroy the bulk of it. Everything must be removed, and we need to do it as quickly as possible," he added. He raised his eyebrows, slightly. An instant later, and after a moment or two of complete silence, the room had been stripped bare and all the other angels were gone. The sudden change to the appearance of the room leaving Lara and Tris both open-mouthed with surprise.

"A little time-slowing," Mykael said, in answer to their unspoken question, as they could once again clearly hear the sound of the 'lockdown' warnings.

"What about the computers?" Tris asked, indicating the bank of six computers on the far side of the room. "There might still be stuff on the hard drives." Mykael seemed to nod slightly. An instant later there was complete silence.

"Either of you any good at disassembling a computer?" Mykael asked. Both Lara and Tris shrugged a little unsurely. An obvious indication that, while they both might make use of computers, they were clearly not all that familiar with their inner workings. Mykael sighed a little, and then moved over to the nearest computer. "Just grab one of those screwdrivers from over on the bench, and then copy what we do," he instructed.

Lara and Tris hurried to do as they'd been asked. In less time than expected, they had each extracted a drive from a computer, while Mykael and Andrew had completed doing the same for the other four.

Mykael reached out a hand to take the two drives from them, and then the two that Andrew had removed.

"Wait here, and don't move a muscle, he instructed. As he disappeared, the sound of the warnings recommenced. Tris felt Lara tighten the grip on his hand, the action an obvious sign of her sense of nervousness and unease about them being without Mykael's protection; even 'though Andrew was still with them. An instant later Mykael reappeared… empty-handed.

"Why didn't you just wipe the computers?" Tris asked with a sense of bemusement. "Like you do with cell phones and cameras and stuff like that?"

"Because I couldn't trust that they might have ways to restore what had been wiped," Mykael replied. "And anyway, it's likely that Lieutenant Colonel Harris McMahon and a few others, will also have some of the data backed up on their laptops. I'll get Ithuriel to sort out a squad to get rid of whatever we can, in that regard, over the next few days."

"But won't they notice that these computers have been opened?" Tris questioned, pointing to the open backs of the four computers."

"Of course," Mykael replied. "Just as the same as they'll notice that everything else has been removed." He reached out and took a hold of Lara's free hand. "Now, much as it might be fun to hang around and watch the stunned reactions when they return, we've probably accomplished all of what was needed for the moment, so let's just head home."

***

Having just taken a seat to start eating his order of a Big Mac, fries and a medium-sized Frozen Coke, Rylan suddenly felt a sense of danger as a dark shadow suddenly loomed over him. He could tell, simply by the stature of the man, the colour of his trousers and the way that he stood, that it was the same police officer that he'd encountered, and escaped from, a week or so earlier. Perhaps, he quickly thought, he should have found a different McDonalds to go to, rather than the one that was so obviously a part of the officer's patrol area. For a few moments, he tried to ignore the man. Continuing to work his way through his Big Mac as if not noticing that anyone was close to him.

"Well, kid," the police officer suddenly announced. "I've done a bit of a check around the schools in this area and none of them seem to have a kid enrolled by the name of Christopher Makin. So, for a start, how about you tell me your real name?" Rylan shrugged and remained obstinately silent as he concentrated on hurriedly finishing the last of the burger.

"Hows about you look at me when I'm talking to you," the police officer suddenly demanded. Tris kept his gaze steadfastly on the table in front of him.

"I'm homeschooled, so I won't be on any school roll," he murmured. "I told you that the last time."

"Okay, on your feet," the officer suddenly demanded. Rylan looked up at him with almost a sense of disbelief.

"What for?" he nervously queried.

"It's the middle of the day and I've got reason to believe you're either a truant, or a runaway," the officer retorted. "I'm just going to keep you from taking off on me again, while I check out if there's anything on file about you; given that you were so keen to do a runner on me, the last time I spoke with you. Most of the local precincts have details of missing children, runaways, persistent truants, and such. I'll radio through a description of you and see what they can find. It's probably for your own good." Tris immediately wondered if his parents would've contacted the police about his absconding from his visit to the psychiatrist. Although, given the way he'd been abused by his father, and what else he could relate to the police about events at the church, he still felt that that wasn't all that likely. With an almost exaggerated sigh, he got to his feet, leaving his carton of fries and the Frozen Coke on the table. The policeman immediately pushed him hard up against the divider between the booths, as the general hubbub of noise in the McDonalds was quickly hushed by a morbid interest in the sudden confrontation.

"Hands on your head!" the officer demanded. Rylan did as instructed, as almost everyone turned to look at him, only to find that his left wrist was suddenly manacled. His left arm was then pulled down behind his back, before his right arm grabbed and also brought down, so that his wrists could be cuffed behind his back. The handcuffs were then tightened so that they securely trapped his skinny wrists.

"I'm not risking you taking off on me, again," the police officer said gruffly, as he then grabbed Rylan by the upper arm and began to escort him out to a waiting patrol car, holding his arm high so that Rylan was forced almost onto his tiptoes to keep from being lifted off his feet. The man perhaps feeling secure in the knowledge that, with the back area of police vehicles being centrally locked, he could then take his time with his interrogation without the risk that the boy might, yet again, make a fool of him by taking off, unexpectedly. Big burly police officers chasing after small, innocent-looking children did not tend to go down too well with the general public... not unless the child had clearly committed some heinous crime. Admittedly, this kid looked far too innocent to have ever committed any wrongdoing, yet there was something about the whole situation that bothered Officer Grif Malone. A look in the kid's eyes that spoke of some trepidation as he was escorted out to the waiting squad car. Rylan, for his part, waited until he'd been placed in the back of the vehicle and then leaned towards the door just before it was closed.

"Can you go and get my fries and Frozen Coke?" he asked politely. "That's all I've got to eat, for today." The policeman seemed to pause for a moment, then sighed a little resignedly and glanced back towards the eatery, feeling a sense of exasperation; yet aware that he was, in reality, just detaining a child for further investigation; not arresting a hardened felon. Admittedly, the fact that the requested items might be the kid's only meal for the day, suggested that, as he'd suspected all along, he was most probably a runaway. With a shake of his head, he slammed the door shut, checked that it was securely locked, and then headed slowly back inside.

The moment the officer had gone back through the doors to the McDonalds, Rylan visualised being back inside his hideaway, looking towards the door and was delighted to find that instantaneously that was where he was. Unfortunately, he still had his hands in restraints. For a moment he wondered about the possibility of going downstairs to find George. The only problem with that idea, he quickly realised, was that during the day George was often out wandering the streets in search of bottles and cans. If the old man wasn't there, then he didn't want to go wandering around downstairs while handcuffed in case, as he'd been warned, there were people there who might take advantage of his restrained state.

Eventually, and perhaps just out of curiosity, he wandered over to the door and visualised himself as seated, back on the couch, without the handcuffs. To his intense delight, he found that he was suddenly on the couch with his hands free, even as the handcuffs clattered noisily to the floor close to the door. That set him thinking.

Obviously, when he transported himself, it seemed that he always had his clothes. Perhaps that was simply because, in his visualisations, that was how he automatically imagined himself.

That must have also been why he'd unexpectedly brought his attacker with him, the first time he'd discovered his 'jumping' ability. And why, this time, he'd remained handcuffed. He hadn't thought to purposely visualise himself as being without them.

For the next ten minutes, he experimented. Quickly learning that, in most cases, if he was holding something, and just thought of his hiding place, it would also transport with him. Just as he'd already discovered when bringing home food, and the time when Xavier J. Hernandez had had a grip of his ankle. If he purposely thought about not having an item, it would be left where he'd been standing. In one of the experiments, he'd purposely visualised himself as transporting in just his underpants and was not too surprised to find that the rest of his clothing was simply left in a crumpled heap on the far side of the room where he'd originally been standing. He hurried back across the room and hastily got himself properly dressed. Perhaps as much to ward off the sudden cold, as to lessen the chance of his being discovered so scantily dressed, and with his wings showing. Before putting his shirt and jumper back on, he hurried through to the bathroom to check on how much his appendages had grown. To his surprise, they now reached well over halfway down to his waist. Finally bundling himself back into the warmth of his shirt and jacket and ignoring the fact that he was badly in need of a wash and a change of underwear, he quickly made a mental note to always visualise himself as properly clothed.

Still, he surmised, the practise in visualising made him wonder about the possibility of simply being able to think of other places and just 'jump' himself there. With a slight sense of anxiousness, he stood facing the window and visualised himself as standing in the corridor. It worked! He 'jumped' back into his room and immediately decided to try for a bigger 'jump'. Not wanting to head anywhere where he might be seen, he thought of the foyer, which was usually unoccupied. Simply because, most of the usual derelicts living downstairs tended to want to stay well out of sight of the street.

In an instant he was there, looking out at the wire-net fencing outside the building. Immediately on hearing voices from somewhere behind him, however, he hastily returned to his room. Hoping that his sudden appearance, and then equally abrupt disappearance, had not been noted by anyone… not even George.

Back in his room, he thought of the alleyway where he'd first found the open door and was instantly there. With a nod of his head, he quickly returned to his room. Realising as he did so that, when he ran out of the money he'd acquired from Xavier J. Hernandez, getting food from the dumpster behind the café would now be a much easier task. There was, of course, a risk in just appearing beside it. More particularly, if someone else was already there who might see him just suddenly appear. But the return could now also be instantaneous.

CHAPTER EIGHT

Diversions....

Mykael waited until everyone was silent, and then exhaled softly in preparation for explaining the extra plans he and Ithuriel had in mind for ensuring Lara's safety. They were using the schoolroom over in the big house, so that they could accommodate everyone who'd be involved in some way, as well as those who were merely curious as to what was about to take place. That included Steve and Evelyn Robertson, Colin Watters, Monique and Robert Wells-Henrikson and Hugh and Gladys Gibbs as well as the seven former angel-children and all the children and adults now living on the island.

"Well," Mykael finally drawled, "while we've managed to get the bulk of what the military had as records of Lara's existence and development now securely locked away, we still have some work to do with regard to getting the military distracted away from the farm, and perhaps also this island and the local village. The operation for this to happen will, therefore, take two different approaches. And having already discussed the matter with some of those concerned, this is what we plan to have happen." He glanced quickly around the room before continuing.

"Firstly, we'll be confusing the issue of the GPS signal, by spreading a few duplicates of it throughout the world. Colin Watters will explain more about that in a minute. Our second approach will be to have several fake sightings of Lara in various places well away from here. For that, Monique and Robert will help with providing the necessary publicity; but at the same time, with a plan of creating some considerable degree of sceptism. We will also, however, need to have trustworthy people to report the sightings to them. So, to that end, Hugh and Gladys will be having a second honeymoon in Europe, as part of our operation to have sightings in Sweden, Germany and Poland. Amanda's parents have volunteered to travel to Australia and New Zealand for a short visit with the friends they'd made there over the last year or so, along with a brief stopover in Hawaii, and the Housemans have agreed to be our eyes in Canada. Lara, in one form or another, will also make appearances in Brazil, the United States, Spain and Italy to name just a few places, because, given the important influence of the Catholic church in those regions, it's likely that the sightings will very quickly be believed by the masses, even if the church, itself, is reluctant to make any definitive comment. While, as I previously mentioned, Monique and Robert will obviously be providing the sceptical counter-balance by promoting such sightings as merely symptoms of ongoing copycat hysteria."

"I could do another appearance in Wichita?" Tris offered almost mischievously. Mykael gave a slight shake of his head.

"I doubt that'll be necessary," he murmured. "Once these other sightings are made, I'm sure that there will be more than enough interest generated about your previous appearance."

"So do I have to actually go to all of these places?" Lara queried a little anxiously.

"Not unless you really want to," Mykael replied. He gestured towards Alexei, who in turn gestured to his brothers. In an instant, there were seven identical copies of Lara to be seen. All of them dressed in exactly the same clothes as Lara was currently wearing and appearing almost indistinguishable from the original.

"And I'm only doing this once," Tristan murmured, giving a slight laugh to show that he wasn't annoyed by what he'd been asked to do. "And only because Mykael feels that it's necessary." He then shook his head a little, so that his imitation of Lara's long blonde hair swirled out around his shoulders, and gave a slightly girlish giggle. "And I certainly have no intentions of sauntering along any strange beach in a bikini while doing it!" he added, pretending to flounce along as if on a catwalk for a few paces. "Once was enough!"

"Just be thankful you're just transforming into a little girl with wings and not some aged harridan," Ithuriel teased.

"Or someone built like Dolly Parton," Colin Watters added. Perhaps in reference to the fact that, with them all being identical copies of Lara, there was no perceptible chest development on any of the 'clones'.

"Getting matters back on track," Mykael softly continued, suppressing a slight smile as each of the angel brothers quickly reverted to their normal appearance. "Our first issue, however, will be to do with the GPS signal. And for that, I'll hand over to Colin Watters to explain the little side-project that he has been working on." At this prompting, Colin Watters got quickly to his feet and wandered to the front of the room holding a container about the size of a shoebox. Placing the box on the table in front of him, he picked out Lara's necklace.

"This," he said, waving the necklace towards the gathering, "is the original necklace. As you all know, it's putting out a special GPS signal, which is what the military had been using to track Lara. As a good many of you will now understand, its signal is not detectable when it is inside a lead-shielded box or within the confines of the island, due to the anti-snooping devices that Steve Robertson had installed way back when there were all those problems regarding the press hacking into the personal cellphones of public figures as a way to get the latest news scoops." He tossed the necklace across to Mykael, before continuing.

"Mykael has assured me that he has decided on a very safe place to put it, so I will leave that matter in his hands, if you excuse the slight pun." Mykael gave a quick nod.

"And I'll be putting it somewhere that, while it will not only still be active and therefore traceable, it will present a rather difficult problem for any U.S. military group trying to gain access to it," he murmured, before gesturing for Colin Watters to continue.

"Now, in this box I have eight more necklaces, for want of a better description." Colin Watters quickly picked up a couple of very small box-like devices with thin straps attached. "These little beauties put out the exact same frequency of GPS signal," he quickly explained. "So we're going to attach them, by straps, or by other means where necessary, to animals that tend to spend a lot of time in migration, or in simply travelling extensively. I'm thinking of albatrosses, whales, and sharks and such. We'll give the U.S. military a good number of wild goose chases, that will hopefully take them all over the planet."

"We could possibly attach one to a satellite or…or a rocket going into orbit," Tris eagerly suggested. "There's that new launching facility in New Zealand that's fairly busy doing that sort of thing."

"That's a very good suggestion," Colin Watters murmured. "Especially if they believe that they're tracking an angel."

"And while that is happening," Mykael quickly continued, after a nod of agreement at that particular idea, "not only will there be a whole lot of fake 'Lara sightings' all over the planet, but Ithuriel, Gabriel, Ariel and I will also be tracking the various military groups that think they're tracking Lara, and wiping the hard drives of any of their computers that might contain anything relating to her."

"So, essentially, you'll be trying to lure them out into the open, with the angel sightings and false signals, as well as confusing them?" murmured Steve Robertson. Admittedly, the question was essentially rhetorical.

"You got it in one," retorted Colin Watters. "I also tend to think, and Mykael agrees with me in this, that the whole Lara issue, for want of a better description, will, so far, have been kept strictly under wraps to avoid the possibility of a public outcry. I mean, I'm sure you can imagine the ruckus that would erupt, in all aspects of the media around the world, if it ever became known that the U.S. military were keeping a young girl captive, after buying her from her parents. Regardless of the fact of her also having wings. In fact, I'd even be tempted to suggest that it's highly likely that even most of that lot that came ashore up at that beach by the farm, a week or so ago, had no real idea that they were searching for anything other than what they were told. That is, that it was some sort of item of electronic hardware attached to a parachute or balloon. That means that the number of people who really know what Harris McMahon and his subordinates are searching for, is likely to be quite limited. Obviously, they'll also be the ones most prominent in the continuation of the search, and, therefore, the individuals we should continue to be targeting for what they might have recorded."

"So when is it all going to happen?" Tris asked eagerly. "Like, can me and Lara do some of the sightings?"

"Let's just get the decoys up and running, for a start," Mykael replied, smiling at Tris's obvious enthusiasm. "That's likely to take a day or two, at least. Particularly if we want the decoy signals to be well-spaced around the planet."

"And well away from here, and my parents' farm," added Steve Robertson rather softly.

"Well, what about when you get rid of the last bracelet?" Tris asked. "The real one! Can we..." he indicated himself and Lara, "...know where it'll be?" Mykael was quiet, for a moment or two, as he seemed to be considering the idea.

"Please," Tris pleaded. Mykael sighed and then nodded.

"Okay," he said with almost a slight laugh. "But keep in mind that you'll have to watch from a distance. Where I'll be putting it, is an extremely dangerous place."

"So where will we be going?" Tris asked eagerly. Mykael inclined his head briefly to one side.

"That, I'm keeping a secret," he murmured. "You'll just have to wait until we go there." He quickly turned to all the angels who'd once been children living on the island – Alexei, Gofraidh, Tristan, Aerynn, Taylor, Conlaodh and Andrew. "I'd like you all, with Ithuriel's guidance, find appropriate places to attach the eight new devices," he quickly explained. "Before we get around to making any 'Lara' appearances, we may as well start by have that covert U.S. military group chasing impossible GPS signals from all over the planet. As Colin mentioned, earlier, you will need to choose animals that tend to travel long distances and would be reasonably hard to track. As I said earlier, I'm thinking of sharks, whales, orcas, and maybe albatrosses or other large migratory sea birds..." He paused a moment. "At any rate, just make it difficult for them to be tracked. The longer we can keep Lieutenant Colonel Harris McMahon and all his little subordinates running around out there chasing their tails on various wild goose expeditions, the better."

"So, we should head off now?" Ithuriel asked, gathering up the box containing the eight dummy GPS devices. Mykael nodded rather nonchalantly.

"If you wish," he replied. "As I said, just be creative with where you place them. The harder they are to track down, the better. And if one of you can manage to get one into orbit, that'll be fine. Just don't put yourself at any risk. Then, when you've finished, meet me back at the church. Let's say by… this time tomorrow, so that we can start the planning of phase two." Everyone watched as Ithuriel tossed a GPS device to each of the other angels; each of them simply disappearing the moment they'd grabbed it.

"Now, you two," Mykael instructed, indicating the two child angels, "can come with me." With the bracelet still in his right hand, he reached out and held each of them by the hand, Lara on his right, Tris on his left.

An instant later they were high in the air over a woodland area that seemed to have a smallish town to one side. A town that seemed of a similar size to Oakton, Tris quickly noted, but for some reason appeared to be strangely deserted. No cars, or people, or movement of any kind could be seen. Not even in the amusement park with its large Ferris wheel. Some distance below and out in front of them, was also a rather large concrete building of some type that seemed to be not fully completed, or was quite damaged and broken in some way. However, like the town, it also seemed strangely deserted. Appearing to show absolutely no sign of life or activity.

"Where on Earth are..." Tris began a little hesitantly.

"Pripyat," Mykael quickly interrupted. "Which is a town in the northern part of the Ukraine."

"But, isn't that near Chernobyl?" queried Tris with some degree of anxiousness. "You know, where that nuclear power station went into meltdown?"

"Exactly," replied Mykael. "That's why there's no one here. In fact that big building you can see directly to our left is the

Chernobyl power station. Which is also why we are way up here." He drew them in a little closer. "Which is also where you two will stay!" he added rather sternly. "Not unless you want end up with rather hot bottoms!"

"From the radioactivity?" Tris quickly queried just a little nervously, looking down towards the massive broken structure of the nuclear power station.

"No," Mykael said sternly, even as he also seemed to smile a little. "From my right hand!" Tris was silent for a while as he looked, with some slight embarrassment, at Mykael, and then at Lara. Wondering a little, as he did so, if Mykael was just teasing or whether would really carry out such a threat. More especially if it also meant spanking a girl-angel.

"Who's to know what I might do, if it concerned ensuring the ongoing safety of the two most precious children on this planet!" Mykael added, as if somehow reading his thoughts.

"So what are you going to do with the necklace?" Lara asked. Not appearing too put out by the slight reprimand and threatened punishment. Mykael gave her a warm smile and looked down at his right hand, which was still holding the GPS tracking device.

"Well, given that it's still putting out a good strong signal, I'm going to place it on top of the Number four reactor… the one that actually exploded. Which will mean that, not only will it very quickly become far too radioactive to be touched, but, given where it will be, any U.S. military group tracking it, will have a very hard time trying to convince the Ukrainian Government, and perhaps also the Russians, that it has anything whatsoever to do with some new atmospheric monitoring device off a weather balloon. Given the current state of tension between those three countries, and the likelihood that the U.S. military will not want to let on about its true purpose, I'd be tempted to say that it's destined to remain there for a very, very long time." He looked about for a moment, as if checking whether there was any way in which they might be seen.

"Okay, you two wait right here," he then instructed. "I'll be back in an instant." He seemed to shimmer slightly, and then blink into invisibility for just the merest second, before showing them that the necklace was no longer in his right hand.

"All done. Now, let's get back home!" he announced. "With all the extra GPS signals causing general confusion, we can start tracking the military personnel involved. Then in a few days, we can plan on adding the angel sightings, just to keep things really mixed up."

***

Rylan sat up and threw off his blankets, as there was a sudden, quiet knock on the door to his hideout. A little cautiously, he wandered over and put his ear to the door.

"It's just George," he heard the old man say quite softly, as if not wanting to be heard by anyone downstairs. "I've brought you a little something to eat."

Opening the door a little, Rylan saw that George was waiting against the far wall with a brown paper bag in one hand.

"It's just a few pies that I managed to score," George quietly said, as Rylan indicated for him to come in. "They're best before yesterday, and they're cold, but they should still be quite okay to eat."

He placed the bag on the bench, grabbed a pie out of it and then wandered over to sit on the couch. After a moment's hesitation, Rylan did likewise. In some ways, pleased for a bit of company as much as the extra food. Spending most of his time alone in his hideout could get pretty boring.

"So how's about you tell me about your future plans," George eventually suggested when he'd finished eating. He brushed a hand across his mouth to wipe away a few stray crumbs. "Like, how long do you to plan to be living on your own. And don't worry. As I said when you first arrived, I ain't about to go running off to the police, or social welfare, about you. Not if you don't want me to. I'm just curious, that's all." He sighed softly. "And a little worried. 'Specially as you don't come across as any sort of streetwise kid, and, to be brutally honest, this ain't a very nice area of the Big Apple for anyone to be, who ain't too sure where he's headed and don't fully understand the dangers… more especially at your age. Which obviously puts you at quite some risk, if you get my drift. Particularly from those 'round here who tend to be on the lookout for strays and runaways, and possible ways to exploit them for their own profit."

"But I don't have anywhere else to go," Rylan murmured. "At least, not where I'll be safe."

"Wouldn't some sort of orphanage be better than being out on the streets, if you can't go home?" George queried. Rylan gave a small shake of his head.

"I'm not normal," he murmured, half wondering whether he should let George in on his secret. About his wings and his ability to teleport. Or as he now called it… 'jump'.

"Even more reason for you to find somewhere safe and have someone to care for you properly," George countered. Rylan quickly wondered if the comment meant that George had figured out that he was gay; that he liked boys, or at least that he felt that he had had some attraction towards other boys. As he mulled over George's comment, three names from Oakton Middle School came quickly into his thoughts… Matthew Ryan, Christopher Makin and Skylar Jeffries. They were boys from various classes that he'd been in that he would've really liked to have been friends with, and maybe even more. Although in Skylar's case it might simply have been because of his close resemblance to Finn Wolfhard from the first Stranger Things season on Netflix. He had, of course, had to keep those feelings entirely to himself, for fear of being further rejected and ostracised. There had seemed no point in his being careless enough to provide the undeniable 'proof' of what everyone was already saying about him. Even being seen to be too friendly towards those boys would have also caused them major problems, given the way other pupils could be so quick to make nasty judgments. And that would've only made the three boys hate him even more. Perhaps even have led them into beating him up, just to prove to everyone else that they were not in any way connected; that they were not his 'boyfriend'.

At the same time, going to an orphanage would simply place him in even greater danger. More especially with his now having wings. With the close living that would be necessary, there would be no way that he'd able to keep them a secret for very long, even if he did have the ability to 'jump' away from danger. And if he ended up sleeping in a dormitory situation, night times would simply become a nightmare if older boys ever figured out that he was gay, no matter how much 'protection' might be offered by those running the place. Tears welled in his eyes as he suddenly realised just how alone he was and how little choice he had in matters.

He suddenly felt a hand on his shoulder, but didn't shrug it away. George had already proved himself to be a trustworthy friend. He quickly wiped at his eyes.

"Some of the homeless shelters tend to have a few kids staying," George said consolingly. "Not all of them mind you. But those that do will often turn a blind eye to the situation, with regard to the police and social welfare. Especially if there's an older adult staying there who's willing to take on some responsibility for the day-to-day welfare of a kid. Tell you what, I'll put out some feelers and see what I can find out. In the meantime, if you need me, or even just want a bit of company, I'm usually downstairs by five, most evenings. And don't worry about the other old fellows like Alf. They've sort of guessed that you're still around, somewhere, but I've told them that I'd look out for you, so they won't worry too much about you being here."

After giving Rylan's shoulders a quick squeeze, he got to his feet and wandered over to the doorway.

There's a couple more pies in the bag," he muttered. "You keep 'em for tomorrow. I can always find more." Rylan nodded.

"Thanks," he murmured as he again wiped at his eyes.

"You just lock this door properly when I'm gone," George replied. "And stay off the streets as much as possible."

***

"Sir, I think we're picking up Angel-girl's GPS signal, once again," Sergeant Oliver Childers cautiously announced, looking intently at the screen in front of him.

"Where from?" Harris McMahon immediately demanded.

"It's from near the Antarctic... and… and also near Hawaii," Sergeant Oliver Childers replied a little less surely, as a second listing of coordinates suddenly popped up at the bottom of the screen.

"It can't be in two places at once," Harris McMahon snapped. "That would be impossible. One of them must be some sort of an atmospheric echo."

"And now another one has just popped up," murmured Sergeant Childers warily. Not wanting to upset his superior officer. "This one's coming from Eastern Europe."

“Whereabouts?” Harris McMahon queried angrily. Oliver Childers gave a slight shrug.

“Given the coordinates it’s showing, I’d say somewhere in the Ukraine. Sort of near to Pripyat,” he said cautiously. “Which could be a major problem.” He hurriedly focussed in on the new reading, in an attempt to get more exact coordinates.

“Why?” Harris McMahon muttered. Watching as the junior officer hurriedly flicked coordinates and images across his screen. For his part, Sergeant Oliver Childers seemed a little bemused that his superior officer would be unaware that Pripyat was the hastily evacuated, and now completely deserted, small town closest to the site of a major nuclear disaster that had affected the whole of Western Europe. A reactor ‘meltdown’ of such severity that it had resulted in the hurried evacuation of all the surrounding countryside; the residents of the town of Pripyat even having to leave all their personal possessions behind, because of the risk of radiation contamination.

“Because from what I’m reading here, it would indicate that Angel-girl’s possibly in the middle of the Chernobyl nuclear reactor,” he sighed. “If that’s her actual signal.” He paused and looked at the other indications. “It could be one of the others, Sir,” he hastily added. “Because there are now at least five signals showing up from locations all over the world.” Lieutenant Colonel Harris McMahon was quiet for a while. He gave a slow, exasperated shake of his head.

“Lock onto one that appears to be moving and give us some coordinates,” he eventually snarled.

“Which one, Sir?” the junior officer nervously queried. In response, getting a rather black look from Harris McMahon.

“Any one of them, damn it! I don’t really care! Just choose the one that’s nearest!” the Lieutenant Colonel snapped. “It looks like we might just have to track them all down and eliminate them one at a time." He started towards the door, and then turned, abruptly. "And while you're at it, call Sullivan and get him to check with the squad we've got searching for her twin. Find out if they've had any success, as yet. If we can locate the boy, we might be able to use him as bait to trap his sister!"

***

Skylar sat quietly in a side room at the police station, waiting to find out whether he would soon be safe from the Network and on the way back to Pinehurst to be reunited with his mother. Cooper sat beside him and appeared to also be deep in thought. Skylar assumed that perhaps his companion would also be wondering how long it would take to make contact with his parents or guardians.

Admittedly, their escape had been fortuitous, to say the least. There had been eight children on this particular assignment and by a chance of luck, after they'd completed their usual humiliating 'parade', they'd become waiters for finger foods; that extra 'duty' being, as usual, just a chance for the potential 'clients' to peruse them all a little more closely. When ordered to get more hors d'oeuvres from the kitchen, Skylar and Cooper had noticed an unattended door and after managing to evade Angelo and Reggie, who were also acting as their minders, had made a quick escape out of a rear door of the kitchen area. After that, it had then taken them quite a while to find a way through a maze of corridors to an exit. All the time, wary of being caught by the security guards that seemed to be present at all the main doors, or by Vittorio, Angelo, or Reggie… or indeed any of the other 'assistants' who were sometimes used to keep watch on them.

Eventually, they'd found their way down to the underground parking garage where the truck was parked and, on finding the garage entrance unlocked, had then managed to get clear of the building. Once they'd bypassed the main gate, by finding a gap in the fencing well away from the security guards, they'd contrived to hide from recapture, by making use of the cover of the tall hedge that bordered the road, and kept the premises safe from prying eyes.

In a major stroke of luck, once they'd reached the main road, it hadn't taken more than a few minutes until they spied a passing police cruiser on a routine patrol and flagged it down. The fact that they were so scantily dressed seemed to have the two officers keen to know more about their situation. The officers appearing to, at first, think that they might have been the subjects of some childish prank; such as had been occurring in parts of Europe where young teenagers sometimes dared each other to walk through various shopping malls or supermarkets in just their underwear. Their explanation of being kidnapped, held captive, and then forced to work as slaves at secret private functions in preparation for being 'sold', however, resulted in them being taken straight to the police station so that arrangements could be made to have the venue, and their allegations regarding it, checked out.

Now, with each of them pulling the blanket they'd been given a little tighter around their shoulders, as much for extra warmth as to avoid feeling so exposed to the gaze of other people at the station, they waited for those promised events to take place. Hoping for someone to come and tell them that their parents, or even just the local Social Services Department, had been contacted and that they would soon be free from the clutches of the Network.

Even though they were now in one of the interview rooms and well away from the gaze of others in the station, they still felt just a little embarrassed in the fact that, beneath the blankets they'd been given for warmth, they were still wearing just their 'display wear'.

"We're just working on locating your parents' addresses and phone numbers," Officer Graham Stillwell quietly advised them, giving them a warm smile as he suddenly entered into the room. "And given that it's a kidnapping situation, we've also notified the FBI of the circumstances. You know, about the idea of this Network group having kidnapped you and other children. They've said that they'll send someone right over to sort out the problem. They'll also take care of checking out the venue that you say you escaped from. One of the top brass, it appears. So don't you worry, we'll soon have your friends rescued, and you all safely reunited with your parents."

"Thank you," Skylar murmured. His voice sounding as little more than a whisper, as tears of relief flooded into his eyes.

"I'm not sure where I'll end up," Cooper muttered a little more forcefully. "I doubt my stepparents will end up welcoming me back with open arms."

"Why not?" queried Skylar, with some mild sense of surprise. It seemed strange to think that a family would not welcome back a kidnapped offspring. More so if the child had been rescued from the likelihood of being auctioned off into a life of prolonged abuse.

"It's complicated," Cooper muttered as he gazed at the floor. He sighed a little resignedly. "I've been living with my step-dad and his new girlfriend. I don't think either of them wants me there. Not now that they've got James and Becky."

"Becky?"

"Yeah," Cooper sighed. "My baby sister, Rebecca. I've also got a step-brother, but he's only four."

Well, what about your real mom?" asked Skylar. Cooper gave a further shrug.

"She's dead and my real dad buggered off before I was even born, so I was told." He sighed a little resignedly. "He was my mom's first boyfriend. She was only seventeen, but when he heard she was pregnant, he evidently took off like a scalded cat. I don't even know his name. And then Mom's parents kicked her out. Didn't want the shame of her being an unwed mother, I presume."

They both fell silent. Listening to the sounds of activity beyond the room in which they were placed. In some ways, it almost seemed that, since they'd been told that the FBI would be taking over their situation, the local precinct felt no further need to be involved. Certainly no one had returned with the promised hot drinks and warm clothing that had been promised when they'd first arrived. Or perhaps it was just that, with it being a Saturday night, the precinct was busy with the usual weekend parade of drunks, brawlers, pickpockets, and other sundry miscreants.

Eventually, after about an hour or so of waiting, the door opened and two men in business suits, rather than uniforms, came into the room. Skylar and Cooper quickly, and correctly as it turned out, assumed that they would be the members of the FBI taking over their case. Especially as they both seemed to dismiss Officer Stillwell's account of how they'd been found, and their circumstances, with a mere nod of the head and indicated that the two boys were to immediately come with them. Wrapping the blankets tightly around themselves as they left the interview room, Skylar and Cooper followed, almost eagerly, after the two FBI agents; at the same time, also well aware of the curious looks that they were getting from others in the building.

Once outside, they were directed towards a large dark-coloured car and ushered into the back seat. To their immediate dismay, Vittorio was already seated inside and obviously waiting for them.

"You two are certainly going to regret trying to make an escape," he hissed as he quickly handcuffed each of them and ran a connecting chain around a bar between the front and back seats to prevent the possibility of another attempt to escape. "I don't like it when my property doesn't do as it's told! Especially when I have to cut short an 'entertainment'."

***

Skylar rolled over a little cautiously, as he felt a hand gently touch his shoulder. It was Noah, holding a cup of water. Skylar winced as he sat up to take the cup in his handcuffed hands so that it wouldn't spill. Even that small action proved difficult, because he hurt all over, it seemed.

"Here, drink this," Noah murmured, as he helped Skylar get a proper hold of the cup. "I've also got you some biscuits and a snack bar."

Skylar took a sip of water and looked across to where Cooper was still quietly sobbing, his handcuffed hands hiding his eyes as he lay huddled up on another of the mattresses. Peter was, likewise, trying to coax him into sitting up to have something to eat and drink. The marks of the severe beating he'd received stood out very clearly on the areas of his rather pale skin that were visible.

"I know it looks bad, and it still hurts like hell, but you both got off rather lightly," Noah murmured, as he seemed to be aware of where Skylar was looking. Skylar shook his head, trying to figure out how getting thirty vicious strokes of a wide leather strap, in beatings that had covered them from the middle of the back all the way down to the back of the thighs, could be considered 'light'.

"How?" he murmured a little cynically, even as he half-guessed the gist of the boy's comment. Noah responded with a shake of his head.

"If it hadn't been that Vittorio is keeping you two as a part of that special 'innocent' group he's been going on about, he would have used something far more vicious than just a strap. And he might not have stopped at just giving you a leathering," he said softly.

Skylar quickly understood what the boy meant. He was still 'innocent', and that was something for which he could be thankful. Cooper, likewise. Nevertheless, the punishment that they'd received had not only been painful, but extremely humiliating in that it had been carried out in front of all the other captives, as a warning to all of them to not be so foolish as to try to abscond.

After being returned to Vittorio, he and Cooper had then been taken back to the holding house and kept in handcuffs. It was then that he and Cooper had found out the purpose of the hooks on the wall. Once their handcuffs had been secured over them, so that their toes only just touched the floor, they were left hanging… still dressed in just their 'display' attire.

Despite the fact that the boys often showered communally, and so were quite used to seeing each other undressed, their humiliation had been further increased when, after the other children had arrived back for their 'assignment', all of them, both boys and girls, had been ordered to the basement room to witness the punishment of the two 'runaways'.

Vittorio had then punished them quite viciously, as much as an example to the other children as to Skylar and Cooper. Taking a 'run-up' of a couple of steps for the delivery of each hit. Alternating between each of them for a total sixty strokes… thirty each. The strokes being delivered in lots of five, so that they each had a short time to reflect on their pain while the other boy was punished, before facing more torture. While the majority of the leathering was across their behinds, some strokes also ranged from the middle of the back to the thighs, leaving the whole area not only well reddened but also covered in welts. Their 'display wear' providing scant protection from the viciousness of the punishment.

For Skylar it was a reliving of the nightmare he'd suffered at Pastor Isaac's boot camp and, just like Cooper, he'd screamed, pleaded and sobbed for the entire duration of the chastisement. Begging for the brutality to end. Afterwards, when their punishments had been completed, and the girls had been returned to their quarters, they'd simply been left fastened to the hooks for the rest of the night. Stretched out almost on tiptoe, until their legs and arms also ached and throbbed. Unable to do anything at all to alleviate their hurt and humiliation, and knowing, from Vittorio's last instructions, that for any of the other boys to get them down, or offer them help in any way, would only invite further vicious punishment… for them and whoever assisted them!

In the morning, Vittorio had inspected the welts and bruises that had resulted from their punishment and had decided, after advising them of what could still happen if they continued to be disobedient, that he felt that neither of them required further physical chastisement. After which, they'd been released from the hooks, and allowed to go to sleep. Perhaps, Skylar surmised, it was more that Vittorio didn't want them to still be too badly marked when it came time for their next 'entertainment' session. More especially as he seemed to gain some perverse sense of satisfaction out of stating to the prospective buyers at the 'entertainments' that his 'merchandise' was always 'unblemished' and 'obedient'. Making it obvious that, much in the way that child slaves who were destined to be offered for sale in past times were not whipped, but paddled, so that did not have visible indications of being disobedient, he certainly didn't want marks of any recent punishment session to be too visible to his clientele. Not unless such a punishment was to be part of the entertainment. For which discipline he always preferred to use a flat, wooden paddle that stung, and quickly reddened the skin, without leaving discernable bruises or welts!

Nevertheless Skylar still felt rather humiliated in that, while all the other boys were now dressed in jeans and T-shirts, he and Cooper had to remain in their display wear, and still in handcuffs, with the marks of punishment on display as a warning for everyone to see. Thankfully, while sleeping, they were at least allowed a blanket as extra cover. They were destined to remain like that for the rest of the day, or at least until Vittorio felt absolutely sure that they'd properly learnt their lesson and wouldn't, in the future, be likely to cause any more problems.

***

Rylan tried to avert his gaze as he sensed that he was being closely watched. The dark-skinned man with an ostentatious assortment of bling — a swag of gold chains around his neck and what looked like seriously expensive diamonds in various piercings in his ears — who'd followed him into the McDonalds, had not bothered to join any queue in order to acquire a meal, but simply seemed content to sit at a booth and observe him from a distance. Watching as Rylan had made his food order, waited for it to be readied, and had then retreated to a vacant booth reasonably near to the bathrooms. Rylan felt decidedly uncomfortable at the man's scrutiny, because his intentions and manner seemed furtive; the complete opposite to that of the police officer who'd suspected him of truancy. There was nothing of the belligerent officiousness of those previous encounters, where the police officer had simply confronted him, quite directly. This man's manner seemed far more sinister; more like a silent snake, or a fox, menacingly stalking its prey; waiting for an opportune moment to pounce.

Wary of what had happened when he'd been followed by a group of teenage boys, a couple of weeks earlier, Rylan decided to stay where he was for a moment. It was unlikely, he reasoned, given the security guard by the door, that the man would cause him any problem while inside the place. In which case, there seemed no sense in going outside where there would be a lesser chance of someone coming to his assistance if the man did try something untoward.

He continued eating. Trying to ignore the growing sense of danger that he felt, by keeping his focus steadfastly on his food and on the table in front of him. A movement caught his eye as the dark-skinned man suddenly moved closer. Quickly sliding into the seat on the opposite side of the booth.

For a minute or two, the man said nothing; just sat there watching him. Nevertheless, Rylan couldn't help but feel even more nervous about his presence and of being the focus of such close scrutiny. Casting a quick look about, he thought of simply picking up his food and heading to the bathrooms, but then felt uneasy about disappearing so blatantly. Especially as he sensed that the man might simply follow him. An inner sense seemed to tell him that it would be unwise to get caught in a confined area with someone exuding such a sense of menace.

"You with your parents?" the man suddenly hissed. Rylan kept his gaze lowered and made no reply. Nevertheless, his lack of response seemed to supply the answer that the man required.

"I thought not!" he murmured. He took out his cell phone and quickly took a snapshot of Rylan. Not that there was too much to see, given that Rylan, as usual, had kept the hood on his jacket up, and forward, to try to keep his face from being seen and perhaps recognised by anyone who might know his parents and inform them of his whereabouts.

"If you're a runaway, I can help you?" the man suddenly whispered, his voice low and almost conspiratorial. "I look after lots of young kids who're runaways." Again, Rylan did not reply but, having finished his Big Mac, took a quick sip of his frozen coke and then started nibbling from his cardboard carton of fries.

"You'll be needing my help kid, if you want to survive on the streets," the man suddenly hissed, reaching out a hand to grab at Rylan's wrist. "And I know you're on your own, 'cause I already seen the police try to take you in." Rylan quickly twisted his hand free of the man's grasp.

"I can give you a place to stay and a chance to earn some money," the man whispered, his voice suddenly quite stern. Yet again, Rylan gave no hint that he'd even heard the suggestion.

"You need me!" the man added. In some ways sounding as if he was not used to his offers being refused, or simply ignored. Or perhaps it was just that he felt that having a heavy-handed manner would be more likely to create acquiescence in a child he hoped to acquire. Rylan continued to ignore him and simply picked up his frozen coke drink once again. Ready to throw it in the man's face if he again tried to grab him. Figuring that doing so would immediately gain everyone's attention and allow him the chance to escape to the bathrooms. If he could get there, without being grabbed, and before the man could follow, he could simply disappear. Looking sideways however, he suddenly noticed George wandering slowly by, outside the window beside the booth. With a plastic bag casually dangling from each hand, he appeared to be on his way home.

"I gotta go!" Rylan said, as he hurriedly gathered up his drink and his cardboard packet of fries. "I gotta meet someone!" Leaving the man a little surprised by his sudden burst of activity, he slipped from his seat, hurried out the door and called George's name. The old man turned and immediately stopped to wait for him.

"Well, Rebel," murmured George, when Rylan reached where he was waiting. "I see you got yourself a bit of a feed." Rylan quickly handed him the remainder of the fries.

"There's a man in there who I don't like the look of," he said, glancing back towards the McDonalds. "I think he wants to grab me, or something," he added. Quickly noticing that the dark-skinned man had followed him outside, but now remained just outside the main doors, still just watching him. George shifted one of the bags he was carrying over to his other hand to make it easier to grab the packet of fries. He glanced surreptitiously around as he did so, without making it seem that he was actually looking towards where the dark-skinned man was waiting.

"He's definitely not someone you ever want to get mixed up with," George murmured, before giving Rylan both of his bags to carry, so that he could eat the fries more easily.

"He's scary," Rylan whispered in reply as he then looped both the bags over the crook of one arm so that he could still hold his drink. "He kept saying that I needed his help and that he could help me get money and give me a place to stay, but there's something about him that I don't trust."

"I think your senses are giving you the right feelings, Rebel," George murmured as he grabbed another fry in his grubby fingers and quickly swallowed it. "TakerZ is a pimp of the worst kind. He gets young girls, and some boys, working for him, if you gets what I mean, and takes most of their money. Once you're with him, you don't get to leave. Well, at least, not without some real hassle. You must stay well clear of him... and others like him."

"But what if he follows us?" Rylan whispered, already noting that TakerZ had moved a little closer to where they were standing. "He'll find out where I'm hiding."

"I got ways to lose them sort," George murmured. "You just stick close." They started walking. Trying to appear casual and unconcerned, even 'though Rylan felt an intense nervousness in knowing that the dark-skinned man was still following them. He worried that, if the man just decided to grab him, would George actually be able to help? After all, he wasn't a young man and at times seemed a little frail.

For a short while, they simply wandered along on the sidewalk. Fully aware, however, that the pimp was still following at a discreet distance, until George turned rather abruptly into a shop doorway, dragging Rylan with him with a free hand.

"This way," he muttered quite casually, almost as if they were just going shopping. Once through the doors, they headed a small way into the dimly lit shop. It took a moment or two for Rylan's eyes to adjust to the subdued lighting.

"Afternoon, George," a woman behind the counter a short way into the shop suddenly intoned rather wearily. "I see you got a little follower today?" George nodded.

"This is Rebel," he muttered glancing back towards the doorway. "He's a kid I'm keeping an eye on. Unfortunately, he's started to attract a bit of interest from TakerZ, if you catch my drift. That lowlife's been following us ever since we passed the McDonalds." The woman seemed to give Rylan a quick once-over. Perhaps, like many others, at first just a little confused by his androgynous appearance, but fully understanding of George's concerns for the child in front of her... whatever gender it might be.

"I take it you need to lose that 'son of a bitch'," she murmured, also glancing towards the door and raising her eyebrows rather knowingly. George nodded. The woman, in response, gave a slight sideways nod of her head that seemed to indicate that they should proceed further into the shop. She then quickly wandered over to the door to the shop and closed it; turning around the 'open' sign to read as 'closed' to anyone outside. It would be just a temporary closure to ensure that George and Rylan got a head start on their follower.

Taking Rylan's hand, George led him to the back of the shop, through a small kitchen area and then out through a rather sturdy door. Rather than being back on a street, however, Rylan was surprised to find that they were now in a rather small, fully enclosed courtyard. After a slight hesitation, George then headed diagonally across the small space to another door and then led Rylan up a series of stairs, across a strange enclosed walkway, down a maze of several corridors, and finally down some stairs. After that, they seemed to move from building to building, by various unexpected turns, all with an air of George knowing exactly where he was headed, even as voices were heard from various rooms around them. Occasionally, they'd pass by people who would casually nod to George and appear to regard Rylan's being with him with mildly bemused curiosity. Quietly understanding that there was nothing untoward in what they were seeing. The old man was simply helping someone out of a difficulty.

On unbolting and opening a final door, Rylan was surprised to find that they were now on the opposite side of the alley from where an open door had eventually led him to his sixth-floor hiding place when he'd first escaped from the police. He glanced to his left towards the wooden fence and its small gap; the hole through which he'd scrambled in order to evade capture. With a quick glance towards the busy street at the other end of the alley, George hurried him across the alleyway and after a bit of fumbling with some strange sort of key, through the same door that Rylan had used when he'd first arrived.

"I'd suggest you stay well-hidden for a while," George murmured, eventually directing Rylan towards the stairs that led up to his sixth-floor hideout. "For at least a day or two. If you do have to venture out, for any reason, I'd also avoid going anywhere near that particular McDonalds, if I were you. Taker Z will be keeping an eye out for you, of that you can be sure. If you stay out of sight, I'll try to get you some extra food to keep you going for the next couple of days."

CHAPTER NINE

A Coincidence....

Lara looked across the pool complex to where Matthew and Melanie were, as usual, sitting side-by-side on the steps that were part of the little alcove leading off the main pool, holding hands. Not that there was any sense of jealousy in her gaze. Since her rescue, Tris was totally her 'Prince Charming', as it were, even if he still seemed more than a little reticent about indulging in such innocent displays of affection with her. There was also the consideration that everyone else seemed to assume that, because they both had wings and were of a similar age, and now seemed to go everywhere together, that they were, by a vague extension of that idea, obviously 'boyfriend and girlfriend'. Perhaps, in some way, she figured that they were also correct in that assumption, even if Tris hadn't quite realised it as yet. She continued watching. Feeling a sudden small sense of delight when Tris, perhaps sensing her feelings, seemed to timidly reach for her hand; touching it for a few moments, before quickly withdrawing his hand.

"Carwyn said something rather funny the other day," she eventually said rather softly. "He said that when you first rescued Matthew, it was because his stepdad thought he was gay, but now he isn't. How does that work out?" Tris sighed softly.

"He was a bit mixed up, when he first came here," he replied. "His stepdad had confused him a fair bit by taunting him about it. Like, I think Matthew wasn't too sure about it all, but his stepdad kept telling him that he walked and talked like he was… you know… gay, and then started punishing him for it, which just got him even more confused. So much so, that I think he started worrying that maybe other people could see something different about him, but, at the same time, he didn't know what it was. Then, when I rescued him, I think it was also difficult because, for a while, he was still a bit uncertain about whether we were just friends or if he was..." Tris shrugged, leaving the sentence unfinished.

"You mean, he thought he was in love with you?" Lara queried a little bemusedly. Tris gave another slight shrug of his shoulders.

"I don't think it was actually like that," he murmured, even as he blushed a little in embarrassment. "It was more because I was... like... his only real friend for a while. Especially after I got him away from his stepdad and he ended up staying up at the farm." He didn't bother to mention that the situation was, in some way, reciprocal, in that Matthew had also been, at that time, 'his' only friend. "Later on, we got his mum there as well. They seemed happy being at the farm, but then Mykael and Mr Robertson arranged for them to come and live on the island, mainly because Matthew didn't ever want to go back to Oakton. Not when everyone in his church had heard the nasty things that had been said about him, and seen a video of him getting punished. Then, when he came to the island, on the first day of school, he met Melanie... and... well..." He gestured towards the far side of the pool. Any other explanation was rather unnecessary.

"So what was so bad about the video that he didn't want to go back home?" Lara asked. Tris exhaled softly.

"It showed him getting beaten. Like, strapped across the bare backside," he explained. "Like, with him half-naked! And screaming and pleading for it to stop, because of how much it hurt!"

"And his stepdad did that to him? And videoed it?" Lara exclaimed, somewhat shocked.

"Along with a couple of other men, one of whom was actually the pastor of a church in Oakton. He was in charge of the camp where it all happened. They used to get the parents to send their kids to a 'boot camp' where they 'disciplined' them. It was, supposedly, to teach them right from wrong, but instead of having just physical discipline, like marching and exercises, they were really just using the camp as an excuse to film the children getting punished with straps and paddles and stuff. They were then selling DVDs of what they'd done to each kid, through the Internet."

"So how did you get involved in it all?" Lara asked. "You know, like, how did you find out about what was happening with Matthew?"

"I had to go to Oakton because my real mum's sister tried to make a claim to adopt me," replied Tris. "And then it turned out that her husband was the same pastor who was running the boot camp. Pastor Isaac and my auntie were trying to make it so that I had to live with them, 'cause, as you know, Mum and Dad... like, Joshua and Amanda, are really just my Godparents. They adopted me after I came out of hospital after the plane crash. My real mum and dad had stipulated that in their wills, because they knew I liked coming here."

"So you weren't with them when they died?"

"I was," Tris replied. "But for some reason I survived."

"You survived a plane crash?" Lara exclaimed with some astonishment.

"Yeah. And I was the only one who did," murmured Tris. "That's why I ended up being called the 'miracle child'. Only, I didn't have wings back then."

“They grew later?” Lara queried. Tris nodded. Feeling sure that he’d explained all about the wings part to Lara at some previous time.

“Yeah,” he murmured. “Anyway, getting back to how it all worked out. When I went to Oakton, I met Matthew and his friends at the local mall and then ended up going to his school. We, sort of, became friends, even ‘though I was only there for just a few days. I think it was more because he realised I was a bit lonely. Like, what with me being new to the area. I suppose, in a way, he was too, because the friends he usually hung out with were all in other classes at school, and I was put in his class. I mean, I wasn’t going to be there all that long, because Mykael was already working out a way to get me back here and yet make it seem as if I was dead, so my auntie wouldn’t ever try to get me back again.”

“And did that happen?” Lara asked. Tris gave a further quick nod.

“Yep,” he continued. “Mykael arranged it so that, after I’d been there for just a week, there was a tornado that he could use to have me disappear. I had to ride my bike into where it was, while pretending to get away from it, so that he could make it seem as if I’d got caught up in it.”

“Wasn’t that dangerous?” Lara exclaimed. Having lived all her life in America, she was well aware of the dangers that tornados presented to both people and property. Tris responded with a semi-casual shrug. The whole episode had not seemed all that dangerous at the time… just incredibly noisy, and horribly wet and windy.

“It probably looked that way,” he muttered. “At least to anyone who didn’t realise what was really happening. But Mykael and Ithuriel and a whole lot of other angels created this sort of weird bubble of air within the tornado so that I was quite safe.

I had to let my bike, and my school backpack and jacket and shoes and stuff go off in the tornado so that they'd be found a bit later. Like, when people started searching for me. Then I ended up staying at the farm with Grandma and Granddad for a few days while Mum and Dad went over to Wichita to pretend to help search for me. Eventually, the police, and everyone else over there, just decided that I must be dead, even 'though they never found a body."

"But your mum and dad knew you weren't, obviously?" Lara said with a nod of her head, in essence making the question rather rhetorical.

"Of course," Tris replied. "They knew I was staying up at the farm. But they had to put on a big act of being upset and angry that I was missing, and most probably dead because my aunt and uncle hadn't taken proper care of me."

"And what happened then?" Lara queried. "Like, how did you meet up with Matthew again?" Tris gave a shrug.

"Some things happened to me back here which meant that I ended up in a coma," he murmured, glossing over all the problems that had actually occurred, to avoid having to mention about the influence Ahaitan had begun to exert on him, perhaps deciding that it wasn't a time to frighten Lara with further stories of turned angels and demons. "Anyway, afterwards, I didn't remember anything about what had happened to me. Like, my going to Oakton, or the tornado, or being with my aunt and uncle, or anything. I didn't even remember getting my wings. Nothing at all of what had happened since the plane crash. At least, not until late one night when I woke up and sort of heard Matthew making a prayer to be saved from getting hurt. It was sort of similar to what I did with you. But then, when I got him back here, because of my having been in a coma, while he knew who I was, I had no idea whatsoever of who he was. Even though we'd met up in Oakton, and I'd been in his class for a few days."

"So then you started to figure it all out, I presume?" Lara said, canting her head a little to one side as she also gave a slight shrug.

"Yes," Tris sighed. "I began to realise that there were a lot of things that I'd forgotten about, or that had been erased from my memory. Some good, some not so good." He paused a moment, remembering some of the bad things that he'd been told that he'd done, the problems he'd created for everyone, and the way he'd been ostracised by almost everyone on the island except Amanda, Joshua, Andrew, his grandparents, and Carwyn. "Anyway," he eventually continued, "Mykael decided that Matthew had to go back to Oakton. I was upset about that, of course, because he was my only friend at that time, but then Mykael sort of hinted that that was how it had to be for things to work out properly. I didn't want to understand that, of course. But then, when Matthew's stepdad and Pastor Isaac started on at him about him being gay, and said he was going to be sent to the camp, I ended up rescuing him again."

"How did he know to call for you?"

"I had visited him a couple of times, after that first rescue. It turned out that his stepdad had been mistreating him every time his mum was away. He was pretty upset about that, so I told him to just call to me for help if he ever really needed it... the same way you did. That ended up being when he was being humiliated at the church and was about to be sent to the camp, for even more severe punishment. He was even made to wear a yellow dress in front of the whole congregation and they all chanted about sending him to the boot camp. I stayed invisible and went with him, so that I'd know where it was, and then took him to the farm. That's why Granddad made that funny comment when I first took you to the farm."

"You mean, about 'this one not being comatose?"

"Yeah. Because when I took Matthew to the farm, he was unconscious from 'be'ing and was still wearing the yellow dress. So, at first, everyone thought he was a girl. Anyway, afterwards, when Matthew was safely in bed, I decided to do a bit of a spying to find out what was at the camp; sort of like we all did with Mykael at the military base. That's when I worked out that they actually filmed all the punishments, and other stuff, and had DVDs of it for sale through the dark web."

"DVDs of Matthew?" Lara queried, looking across to where Matthew and Melanie seemed almost close to exchanging a kiss.

"Well, no. They were still just setting that one up. Like, getting ready to film it. But there were quite a few of other kids, and they were all similar. The DVDs would have a picture of the kid on the front cover, sort of smiling, but then, when you opened it up, the picture on the actual disc always showed a back view of them, naked and all bruised from being beaten. They'd have words written on the back of the cover about what the kid had supposedly done wrong, and the kid's name on the front of the video. Like, there was one was of a kid called Skylar, who looked a bit like Finn Wolfhard from Stranger Things. He'd supposedly been sent to the camp just because he'd sneaked out his bedroom window one night to hang around with some older kids. Another was of a girl, Julia, I think her name was, who'd got caught smoking dope. The worst one was of a kid called Rylan. Matthew knew him from school and said that he really was gay… like really gay! What they did to him at the camp... well, what they filmed of it anyway... was really nasty, but now, no one knows where he is. After being sent to the camp...

"Have you got a picture of him?" Lara suddenly interrupted. "Of Rylan?"

"Not here," replied Tris a little bemusedly. "Why?"

"Because my brother's middle name was Rylan. I just wondered if it might be him. You have to admit, it is an unusual name, and if he was at school with Matthew the age would be about right."

"Well, I didn't ever actually meet him, like, face to face, but..." Tris began and then paused. Suddenly realising whom it might have been that Lara had reminded him of, when he'd first rescued her.

"But you don't have a picture of him? Like, here?" Lara asked. Tris shook his head.

"No. But Mr Watters will still have all the pictures on his computer," he quickly continued. "He's even got copies of the original DVDs."

"Can we go and see them?" Lara queried. Tris looked a little bemused at the suggestion.

"I don't think it would be a good idea for us to see the DVDs," he murmured. "They're not very nice. Anyway, Mr Watters probably wouldn't let..."

"I don't mean the actual DVDs," Lara interrupted, with almost the hint of an amused laugh at the preposterousness of the idea. "I just want to see the picture you said was on the DVD cover. You know, the picture of Rylan." Tris quickly nodded an understanding of what she was suggesting.

"Oh. That shouldn't be a problem," he hastily replied.

"Can we go now?" asked Lara.

"Sure," replied Tris almost eagerly. He reached out for her hand, knowing that it would be no surprise to the others in the swimming complex if they just vanished. "I suppose, now that you no longer have your GPS tracking necklace, I should also properly introduce you to the shopkeeper and the one or two other people over in the village at the same time. Like, the ones that do know about me and all the other angels. I mean, they do know about you and have seen you at the meetings Mykael had, but this would be properly meeting them." He paused a moment and looked around the complex. "But you'll need to keep your wings hidden until I tell you it's okay to show them. Not everybody in the village knows about us angels, obviously. Just a few people that we know we can trust."

***

"So what do we have here?" Hugh Gibbs asked, as Tris, having checked that the shop was empty, made himself and Lara visible. The elderly shopkeeper hurried over and locked the front door to the shop. He then quickly pulled down the shades and turned the sign around to indicate that the shop was closed for a lunch break.

"This is Lara," Tris quickly explained. "My new sister." He quickly turned to Lara "And you can show your wings in here if the door is locked. Mr and Mrs Gibbs know all about us angels."

"So we're privileged to have a visit from the newest little angel on the island," Hugh Gibbs responded with a broad smile. "A beautiful little girl this time." He turned towards the doorway that led to the living quarters. "Gladys, we have special visitors," he called. He turned back to Tris and Lara. "She's just packing for our second honeymoon," he softly continued. "Steve Robertson is paying for it and the Watters have said that they'll look after the shop for us while we're away." A moment or two later, the Robertson's old housekeeper, came hurrying into the room.

"It's so good to see you, Tris," she gushed, before quickly turning her attention her attention to Lara. "And you're the new one. Lara, isn't it?" she asked with a smile.

"Yes," replied Lara a little cautiously. "Tris's parents have adopted me."

"And you have wings too, I see," replied Gladys, in a statement of the obvious.

"I rescued her from the Americans," Tris said rather proudly. "Like Mykael said at the meeting, she was being held captive in some secret military hospital."

"So, is there something that you would like from the shop?" Hugh Gibbs keenly queried. Both Tris and Lara immediately glanced towards the section of the counter that held the containers of sweets.

"We'll call in a bit later for some, if that's okay," Tris replied. "We've actually come over to the village to have an important talk with Mr Watters. We think we might have found out something about Lara's twin brother."

"Well, you've probably timed it right," said Hugh Gibbs with a smile, as he glanced at his watch. "He should just about be closing up for the mid-afternoon. Opening again at about five. But you'd best check before you go running in there with your wings showing. Even as an ex-policeman, he doesn't always keep too strictly to the hours."

"Will do," Tris advised. He turned to Lara. "We can either 'be' to Mr Watters place, or give you another test of wings invisibility by walking there," he continued, making his wings disappear. Lara hastily did the same.

"You may as well give the village something new to talk about," Hugh Gibbs added with a smile, as he unlocked the front door and quickly turned the sign around to say that he was open for business. "A new child on the island is always a handy source of gossip, for some. Even if they don't know the full truth of the matter."

Taking Lara by the hand, Tris led her out onto the street to walk the few doors to the newly renovated public house, aware that their progress was being watched by a few of the elderly villagers, who were perhaps already wondering why they hadn't seen the two children arrive by boat, or on the bus. Reaching the public house, they entered and spotted Colin Watters in the process of wiping clean a couple of the tables.

"Just head yourselves upstairs," the ex-police Detective Sergeant said rather casually, and almost without looking up, not seeming fazed by the two unexpected arrivals. "If you could ask Alice to put on the kettle, I know I could just murder a cup of tea."

***

A short while later, after the obligatory cups of tea, with hot chocolate for Tris and Lara, they were seated in the ex-detective sergeant's study.

"What we came to ask was if you still had those photos from the covers of those DVDs that I got from Oakton?" Tris quietly asked. "You know, the ones from the boot camp."

"They'll be in a file somewhere here," Colin Watters replied, gesturing towards the shelves above his work-desk. "Any particular reason why you need to see them?"

"Lara wants to see the one of Rylan," Tris hastily explained.

"I think he might be my twin brother," added Lara softly. Colin Watters looked at her with a hint of surprise.

"Your twin brother?" he queried. He gave her a quick scrutiny, then stood and quickly began sifting through some boxes on one of the upper shelves.

"My brother's first name was actually Lawrence," Lara explained. "But he hated it and always used his middle name. Which was Rylan."

"And you think that this Rylan might just be your brother?" Colin Watters queried, as he seemed to locate the small flat box he was looking for and placed it on the desk

"When Tris mentioned that the boy in the video was rather gay, I just thought it might be him. Because I think that's why my foster parents didn't want him. Even though I haven't seen, or heard anything about him for about four or five years. I mean... the name's unusual enough for it to possibly be him."

"Well, here they are," announced Colin Watters, as he pulled a manila envelope out of the box. "Now, let's see if it is a face you remember." He pulled the photos out of the envelope and offered the one of Rylan to Lara. "Does that ring any bells?" he asked. Lara looked at the face for a moment.

"It looks a bit older than I remember him, but I think it is," she eventually murmured rather softly. Tris looked at the photograph for a moment, and then at Lara, suddenly remembering an instance of seeing a long-haired boy sitting on his own in the Oakton Middle School student cafeteria and immediately realising why Lara's face had seemed vaguely familiar when he'd first brought her home.

"So... so, he... he's your twin?" he half-stammered. Lara tilted her head slightly.

"Well, we're not totally identical, or anything," she said softly, giving the photo further scrutiny. "Otherwise he'd be a girl..."

"He's seriously gay, according to all the kids in Oakton," Tris countered with a wry smile. "Maybe that's close enough."

"I know," Lara replied with a soft exhale of breath and a slight, almost resigned, shake of her head. "As I said, I think that's why my foster-parents decided not to adopt him as well as me, because, even when he was five, he seemed to be a bit that way, if you get my drift. So I think, in the long run, it was simply because they didn't want to risk taking on that sort of problem. You know, of adopting a boy who might eventually cause them considerable embarrassment when he got older. We wanted to stay together, of course, but the Holts didn't want him. I was really upset when I had to leave without him."

"So did you see him after that?" Tris questioned. Perhaps pre-empting the question that Colin Watters was also about to ask. Lara gave a slight shrug.

"It was... sort of, difficult," she replied. "A couple of weeks after I went with the Holts, they suddenly changed their minds about adopting him. I think it was because they realised that I was really upset about us being separated. But when they went back to the adoption agency in Boston, they found that Lawrence had already been placed with some other people. After that, it was supposed to be arranged that we would get to spend some time together every few weeks, but then, when we did, it always seemed pretty stressful for us to have to separate, afterwards. Especially, because each time we'd only see each other for, like, just an hour or so, and even then, for some weird reason, we were never allowed to be alone, together. But then, the people who had Lawrence decided to move from where they were living and go west, somewhere. You know, like, move to another state, so we didn't get to meet, after that. What was weird was that no one even bothered to tell me they were going to shift, or where they'd actually gone to when they did. All I was eventually told was that Lawrence's parents had left Holyoke and moved somewhere out of the state. My foster-parents then just decided it was probably for the best. I think it was because they felt that Lawrence was being difficult, what with him already refusing to answer to Lawrence when we were together, and with how he was developing with his sexuality; like, always wanting to play dress up, especially when his parents came to our place in Fitchburg and he could try on some of my clothes.

"The name change being the reason why he ended up being called Rylan?"

"That was totally his choice. As I said a moment ago, it was his middle name. He always preferred it to Lawrence, which he absolutely hated for some weird reason… especially when it got shortened to Lawrie. I think it was because of the Lara and Lawrie thing. You know, them being too similar."

"I think we need to take this to Mykael," Tris suddenly suggested. Lara looked a bit surprised.

"Why?" she asked.

"Because if Rylan's your twin, then it's possible that he's also… you know, like you and me. It's quite likely he'll be growing wings." He quickly turned to Colin Watters and handed him Rylan's picture. "Can you print off a copy of this one for us? Please. If you've still got it on your computer?"

***

"We have something we need to tell you," Tris announced a little breathlessly, as he and Lara hurried over to where Mykael was busy talking to Andrew outside the island's church.

"I've found out something about my twin brother," Lara said rather softly. "It looks like he was in one of the videos that Tris said those nasty men made at the boot camp."

"He's the gay kid, Rylan," Tris quickly added.

"Also known as Lawrence?" Mykael queried. Lara quickly nodded.

"We're twins," she eagerly replied. "Only he doesn't like to be called Lawrence." Mykael nodded sagely.

"That might explain a few things," he mused.

"We were just thinking that he might also be starting to…"

"Grow his wings," Mykael interrupted, competing the sentence that Tris had begun.

"So you already know about him?" Lara questioned, perhaps feeling even a little miffed that Mykael had not previously made mention of it.

"Not properly," Mykael replied. "I had, however, already worked out that the military group who were searching for you, were also onto something unusual when they began concentrating a search in New York for a boy by the name of Lawrence Daniels. Now, I see the connection. And you're most probably right. He could be coming into his wings. Which would be exactly why the military are looking for him. While they might not be certain that that is the case, they'd be willing to take the chance that, given what you are, he might also be something special. In the circumstances, it wouldn't have taken them too long to search out your adoption records and talk to the Holts about the circumstances of your adoption."

"It could also be that they might want to try using him to entice Lara to come to them," Andrew added. "Especially now that it appears that they've given up on most of their searching out GPS signals."

"So are we going to find him?" asked Tris eagerly. Mykael gave a slight nod of his head.

"Gabriel, Raphael, Illyriel, and I are still fairly tied up with the Middle East problem at the moment," he replied, giving a rather weary shake of his head. "So many misguided fools who misinterpret their holy wisdom and then think that killing innocents is a way to a better life," he mused almost to himself. He gave a further sigh. "I suppose, for a start, it'll have to be up to you lot to sort out," he added turning to Andrew. "Particularly with your skill in being able to see and sense angels. Ithuriel should also be available to help, when he's finished with organising the 'Lara' sightings, and you could always call on Conlaodh or Taylor for extra support, if needed. Given Conlaodh's sensitivity, and with all the unnecessary killing of innocent children in the Middle East, I feel sure he'd rather be elsewhere occupied. The same with Taylor."

"We can help, too," Tris earnestly announced, hastily indicating himself and Lara. Mykael looked at them both for a moment.

"Without wishing to dampen your enthusiasm, we will need to be a little discrete, particularly given all the recent 'angel-sightings' of Lara over the past week or so." He looked directly at the girl-angel. "While it's unlikely that you can now be photographed, it might be a risk to take into consideration, given that you are still very much a novice with some of your abilities. If you did end up being seen in New York for example, that could likely result in even more emphasis on a search for your brother by the very people we really don't want to have finding him." Lara and Tris hastily exchanged a look.

"I can always just stay here," Lara said, perhaps more just a little despondently at the prospect of being away from Tris for a while, than for not being included in the search for her brother.

"That would probably be for the best," Mykael murmured. He turned to Andrew once again. "As for how to begin your search for Rylan, you could probably start by visiting the boy's stepfather," he suggested. "Even if he is in prison, you could still possibly find out more about the reasons why they took him to New York and whereabouts they were staying. Given that it's quite likely that Rylan's mother is still at the same address, it might just give you a bit of a head start in your search."

"We could perhaps take Tris along with us for that," Andrew proposed. "Especially if we look in on Pastor Isaac as well. Another visit from an avenging angel might just help start him talking." Mykael appeared to consider the proposal for a moment and then nodded, even if the idea of Tris as an avenging angel seemed a little amusing.

"I'll leave that to your discretion," he eventually said. "Just make sure that you keep any visit to the prison discrete. There's no sense in attracting unnecessary attention from either the prison authorities, or any other entities who'd be best kept well out of this little matter."

***

"So, how are the sightings going?" Lara eagerly asked as Ithuriel became visible at the front of the church.

"It's actually a bit of fun," Ithuriel replied, with almost an impishness that belied his status as a senior angelic guardian. "We started with one in Sweden, which was Gofraidh in your guise. Monique and Robert are now helping to make that story develop, news wise. After which we'll add a couple more in other parts of the Northern Europe when Hugh and Gladys get over there. Aerynn's currently in China, while Alexei and Tristan have since added sightings in various parts of Australia. Conlaodh and Taylor decided to make brief appearances in New Zealand, as a break from working in Syria. After that, I might get them to look at doing the same in parts of Russia, and Alexei's then going to head to Italy. All of it is, of course, creating quite a bit of Internet activity with ever-increasing arguments of biblical revelations about the 'coming of days' being refuted by counter-claims of it being 'fake news' by the usual naysayers."

"And the necklaces?" queried Tris rather impatiently. Ithuriel gave a slight shake of his head.

"That's got the military totally flummoxed, it seems," he replied. "The last we heard, they'd got some small frigate chasing a whale all around the southern oceans, and heading down towards the Antarctic, another group was tracking signals from a couple of albatrosses somewhere across the Indian Ocean, while a third group was trying to figure out how the GPS signal could be coming from a satellite that had just been placed into orbit."

"And what about Chernobyl?" Tris asked. "You know, like, where the real necklace is?"

"They seem to be avoiding that one for the moment," Ithuriel murmured. "Perhaps it's just a bit too hot for them to pursue." He grinned a little at his joke.

"You mean radioactive?" Lara quickly queried, not quite catching his attempt at humour. Ithuriel gave a nonchalant shrug of his shoulders.

"Well, that too, I suppose," he muttered. "But I was really meaning the political situation. Given the tension between the Ukraine and Russia over rebel activity and the takeover of the Crimea, I think the U.S. military don't want to be seen to be taking sides in any way, even if that's not what they intend. At the same time I think that they're starting to realise that their tracking of the GPS signals is a lost cause."

So what do you think they'll do?" Lara cautiously asked.

"Well... they already seem to be stepping up their search for your brother, according to what I overheard on a recent visit to spy on Harris McMahon," Ithuriel replied. "It seems that they think he might still be in New York, because they know that's where his mother is. And obviously, she's looking for him as well."

"So shouldn't we start looking too," Tris almost demanded. Ithuriel sighed softly.

"If they locate him, we'll soon know and can simply do a rescue," he replied. "But if you're really worried about the situation, I'll have a talk with Andrew about getting something happening. And in that regard, as Mykael suggested the other day, it might be best to start with a visit to the prison that Rylan's father is in. It could just give us a better idea of where to start looking in New York. After all, it's a pretty big place, with a lot of people and a lot of places in which one small boy could hide."

***

Rylan tensed as a hand was suddenly laid on his shoulder. Looking around, as he tried to dodge away from its grasp, he quickly saw that it was the same man who'd accosted him in the McDonalds a few days earlier. For a moment, he thought about simply disappearing to his hideout, but quickly realised that that would not be the best thing to do when he was in the midst of a crowd. He also didn't want to risk the chance that the man might teleport back with him, when there was no guarantee that he'd simply fall to the floor in a comatose state, as Xavier J. Hernandez had done.

In truth, at the first touch, he'd thought it might be the policeman. He seen the patrol car a number of times in the past few days, but had so far managed to avoid being spotted by keeping hidden within the crowd of pedestrians. Somehow, he also sensed that the police officer was definitely still keeping an eye out for him. At the same time, being arrested wouldn't be a big problem; not now that he knew that he could instantly disappear from any car, interview room, or cell into which he was placed. In fact, the idea of disappearing from a locked cell almost seemed amusing; especially giving the consternation it would create.

Nevertheless, as George had suggested, he'd been avoiding the McDonalds he'd previously gone to and was now using a Subway franchise situated quite near to one of the transport hubs to get meals. Not that he'd be able to continue doing that for too long, given that the supply of money he'd taken from Xavier seemed to be dwindling rather rapidly. After it was gone, unless he found another source of money, he would be back to scrounging in the dumpster at the back of the café, or relying on George to feed him.

"Leave me alone! You're not my father!" he quickly shouted, as he tried to squirm away from the man's grasp, the hood of his jacket slipping off his head as he did so. For a moment they simply eyed each other. With his showy assortment of bling, the man reeked of being a street gangsta of some type, or at the very least, someone of equally dubious intent. George had called him a pimp and Rylan now understood exactly what type of situation he'd end up in, if TakerZ — real name Devondre Hubert Cronfeldt — got a hold of him. Everything about the man clearly spelt danger, just as it had also done in the McDonalds when he'd first tried to coerce Rylan into going with him. Making him the sort of person that Rylan knew he had to avoid at all costs.

"You keep your hands off me!" he shouted as TakerZ reached out to grab him once again. "Help! This man is trying to hurt me! Help me!" he shouted, in the hope that it would attract the attention of others around him. For a moment, he felt the man's hand loosen its grip just a little and then start to clench a little more strongly.

"You will come with me!" TakerZ hissed half under his breath, as he fingers pinched hard into Rylan's shoulder. Rylan quickly wriggled away from his grasp for a second time, dropping the last of his food in the process. He looked around for an escape and quickly noted that a large African-American woman had suddenly seemed to notice his plight. She wasn't the only one to take note of the unexpected confrontation, obviously, but she seemed to be the only person who also seemed willing to become involved in his plight, as she waddled hastily in his direction.

Appearing to rather effectively block the path that it seemed his assailant had planned to take with him.

"Hey! You! Take your hands off that little girl, you ugly ape!" the woman yelled, as she came closer. As the man again reached out to grab Rylan, the woman got close enough to swing her large handbag against the side of the man's head, with a resounding thump. For an instant, taken by surprise by the force of the blow, TakerZ seemed a little stunned, but hastily released the tentative grip he'd had on Rylan's shoulder. A further blow from the handbag clattered into the side of the man's face, as other people in the throng finally began to be stirred into action over altercation and, perhaps persuaded into helping by the woman's actions, began to close in on the man. At the same time, Rylan felt the woman's hand grab his wrist in an almost vice-like grip.

"You come with Mama Hattie," the woman rumbled far more softly, as TakerZ gave the two of them a menacingly dark look and then hurriedly dodged away through the crowd. Perhaps anxious to avoid any close police presence that a crowd disturbance might create. "Mama Hattie take you to where you be safe." As the crowd began to slowly disperse a little, even as people still seemed to be giving him some cautious scrutiny, and wondering just a little if it was perhaps against his better judgment, Rylan let Mama Hattie lead him, in her slow waddling way, along the sidewalk. Now keen to at least have the protection of someone who, like George, seemed willing to want to help him.

After walking for about a couple of blocks, and making a couple of turns, they finally reached a shelter for the homeless that appeared, from the sign out front and the imposingly tall, stone building beside it, to be run by some church organisation. Still with his wrist in a vice-like grip, Mama Hattie quickly ushered him up the steps, with surprising grace for a woman of her size, and into the foyer of the building.

"I see you a found yourself another little stray, Hattie," the woman behind a counter just inside the door to the refuge said with a wry smile and a slow shake of her head as, still clutching Rylan by the hand, the large woman waddled into the warmth of the interior. "A bit different to the others, this one," she added.

"Colour makes no difference to me if a kid's in trouble," Hattie rumbled. "I think TakerZ was trying to add her to his collection, and there ain't no way I'm letting someone as young as this little one appears to be get caught up in his vicious ways. She'd probably be dead within a week! Especially with the nasty way he treats his girls and the scumbags he gets as clients!" She hurried Rylan into the interior of the building and into a long, narrow room that seemed to have two rows of rather basic looking beds and cabinets set out along the walls.

Mama Hattie slumped herself down on one of the beds and indicated for Rylan to sit beside her.

"This is the female room," she announced. "So you'll be safe with me for a while." She waited until Rylan was seated. "Now, girl, how about you a tell me who you are, and where you're supposed to be," she said brightly. "And don't panic, I ain't a fixing to involve the police in this. Not unless you really be awanting me to." Rylan felt a slight sense of relief, and also some amusement, at the way the Mama Hattie referred to the police with a sense of disparagement by putting an extra strong emphasis on the first syllable of the word. At the same time, he felt just a little nervous about what would happen when she found out he was a boy. He sighed, as she patted his hand lightly as if to spur him into a reply.

"My name is Rylan Daniels, and I used to live in Oakton, near Wichita. But I'm not going back there, because my dad hurts me all the time." Rylan quickly explained in almost a whisper. "And... and I'm... I'm actually a boy." Mama Hattie immediately looked at him with some surprise, at the same time cocking her head to one side for a moment and then breaking into a broad smile. Reaching out, she pushed the hood of Rylan's jacket back a little further onto his shoulders and then ran her fingers lightly through his long hair, brushing it to one side so that she could see his face more clearly.

"Well, you sure is a mighty pretty little thing for a boy," she rumbled rather softly. "And I'm a thinking that that might not be a such good thing, if you be out on the streets."

Rylan nodded, and sighed a little resignedly. Mama Hattie reached out, lightly patted his hand once again, and then seemed to study him for a moment or two.

"You know, you be looking like serious jailbait, kid. Especially to some of the low-lifes out there," she continued. "Now if that be somethin' you want, then you just stay as you are. But if you be awanting to keep safe, then I suggest that we all change how you look. Mind you, that don't mean that you be totally safe, but it might sorta lessen the odds of you a getting hurt, just a tad." Rylan shrugged a little. Something in the caring way that Mama Hattie had said 'we', regarding the comment on changing how he looked, seemed to have him feeling that, like George, she might be someone of considerable help to him.

"My parent's are probably still searching, but I don't want them to find me," Rylan said with some emphasis. "They brought me to New York to see some special psychiatrist. But he was just the same as Pastor Isaac, my dad, and the other man at the camp, 'cause I know the look in their eyes. Like, how they enjoyed seeing me without any clothes on, and seeing the welts and marks that a strap leaves on my skin. Edward J. Stanford was no different! I knew it from how he looked at me when he started taking all the photographs. He just hadn't got around to hurting me, yet."

"Well, I can tell you now, kid… TakerZ, and other low-life rubbish like him, ain't no different. They don't care who they hurt, just as long as they can gets some money off of it," Mama Hattie rumbled in response. "And to be blunt, to people like him, I don't think it would really matter whether you be a boy or a girl, if they could see a profit in it." She paused a moment, then put a hand under his chin and looked him squarely in the eyes. "You understand what I'm getting at?" she almost demanded. Rylan nodded.

"I know what that means," he whispered, trying to avoid returning her gaze. "Cause I'm... I'm... I think I'm..." He didn't want to say the word outright in case it made it seem more definite. He also worried that this woman might think less of him for being that way.

"You sure you're not just a bit too young to know that for sure?" Mama Hattie interrupted. Rylan simply shrugged.

"It's why my dad always wanted to do bad things to me," he eventually murmured.

"Even more reason for you to be kept safe!" Mama Hattie wheezed. Seeming to fully understand from his previously unfinished comment, and timid reactions, that not only was he possibly gay, but had also been abused as a result. She exhaled softly and looked around the room. "In fact, boy or not, it might be best if you sleep right here, where I can keep an eye out for you," she added, indicating the bed next to hers. "Cee-Cee can just move over one."

"I... I've got a bit of money," Rylan offered, fumbling in the side pocket of his jeans for his wallet, which still contained the little of what was left over from the money he'd taken from Xavier J. Hernandez. Mama Hattie quickly pushed his hands aside.

"I don't needs your money, Honey," she murmured and then seemed to chuckle a little at the unintentional rhyme. "You just keep a hold of that for yourself. There's no cost for you to stay here, and haircuts, now them I can also do for free. I used to have a job as a hairdresser, once," she laughed a little more loudly, her voice a rich, throaty rumble. "Least ways, until I got too big to get around the customers all that easily." Waddling over to a set of drawers beside one of the beds, she reached in and grabbed a pair of scissors, a squeeze bottle of water and a comb.

"I tend to stay in one place, nowadays," she murmured. "Doing free haircuts for those that stay here. The church don't seem to mind, 'cause I also help keep a bit of an eye on who comes into the shelter at night. We try to keep this place more family based. Don't need no winos, stoners, junkies or crack-heads messin' it up."

"Are you sure they won't mind if I stay?" Rylan asked just a little anxiously. He'd previously avoided the church shelters, feeling sure that they'd immediately notify the police, or at least someone concerned with child welfare, if he seemed to be on his own. But, somehow, he felt at less of a risk of that, given the amiable way in which Hattie's arrival at the shelter with him in tow had been viewed with an air of almost mild amusement, or perhaps bemusement, given his fairness. It immediately reminded him of what George had once said about children without parents staying in the shelters… 'those that run them will often turn a blind eye to the situation, with regard to the police and social welfare, if there's an older adult who's willing to take on some responsibility for the day-to-day welfare of a kid'.

"If you be with Hattie, it won't be a problem," the woman rumbled, seeming to understand where his thoughts had headed. "You'll just be another one of my children. Although a bit younger than most of 'em." She then beckoned for Rylan to follow her. "Come on," she said brightly, waddling across towards a doorway that seemed to lead to the kitchens and bathrooms. "If we go out the back, it'll save us having to sweep up what we cut off. Afterwards, you can help me out in the kitchens. Get you in everyone's good graces. That way, we also keep you off the streets and outa sight for a while. Taker-Z won't like it that I took you from him. So he'll certainly be on the lookout for you for the next day or so. You can bet your sweet little boots on it."

"Will he come here?" Rylan asked somewhat nervously.

"Not if I'm with you," Mama Hattie rumbled. "Mind you, I wouldn't go wandering off anyplace on your own for a while. As I just said, you can bet your boots that he'll be keeping a lookout for you. We can be sure of that. Especially for if you be alone. Now, let's get this haircut done. Afterwards, you can have a quick wash to freshen you up a bit while I sort you out some fresh clothes to wear. Hopefully, a change of clothes and a haircut might make you a bit harder to recognise."

As Rylan glanced a little nervously towards the men's bathroom, Mama Hattie seemed to follow his gaze.

"I think it might be better if you use the girl's bathroom for all your washing," she rumbled. "There's not likely to be anybody using it at this time of day. Anyway, you can always use the disability cubicle if you're worried about anyone walking in on you. Ain't nobody staying here who makes use of it at the moment, anyways. Just make sure all the women are gone before you go for a wash. Okay? We don't need any of them making complaints about you."

***

TakerZ stamped his feet to ward off the cold, as he waited, somewhat impatiently, for his phone call to be answered. He didn't usually like ringing from a public phone, but given the likelihood that the FBI, or some other crime-fighting agency, might be bugging the other end, he didn't want to use his personal cell-phone just in case the call could be traced. Much as he'd originally thought about trying to add the unknown girl to his stable, he now felt some doubts about doing so. In a way, she seemed just a bit too young for him to be able to have simply 'streetwalking'. Having her out in public would inevitably attract police attention that he certainly didn't need, and keeping her locked up somewhere would mean that she'd also have to be closely supervised, which he didn't really have time to do. Not if he wanted to be able to keep a proper check on the rest of his street-girls. At the same time, he was well aware that there were other ways of making a good bit of money from young runaways. Especially if he could sell them on to the new paedophile trafficking group with whom he'd recently made contact. A secret organisation that had recently surfaced through the Dark Web called the 'Network', who were always on the lookout, it seemed, for good-looking pre-teen runaways. Eventually the phone was answered and, for a moment or two, he quickly exchanged the usual cautious greetings that also served as passwords and a means of verifying identification.

"So what are you offering this time?" the voice on the other end eventually asked, once his credentials as a pimp and a procurer of young runaways had been established.

"I think I've seen someone that might be of interest to Vittorio,"TakerZ murmured. He kept his voice rather low so that there was little chance that his conversation would be overheard.

"Such as?" the nameless voice drawled.

"A rather pretty girl," he quickly replied. "Looks like she's definitely a runaway. She certainly seems homeless, and I've spotted her a few times just wandering the streets."

"How old?" snapped the voice, rather abruptly. "At the moment, Vittorio won't be interested in anything too mature." TakerZ thought for a moment.

"About ten or eleven I'd say, twelve at the most, and quite slender. It also doesn't look like she's into puberty, as yet, if you catch my drift. Nothing showing up top from what I've seen."

"So have you got her with you?"

"Not as yet. I almost grabbed her, earlier today, outside a Subway franchise near 53rd and 5th, but then some fat, ugly bitch interfered. Hollering and shouting at the top of her voice, fit to wake the effin' dead. Made it too public to do an easy snatch. That's who the kid's with at the moment, I'd guess."

"You still think you can get her?"

"I'll track her down easily enough. It'll be just a matter of finding out where the woman has taken her and then arranging a suitable time for the grab. Just as long as you can arrange to pay the usual amount!

"That'll depend on what she looks like."

"She's a cutie. Best I've seen in a while, in a tomboyish sort of way. And, I dare say, probably untouched."

"In that case, she could be quite useful for some special event Vittorio's got coming up."

"So when I get her, I just keep her knocked out, and then contact you?"

"Precisely. But make doubly sure she's still an innocent, okay?" the voice almost demanded. "No trying to make a little side money from her before you hand her over, or having a bit of fun with her yourself! Understand? She has to stay totally innocent and untouched. Otherwise she won't be worth anywhere near the full amount!"

"Okay, okay, don't worry," TakerZ huffed, not enjoying being talked down to in a manner that, in some ways, seemed like a reprimand. "I won't touch her. Vittorio gets first dibs. Okay?"

CHAPTER TEN

Safety Concerns....

Rylan quickly stripped out of the outermost of his 'borrowed' clothes in readiness for a shower. Over the last couple of days, and after his time in his hideout, it had felt rather nice to be able to keep clean by having a daily hot shower; even if it did mean his having to wait until all the other women in the shelter had left for the day, in order to use the female disability shower.

Having set the shower to warm up, as he'd done for the past couple of days, Rylan looked at his new image, which he liked in some way, in the bathroom mirror. Almost automatically, he rubbed his right hand gently across his scalp, feeling the softness of the inch-long stubble of his new haircut. In a way, compared with how it had been for so long, it seemed strange to suddenly have his hair so short; much like a military 'buzz-cut'. Not that it made him look tough in any way… far from it. Even Mama Hattie had murmured after she'd given him the haircut that he still looked rather too pretty for a boy.

As he turned his head from side to side, gazing at his reflected image, he even felt that he looked just a little bit like 'Eleven', the girl who could do all the strange thing with her mind that he'd seen in a recent Netflix television series when he was with the Fulchers, especially with the way the hair at the front seemed to come forward a little onto his forehead; a bit like a widow's peak.

Admittedly, his hair was a great deal lighter than Eleven's… almost white blonde compared with her dark chestnut brown.

Outside the bathroom, all was silent. He knew that Cee-cee and Mama Hattie, also known as Big Hattie, would be out there, somewhere. Most probably, in the kitchen helping with lunch preparations. Not that there would be all that many to feed. Given that it was almost lunchtime, a good number of the overnight 'guests' had, as usual, already left for the day. Many of them, however, would be back by nightfall. Once they'd finished whatever they'd had planned for the day. Even if it was simply scrounging around for cans and bottles for recycling, begging, busking, working part-time, or whatever else they could do to raise just a little extra money. That was why Mama Hattie had decided that late morning was the safest time for him to use the bathrooms.

Over the last couple of nights, none of the women had seemed to be all that put out by the presence of a young boy in the female dormitory. In some way, it seemed that whatever Mama Hattie determined was accepted without comment. And if she'd decided that Rylan would be safer sleeping in with the women and teenage girls, then that was simply how it would be. Perhaps they also felt that he was far too young to pose any sort of threat. In fact he doubted that a good many of them, more especially those who didn't tend to stay around for the day, had even realised that he was a boy, despite his short hair. Not that they ever paid him too much attention to him or questioned Mama Hattie about his being there. Most of them seeming content to just wander in at dusk, make the most of the free meal provided, and then settle down for a quiet night of playing cards, watching television in the community room, reading, or just talking quietly.

In a slightly amusing way, it had also taken Cee-Cee some puzzled moments to work out exactly what he was, when they'd first met. Partly because he'd had his hood pulled up, but also because, even with his hair so short, he still presented a rather androgynous appearance. Nevertheless, he felt pleased that she had not objected to having to shift over a bed, or even in the fact that he was a boy sleeping in the female dorm, especially as he felt safer in sleeping close to Mama Hattie. Perhaps it was that, at almost sixteen compared to his eleven years-of-age, Cee-Cee also didn't regarded him as much of a threat. At the same time, he quietly wondered how they'd all feel if they discovered his secrets… his wings and his ability to 'jump'. Whether they'd be scared and regard him as some dangerous mutant, or freak... or a... was he possibly an angel? He wasn't quite sure of that, either. That's what made it a little awkward. It was difficult to think of how other people would view you, when you didn't really know what you were, yourself.

Having checked that the water was at a nice temperature, and thankful that the disability shower in the women's bathroom had a lockable door, he quickly stripped off his underpants, tossed them onto the pile of his other clothes and stepped into the warmth of its spray. It felt invigorating to have the water sluicing over him, almost as if it somehow also washed away all his cares and worries. As he reached for the soap and began to wash, he mulled over his situation. He was safe, for the moment, as long as he stayed out of sight. He had a 'protector' in Mama Hattie, and most of the other people helping to run the shelter also seemed to care for him in some way, given the friendly way they smiled at him when he was helping in the kitchen, or doing other small chores.

Admittedly, he hadn't been out of the shelter for the past four days. Mama Hattie had advised him that, even with his new haircut and different clothes, it would be best for him to stay completely out of sight for a while. To lie low, perhaps in the hope that TakerZ would eventually decide that he'd fled the area. Admittedly, as a 'just in case' plan, he'd already made a good visualisation of the area at the back of the shelter. Memorising the view from where the backdoor opened out into the small, semi-enclosed courtyard where, on his first day in the shelter, Mama Hattie had sat him on a chair to give him his haircut.

At the same time, he hadn't felt hemmed in by not being out on the streets. Or even of not going back to his sixth floor hideout. Being safe in the shelter, even if Mama Hattie did expect him to help out in the kitchen and with other small daily chores, was certainly much better than being on his own; regardless of the fact that it meant having less privacy. Regular food, hot showers, television, the chance to wash his clothes, and the companionship of Mama Hattie and Cee-Cee certainly made life a lot more tolerable.

Having eventually finished his washing, for a few moments, he simply stood and let the water course over his wings and down his back. Noting, as he did so, that his wings now reached almost to his waist. Not quite there yet, but at the rate they were growing, he felt sure that it wouldn't be too long before it would be impossible to hide them under something as simple as a bulky jumper and a coat with a hood.

With a sigh, he reached across and shut off the shower, and then shook his arms and his head, and also ruffled his wings a little, to rid them of excess water. Having wiped the water from his eyes, he looked around and quickly realised that he'd forgotten to grab a fresh towel. For a moment he felt a sense of panic. If he simply put on his clothes and they ended up wet, Hattie would surely notice.

Rather cautiously, he opened the door to the disability shower and stepped out into the main area of the women's bathroom. As expected, there was no one else about, but unfortunately, neither was there a stack of fresh towels. Mama Hattie usually collected the towels for washing at nine-thirty and, over the last few days, he'd been tasked with supplying fresh towels for the bathrooms in the mid-afternoon, Mainly because the bathrooms were not usually required for showers for most of the middle period of the day.

Wandering over to the main bathroom door, he guardedly called out for Mama Hattie. To his relief, her reply was almost immediate.

"You be a needing a fresh towel, Honey?" she called, from somewhere in the main room, seeming to immediately sense his problem.

"Yes. I forgot to bring one with me," Rylan replied. He waited a moment, and then quickly aware of his nakedness, hurriedly retreated into the disability shower. He quickly hid behind the door; holding it open by just a small crack, feeling sure that Mama Hattie would fully understand his sense of modesty. A moment later, she waddled into the bathroom with a stack of towels. After a quick glance around, she realised where he was and came over to hand him a couple of towels through the gap in the doorway.

"Thank you," Rylan said a little breathlessly as he grabbed them and hurriedly threw one around his shoulders.

"It's no problem, Honey," Mama Hattie rumbled. "I'm just pleased that my little 'Milky Bar Kid' wants to keep himself nice and clean. Which is certainly more than you can say for some of the males who doss down in this place. At any rate, you just make sure you dry those pretty little wings properly. The ones that you've been trying to hide from me for the last three days! When you be dressed, lunch will be on the table."

Rylan stood in stunned silence for a moment, clutching the towels to his chest. Just listening as the door to the bathroom swung shut with a slight thump, leaving Hattie to slowly amble her way back towards the dining area. His thoughts were in turmoil. How had she realised that he had wings? For how long had she known? Did anyone else know? Had she told anyone else? At the same time, he felt a little puzzled. By the nonchalance of her actions, it almost seemed as if the idea of a homeless boy having wings seemed of no great consequence to her. And what on earth was a 'Milky Bar Kid'?

***

Tris looked about him, thankful that he, Andrew, Taylor and Conlaodh were still invisible. Now that Taylor and Conlaodh had finished their Lara sightings, they seemed more than ready to help out with taking part in the quest to find her brother. Perhaps that was because it certainly a more inviting proposition than heading back to the Middle East situation. The first step of this new quest was, they decided, to visit Pastor Isaac, William Daniels and Scott Ryan in prison.

Despite their not yet being close to the main area of cells, the prison still gave off a quite foreboding atmosphere. An unveiled threat of menace, violence and thuggery that seemed almost a little overwhelming. And it was not just from the captive inmates, a good many of whom seemed quite docile and cowed by their surroundings. The more threatening factors appeared to come from the belligerent stances and angrily shouted instructions of the prison guards. Their behaviour simply creating an atmosphere of barely-veiled aggression, which was also enhanced by the range of firearms clearly visible beyond the confines of the actual containment areas. To his surprise, of the few prisoners that he could see, many were in short ankle chains; a move obviously designed to prevent them from progressing anywhere at anything much above a slow shuffle.

"I wouldn't want to ever be stuck in a place like this," he whispered, moving a little closer to Andrew, as the mood of the place seemed to become palpably oppressive. "Even for just a visit."

"If you ever came here without a senior guardian, you also wouldn't be flying or 'be'ing for quite a long while, either," Andrew murmured, putting an arm protectively across his shoulders. Tris looked up at him with a quite curious expression, perhaps half-wondering why anyone would ever want come to a place like this, if they didn't have to, and also wondering how doing so could affect his abilities.

"Why?" he eventually queried bemusedly.

"Because if you did, either Mykael, or Ithuriel, would probably ground you to the island for a very, very long time," Conlaodh whispered. "No 'be'ing or flying!"

"And I dare say you might not be able to sit down too comfortably for a fair few days either," Andrew murmured.

"You just ask your Uncle Alexei how it feels to be draped over Mykael's knee for a good old-fashioned butt-warming when you're only twelve," Taylor added with a chuckle. "According to what Tristan once told me, Alexei certainly had four rather red cheeks that day."

"Let's just get on with finding Pastor Isaac," Tris muttered, once again feeling embarrassed at the thought of such punishment, or even just his being teased about the possibility of being on the receiving end of it. While he understood that they were currently in a place of confinement, and by obvious extension, punishment for serious misdemeanours, something about the place also reminded him, just a little too unpleasantly, of the viciousness and cruelty he'd suffered in the 'containment room' at the boot camp.

"I would say the pastor, and his cohorts, are quite likely to still be in isolation," Andrew mused. "Especially with how a good many of the other inmates will be feeling about the sort of activities they got up to." He gestured to the others. "You all stay here a moment, while I go and do a little reconnaissance." As he disappeared, Tris moved a little closer to Conlaodh and Taylor, feeling thankful for their protection and the fact that they were still outside the main area of cells.

In less time than expected, Andrew returned and tapped the side of his head. Almost immediately each of them had a visualisation in their head of a short corridor with rather subdued lighting. In an instant they were actually there.

"As I was sure would be the case, all three of them are still in solitary," Andrew whispered. "And as I said a moment ago, I should think that it's more for their own protection, than for any wrongdoing since they arrived."

"So who do we visit first?" Taylor asked.

"Why not start with the pastor," Andrew suggested. He nodded towards Taylor and Conlaodh. "It might even be best if we just let Tris be visible, for a start," he suggested. "No sense in making too big a show, if we don't need to."

An instant later they were all standing, still in a state of invisibility, to one side of a small, concrete cell. At one end of the room, the small window that was set up high in the wall gave a view of the sky and not much else. Beyond that, the room was very simply furnished; a small metal table with a central leg firmly attached to the floor, combined with a seat that was also attached to the table support, was set to one side of the room. Along with a toilet and washbasin in one corner and a bed that was attached to the opposite wall. Pastor Isaac, still unaware of their presence, was sitting at the table, writing in a small exercise book. Eventually, at Andrew's prompting, Tris made himself visible. Pastor Isaac looked up, seeming quite unperturbed by the unexpected appearance of a child-angel.

"You, again," he murmured almost a little wearily.

"I need to ask you about Rylan Daniels," Tris responded. Perhaps feeling that there was no point in simply engaging in small talk in such a situation. "Like, if you know anything about where he might be?" Pastor Isaac seemed to study him for a moment; his face somehow reflecting an innate sense of curiosity.

"Were you an angel when you first came to live with us?" he softly queried. "You know, with me and your Aunt Jessica?" The question took Tris a little by surprise. Nevertheless, he nodded a reply.

"That's why I needed my door locked," he added. "My wings are always visible when I'm asleep."

"And why you could not be filmed, no doubt," Pastor Isaac murmured, giving a slow shake of his head. Tris hastily nodded, deciding not to mention anything about having his guardians present at that time.

"Do you know anything about where Rylan Daniels could be?" he repeated. "It's important that he is found." Pastor Isaac gave a slight shrug.

"All I know is that he went missing when William and Molly took him to New York," he muttered. "They were supposed to be taking him to some top-notch psychiatrist to get his head sorted, but he did a runner on them, according to William." He sighed softly and nodded towards the next cell. "You'd best ask him about it, because I only know what he told me when he came back to Oakton to assist with..." he added, before leaving the rest of his comment incomplete by lapsing into a long silence.

"Do you forgive me?" he suddenly asked. Tris glanced towards the vague opaque outlines where Taylor, Conlaodh and Andrew were standing, with a look of bemusement. In response,

Andrew seemed to give a half-shrug. Tris quickly turned back to the pastor.

"That... that's not... not for me to say," he hastily stammered. "Those sort of decisions would be for angels of much greater importance than me. I just... I just need to find Rylan Daniels. It's important, because he needs my help." Pastor Isaac seemed to ponder on that revelation for a moment.

"Are you taking him to be with Matthew?" he murmured. Tris hastily nodded a reply and then quickly faded before he could be asked further awkward questions. In some ways what the pastor had asked was true. Once they'd managed to find him, Rylan would be coming to live on the island, which was where Matthew was now living. Even if many people back in Oakton firmly believed that Matthew Ryan was dead. Andrew nodded and an instant later they were all back in the corridor, with Andrew quickly indicating towards a door a little further along from where they were standing.

"We may as well see what we can get from William Daniels, next" he suggested. "I'd be tempted to think that Scott Ryan will probably know little more than the pastor, regarding Rylan."

"So how do you want to approach this?" Taylor asked. "Do we just send Tris or..." He left the suggestion incomplete. Andrew stayed silent in thought for a moment or two.

"Let's just play a few mind games," he eventually whispered. In an instant, he, Taylor and Conlaodh seemed to resemble turned angels. Their skin now had a reddish hue, which was complemented by their having jet black, leathery wings and gleaming yellow eyes. Tris looked at them in astonishment. Quickly realising that, if he hadn't already known who they were, he would've found their presence and appearance rather frightening.

"What about me?" he asked. Any thoughts that he would end up looking equally ferocious were quickly dispelled as, at a glance from the three adult angels, he was instantly transformed into an image of Matthew, complete with the little yellow dress, knee length socks, an Alice-band for his hair and T-bar shoes.

"That's not fair," he muttered, quickly pulling at the hem of the dress to ensure it fully covered the thin, nylon panties. "Why do I have to end up like this?"

"Because William Daniels thinks you're dead," Andrew whispered. "And he also knows that they had you dressed like this when they were abusing you. Your disguise will be equally as frightening to him, as how we now look. Especially when, as far as he supposes, you probably died of hypothermia out in the snow near the boot camp!" Tris gave a slight shrug.

"You might have at least warned me," he muttered. "Or at least let me wear some of Matthew's normal clothes."

"Would you prefer to appear as Williams Daniels last saw you when you were disguised as Matthew?" Andrew asked with a slightly conspiratorial smile. Tris hurriedly shook his head, even as he remembered that the man's last view of him would've been in the containment room at the boot camp; semi-naked and with a decidedly red and welt-marked bottom!

"No. It's just that..." he began, before lapsing into silence.

"Don't worry, it's all just an illusion," Taylor whispered. "Even with the way the clothes you were wearing have been transformed." Tris looked down at the dress and then fingered the material.

"You mean, this is just an illusion created from my jeans and...?" he questioned. Perhaps also keen to be away from the idea of his being seen, by anyone, in a state of undress. Taylor nodded.

"Even my underwear?" Tris queried. Again, Taylor nodded.

"Once you've got him scared, call on us to appear," Andrew murmured.

"How do I do that?" Tris queried. "Like, get him scared?" Andrew smiled at him a little conspiratorially.

"Just the ability for you to suddenly appear inside a locked cell will have him wary of you. You then just have to act as if you are angry with him for mistreating you. Understand?" Tris nodded and, again, pulled at the hem of the dress to try to make sure it covered him properly.

"Now, are you ready?" Andrew asked. Tris gave a shrug that was quickly taken as a 'yes' and an instant later all four of them were in the small room that was William Daniels' new home, and would be for some considerable time. Much as for Pastor Isaac, it was a quite sparsely furnished cell.

"Okay," Andrew whispered. "You're on first." A moment later, Tris began to become visible. Sensing something unusual happening in the middle of the room, William Daniels casually looked up from the book he was reading and then stared at Tris in horror.

"You... you... ca...can't be. You... you're dead!' he stammered, as he dropped his book and backed away on his bed towards the wall. Trying to get as far away from Tris as was possible within the confines of the room. "You can't be real!"

"Real enough to come back here whenever I want," Tris growled, in his lowest, most sinister sounding voice; quickly catching on to a further way to make Andrew's suggestion work. "And to bring friends to torment you," he added, with a glance towards the vague outlines of the adult angels. He slowly turned back to face William Daniels once again, as Andrew, Taylor, and Conlaodh made themselves visible. Tris watched the man's eyes grow even wider with fear.

"Now," he growled. "If you don't want us coming back here to torment you every night, you need to tell us everything you know about Rylan."

"Rylan?" William Daniels croaked. "I... I don't... understand? I... don't..."

"We need to capture that boy as soon as possible" Andrew interrupted, moving menacingly closer. "We know you took him to New York, so we need to know where he is and what you had planned for him. He belongs with us!"

"I... we... that is Molly and me, we just took him for some special psychiatric care because of him being... you know," William Daniels almost pleaded. "I... I wasn't going to continue to hurt him again. Not after the boot camp thing didn't work."

Andrew immediately remembered what Mykael had shown him of the recordings from the boot camp office. In particular, of William Daniels' boasting of how good it would've been to have Matthew and Rylan together on film. There had certainly been no thoughts of remorse, or of any sense of caring for the wellbeing of either of them.

"We don't need your lies!" he bellowed, the sheer force of the comment immediately causing William Daniels to cower back against the wall beside his bed; his face turned to the side; trying to avert his eyes from the demonic images confronting him, but somehow unable to do so.

"We want the complete truth!" snarled Andrew, the power of his voice seeming to come from the depths of Hell. "Not whatever you think will simply reduce your guilt!"

"It... it was all Pastor Isaac's idea that... that we should send Rylan to the boot camp," William Daniels half-croaked. "The... the kid was so obviously gay that everyone in Oakton knew it and... and then, when Pastor Isaac found out that I was already abusing him, he suggested that we could make a lot of money out of him by filming it. Like, what I was doing to Rylan, along with the beatings and stuff."

"So why did you suddenly decide to take him to New York?" Andrew demanded. William Daniels seemed to swallow nervously.

"When he came back from the camp, he was still bleeding quite badly, so we couldn't afford to let anyone see him," he said as his voice trembled. "We were also worried that if the school found out about any of it, they would call in the police and then…"

"Which would have made your previous ongoing abuse of him, beyond just the beatings, rather obvious," Andrew interrupted. William Daniels seemed to nod slightly in dejected agreement.

"Molly suggested that we put him into fulltime psychiatric care, to get him out of sight for a while," he continued. "But in the end, we didn't, because it was going to be too expensive, and, given his young age, he would have probably had to undergo a full medical check before being admitted."

"Which would have, once again, revealed the extent of your abuse of him," Andrew said sternly. Once again, William Daniels gave a cautious nod.

"It was then that were told that, if he was seriously mixed up, we should take him see to a New York specialist, by the name of Edward J. Stanford. Which is what we did so that..."

"As a means to cover up the truth?" Andrew interjected. "That not only had you been abusing him, but that you were keen to continue doing so?" They weren't questions that actually required an answer. The truth was self-evident.

"We took him to see Edward J. Stanford, but after three visits he suddenly just took off," William Daniels muttered, almost as if trying to place the blame on Rylan. "Molly's still there trying to find him, and I came back here, to Oakton, to work, because we needed the money." He reached for a note pad and hastily scribbled an address, before thrusting the sheet of paper towards Tris. “Here,” he said. “This is where Molly will be staying. You can check with her to see if she’s found anything.”

“While you’re busy writing, you may as well write a complete confession of everything you did to Rylan,” Conlaodh suggested. “And not just from his time at the boot camp. We already know all about that! We want you to write down everything that you did… from when you first started abusing him!”

“But, that would...” William Daniels began. Quickly realising that what was on the videos from the camp didn’t really show anywhere near the full extent of his abuse of Rylan. Abuses that, when added to his present sentence, would probably have him jailed for life!

“We can always pay you more, rather less friendly, visits?” snarled Conlaodh with an air of menace that totally belied his usual quite gentle nature. “And bring more of our ‘friends’!” As the three demons seemed to crowd closer to him and take on even more hideous appearances, William Daniels opened the note pad he’d used to scribble down Molly’s New York address and picked up a pen. For almost fifteen minutes, the four angels watched in silence as he hastily scribbled out a testimony of all the abuses he’d inflicted upon his adopted son, prior to making arrangements with Pastor Isaac to take Rylan to the boot camp, and also a full catalogue of the abuses he’d enacted upon him there and afterwards.

“Now sign it, and date it!” Andrew demanded when he seemed to have finished. “And add that you wish to have this confession of your abuses against Rylan taken into consideration… as a means of properly clearing your conscience and atoning for your sins.” William Daniels hastily complied, and then handed him the confession. With glances towards Taylor, Conlaodh and Tris, Andrew indicated for them to fade into invisibility.

Once in the corridor, Andrew, Taylor and Conlaodh quickly reverted to their proper forms, leaving Tris still as an image of Matthew… little yellow dress and all.

"Hey," Tris immediately clamoured. "I don't want to stay like this." Andrew glanced at Taylor and Conlaodh, as they all seemed to grin slightly.

"I just thought that, while we've got you looking like Matthew, you might just like to pay a quick visit to his stepfather," Andrew said with a wry smile. "Just to let him know that you're still around," he added, giving a somewhat amused raise of his eyebrows. Tris seemed thoughtful for a while.

"Only if you change me back to what I'm supposed to be, immediately afterwards," he muttered rather bluntly. "I certainly don't intend to go to New York looking like this!" Yet again, he pulled at the hem of the dress in an effort to force it to cover a little more of his thighs, rather than the dress being almost like a miniskirt, and hastily glanced in both directions of the corridor, hopeful that no one else, such as a prison guard, would suddenly come wandering along.

"We won't be interrupted," Andrew murmured, immediately understanding his concerns.

"And I'm not going home like this either!" Tris added rather emphatically. Perhaps just a little wary of how Lara would react to seeing him in such strange attire, given that her twin brother was already 'batting for the wrong side', as it was sometimes said.

"You won't be on your own. We can become the demons that Scott Ryan once thought you were," Conlaodh added with almost keen enthusiasm. He and Taylor quickly took on child-angel guises, with Conlaodh somehow making himself appear as a rather close image of Tris. Feeling just a slight sense of relief, in that he wouldn't be on his own, Tris sighed and prepared to visit Scott Ryan.

Like with William Daniels, Scott Ryan looked at Tris, as an image of Matthew, with a sense of horror.

"But it's not possible," he exclaimed, as he hastily scrambled off his bunk and retreated to the farthest corner of his cell. "You... you... you're dead!"

"Not quite," Tris exclaimed. "But seeing that the last time a friend came to rescue me, you thought he was a demon, I just thought I'd bring a couple along so that you would know what to look for, the next time you're discussing matters with Pastor Isaac." Conlaodh, Andrew and Taylor immediately made themselves visible. Firstly, as boy-angels, with Conlaodh still managing to show a quite remarkable resemblance to Tris in his normal form, before Andrew and Taylor, once again became vile-looking demons. They moved threateningly close to Scott Ryan, as if preparing to grab him.

"Just thought that you'd like to know the difference," Tris said almost a little mockingly, as a dark stain spread across the groin area of Scott Ryan's prison attire. A moment later, the four angels disappeared from the cell and were suddenly back in the church on the island. With Andrew, Conlaodh and Taylor all looking like their normal selves.

"I need to get this photocopied, for Mykael's records, and then get the original back to the prison, where the authorities can find it and start acting upon it," Andrew suggested, glancing down at the pages of confession William Daniels had given him. "Then we'll need to make arrangements with Mykael for visiting New York."

"Can you get me back to normal, first?" Tris muttered, as he realised that, while he was back to looking like his proper self, he was still wearing the yellow dress, white socks, Alice-band and T-bar shoes.

"But you do look quite cute," Andrew teased. "I just thought...." He quickly lapsed into silence as Tris kicked off the T-Bar shoes and began trying to struggle out of the dress; something that wasn't too easy given the way it buttoned at the back and also because it was really just an illusion created from his normal clothes, so, in reality, the fastenings didn't quite match up.

"Okay, okay," Andrew quickly continued. "There's no need for you to go home completely naked!" In an instant, Tris was back in the clothes he had been wearing earlier. His trainers, however, were now lying on the floor, having transformed back from being T-Bar shoes.

"Thank you," he murmured, sighing with just a hint of exasperation as he began levering his trainers back onto his feet, without bothering to undo the laces. "While I do understand why looking like Matthew in a yellow dress was important for what we were just did, I'd much rather be me! Dressed normally!"

***

"The crew have managed to get a bead on another of the GPS sources, Sir," Sergeant Oliver Childers announced rather quietly. He stayed well clear of his senior officer. Well aware that Harris McMahon was most likely still in a foul mood after it had been revealed that, the previous day, they'd simply been tracking a whale shark.

"And what is it this time?" Harris McMahon snapped irritatedly. "Another damn whale shark? Or maybe this time it's a bloody dolphin?" Sergeant Childers gave a slight shake of his head and retreated a little towards the door.

"A bird, Sir," he replied. "Some type of albatross, it seems. We haven't bothered to capture it because it's supposedly bad luck to kill an albatross, but from the close up camera images, it seems to have some small device attached to one of its legs." Harris McMahon sighed, and gave a slow shake of his head.

"Which means all the others that we're tracking are most likely also decoys," he quietly fumed. "Including the one that's in bloody orbit!" He exhaled with a clear sense of exasperation. "Given that there now also appear to be sightings of the girl everywhere from Afghanistan to Zaire, we may as well return home and stop wasting time on such fruitless searches."

"So we're giving up?" Sergeant Childers cautiously queried.

"Not in the slightest," McMahon snapped, immediately irritated by the mere suggestion of failure. "We're just changing focus. We'll just put more of our resources into tracking down Angel-girl's brother. As I previously mentioned, he might be like her and even if he isn't, we can probably still use him as bait to lure her to us. From what the Holts have said, the two children were very close before they were separated, so it makes sense to use that to our advantage."

"So now we concentrate on New York?" Sergeant Childers tentatively asked. While that seemed an obvious course of action, he didn't like to pre-empt his superior's decisions. Harris McMahon gave a slow shake of his head, more in exasperation than as any answer to the query.

"It'll be better than wasting our damn time out here," he muttered angrily. "And, according to our last reports, that's where the boy's mother has been concentrating her search."

"And what about the father?" queried Sergeant Childers.

"He's still a guest of the government, according to all reports," Harris McMahon replied. "And likely to be so for some considerable time, given that he's pleaded guilty to selling indecent DVDs of children being abused."

"Including Angel-girl's brother?" Sergeant Childers queried.

"Most likely," growled Harris McMahon. "According to all the reports on the boy's background… at least what we managed to get from the adoption agency, and his records at Oakton Middle

School, the kid's seriously gay. After some issue with a church camp his father was associated with, he was taken to New York by his parents for specialist psychiatric treatment. It seems, however, that he absconded after two or three sessions and it's now thought that he's probably been living on the streets since then."

"And the search we've already got going? Have they come up with anything?"

"Just bits and pieces, similar to what I've just told you," Harris McMahon sighed, giving a further slow shake of his head. "There's even a report that a police officer spotted a kid matching his description in a McDonalds and tried to arrest him for being truant. But, somehow, despite being handcuffed, the kid managed to escape from the back of a locked squad car, after he'd asked the officer to go back and get what was left of his meal. Which, when you think about it, is sort of similar to what happened when Angel-girl absconded."

"Anything else?" Sergeant Childers continued. Harris McMahon exhaled softly.

"Just some casual hearsay that he might now be hiding in one of the homeless shelters," he muttered.

"So we should tell the squad to concentrate on them, Sir?" Oliver Childers asked. "Like, the homeless shelters and places like that?" Harris McMahon gave a further exasperated shake of his head.

"No. We'll just sit back and wait until he comes to us," he drawled sarcastically. "Of course we concentrate on them!" he retorted sharply. "We need to get a hold of that kid before anyone else has a chance to. And from all reports, there are already other people out there trying to find him. And, in this instance, I don't mean the damned police!"

***

At the sound of footsteps on the stairs, the boys in the basement room all sat up, looking rather nervous. A moment later, the door was unlocked and Vittorio stood in the doorway, holding a short leather strap in one hand.

"I need four boys for a little session tonight," he announced, casually surveying the faces in front of him. "It's nothing too onerous. Just another photography session for Maxwell Keane." He seemed to hold his gaze on a few of them for a minute or two, appearing to be making various choices.

"Okay," he eventually muttered. "Stand up when I call your name." He again perused the group of boys. "Let's make it Noah, Cooper, Luka and… and… Skylar," he eventually decided.

As the other boys had done, Skylar scrambled quickly to his feet, anxious to avoid the possibility of upsetting the man and consequently ending up on the receiving end of a thrashing. Vittorio beckoned them all to come closer. Once the four boys were standing in front of him, he seemed to make a couple of quick decisions.

"The parings can be Noah and Luka, Skylar and Cooper for a start. Maxwell may change those around, but let's have it start that way." He sighed rather ostentatiously, and slapped the short piece of leather he had in his right hand onto his open left palm. "I'll expect you properly showered and ready for inspection in thirty minutes. So, don't keep me waiting." He turned to go, then stopped in the doorway and turned to look at them. "There'll be no special costumes tonight. You'll just be wearing white display pants, jeans, sneakers and a plain white T-shirt. I'll have a fresh selection of clothes for you after I've done my inspection, so just make sure that you're totally clean!" He turned and headed back up the stairs.

The four boys began to follow after him, heading for the showers. After all, with little else to do downstairs, there was no sense in being tardy and risking punishment by taking longer than the thirty minutes specified.

"Why does he always need to inspect us?" Skylar whispered as he drew level with Noah.

Probably to make sure we're hairless," Noah murmured. Perhaps not wanting to say anything too loud in case Vittorio overheard him.

"Why?" Skylar queried. Noah gave a slight shrug.

"So we don't look like we're starting puberty, yet," he whispered. "According to Peter, Vittorio feels that he can charge a lot more for us, if we look younger." Skylar nodded an understanding. Perversely, he could perhaps also understand Vittorio's logic and reasoning.

"So who's Maxwell Keane?" he asked as they entered the bathroom and began to get undressed, none of them feeling any reticence about stripping off in the company of the other boys, given how often they were 'inspected'.

"Just some dodgy Republican politician," Noah murmured with a sigh. "I've seen him on TV a couple of times, when they've been going on about various issues regarding Congress and the Federal Court. Like, gun reform. He's an ardent NRA supporter and a bit of a racist, which is why he likes little white boys like us. Peter's evidently done a few sessions for him in the past, and I've done one. As I said, he's pretty harmless. Doesn't even touch you. Well, not all that much."

"So what will we have to do?" Skylar asked nervously, as Noah reached in and turned on the water in the cubicle they would share. Luka and Cooper were already sharing the other cubicle. Noah gave a further shrug as he reached out to test the water temperature.

"Not too much," he casually replied as he grabbed a bar of soap from the rack. "Maxwell just likes to take photographs."

"Photographs?" Skylar echoed. Noah nodded and stepped into the warm water, allowing room for Skylar to move in beside him.

"If it's like the last time, he'll take photographs of us as we strip down to our display wear, and then have us wrestle with each other on this large, padded mat. That's why Vittorio paired us up."

"So we just have to wrestle each other?" Skylar muttered, trying to get the concept fully worked out in his head. "And that's all?" Yet again, Noah shrugged.

"Pretty much," he said. "Apart from the fact that all we'll be wearing will be white briefs, and Maxwell may have some other friends there with video cameras."

"So we have to wrestle each other, in just…?" Skylar exclaimed, also grabbing a bar of soap and proceeding to wash under his arms. "While they take photos and films of us?" Noah exhaled softly, and perhaps with just a hint of exasperation, given that he felt that he'd already made it quite clear about what they'd be doing.

"Well, it's certainly a lot better than what we could be asked to do," he replied a little bluntly. "At least we won't have anyone fondling us, or sticking fingers into awkward places. The only difficulty will be over how we start to react when we're clambering all over each other, if you catch my drift."

"So that's all that will happen?" Skylar murmured.

"Pretty much," Noah replied. "Although Peter said that, sometimes, you have to wrestle in water."

"You mean, in a swimming pool?" Skylar asked.

"More just a shallow paddling pool," Noah replied. "Although Peter did say that you get wet everywhere! Which can get a little embarrassing, to say the least. Especially if you're just wearing white display pants."

"So that's all?" Skylar queried. "Like, just wrestling?" Noah shrugged as he poured some shampoo onto his hand and then massaged it into his hair.

"I think Peter said that, on one occasion, they had to spank each other," he muttered. "Like, he had to spank Cameron, I think... or some other boy; mainly because one of the guests wanted some extra photos." He paused a moment to wipe shampoo away from his eyes. "Anyway, at least it's better than being sent to Dracula," he murmured as he leant under the shower to start rinsing his hair.

"Dracula?" Skylar queried with some bemusement. Noah nodded, even as he scrubbed at the water sluicing through his hair.

"Just a client who likes to bite," he replied. "You just ask Peter what it's like to end up with little bite marks all around your neck and arms... and even on your bum cheeks."

***

"Mama Hattie, she says for me to tell you to hide," Cee-Cee whispered as she hurried into the television lounge where Rylan was watching a repeat of Ellen. "There be some mean-ass woman asking 'bout you at the main office. She reckons it might be your mama, or a social worker, or something. But, whatever she be, she certainly sounds like trouble." Rylan immediately looked a little nervous. He scrambled out of the old armchair and hurried through to the female dormitory to grab his hooded jacket.

"Not the police?" he queried as he turned to see that Cee-Cee had followed him. She gave a quick shake of her head.

"No, just a mean-ass woman," she murmured, glancing back towards the door. "Mama Hattie overheard her talking to the supervisor. She was waving some picture around, and asking 'bout you! Like, if anyone here had seen you recently?"

"Did Hattie say that I was here?" Rylan asked anxiously.

"Course not," Cee-Cee said, hurrying over to cast a quick look around the edge of the doorway towards the main office. "She's not stupid. She just knows that the lady probably be your mama and that she means big trouble for you. So, Mama Hattie, I think she gonna tell your mama and the supervisor that you went off to St. Vincent's."

"Where's that?" Rylan said, looking rather surprised. Cee-Cee flexed her shoulders a little.

"Cross town someplace, I guess," she replied, her upturned hands seeming to convey a sense of not knowing. "I just knows it ain't anywheres 'round here. Mama Hattie, she knows all the shelters."

"So where do I go?" Rylan asked. Cee-Cee gave a shake of her head.

"Anywhere where you won't be seen if that mean-ass woman wants to nosey around for a bit," she replied, and then paused for a moment as if thinking through one or two ideas. "Follow me," she eventually murmured, hurrying towards the far end of the room. She hurried Rylan past the kitchen and bathrooms, down a corridor and out the back door of the refuge into the semi-enclosed courtyard. "We can go in there," she said, pointing to a side door into the church. "Plenty of good, dark places to hide in a church."

"In a church?" Rylan queried a little disbelievingly. As far as he could remember, there certainly weren't any places to hide in Pastor Isaac's church back in Oakton. Not even down in the basement!

"Sure," Cee-Cee replied. "Churches have always been sanctuaries. Places where you could be safe." Rylan shook his head as he hurried after Cee-Cee. The only church he'd ever been to had most certainly not been a safe place.

They hurried across the short distance to the church and into a side entrance. Stepping into the coolness of the interior, Rylan immediately gazed up at the high, vaulted ceiling. He stopped still for a moment; this place was nothing like the last church he'd been in. He shuddered at the thought, remembering the humiliation of being 'outed' and shamed in front of the whole congregation. That was not to say that he hadn't been aware that it was already fairly common knowledge, at least around Oakton Middle School, that he was gay. It was more the way Pastor Isaac had talked about it to the congregation. The nasty words he'd used to paint Rylan as being a perverted abomination… almost inhuman. Describing his supposed behaviour as being akin to that of an animal. A degradation that had led to his being sent to the boot camp, to be systematically abused and brutalised, by his father, a man called Scott Ryan, and the pastor, as a supposed 'cure' for his 'problem'. His tormenters appearing to find some considerable delight at not only seeing him naked, but also the way in which he reacted to all the pain and humiliation that they inflicted upon him.

In contrast to garish modernity of Pastor Isaac's church, with its state-of-the-art multi-speaker sound system, lavish décor, plush padded pews, broadcast cameras, and large viewing screens, the inside of this one seemed quiet, austere and dark. Its main illumination coming from sunlight filtering through large, multi-coloured, stained glass windows, the single light that shone out above the multiple keyboards and polished pipes of the pipe organ upstairs above the entryway, and the sombre glow cast by the small clusters of lights hanging on long, thin chains from the ceiling. And yet, curiously, that same subdued darkness seemed to have a rather calming influence. Not seeming to be in any way foreboding or menacing; almost as if announcing that the inside of this church was a place totally removed from the hectic turmoil and dangers of the rest of the world, outside.

"Quick, in there," Cee-Cee exclaimed as, having him ushered him across to the far side of the church and having glanced around to check no one else was around, she opened the door to a small cubicle and hastily pushed him inside. "It's a confessional!" she added in answer to his slight look of confusion. "A place where people come to confess. You know, like, to tell a priest of their sins and ask for forgiveness. So that he can give them their penance, so God will like them again. Anyways, you just stay in there and keep quiet until I come back for you."

"But what if someone needs to do one of those confession things?" Rylan quickly asked. "You know, to tell a priest man what it was that they'd done that was wrong?"

"They won't be having a service until later on this evening," Cee-Cee retorted. "And if some ol' priest comes along, just tell them that you need to confess something."

"But what will I say?" Rylan asked. Cee-Cee gave him a wry smile and shook her head.

"You mean to tell me you ain't never done nothin' wrong?" she almost laughed. "Most boys your age will certainly have done somethin' that they be needing to confess. At least all the ones that I know do! And some of 'em are a darn sight younger than you. And if you seriously ain't got nothin', you just keep making stuff up. Anything at all! The more badder, the better."

"But, what if I run out of things to say?" Rylan queried. Not feeling too sure of just what it would be wise to reveal of his past to any 'Man of God'.

"Then just ask if there's somewhere private where you can pray. Like, on your own. Just be a little wary of Father Thomas, however. According to a couple of the boys, he can sometimes be a just a little bit too free with his hands, if you catch my drift." Not nasty like... just a bit too 'touchy'. Like, with stroking your arms and hair and such. Rylan nodded, and carefully got himself seated. Hoping that his sojourn would not be for too long and would not be interrupted by any 'Man of God', no matter how well-meaning they might purport to be.

"Anyways, I'll be back for you as soon as Mama Hattie says that it's okay," Cee-Cee whispered as she began to quietly close the door to the confessional. "She just wants for you to be safe." She paused a moment and then looked at him a little bemusedly through the half-closed door. "And so do I. Even 'though you be a little whitey!"

***

For long while Rylan simply stayed where he was. Somehow enjoying the solitude and sense of calm that seemed to pervade the building. In a weird way, it reminded him just a little of nighttime in his hideout, with just the light of a single candle. It also gave him time to think through his situation. Like, what would happen if his mother did find out where he was staying? Or worse still, if TakerZ eventually worked out where he was? Something about the man had him worried. He didn't seem the type who'd be too put out if he had to go into the women's sleeping area to get what, or whom, he wanted.

Thankfully, in the time that he waited, no one bothered to come to check the confessional. At the same time, he'd wondered whether any priest, if one had turned up to hear his 'confession' and he'd told them a true account of his past, would've simply have thought he was trying to be impudent by making up an impossible catalogue of rude acts and abuses. Not that anything to which he'd been subjected could've been considered events over which he'd had any control, or had willingly enacted.

And then there was Hattie, or Mama Hattie as Cee-Cee called her... and not without good reason, given the diverse group of teenage children that turned up at the table at dinnertime to spend the evening in her care. Some of them were obviously still trying to attend school. Some of the others... well, who was to know where they went, or what they got up to, during the day?

Despite her obvious different ethnicity, and the fact that his simply being with her seemed to invoke looks of some curiosity, Rylan still felt that he could trust Mama Hattie almost implicitly. Certainly not like the special psychiatrist, to which his mum and dad had sent him, to 'sort out' his problems. Edward J. Stanford, Doctor of Child Psychology the bronze, polished plaque outside his office had said... if that was what he really was. But then, nothing in his life had been easy to understand since his return home from the abuses of the camp.

After keeping him locked in the basement for almost a week, perhaps because his parents had been scared that Pastor Isaac's threats might not have put him off going to the police, they'd eventually smuggled him out of the house in a large cardboard box, which supposedly contained linen, for the trip to New York. Not that he remembered much about it, given that he'd slept for most of the trip as a result of some pills he'd been forced to swallow.

The moment they'd arrived in New York, and settled into an apartment, his dad had informed him that further treatment for his 'problem' had been scheduled. This time, however, instead of the beatings and abuse he'd endured at home, in the church basement and at the boot camp, it was supposed to be of a proper medical kind. The alternative, of his being placed in a residential psychiatric home, had certainly not held any appeal, and, a little to his surprise, the first couple of sessions with Edward J. Stanford had been, more or less, just as he'd have expected proper treatment sessions should be.

He and the psychiatrist had simply talked; discussing reasons of how, why and when he had first come to believe that he was gay. It was all just as his parents had said would happen, and, in a way, he'd felt no difficulty in being with the man, and explaining the thoughts that were inside his head; strange thoughts that fringed on how he felt far more attracted to being liked by boys rather than girls.

Nevertheless, his sense of ease with the sessions had only remained that way until the third session, when Edward J. Stanford had suddenly decided that, as an important part of the treatment, he needed to take photographs of him; both in his underwear and also naked. While he'd allowed that to happen, perhaps coerced by Edward J. Stanford's smooth explanation of being able to visually identify various physical traits in his body shape that were, supposedly, evidence of his mixed-up sexuality, by the end of the session, and by the awkward ways in which he'd been asked to pose, Rylan knew for certain, simply from the look on the man's face as he took the photos, that he was simply another pervert. A man no different in all his aberrant desires for young boys, than Pastor Isaac, Scott Ryan, and his own father. The man's actions just hadn't progressed that far, as yet.

In a way, knowing the gay feelings he'd once had towards other boys had made him feel ashamed. That was why, shortly after he'd turned ten, and about a year or two after the family had first moved to Oakton and become regular members of Pastor Isaac Scott's 'New Christian Mission', his dad had started taking him down to the basement, for special little man-to-man talks. Not that he and his dad had actually talked all that much. The first session had simply begun with him being spanked, supposedly as a means of curing him of being 'gay'. A punishment that was repeated the very next day, followed by some inappropriate touching and fondling that somehow seemed to undermine the whole purpose of the discipline. Along with the threat that he should tell no one about what was happening; not even his mother!

At a further session, a few days afterwards, he'd also been given some tablets to take. Waking up a good three hours or so later, to find that he was laid out on his own bed, partly undressed, he soon realised that any ideas of a man-to-man 'talk' had gone well beyond just the usual spanking and touching. The 'talks' that had then followed had soon escalated into a regular pattern of quite painful abuse, sometimes without the need for him to be sedated, and including sessions where his dad would also force him to dress up in girl's clothes, before abusing him.

If the kids at school who repeatedly ostracized, teased and bullied him, thinking that they were hurting him and making his life a misery, they were not to know that the hours he spent in school were actually a respite from the far worse abuse, both verbal and physical, that he suffered at home.

And yet, through all the time of it happening, he'd believed that it was something that his mother knew nothing about. For months, it seemed, he'd hoped that one day she would discover the truth, be totally horrified by what was happening to him and that it would all end. He'd kept that thought in his head, each time his father took him downstairs, knowing that to try to run away would only make his punishment worse. At least until the day, just a few weeks before his eleventh birthday, his mother had come down to the basement and caught them together. Rather than being shocked at what was taking place, she'd made no attempt to intervene. Instead, she'd simply watched for a minute or two, then shrugged and headed back upstairs.

Afterwards, she'd simply said that, if he intended to grow up as gay, then he'd have to get used to that sort of treatment. That day of shame, as it turned out, was merely a prelude to what he'd eventually suffered at the boot camp.

***

When Cee-Cee finally arrived to collect him, he was surprised to find that almost two hours had passed. Now, sitting on the edge of his bed, he felt a little comforted by not having had to reveal anything to anyone in the church about his past. While Cee-Cee had told him that priests had to keep secret whatever they were told in a confessional, he still felt that his revelations might too easily have brought the police into the situation. At the same time, he sensed an air of tension in the room. More especially with the way Cee-Cee stayed by the door to the foyer. Seeming to be keeping a nervous watch on what was happening out there.

"We have us a bit of a problem," Mama Hattie murmured, as she eventually waddled back into the room and lowered her bulk onto the edge of her bed. Having quickly indicated for Cee-Cee to go back over to the door to check that there was no one still hanging about in the foyer asking about Rylan. The bed creaked, a little ominously, under her weight. She patted an area of the blankets beside her, the action seeming to beckon for Rylan to come and sit beside her.

"It seems your mama is searching all the shelters for you," she rumbled, when Rylan was close beside her. She reached out to put a rather massive arm around his slender shoulders and drew him a little closer. "'Cause someone had told her that they'd seen you down near the Mission, early last week. It seems that she's started checking all the shelters. Going around them regular like, on the offchance that you'll eventually turn up at one of them. And a couple of them mentioned that, while they hadn't seen you, they were pretty sure that you were staying here. From the way she was mouthing off, she seemed quite sure that we had you hidden away here, somewhere. As a further problem, it seems she's not alone. From what I hear'd, some other military type spooks have also been looking out for you, as well as that a-hole TakerZ."

"Why?" Rylan questioned. Seeming puzzled at the idea that so many people would suddenly be looking for him. While the possibility of his being wanted by the police and his parents he could understand, and TakerZ, now that he had some idea what the man wanted him for, the idea that the military would be after him however, made no sense at all. Not unless they had somehow worked out that he was 'different' to normal humans. As he sat with his thoughts in turmoil, Mama Hattie sighed softly.

"With your momma, I can understand why she be looking for you. Now whether you want to be found… well, that's between you and your momma. With TakerZ, however, it'll be because he knows that, as a pimp, he can make money out of you, somehow. And you definitely don't want to get involved in any of that sort of thing." She sighed, patted his hand once again, and was silent for a moment. "With the military, that… well, I really don't know," she eventually rumbled with a slow shake of her head. In some ways, simply echoing his own bewilderment at that state of affairs. "Even given what you might be. Though it does seem, from what they been asking, that they not be there just to help your momma. In fact, I seriously doubt your momma even knows they be lookin' for you."

"So will I still be safe here?" queried Rylan, more than a little anxiously. Big Hattie shuffled her rather solid bulk a little across her bed, making it shake and creak a little, and then once again reached out to pull him close.

"Rylan, you stand out like the proverbial sore thumb," she muttered, giving him a further affectionate squeeze and then tousling the short spikes of his white-blonde hair, before looking around to see that there was no one close enough to hear. "In case you hadn't noticed, most of the 'guests' in this place be sort of dark skinned and you jus' a skinny lil' white boy; even if most times you be half hidden inside your coat. Now that don't mean that I don't cares for you, 'cause I do; you being a very special sort of kid, 'n all. But, I also thinks I be needing to get you well outta sight for a little while. If your mama, TakerZ, and them others, are searching all the shelters, who knows when the police might follow." She again glanced around the room. Almost as if singling out certain of the absent 'guests' who would be back by nightfall. "And in that regard, a few of them that stay here ain't too much on the good side of the law, if you catch my drift," she murmured. "And I certainly wouldn't put it past a couple of them to be okay with 'ratting you out' just to take a little heat off of themselves, or to get themselves some credit with the authorities, if the needs be. Especially if they be thinking you might have the police looking for you."

"So, where do I go?" Rylan asked, his eyes quickly starting to water up. The last week or so with Mama Hattie had been one of the few times in the past five years, apart from his time with the Fulchers, and old George, that he felt that he'd found someone who genuinely cared about him; someone who actually wanted to 'mother' him and treat him with kindness, and who hadn't looked down on him and judged him as worthless. Someone who also hadn't wanted to just exploit him for what he was.

"Well, I'm guessing that the shelters ain't going to be too safe for a week or two," Mama Hattie softly mused, almost to herself.

She waggled her head a little from side to side, in an action that wasn't really a 'no' or a 'yes'. She gave him a further quick squeeze. "Leastwise, until they think you be well gone from here. So, for a while, we might just have to have you go underground," she eventually said.

"Underground?" Rylan echoed.

"There be some places a few of the less reputable 'guests' who sometimes turn up here go to when the heat be on," Mama Hattie replied. "Especially when they be wanted by such as the police," she added, in response to Rylan's rather puzzled look. "Or they just want to disappear for a while because of drug debts and the like. The subways have some tunnels and tracks that are generally not used too much anymore, so they can be a bit of a secret hiding place. If you don't mind being in the dark for a bit." She beckoned Cee-Cee over.

"How about you go tell Dumper that I'll be needing his help to hide someone for a few days" she said, when the girl was close. "Tell him that I'll meet him at about six tomorrow morning at his usual haunt. Tell him that it be important and not to be too surprised about who I have with me."

***

Rylan looked about him with a sense of trepidation, coupled with curiosity. He was standing on a long curved platform of what was obviously an underground station. Even in the dim light of Dumper's torch, he could see that its construction seemed to have resulted in an amazing brick and glass tile patterning over the arched walls and ceilings. Intricate designs that appeared to continue up the stairway that had presumably once led up to the streets. Perhaps more strange, however, was that it was totally deserted. With almost no sound, apart from a distant rumbling which seemed to be coming from somewhere beyond the walls.

"It's the old City Hall Loop," Dumper advised him. "It's where the underground used to end."

"So don't they use it any more?" Rylan quickly asked, as he pulled his coat around him for extra warmth and adjusted the positioning of the back pack that Hattie had given him — containing a few days supply of food and a torch, as well as some money — on his shoulders. Dumper gave a shake of his head.

"Not for people," he murmured. "Though some of the trains sometimes use it as a quick turnaround, so it's best if you don't base yourself here 'cause sometimes they also take tourist groups through here. They're also keen to prevent it from being damaged, so they do reasonably frequent checks of the place. Some sort of historical heritage thing, I guess. Anyway, it's better if you disappear into the dark. If you're hiding, it's better to stay well away from where you'll be too easily spotted."

"So I stay in the tunnels?" Rylan asked looking towards the darkness of the hole to his left. Dumper seemed to shrug his shoulders a little.

"Well, you can go onto the platforms when you want to get food and stuff," he muttered. "Just don't get seen to be hanging around the same station all the time. Otherwise the station crew will think that you're begging, or pickpocketing, or doing something else that might be illegal. And that'll only get you arrested, or chucked out on the streets. And when you go into the tunnels, try not to be seen doing so. 'Cause that'll just end up with them sending the track maintenance crews after you." Tris quickly nodded, as he again looked towards the tunnel mouth.

"But isn't it dangerous being in the tunnels" Like with the trains coming through?" he queried nervously. Dumper shrugged.

"Just keep yourself well to the side and low down when anything passes, that way you'll give yourself plenty of clearance. You'll also find little alcoves spaced out in some places that you can hide in. They used to be so that anyone checking the lines would have a safe place out of the way of the trains, but nowadays, they just tend to shut down the whole line while they do maintenance. Usually in the early hours of the morning."

"Well, what about the power?" Rylan quickly asked, looking up towards the roof and seeing no sign of overhead wiring. "You know, what the trains run on? Where does that come from?" Dumper hurriedly pushed him forward, towards the edge of the platform, and indicated down towards a strange box-shaped line that was spaced just outside the nearest rail.

"That's the third line," he said bluntly. "It supplies about 600 volts of power for the trains, so is best avoided." Tris quickly scanned the third line to where it disappeared in the blackness of the nearest tunnel.

Isn't it dangerous?" he quickly queried. "Like, if you accidentally fall on it in the dark?"

"It's under-running," Dumper quickly explained. "That means that the trains have a special shoe-thing that picks up the power from underneath the rail, somehow. Just stepping or falling on the boxing won't generally be too dangerous. Still, it's best to avoid doing that, if you can. No sense in tempting fate, as they say."

"Do you come down here a lot?" Rylan asked tentatively. In some ways hoping the boy would say 'yes' and that he might have some company. Dumper gave a quick shake of his head.

"Only if I owe somebody money, or I'm on the wrong side of one of the local gangs for some reason," he muttered. "Most of down here's a bit too dark for my liking. I like to know what's around me." Rylan shuddered. In some ways he felt the same.

Still, Mama Hattie had said that it might only be for a week or two… three, at the most.

"So I should stay in the tunnels, rather than hang around the platforms?" he queried, as much to keep Dumper with him as for gaining information.

"It would probably be best," Dumper said, giving an exasperated sigh that seemed to suggest that, having done what Hattie had asked of him and delivered this strange little white boy to the underground, he really wanted to be on his way. "And, as I said, just try to avoid getting seen by the maintenance crews. If they suspect that you're hiding down here permanently, and not just passing through, they're likely to send out a squad to track you down. After all, the last thing they'll want is to be dealing with the result of some little kid trying to take on a train, especially if it ends up holding up the regular timetable. If even a part of the underground has to shut down, that creates real problems for the whole of the city. Just like they had with 9-11, and Hurricane Sandy."

Tris was suddenly reminded of all the news reports of the flooding that Hurricane Sandy had caused, and the television coverage that had monitored the situation. With large sections of the underground completely swamped as a result of an unexpectedly high tidal surge. Not that there'd been any reports of that sort of weather being likely to hit New York in the next few weeks.

"You should also watch out for gang kids," Dumper suddenly continued. "They sometime use the tunnels as short cuts. Especially when they're transporting drugs. If you see them, you'd best hide, or run. They're fairly easy to spot 'cause, like most bullies, they tend to travel in packs, and if you're on your own, they'll probably try to take whatever you've got. Or beat you up, just to be nasty." Rylan nodded. At the same time, he was also starting to think of what visualisations he could make. His being able to 'jump' would be one easy way to avoid trouble, if he made enough visualisations. He quickly looked around and stared at the stairway for a moment. Making sure that he'd be able to remember it.

"Well, I gotta go," Dumper suddenly announced. "Take care, kid." He started towards the stairs and then stopped. "I'll pop back a few times, in the next few days, to see how you're getting on… if I can find you. You know, just so's I can let Hattie know that her little 'Milky Bar Kid' is still okay." He hurried away out of sight. Halfway up the stairs would be the exit to the maintenance door that they'd used to sneak in.

***

"Okay, All of you, on your feet," Vittorio loudly announced. The dozen or so children waiting in the basement prison scrambled hastily to their feet. All of them anxious about not being the last one to obey the directive, with the likelihood of then suffering the painful consequences of their tardiness. Vittorio waited until they were all watching him in silence. Angelo and Reggie quickly moved to be on either side of the group of children.

"Now, because I feel we might just end up with more problems of silly little children thinking of running away, despite the severity of the punishments that've been dished out," Vittorio smugly intoned, "I'm about to give you a small demonstration of why such ridiculous ideas of escape will be a very dangerous thing to do from now on." He moved towards the doorway and then turned to gesture to the children. "Follow me upstairs and don't try anything stupid!" He hurried out of sight. The children quickly followed with Angelo and Reggie keeping them moving.

Once upstairs, Vittorio led them out of the house and into the back yard, where Miguel had a flatbed truck idling. On the back of the truck was what appeared to be a shop manikin propped up in a seated position on a hay bale.

"Now for a little demonstration," Vittorio announced. Clambering up onto the flatbed of the truck he took a strange looking necklace from the box he was holding, made an ostentatious show of it to all the children and then fastened it around the neck of the manikin. Jumping back down, he came over to stand in front of the children. Producing from the box, as he did so, a device that looked very much like an old-fashioned mobile phone... complete with a short, stubby aerial.

"This is a proximity detonator," he said, making a display of flicking a switch on the device. As he did so, a green light showed on the device and also on the necklace. "Now, while the necklace is within a range of about one hundred metres, the light will stay green. When the necklace gets out of range, the light will flash red and... well, I think it's best you see for yourselves what will happen." He nodded across to Miguel who quickly got into the truck and began driving away down the long driveway that led away towards the hills that surrounded the farm.

The children watched as the truck disappeared in a cloud of dust. Heading out towards the hills. As it reached a distance of about one hundreds metres from where they were standing, the light on the device Vittorio was holding suddenly started to flash red. A moment or two later there was a muffled bang, much like a shot from a gun. Even at a distance, the children could clearly see that the manikin had been decapitated. Its head looping almost lazily into the air from the force of the explosion, to fall on the dirt road somewhere behind where the truck had now stopped.

"Understand?" Vittorio demanded, as the children stared in disbelief, the realisation dawning on them. There would be more necklaces! One for each of them!

"You mean, you would kill us rather than let us escape?" Persia queried, although from the look of shock on her face she already knew the answer.

"If the needs be," Vittorio replied. "After all, if any of you ever got a chance to talk to the authorities, or the media, there are a lot of very important people who would stand to lose a great deal more than any of your measly lives are worth. People who pay me extremely well to provide for their particular needs."

"So we all get a necklace?" Peter nervously asked, fingering the beaded necklace that, like all of the captive children, he was already wearing. Vittorio nodded.

"Only when you're on an assignment," he replied. "And when that happens, each Keeper, given that they'll keep you from taking off, will be padlocked into place, and this little device..." He held up the proximity detonator. "... this cunning little device will be in the cab of the truck while you are travelling. Any of you stupid enough to try to make a run for it when we have to stop, well... you've all seen what will happen." He glanced around the group as if waiting for further comment. Noticeably, there was none. "So, now that you fully understand the situation, you can all head back downstairs. Sometime in the next few days, a good many of you will have an extra special assignment to attend. The one I've been keeping a number of you on hold for." He indicated for them to head back to the house. In a very short time all the children were back downstairs. Once they were seated on the mattresses, Vittorio turned to address them once again.

"Angelo and Reggie will bring down some food for you in about an hour, and then we'll separate you into two separate rooms. Boys in here, girls next door. After you've been separated, you should all try to get some sleep. We've got a fair bit of driving to do over the next day or so, 'cause, before the big event, I've possibly got a couple of smaller entertainments lined up for some of you."

As he turned to head back upstairs, he suddenly stopped and returned to the doorway.

"And just so you know," he announced. "The control device also has a special detonation code. If we get stopped, and it looks likely that you could end up telling people too much, a pre-set combination of buttons will set off all the Keepers, instantaneously and regardless of distance. Understand?" He turned and headed up the stairs and out of sight, leaving the children in a state of stunned silence. The only sound being the slamming of the door at the top of the stairs.

CHAPTER ELEVEN

Some Information....

"Good afternoon," Andrew politely said as soon as the door was opened. "Mrs Molly Daniels?" Much he knew that they had the correct apartment, given it matched the address they'd been given by William Daniels, it still seemed to be best to make the enquiry a question. Much as he'd anticipated, the woman nodded. Nevertheless, she remained standing just inside the doorway.

Andrew quickly reached into the inside pocket of his coat for the identity card that had been prepared for him by Colin Watters. Having undertaken Mykael's suggestion to visit the prison where William Daniels, Pastor Isaac and Scott Ryan were being held, to see what they knew about Rylan, Andrew and Tris were now commencing their New York search for Rylan by, firstly, going to see his mother. The ruse being to find out exactly what she could tell them about Rylan's disappearance by having Andrew pretend to be a representative of a 'local schools' truancy authority'. He quickly waved the false identity card in front of the woman; carefully not allowing her to get too good a look at it, before tucking it back into the inner pocket of his coat.

"Good morning. My name is Arthur Megson and I work for a number of local schools as an enrolment and truancy mediator," he announced rather stiffly. "May I come in, so we can conduct this interview regarding your son's absence from school in a more cordial manner?" He glanced towards the doors of neighbouring apartments. “And without all your neighbours listening in?” He waited a moment for her reply, and then, when she seemed to hesitate a little, continued. “I would certainly prefer that it not be necessary for me to have to return with an official police warrant.”

Perhaps wary that a refusal might result in the police also becoming suspicious of her failure to cooperate, Molly Daniels sighed, the action a clear expression of her annoyance at the intrusion, and then stepped to one side to allow him to enter the small apartment. Remaining in a state of invisibility, Tris immediately followed Andrew inside. It would be his task to surreptitiously check through the rest of the apartment, to see if he could discover any other detail related to Rylan’s whereabouts. Given that the place appeared remarkably small, and quite sparsely furnished, that task would obviously not take too long. Unbeknown of the fact that there was also an extra visitor, Molly Daniels indicated for Andrew to have a seat at the small table a little to one side of the kitchenette.

“I realise that this may seem an unusual way of dealing with things, but having an officer of my type working for several of the local schools, saves the police a lot of unnecessary work in having to check up on children who may not be attending school when required to do so,” Andrew hastily explained, as a reason for his presence as Arthur Megson. “As you would understand, it certainly eliminates the waste of valuable police resources on such trivial matters when there is so much real crime that needs their attention. Now, given that the school authorities in Oakton have recently notified the New York school districts of you and your husband moving to this area, I’m just here to check up on your son. More particularly, because it appears that hc hasn’t yet been enrolled at any local school, as I’m sure you understand is required by law. Nor has there been any notification of his being homeschooled. So I was hoping to be able to talk to him to find..."

"He's not here!" interrupted Molly Daniels rather bluntly. "And I have absolutely no idea where he might be!"

"Perhaps you need to explain that situation just a little more fully," Andrew suggested rather officiously. "After all, I can hardly write in my report... 'He's not here!' Can I?" In response, Molly Daniel shrugged, and then exhaled noisily and slowly.

"William and I shifted here, from Oakton, so that we could get some proper psychiatric counselling for Rylan," she began. "We were always planning to send him to one of the local schools, but sorting out his 'problem' seemed far more important for the time being."

"And that being?" Andrew quickly asked. To his mind, it seemed the sort of question that an officer of his supposed occupation would immediately ask.

"He thinks he's a girl," Molly Daniels almost snapped. "It was causing him major problems at his school in Oakton. He bore the brunt a good deal of teasing and bullying from other pupils, which is why we were advised to take him to see Edward J. Stanford. From what we were told, he's supposed to be some sort of top-order specialist in that regard. You know, with sorting out kids with improper orientation; trans-genders and all that sort of stupid mixed up stuff." Andrew wrote the man's name down on the pad he'd brought with him. If necessary, a discreet visit would be enough to ensure that any notes the man might have made about Rylan, as well as any other files or photographs, would eventually be collected and taken back to the island. Molly Daniels seemed to pause a moment to allow him to finish writing, before quickly continuing.

"He seemed quite happy with the first two sessions. But then, after the third session, he seemed to suddenly change his mind about going. William had to be quite forceful in stressing that the sessions were for his own good."

For a moment or two, especially given the knowledge of what had happened at the boot camp, Andrew silently mused on what 'forceful' might have meant in such a situation. Before he could ask about that, however, Molly Daniels quickly resumed her explanation.

"At any rate, when we took him into town for his fourth appointment with Edward J. Stanford, he did a runner on us. I remember it well, because it was a Wednesday morning and, because of a couple of stupid little fender-benders further downtown, traffic was almost at a standstill. Which meant that, as usual, we were running a little late. So, rather than just cruising around the block trying to find parking and then taking him in to his appointment, William and I ended up stopping on a bus stop so that we could drop him off as close as we could get to Edward J. Stanford's offices, at about five to ten. Everything seemed okay by then, and he certainly wasn't complaining about attending. So after waiting to see him go inside the building, at the same time hoping that no buses would arrive and require us to move, William and I headed off for some morning tea. We'd been doing that each time, because Edward J. Stanford had already made it quite clear that he didn't like parents to be present while he was working with a child." She shook her head a little, as if in some sense of mild exasperation. "According to his dictates… 'having parents present during sessions simply inhibits children from being totally truthful'," she murmured, quoting exactly what the psychologist had explained. "We just went along with his reasoning, with the thought that he most probably knows best. But then, when we went back for Rylan at eleven-thirty, we were told that he hadn't turned up for his appointment. Edward J. Stanford seemed most aggrieved by that happening. He said that he'd even arranged to have special equipment brought in to record the session."

"For recording his talking with Rylan?" Andrew quickly asked. Molly Daniels shrugged.

"I'm not too sure. I got the feeling that it might have been film or video equipment," she casually murmured. "Especially with the way he kept harping on about the wasted time he'd spent in setting up lighting for the special equipment. After all, he'd already informed us, when we first met with him, that he always did audio recordings of all his counselling sessions simply as a matter of course."

"So it was more likely that he was planning to video Rylan?" Andrew queried. At the same time making a further note on his pad to check Edward J. Stanford's offices for any photos and visual recordings of Rylan.

"Well, I presume that was what he was on about," Molly Daniels muttered, with a shrug. "Although, as he mainly spoke to William about all those sort of matters, I don't remember exactly what was planned. Anyway, after making some enquiries with people in the offices downstairs, we were able to ascertain that, after Rylan had gone into the building, he'd gone to the bathroom and then, afterwards, had promptly disappeared out the front door. Presumably, when he was sure that we'd be gone."

"And so you started searching for him?" Andrew asked, as Tris, having completed his check of all the other rooms of the apartment, re-entered the room and, still in a state of invisibility, shook his head to indicate that he'd found nothing of importance, before heading over to stand by the door.

"Of course," Molly Daniels retorted almost a little imperiously. "Both William and I spent the rest of that day, and the next, trying to find out where he might have gone. I mean... no one likes to lose a child, but, unfortunately, in a city of this size, finding just one person can be a pretty daunting task. Even more so, if it's a kid who probably doesn't want to be found." Andrew nodded. Something about the woman's manner suggested that she was being a little evasive, making him aware that he wasn't being told the full truth.

"Have you notified the police about his running away?" he asked. Already feeling sure that she would not have done so, for pretty obvious reasons, but knowing that it would be the type of question he'd be expected to ask.

"Well, no. Not... not as yet," Molly Daniels stammered. "It didn't seem... it didn't... we didn't want to bother them with something so trivial."

'I'll bet,' Andrew mused to himself as, even as he wondered at the sheer bald-faced audacity of the woman to even imagine that a runaway child in a big city could be any sort of 'trivial' matter. "And I presume you've checked out the hospitals and all the homeless shelters?" he quickly asked.

"They were the first places we started looking. Especially the shelters, because we did hear that he'd possibly been seen near one of them." Molly Daniels muttered, then sighed. "Although, lately, I've been doing them on my own. William suddenly informed me that had to go back to Oakton for some work project that he was involved with. Something to do with the church, I think. But I haven't had too much contact with him all that recently." For a moment, Andrew wondered whether it was possible that she really didn't know the full extent of her husband's involvement in Pastor Isaac's pornography operation, and was perhaps still unaware of his recent arrest and incarceration. Somehow, both circumstances seemed just a little unlikely.

"And are there any other places that you think he might have gone to?" Andrew enquired. "After all, it is important to get a child back into a proper regime of schooling as quickly as is possible, and certainly before they've had a chance to get too street-wise to care about the importance of such necessities for their future," he added, trying to make his supposed status as a truancy mediator seem more plausible.

"It was suggested, by Edward J. Stanford, that we should talk to other kids out there," Molly Daniels replied a little resignedly. "Street kids and such. You know, the sort you see hanging around the parks and places like that. He said that they'd probably be the first to spot him, and the most likely people he'd go to for help. I've tried to do that, but most of them just seem to ignore you. More especially the younger kids."

"It still sounds a very good idea," Andrew replied, getting to his feet. "Well, when you do find him, do make sure you get him enrolled at a local school as soon as possible. That way, he'll not only be able to settle into a routine, but I'll also be able to keep a proper check on his progress and attendance. And you won't end up facing the likelihood of being prosecuted for his non-attendance at an authorized school establishment. After all, a proper education is of vital importance for a young child." With a nod of his head, he began heading towards the door, then paused and handed her a card.

"My email address is on this. Let us know, immediately, if you have any luck in finding him. That will undoubtedly save you an awful lot of hassle, in future." While he doubted Molly Daniels would ever bother to make contact, the email address that Colin Watters had set up could be kept relatively anonymous and being a 'dot com' address not give away the true whereabouts of its 'owner'… for want of a better description. At the same time, he felt that his mention of a possible prosecution might just stir her into extra efforts to locate Rylan. Which was something that they'd be able to keep a check on.

***

Andrew looked around Edward J. Stanford's office. In a stroke of luck, it seemed that the man did not work on Mondays. Nevertheless, his psychiatric consulting room seemed exactly like many that he'd seen in movies. There being a large wooden desk with a lamp that dominated the room near to the windows, a couple of comfortable leather chairs, a reclining couch for the 'patient', a chair that could be easily wheeled about and a number of filing cabinets behind the desk, with alphabetic labelling.

"So where do we start?" Tris queried. In response Andrew glanced towards the filing cabinets as he began quickly checking the drawers in the desk.

"He'll probably have the files in some sort of alphabetical order," he suggested, gesturing towards the filing cabinets. Tris began checking the first of them. Not bothering with the top drawer — labelled as 'A-B' — and proceeding straight to the first 'C-D' drawer. His quick shuffle through the files soon located a brown coloured folder labelled with 'Lawrence Rylan Daniels', about halfway towards the back of the drawer.

"Got it!" he exclaimed, extracting the folder and taking it over to the desk. Andrew quickly opened it and extracted a sheaf of papers, a couple of headshot photos of Rylan — with his long blonde hair, he did have a striking resemblance to Lara — and three small recording tapes.

"These are probably from the first three sessions," Andrew mused as he held the tape cassettes in his hand. Perhaps wondering why Edward J. Stanford still used such old-fashioned recording methods.

"There's nothing all that wrong with the photos," Tris added. "Although, to be honest, he does look very much like a girl. Almost like Lara, in fact."

"If he's taken anything that's improper, it'd be unlikely that he'd keep it in the main file," Andrew quietly countered, quickly checking the other drawers in the filing cabinets. "Not if there was a chance someone might come across them by accident." All the other cabinet drawers opened easily and simply contained further files in alphabetical order.

"Maybe he has some secret place?" Tris offered. "Like, you know, a safe?" Andrew nodded, then cocked his head briefly to one side.

"Unless he takes that sort of stuff with him," he murmured. They started checking around the walls for anything that might conceal a safe. Nothing seemed all that likely. At least until Andrew noted that a small section of carpet beneath the desk seemed to have a weave, if that would be the best word to describe it, that ran contrary to the rest of the floor. Almost as if it had been brushed in a different direction. Moving the desk chair to one side, he quickly got down on his knees and after a little effort, lifted out a quite large square of carpet mounted on a square wooden panel that slotted into a space in the floor. Beneath it was the top of a safe with a combination lock.

"Now this seems more likely," Andrew mused as he set the carpeted board to one side. "The only problem is that we now have to figure out the combination."

"I can probably do it," Tris hastily suggested, remembering back to when he'd unlocked the door to Pastor Isaac's basement office. He got down on his knees and placed his hand on the lock. After a few moments' concentration, the lock seemed to move of its own volition, rotating in various directions and giving off soft clicks as it did so, until it gave a final louder click and stopped. Andrew pulled at the handle and the door opened easily. Reaching down into the alcove beneath it he quickly extracted a number of manila envelopes. Thankfully, none of them was sealed.

The first envelope, on investigation, simply contained a book that gave a detailed series of accounts. Andrew shrugged and put it to one side. If it was of importance in some way, they'd figure that out later. The second folder was labelled 'Network' and contained photos of six children – three boys and three girls. Most of them were just face shots, including one of Rylan and there was certainly nothing about any of them that could be described as disturbing or improper. Nevertheless, Andrew quickly put it to one side, after extracting the photo of Rylan. The third folder was labelled 'SHJ'. A quick look through the photos that it contained immediately revealed that they'd found the right hiding place. The photos were of a semi-naked child — a young girl in this instance — and had obviously taken in the same room as they were in. Andrew quickly dropped it back into place and picked up the fourth folder. Quickly noting that it was labelled 'LRD'.

"Lawrence Rylan Daniels," Tris murmured from beside him, even as the designation seemed obvious. Nevertheless, Andrew nodded and extracted its contents.

Like the third envelope, the photos it contained were also nothing like what had been in the second envelope. Being, for the first few, photos of Rylan in just a pair of white underpants... back and front views. Some of the rest, however, showed Rylan totally naked, and looking decidedly uncomfortable with being so undressed. The photos including several front, side and back views of his full length.

"Why would anyone...?" Tris began as he noted that one particular close-up view of Rylan, had him seated on the couch, with his back against the wall, and with his legs drawn up and spread in such a way as to have almost every intimate part of his body on display. He left the question incomplete and shook his head. In some ways, feeling just as uncomfortable and embarrassed with what he was seeing, as the expression on Rylan's face also seemed to project. Not that the crudity of it surprised him at all. He was certainly well aware of what some perverted men liked to look at, simply from what he'd seen and experienced at Pastor Isaac's boot camp.

Bundling the photos back into their envelope and putting it to one side, Andrew did a quick check of the remaining two envelopes – labelled 'PGH' and 'REL'. Like the previous two envelopes, they also contain pictures of children in a state of undress.

With a sigh, Andrew nodded, dropped most of the envelopes back into the safe and returned his attention to the 'LRD' envelope. Getting to his feet he searched around for a spare envelope; quickly finding some in the second drawer on the left side of the desk. He quickly took the photos from Rylan's envelope, and the photo he'd extracted from the second envelope, placed them in the new envelope, along with all the contents of the original file that Tris had found in the folder in the cabinets… the recorded tapes, headshot photos and other documentation. He then placed the empty folder back into the filing cabinet and the envelope labelled 'LRD' back into the floor safe, relocked it, and then replaced the carpet square.

"Wait here," he exclaimed, getting back to his feet. "I'll just put this envelope into Mykael's office up at the big house, for safekeeping." He seemed to shimmer a moment and then was gone. Reappearing just less than a minute later without the folder.

"You didn't time it," Tris said, with a wry smile. "You know, like Mykael does." Andrew merely shrugged.

"It wasn't necessary," he replied. "And doing that takes more effort and experience." He put an arm around Tris's shoulders. "Come on," he urged. "Let's go and get something to eat, and then see what we can find in the rest of the city."

"What should we do about the other rude photos Edward J. Stanford's got in the safe?" Tris asked as they were instantly above the rooftop of a nearby building. "They're probably children who he's also abusing?" Andrew shrugged as they alighted to the roof.

"It's nothing we need to get involved in at the moment," Andrew said. "A quiet word to the local police in the next day or so, along with some information about the hidden safe under the desk and its contents, should soon put an end to his sordid little ways." He gave a sigh and looked towards the city centre. "We still need to concentrate on finding one missing boy who's probably wondering what's happening to him."

"So you think he's might already be growing wings?" Tris quickly asked, with some excitement. Andrew shrugged.

"It's very possible," he murmured. "At least that's the feeling I'm getting."

***

"It'll be like searching for a needle in a flippin' haystack!" Tris exclaimed, looking at the bustle of pedestrians clogging Times Square. "There's no way we're gonna just spot him in any of this." He gestured at their surroundings. "And if he's found himself a good place to hide, we probably haven't got a snowball's chance in hell of figuring out where he'll be."

"Not entirely," Andrew said, with a slight rise of his eyebrows. "If, like Lara, he's coming into his abilities and his wings, then, if I can just get close enough, I should be able to sense exactly where he is."

"Provided we can get 'close enough'," Tris countered with some degree of cynicism. Or perhaps it was just a feeling of trepidation in realising just how difficult the possibility of getting 'close enough' to one small boy might be, in a city the size of New York. More especially, one who just might not want to be found!

"We just have to think like a runaway child would," Andrew responded rather casually. "That means, hiding from authority, such as the police, but still finding somewhere safe to stay. Somewhere that gives you the security of a safe place to sleep and food to eat. Like, maybe, shelters for the homeless, derelict buildings with other street kids, and places like that."

"And you do realise just how many of those are there likely to be in a city of this size," Tris repined a little dejectedly. "Especially if, at the moment, we don't even know where any of them are."

"Oh ye of little faith," Andrew responded, with a smile as he reached out to affectionately tousle Tris's hair. "For the homeless shelters, a visit to a few churches should soon give us some starters. Given that they're often the ones running such places, as an act of good faith. And, I'd be tempted to suggest, so that they don't end up with homeless derelicts sleeping in the pews." He paused and looked about for a moment, before carefully getting one of postcard-sized pictures of Rylan out of Tris's small backpack. It was one of a number that they'd had Colin Watters copy from the front cover of the video. "However," he then continued, "given that the homeless shelters are often relatively empty during the day, we might as well just start looking at other possibilities for a while."

"So we should start by asking some of the street kids? Like, maybe those in one of the parks, or similar places?" Tris enquired, seeming to read the rest of his thoughts.

"I think that would be a good idea," Andrew replied. Having checked that there was no one around to notice, he quickly reverted to a teenage version of himself. Morphing into a boy of about fifteen, with long, baggy shorts, a scruffy looking T-shirt, trainers and a cap… facing backwards.

"Why are you doing that?" Tris queried, looking him up and down.

"Because it's unlikely that street kids will talk all that easily with adults, even if I've got you in tow. Especially one who might just look like a truant officer," Andrew hastily explained. "Given how distrustful homeless kids, and teenagers in general, tend to be about adults with awkward questions, I doubt Molly Daniels would have got a straight answer out of any of them, even if she'd bothered to ask, or if they bothered to answer. If we look to be of a similar age, they might just be a bit more forthcoming with information."

"So where should we head, first?" Tris quickly asked. Andrew gave a slight shrug.

"I suppose Central Park might be as good a place as any, seeing that it's still daytime. We can start doing the shelters a bit later on. Like, late afternoon, or whenever it starts to get dark. As I said, a lot of those places will probably be a bit deserted during the daytime."

***

Their first two hours in Central Park proved quite fruitless. Showing Rylan's picture to most of the people in the midday crowd simply resulted in a great many negative responses. And that was only if the person could actually be bothered to look up from their cell phones for long enough to even acknowledge them, or take a proper look at the picture. A good many of them either totally ignored them, or simply glanced towards it, and then continued walking, without any response beyond a shrug. Getting involved in the problem of locating a runaway child obviously being of little interest to them.

"I was right," mused Tris rather wearily, as they eventually wandered towards yet another group of mainly younger teenagers lounging around on a semi-circular arrangement of seating. Near to where there was a small group of skateboarders. “It is like searching for a needle in a flippin’ haystack!” He began showing Rylan’s picture to some of the youths. Explaining, as he did so, that he and his brother were searching for their cousin, who had run away from home a week or two earlier after an altercation with his parents. The first two teenagers simply shrugged and went back to whatever they were doing with their phones. The third, however, immediately showed signs of recognition.

“Yeah. Sure I’ve seen him. Seen him at least a couple of times, in fact. The first was a good week or two ago, if I remember right,” the girl, whose T-shirt supposedly identified her as Angelique, eventually said, giving a casual shrug of her shoulders. She paused a moment, as if studying the picture and thinking through her recollections. “Though, with his blonde hair being quite long, I wasn’t sure, at the time, if he was a boy or a girl. That’s what probably made him stand out.”

“So where did you see him?” Tris eagerly asked. It was the first hint that they might be on the right track in their search. Angelique, if that was her name, gave a half shrug and then exhaled, rather noisily.

“As I said, it was maybe about two weeks ago. Not far from the Subway franchise near the 53rd Street Metro station. In fact, it was twice in about two or three days, as I remember. The first time, he was on his own. Like, he looked like he just getting something to eat. The only reason I noticed him was because, he, sort of, stood out. Not just with his appearance, but because he also looked rather skittish and out of place, somehow. Like, he didn’t know what he should be doing, or where to go, sort of. Then, the second time, maybe two days later, he was with this big old black mama. She was wailin’ into some black guy who’d tried to get a bit too close to your cousin, if you catch my drift. I mean, as you’re no doubt probably aware, he does tend to come across as a serious piece of jailbait! Whichever way you're looking! Given the appearance of the man who'd tried to grab him, it could have turned out really nasty for him if the big mama hadn't intervened."

"So what happened then?" Tris quickly queried. Angelique made a slight sideways cant of her head.

"Don't know for sure. But I think he probably ended up at one of the nearby homeless shelters, with the big black woman. Like, maybe St Joseph's, St Peter's, or any of the other dozen or so shelters linked to churches named after saints. You could also try the Central City Mission, or one of the welfare centres. At any rate, that's the sort of place she'd be likely to be taking him, and I'd start with those close to the Central Bus Station, given that it didn't look like she'd be likely to roam too far from home. I'd also suggest he's probably still with her, given the way she scared off the pimp and then just ploughed her way through the crowd with him in tow. Anyway, I think some of the locals tend to call her something like Big Lottie or Big Hannah… or something like that. And, from what I hear, she seems to take care of quite a few of the homeless kids; always seems to have a lot of them hanging around, evidently. Mind you, your cousin must stand out like a sore thumb, 'cause he's likely the only whitey in her brood, if you catch my drift. Not that she only looks after her own kind. To be blunt, she might be black as, but from what I hear, she seems to have all sorts of kids hanging around at various times. Blacks, Viets, Mexicans, Costas... you name it. It's sort of like she's just some big old mother hen who attracts homeless kids in all the coffee colours from mocha through to long black. And, as I just said, that's what made your cousin stand out when she had him in tow. Like she's a big black woman, and he's like this little fair-skinned, tow-headed kid and, at the same time, it was a bit hard to tell if he was a boy or a girl."

"So, have you seen either of them since then?" Andrew asked.

"Well, a couple of mornings ago, like, real early, I thought I saw her heading out with him. If it was him, he was dressed different, for sure. Like, much more like a boy. I'd suggest that was the big mama's doing, cause his hair was cut real short and he had on this big old coat that reached way down past his knees. I felt that he seemed worried about something, 'cause he looked like he'd been crying, and she was, sort of, half-cuddling him. They looked like they were headed back downtown someplace. Like, maybe towards the West Side."

"And you haven't seen them since?" Tris asked.

"The big mama a couple of times, but your cousin… not even a glimpse," Angelique casually muttered. "It's like the big mama's had him skip town, or something. Not that I blame her for wanting him well out of the way. Not when the spooks came 'round here asking questions about him."

"Spooks?" Tris queried.

"Feds, P.I.s.... or whatever. We call 'em spooks 'cause they try to act as if they're part of the park scene. They seem to think that all us street-kids will trust 'em because they try to act all friendly, like they sort of know where we're at. You know, like that they're the same as us, or understand how we think. But, to be honest, they stand out like a flippin' Jesus freak at a black mass, 'cause it's obvious that they're a fair bit older than they try to act. And with the sort of questions they end up asking, you just know they can't be trusted. Not ever."

"So why do you think these 'spooks' are after him?" Tris quickly queried. "Like, any ideas?" In some ways, he felt certain that she was referring to the military, but it seemed like something he should ask. Nevertheless, Angelique simply shrugged.

"Not really," she said with a sigh. She gestured towards her friends. "We just figured that maybe his parents were rich enough to hire a stack of people to try to find him. That's usually the case when you get a lot of them dumb official types asking questions about a kid. Although, strangely enough, none of them mentioned a reward of any type and there certainly ain't been no posters, or the like, put up anywhere."

"And do you think they might've worked out where he is?" Andrew asked.

"I shouldn't think so," murmured Angelique with a further shrug, as she turned towards the slightly older teenager. "We certainly didn't tell them anything. But then again, the big Mama's probably the only one who would know that for sure."

"And where would we be likely to find her?" asked Andrew just a little anxiously. Perhaps hoping that it would save them from having to search through all the homeless shelters.

"Just go to shelters," Angelique laughed, as she pointed towards a northerly section of the cluster of buildings that surrounded the park. "I'd try St. Barnards, St. Andrews, or St. Josephs, first. Anyway, once you find the churches, you'll be right, because most of the shelters are right next door to a church. If she's still staying in one of them, you sure can't miss her. She's a big, big woman!"

"And what if she isn't?" Tris asked. "Like, in one of those shelters?" Angelique cocked her head slightly to one side and briefly hunched her shoulders.

"Well, if she ain't there, they'll still probably know where she's gone. With wanting to avoid having the 'crackheads', and such 'low-lifes', causing trouble, all the shelters seem to keep tabs on who's actually staying where, if you catch my drift."

***

Mykael picked up the envelope that had been left on his desk. Immediately noting the name hurriedly scrawled in ballpoint pen on its outside... ***Lawrence Rylan Daniels.*** He opened it and began to examine its contents. The first item he extracted simply being a single sheet of paper. A standardized consulting form, headed with the name 'Edward J. Stanford Child Psychiatrist', that listed the boy's name, age, date of birth and a brief description of what had been presented to the Dr. Stanford regarding the boy's sexuality problems. There was also a small photo attached to the paper with a paperclip; a picture that mirrored, in some way, what had been on the front of the DVD of Rylan that Tris had taken from the camp. At the same time, Mykael could easily see the resemblance to Lara in the shape of the boy's face and the way it was framed by his slightly more than shoulder-length hair.

Tipping more of the contents of the envelope onto his desk, he quickly noted the stack of pornographic photos that had been taken of the boy. With an immediate sense of disgust at what were clearly not photos that any reputable psychiatrist would ever need of a child patient, he made to sweep them back into the folder. In doing so, however, one particular photograph immediately grabbed his attention. It was a back view of Rylan in just his underwear, but of more importance was what Mykael felt he could discern between the boy's shoulder blades. Perhaps accentuated by the angle of the lighting that had been used to illuminate the shot, he felt sure that he could perceive the faint outline of two slight ridges in the centre of the boy's back.

He picked up the photograph and studied it more closely; trying to be sure he wasn't just seeing shadows, or some trick of the light, and then hastily scanned through others of the photos for similar views. Eventually sorting out three pictures that were not too sick and revealing — photos that mainly showed Rylan's back — he arrayed them on his desk, and put the remainder back in the folder, before sending a thought out to Ithuriel.

"What do you see in these?" he immediately asked Ithuriel as soon as the guardian appeared. "Look particularly closely at the area between the shoulder blades." Ithuriel gave the pictures some careful scrutiny.

"A child-angel not too far off having wings, I'd suggest," he eventually offered. "Any idea who it is?" Mykael gave a quick nod of his head.

"Lara's twin brother." he replied. "The one she calls Rylan; the boy that Andrew and Tris are currently trying to locate in New York. As is that military group who were after Lara."

"And the pictures are from…?" Ithuriel asked, leaving the question hanging a little.

"The office of a gentleman by the name of Edward J. Stanford. The eminent child psychiatrist his parents were taking him to for treatment," Mykael replied. He tapped his fingers lightly on the folder. "Although, it seems that most of the pictures that are still in here would simply be classified as straight out child porn," he added. "Andrew visited his office and found them, after Rylan's mother explained about the boy not wanting to continue his visits to Edward J. Stanford for counselling sessions. Given the explicit nudity involved, and how the boy was asked to pose, you can certainly see why the kid might want to abscond from any further 'specialist treatment'."

"And why we need to find him, and fast," Ithuriel added.

CHAPTER TWELVE

In Hiding....

Rylan sat with his back to the wall of the small alcove, set a foot or so up in the side of the tunnel, and listened for the telltale sounds of people trudging their way over the sleepers and the ballast at the side of the tracks. Keeping himself quietly alert for the possibility of needing to make use of his special ability, if whoever it was seemed likely to be some sort of threat to his safety. People such as the subway line maintenance workers, who would collar him and hand him over to the police, or the small groups of gang kids who Dumper had said would steal anything of value from him and very likely also beat him up, just for the hell of it.

He sighed as he listened to the soft babble of voices emanating from the platform less than one hundred feet to his left, the light from which cast a soft, comforting glow into the darkness of the tunnel. The sound of the voices was reassuring in that it made him feel less alone in the dark. Not that he was scared of the dark; at least, not any more. Nevertheless, knowing that people were close by made him feel that he wasn't too far removed from the real world.

A sudden gust of wind began to swirl past him, letting him know that a train was about to approach from his right. He pulled his legs back up onto the ledge, keeping them close to his body so that he was completely contained within the small alcove. Not wanting to risk getting hit, or, more importantly, to be spotted too clearly by the train crew. In his short time in hiding, he'd quickly realised that being seen too close to the tracks, especially in one of the tunnels, by some train crew, would only result in his being hunted down so that he didn't pose a danger to himself or the train schedules.

A moment later, the train rushed past. Its brightly lit carriages throwing reflected light onto the tunnel walls. He hastily lowered his head and pulled his hood forward, so that anyone travelling in them would not see the white of his face illuminated by the light from the train. Not that too many people were ever watching out the windows, he'd soon realised. Most of them seemed too preoccupied with their phones, iPads, or newspapers to even be bothered with idle attempts at conversation with other commuters, let alone to look out the windows at the darkness of the tunnel walls. And at rush hour, with many passengers standing, most of them probably couldn't even see as far as their own reflection on the windows.

With his head down, he watched the wheels flash by. The train's progress quickly slowing as, with a raucous squealing of brakes, it approached the platform. Knowing that its arrival signalled the first beginnings of the morning 'rush'! The time when the relatively sparse traffic of pre-dawn transport would begin to give way to an almost constant parade of early morning trains speeding passengers to their daytime employment, or home from night-shift work.

Paradoxically, that would also be a safer time for him to venture out in a search for something to eat, especially as the supply of money that Hattie had given him was now almost down to nothing. He'd quickly discovered that, with the platforms fully crowded, it was easier to sneak a way out to the main vestibule to perhaps buy, or even just snatch, something from a kiosk, before retreating to the nearest bathroom with his 'prize' so that he wouldn't be seen disappearing, and then promptly jumping to his special hiding place.

Admittedly, when Dumper had first shown him the more rarely used tunnels, suggesting which ones would be safest to hide out in, before taking him to the City Hall Loop, he'd been surprised to find that so many other people also used them. Most of them, he'd quickly realised, were simply derelicts, or those with an obvious need to hide out; and, he'd soon come to understand that not too many of them posed much of a threat to his being there. The bulk of them simply ranging from the homeless and disaffected, who generally populated the less used sections of the underground rail system — at least until they were rounded up and kicked out by the maintenance squads — to those with a bit more swagger who were using it simply as a convenient means of getting from A to B without being seen. A few seemed curious about him, perhaps because of his small size and young age. Most just left him alone, perhaps figuring that he probably lived the same way as they did... singular and solitary, and trusting of no one. In the long run, it didn't really matter, just as long as they didn't report him to anyone official. At the same time, he certainly felt a lot safer now that he'd figured out how to use his special ability in complete darkness.

Having had to use his ability to 'jump' — the name he'd adopted for the process which allowed him to simply disappear from one place and reappear in another — to get away from two men who'd tried to waylay him in the men's bathroom at one station, the very first day that he'd been in hiding, he'd spent the remainder of that day finding various places that would be 'safe' from danger and learning how he could accurately transport himself into areas of complete darkness. At first, he'd simply made use of a couple of the little alcoves at the sides of tunnels and his memory of the City Hall Loop. Then, after a day or two of shuffling through the darkness, making as little use of the torch that Hattie had given him as possible, by keeping close to the tunnel walls, he'd stumbled on a secret hidey-hole; a place where he could be totally safe, even while he slept.

One of the little alcoves he'd discovered in the side of the older, less used tunnels, turned out to also have a door that opened inwards to a small room with a series of power boxes. It had a key lock, which no longer worked because the mechanism was rusted into an unlocked position. But by jamming a long piece of wood, that he'd found lying beside the tracks, between the far wall of the room and the door, he found that he could keep it fully barricaded from the inside, giving him a totally safe place to sleep, undisturbed.

That meant far less chance of getting caught unawares by any number of the 'rat-people' or 'gangstas', of course. Because, on being unable to push the door open, they'd probably consider that it must be rusted shut in a locked position. At the same time it did create the chance of his being discovered by the subway authorities if, for some quite unexpected reason, they decided to do some sort of maintenance check of the electrical systems. In a way, given the totally rusted state of the lock and the fact that the tunnel the room was in was less frequently used, he somehow doubted the likelihood of that ever happening.

By carefully using his torch, so that he could visualise the room clearly, he'd then found that, even if the room was totally dark when he went there, he'd still end up standing in exactly the same place as he'd visualised when the room had been lit. Since then, he'd even been able to find a few old cushions and blankets to take there, to make the room a little more comfortable for sleeping.

Since then, he'd also relied on knowing that he could always use his ability to jump to his safe place to avoid contact with the people who he felt were most likely to pose a danger to him. Especially the groups of gangsta kids, who were often armed with guns and high on self-importance, intimidation and bravado! The larger groups, often of about four to five or more, seemed to be the greater problem. He'd quickly come to realise that while they were older than himself, they were generally just teenagers of a similar age to Xavier J. Hernandez and his cronies and, in order to enhance their status, were usually full of aggression and confrontational to anyone they came across. That also meant that, as Dumper had warned him, they were customarily out to steal from anyone they thought might have anything of value; especially anyone they thought they could easily intimidate.

Thankfully, he'd also found that it was possible to sneak onto the trains to get around to different stations. With already being beyond the turnstiles, a good many people obviously assumed that he had a token, or a MetroCard, even if his grubby, dishevelled appearance often caused them to edge away from him a little. Thankfully, none of them had so far appeared bothered enough by his presence to report him to Metro Security.

Once the train had passed, he moved forward and stretched his legs out a little further. Taking care to see that they weren't close to touching the any of the rails, and most certainly not the one on the far side that carried the electrical current. While in some places he had to be constantly wary of the trains, it was not the case in this particular tunnel. Unlike some of the newer areas of the underground, where he'd almost had to lie totally flat on the concrete to one side of the lines while trains thundered, just inches, it seemed, over his head, or hide in one of the little alcoves that were spaced out at various points of the tunnels, this particular line was not used all that much at night. So far, in all the days he'd been hiding, there'd only seemed to be about three or four trains per hour after midnight. And most of the trains running at those times rarely had any passengers in them, from what he could tell. Just a driver, who seldom seemed to give any indication of having noticed him, even if he was caught, for a moment, in the edge of the illumination of the headlights.

Eventually having watched the train depart from the other end of the station, accompanied by its usual suction of air, he sighed, even as his stomach rumbled, and glanced down at his watch. Its luminescent numbering faintly showed that it was still technically pre-dawn... or, perhaps more correctly, very early morning. The morning rush proper would commence in about half an hour or so. It would then be safer to sneak up onto the platform and filch something to eat from one of the kiosks.

Not that he could properly tell too much about day or night down in the tunnels. The only difference seemed to be that the trains on his line, and others nearby, were far more frequent during daylight hours; or, perhaps more correctly, the eighteen or so hours from sun-up to midnight. In the remaining few hours, it all became relatively quiet, with far less disturbance or need for caution.

Reaching down to his side and fumbling in the dark, he located his torch and started giving it a shake. It seemed to have some sort of suspended magnet in its centre, which could be shaken back and forth between magnetic coils to create some sort of power storage, thus negating the need for replacement batteries. Not that he used it all that much. After all, there seemed no point in unnecessarily advertising to anyone that he had such a treasure.

His being seen in a tunnel with such an item had, at first, simply seemed to make him a target for the 'gangstas'. But he'd soon worked out that, if he shone it straight at them, the moment he was spotted, then switched it off, leaving them temporarily light-blinded, and 'jumped' to his hideout, his antagonists were simply left puzzled as to how he could elude them so easily, and not be where they expected him to be.

Obviously, later at night, there were far fewer people around to spot him whenever he emerged from the pitch black of a tunnel and clambered up onto platforms. Some would simply watch him for a moment and then go back to whatever they were doing. Perhaps a few of them wondered at his being so young to be out on his own at such an hour… that was if they hadn't already tagged him as just some homeless street kid.

With the platforms being less crowded, he also knew that it meant that he would probably be more easily identified if he was picked up on the numerous CCTV cameras; the all-seeing eyes of the underground that seemed to record every presence on the platforms, corridors, stairways and entrances. Strange as it seemed, he'd also noticed that lately they seemed to be doing a lot of maintenance work on the cameras, or something. Almost every platform that he'd frequented, over the last few days, seemed to have some technician checking the cameras.

At the same time, it also puzzled him a little that, even when the platforms were crowded, especially when they were filled to capacity with a throng of waiting, embarking or disembarking passengers, not all that many people even seemed to notice him, or pay him any attention. Not even when he'd scurry from a tunnel and up onto the far end of a platform beyond the barriers and signs that notified that access to the tunnels was forbidden.

Of course he didn't really wanted to be living like a mole… for want of a better way to describe his current situation. He'd certainly been far happier staying in the refuge with Mama Hattie, even if he hadn't been able to venture out onto the streets. The dark-skinned, African-American woman had fussed over him like a mother hen, regardless of the fact all her other 'semi-adopted' children were, as she put it, various coffee-coloured shades, while he was just her little 'Milky Bar Kid'.

When he'd asked her what a milky bar was, she'd laughed and told him that it was the name of a white chocolate candy bar that a friend in the airlines used to bring her from New Zealand; the 'kid' part referring to the very blonde-headed child cowboy image that was used to promote the merchandise. Nevertheless, even though he'd stood out so noticeably when with her, he'd still felt safe in her shadow. None of the more shady characters, using the shelters at night had ever dared try to tangle with Mama Hattie. Her hands quickly became like a large clubs when it came to protecting her 'brood'; always 'ready and able' it seemed, along with her loud, stentorian voice, to 'swat' aside anyone who ventured too near to any of them with what might possibly be an air of dubious intent.

In the days he'd spent with her, he'd finally felt 'safe'; perhaps even more so than when he'd been with the Fulchers, or with old George. All that, of course, had come crashing down when his mother had turned up, showing a photo of him to the people who ran the refuge. And she hadn't been the only person looking for him, it appeared. According to what Mama Hattie had murmured, when they'd been on their way to meet up with Dumper, some men in official looking uniforms had also being checking the shelters for him. Nevertheless, while he still hoped that Dumper would arrive sometime in the next few days to take him back to the shelter, after a fairly anxious first day, which had included his bathroom escape, he'd come to realise that, with his ability to 'jump', he would be reasonable safe in hiding, more especially since he'd found and barricaded the power-box room.

***

Tris walked up to the desk just inside the doorway of the St. Barnards Shelter, feeling a little nervous. This area of New York, a good few streets away from the more touristy locations, seemed far less friendly than even the fractious, anonymous bustle of Broadway and Times Square and other more touristy areas. Behind him, Andrew kept a cautious watch while still in a state of invisibility. They had already decided that Tris would present a less worrisome figure to anyone in the homeless shelters, than would an adult. A person who might possibly be mistaken for undercover police or a social worker… or be, in some way, viewed as someone out to cause trouble for some of the 'residents'. It was also necessary for one of them to keep a lookout for Molly Daniels, the military, or even the police. It seemed more sensible for that to be Andrew. After all, there was also no sense in ruining the subterfuge of him being a truancy mediator by the name of Arthur Megson, if that guise might prove useful in the future.

"Excuse me," Tris politely asked, as he presented himself at the sign-in desk in the foyer. The woman standing on the far side gave him a quick, but lazy, perusal. Perhaps wondering if he was yet another runaway hoping for a bed for the night; a kid simply looking for a means to avoid being picked up at night by the police and given over to Social Welfare. Closing down her laptop computer, she slowly wandered over to where he was waiting.

"I was just wondering if you'd seen this boy," Tris said, showing her the picture of Rylan taken from the cover of the DVD. "He's my cousin," he quickly lied, in an effort to make the reason for his search seem a little more plausible. "And I heard from some street-kids over in Central Park that he might have been seen around here somewhere with a woman I think they called Big Lottie… or something like that."

"Yeah, I seen him," the woman sighed with a weary shrug, giving the photograph a rather quick perusal. "'Though, you should know that you ain't the only person who's been 'round here looking for him. We had a woman down here a few days ago claiming to be his mother and also some rather official looking dudes. Military, I'd guess. They were here the day before yesterday, claiming to want to reunite him with his sister, or some such story. " She gave Tris a further quick perusal. "And you're his cousin?' she said, her manner seeming more than a little disbelieving of that fact. Tris wondered if his unusual accent was perhaps the reason why she doubted him.

"A distant cousin," Tris replied. "And I know he's in a bit of trouble. That's why I'm trying to find him. He ran away from his home be... because his mum and dad were not very nice to him. My dad's his uncle, and we want to give him a new home. His sister is already living with us for the same reason. Her name's Lara," The woman seemed to watch him for a while. Perhaps still thinking through whether to divulge any information.

"As I said, I did see him," she finally said. "A week or so ago... or maybe a bit more. A couple of times, at least, I think. But not here! Last I saw, he was hanging with a big black woman who seems to look after quite a few of the street-kids. You were sort of on the right track with Lottie, but Big Hattie's what they generally call her, and she seems to look after quite few of them strays. It was just that he was the only really white kid with her. Like, real blonde hair and white skin 'n all. And nobody seemed all that sure, at first, if he was a boy or a girl, so to speak. I also hear that Big Hattie just calls him her 'Milky Bar Kid'."

"So that was when?" Tris asked eagerly, given that it seemed to immediately equate with what they'd been told by Angelique.

"Well, as I said, the first time was quite a while ago, but just a few days ago I seen him again. It was early morning because I was just on my way here for the daytime shift, and they was down somewhere near to St. Joseph's Church. So it's my guess that that's where he's probably been staying. He was also dressed different that last time; you know… looked much more like a boy. Now I'd venture to suggest that that was some of Big Hattie's doing, cause his hair looked like it was cut real short. Well, what I could see of it under his hoodie. And he had on this big old coat that reached way down past his knees. I also got the impression that he seemed worried about something. Mainly 'cause it seemed like Big Hattie was sort of cuddling him. Anyways, as I said, I was on my way here to start work, so I didn't take too much notice of where they were headed, but I think it was probably down towards the Civic Centre ways."

"And you haven't seen him since?"

"Not a glimpse. Mind you, I have seen Big Hattie at least a couple a times, lately, but not the kid. It's almost like he's vanished, or skipped town, or something. Now, if you ask me, I'd venture to suggest that Big Hattie's most probably got him hiding out somewhere until the heat's off, if you catch my drift. Although, it's likely she'd be the only one who could tell you that for sure. And then I'd wager that it'd only be if she thinks you can be trusted."

"And where would I find her?" Tris eagerly asked.

"Just go down to the St. Joseph's Shelter and ask for her," the woman replied with a slight laugh. "The shelter's right beside the church; two blocks south of here. You sure can't miss her. She's a big, big woman!" she added, pointing with a finger when Tris seemed a little unsure of which way to head.

***

Having been directed to the female dormitory of the St. Josephs shelter, Tris quickly spotted Big Hattie. The woman at the earlier shelter had been right. Big Hattie was certainly a rather large woman. Clinically obese would have been the official medical definition.

"Excuse me," he said politely, as he came close to where she sat, perched on the edge of a bed. The bed creaked a little under her weight as Mama Hattie shuffled her bulk to get a better view of him.

"They told me up at the St. Barnards Shelter that you might be able to tell me where this boy has gone to?" Tris quickly asked, showing her the photograph of Rylan. Mama Hattie glanced at it and gave a slight nod, and then seemed to take some time to look Tris over.

"Now why's a boy like you be asking questions about the whereabouts of my little 'Milky Bar Kid'?" she eventually rumbled rather softly. Not that anything in her tone of voice was all that intimidating. More, perhaps, just protectively curious... in spite of its depth. Tris immediately noted the possessive nature of her reply as an indication that she recognised the boy in the picture.

"Because I think I can help him," replied Tris, giving her a broad smile, while also finding some bemusement at the nickname she'd used for Rylan. "There's a place I can take him to where he would be completely safe. Where his mum and dad would never ever find him... or anyone else, if he didn't want them to. And his sister's already there. Waiting for him."

"Now it's funny you should mention that," Mama Hattie, said, with a smile. "Some of them official looking dudes who were asking after him, said almost the same sort of thing. Like, how they'd take him somewhere safe. It seems that they were also looking for the sister. Wanted to know if any of us had seen her, as well." She gave a slight shrug. "I dunno, about the girl, 'cause I ain't seen her, but the boy is, sort of, unusual in some way. And I'm not just meaning his being more than a little bit mixed up about whether he be a boy or a girl, if you catch my drift." She gave a sigh and eased her bulk into a slightly more comfortable position on the edge of the bed. It creaked a little under the strain. "Mind you, the way the spooks were buzzing around, they must think those two kids are something real special."

"They are," Tris said. "And as I said, his sister is safe with people who can protect her. But, believe me, all the other people looking for Rylan, do not want him for a good reason. They just want to lock him up in a cage. Like they did with his sister… at least until we managed to rescue her. And the same goes for his parents, even though his dad's already in jail for abusing him." Mama Hattie shook her head and sighed. The actions seeming to cause her whole bulk to shudder like a rather unstable jelly.

"He told me as much," she said softly. "Like, about his mother and father and the abuse 'n all. As if the poor little mite don't have enough problems. Like, with him not being sure what he be! That's why I made him to dress down, and be as much of a boy as he can. It be much safer for him that way. Especially out on the streets!"

"So do you know where he would be now?" Tris cautiously asked, hoping that the woman would feel that he was genuine in his efforts to help the runaway. Mama Hattie looked around a little, as if checking who might overhear.

"Well, first of all, he was just staying here. Like, inside all day, 'cause this nasty ol' pimp, TakerZ, was a fixin' to grab him. But then, when his momma also starting comin' 'round all the time asking awkward questions, and then the spooks started sniffing around the shelters, I got a friend to hide him in the underground," she said quite softly. "You know, like where all the old subway lines for the Metro go. Especially the ones that ain't used too much no more."

"So, do you think any of those other people... you know, the official types, know where he is?" Tris queried. Mama Hattie gave a soft chuckle.

"Not that I know of," she rumbled. "Dumper hasn't let me know of anything that might have happened in that regard. And I'm certainly not going to tell 'em anything."

"But you're telling me,"Tris queried a little bemusedly. Mama Hattie seemed to smile at his slight puzzlement.

"But, you be a different kid. I can see that," she softly rumbled. Tris's expression seemed to immediately display an increased sense of bemusement.

"How?" he asked.

"Well, firstly, you're clearly just a child. You're not like the official types who come searching. What with their always trying to be all casual, pretending to be friendly, and yet you just know that they be itching to get all heavy and to start making threats, even as they be asking you the nice polite questions. Just as with the police, you can see it in their eyes. Like, they be used to getting what they want, when they want it, if you catch my drift. So they start playing on their 'good cop', 'bad cop' routines, as if they be thinking you might get fooled into believing their antics. More especially when they get to thinking that you might be knowing something."

"And secondly?" Tris cautiously queried. Mama Hattie cocked her head briefly to one side and smiled.

"I can sort of faintly see those pretty little wings you be trying to hide, Honey," she said, with the hint of a laugh. "Like, maybe you be a little angel or something, I just know. Now, my little

Rylan, I guess he be also headed that way, to my way of thinking. He might not yet have the full wings bit as yet. Leastwise, not anywhere as well-developed as yours would seem to be, but his aura is just the same; sort of real special colours."

"So, do you know where I can find him now?" asked Tris earnestly. "Like, if he's still there?" At the same time, feeling just a little taken aback by the fact that Mama Hattie could understand what he was, know that he had wings, and yet accept it all so casually. Mama Hattie gave another bed-shaking shrug. Given her bulk, for a moment Tris quietly wondered whether it might be strengthened a little more than the others in the room.

"As I said, last I knows, he was still somewhere in the underground," she replied, then looked carefully around. "Somewhere not too far from the old City Hall loop line, I think," she added in a whisper. "That's where I had Dumper take him, when his momma and all those others first be looking for him."

"Can you take me to him?" Tris asked. Mama Hattie smiled and gave a slight shake of his head.

"Now, what makes you think I could be going up and down all those steps and be wandering roun' them ol' subway tunnels?" she laughed, in a manner that again shook the whole bed. "Sorry, Honey, but ol' Hattie jus' ain't that mobile." She looked around the room as if trying to spot someone in particular. "I could maybe get Dumper to take you to where he was. Last he told me, Rylan was somewhere around Broad Street," she eventually murmured. "Not that I can guarantee that he'll still be there. It's good to keep yourself on the move when you be down in those sort of places."

"But can't you take me?" Tris asked again. Mama Hattie gave a throaty laugh.

"Me?" she queried. "Honey, look at me. With my size, does it look like I leave this place all that much? Apart from wandering down to the local shops a couple of times a week?" She shook her head and sighed softly. "At any rate, them damn official types seemed pretty sure that I'd had some contact with him, so I just know they be watching me, for certain, 'case he returns. You won't likely see any of them when you leave, but you can be sure that they'll have someone out there, somewhere, keeping a watch. Sitting at the bus stop 'cross the street, pretending to be reading a paper or something." Tris quickly thought through that item of information. By extension, it was obvious that they'd likely get to know he'd been talking to Mama Hattie. In which case, they might also be curious enough to want to know why. And perhaps follow him.

"Is there a bathroom somewhere that I could use?" he asked, looking hastily around.

"Down that hallway, and turn left," Mama Hattie replied, shifting her bulk to point a large arm towards the back of the sleeping area. "It be the second door on your right."

"Thanks," Tris said, hurrying off to where she'd indicated. Less than a minute later he was high in the air above the building. He sent out a quick visualisation to Andrew, who was instantly beside him. Pointing to the roof of the building, they descended. At the same time, remaining invisible.

"Big Hattie says that he's probably in the underground, somewhere," Tris said with a slight shrug. "Like, down in one of the old subway tunnels. You know, the old parts of the Metro system. Up somewhere near City Hall or Broad Street, she thinks."

"Does she know exactly where?" Andrew asked. Tris shook his head.

"No," he replied. "Just somewhere near the old City Hall loop… or some such thing. But she did confirm that there were other people looking for him, besides his mother. And, that some of them were also looking for Lara. I think she thought that they might be FBI or military or something, and that, because they felt sure that she'd been looking after him, they'd probably be keeping a watch on her in case he returned."

"Which, I take it, is why you didn't just walk out the front door of the place," Andrew said with a knowing nod of his head.

"She also sort of confirmed something else," Tris continued a little excitedly. "She could tell straight-out that I had wings. She said she could see them, or sense them, or something. More importantly, she said that Rylan also had wings, and that it seemed that he had the same sort of aura about him as me."

"Which means that he's definitely at a similar development stage to Lara and also, very likely, starting to wonder why he has wings," Andrew replied. "And that means that we really do need to find him… and fast."

"Well, it should be easier if he's turning into an angel, shouldn't it?" Tris replied. "If we also go down into the Metro system, you should be able to sense where he is."

"It won't be quite that straightforward. Not if he's only been into his transition for a little while," Andrew said, giving a slight shake of his head.

"His what?" Tris asked.

"His change. Like Lara, he'll be growing his wings, but probably doesn't know how to use them. It'll be just like how you started off," Andrew replied. "But as you say, I should be able to sense where he is, although I'll still need to get reasonably close to him at least once, so that I can start to identify his particular signature."

"His what?" Tris queried, yet again.

"What helps me with sensing other angels. Like fingerprints, each of us seems to have a slightly different sensing signature, for want of a better description," Andrew hastily explained. "Just as people look different and sound different and have different fingerprints and DNA and stuff. That's how I can know whether it's you I'm sensing, or Lara, or Conlaodh, or whoever."

CHAPTER THIRTEEN

A Hunt in Progress....

"So where do we start?" Tris queried, as he looked across towards the entrance to the Broad Street subway station. "And, how?"

"We get ourselves inside and start looking and listening," Andrew replied. "Even if we can't spot him straight away, we can at least listen out for anyone mentioning about anything untoward. If Rylan has wings, he'll probably be trying to hide them in some way. Which might make him stand out as a hunchback, or something a bit untoward, to people on the platforms."

"Do we have to pay to get in?" Tris asked, aware that there were turnstiles to be negotiated in order to reach the platforms. Andrew seemed to roll his eyes a little.

"Of course not," he replied with a slow shake of his head. "We just stay invisible and then visualise ourselves somewhere past the turnstiles. Afterwards, we can find somewhere to become visible without anyone seeing us appear."

A few moments later, having entered the subway, visualised themselves beyond the turnstiles and found an alcove in which to become visible, they wandered down onto the platform.

"Now," Andrew whispered. "Keep you eyes and ears open. As I said earlier, even if we can't spot him straight away, we might just hear something that will give us some better idea of where he's hiding. Like, near which of the stations he might be based."

Tris nodded as they then separated and wandered off to opposite ends of the platform.

For quite a while it seemed, neither of them saw and heard anything that would've been likely to help them in their quest. At least, not until Tris overheard a snippet of a casual conversation between two middle-aged women regarding something that had supposedly happened a few days earlier at a different subway station. The words that had caught his attention were… 'and then, after a startled look around, the kid simply disappears again. Right before their eyes!'

He surreptitiously moved a little closer. Wanting to find out more about what had occurred, but also not wanting to appear as if he was actually eavesdropping. Thankfully, neither of the women paid him the slightest attention.

"… but, first of all, Chad said that this kid was just suddenly there," the first woman continued. "Like, just standing in the middle of the men's room on Lexington and 59th… just as if he'd just teleported there from another dimension or something. And then, before any of his maintenance crew could even do anything, or say something, the kid just vanished. Like, one minute he was there, the next he wasn't. Chad said that his workmates were all hurriedly crossing themselves like they'd just seen a ghost or something."

"And you believe him?" the second woman queried.

"Chad's pretty down-to-earth about such matters and certainly not given to telling lies," the first woman solemnly replied, with a shake of her head. Almost as if a little annoyed that her husband's veracity might be being impugned. "And I very much doubt he'd ever bother to make up such a wild story."

"So what did he look like?" the second woman quickly enthused. "You know, the kid?" The first woman gave a casual shrug of her shoulders.

"According to Chad, he was quite small and was wearing a rather grubby-looking coat with a hood. He thought it was probably a boy, given that they were in a men's room. Not that he could be too sure with the big coat he was wearing and with his hood being up."

"And he hasn't seen him since?" the second woman queried. Again the first woman gave a shrug.

"He hasn't said anything more about it. But they're all a bit spooked, naturally. Chad had also wondered if it was a ghost, at first. But since talking to some of the security men, they've evidently heard, from a few of the gang kids they've escorted out of the place, of some strange kid hiding out in the tunnels. The gang kids said that he's got a torch, but whenever they get near to him, he suddenly shines it at them and then, when he turns it off they can't seem to find him; even when they've tried coming at him from all different directions to block every possible way of escape. It's like he can just vanish into thin air whenever he wants."

Any further conversation, however, was quickly lost as, with a rather noisy squeal of brakes, a train hurried into the station and the two women hurried to get on board. Tris quickly hurried to find Andrew.

"I've got something," he said excitedly, once they were together. "And it seems that Rylan's discovered how to 'be'. I overheard two women saying that he'd startled some workmen by suddenly appearing for a few seconds in one of the bathrooms they were renovating. They said that he was wearing a big overcoat with a hood. It seems that he's also been avoiding some of the gang kids the same way. You know, by just disappearing." Andrew nodded sagely and pursed his lips a little.

"Well, that gives us good things and bad," he murmured. Tris immediately looked puzzled.

“Such as?” he queried. Andrew exhaled softly and cocked his head a little to one side.

“If he can ‘be’, then it might be a bit harder to just grab him,” he said. “At the same time, if he is able to use such a skill, it’s highly likely that he’s also found somewhere safe to go to; which, with a bit of luck, I may be able to lock on to. Provided I can just get close enough to him to pick up his angelic signature.” He looked about as the train hurried off to its next stop. “Now, did the women say anything about where he was seen? You know, when he suddenly turned up in that bathroom?”

“I think she said that it was at Lexington and 59th,” Tris replied.

***

Skylar looked up as the door to the basement room banged open. It wasn’t any basement room in which he’d previously been, but the Network seemed to have a good many ‘holding houses’, as they called them, spread throughout the outskirts of various American cities. All of them with soundproof basements in which children could be temporarily contained between ‘assignments’. Many of those that were in cities, also seemed to have access ways, or holding areas, that allowed trucks to back into them and be completely out of sight, so that the captives could be transferred into the truck, or out of them, without risk of being seen. After all, the sight of several handcuffed and gagged children being escorted into the back of a truck, out in the open, would certainly arouse curiosity and likely unwanted police attention; courtesy of a simple phone call from a well-meaning citizen anxious about seeing something untoward.

The holding rooms were all very similar in appearance and function; being sparsely furnished, with just the barest of bedding comforts, most of which appeared to have been purchased secondhand, or salvaged from rubbish tips. Usually being in the form of old, well-stained, threadbare mattresses and yellowed, uncovered pillows, along with some coarse woollen blankets that looked like old army surplus, to keep out the cold. Toilet facilities were also usually very basic. Sometimes just being a bucket with a lid. Showers and any other forms of bathing would usually conducted upstairs, under the watchful eyes of Vittorio, Angelo or any other of the men who helped with supervision. Upstairs was also where any 'special treatment', beyond a simple punitive thrashing, meant to serve as an example to the other children, was meted out.

Most of the time, the boys were kept bare-chested, dressed in just jeans or shorts unless it was particularly cold. Alternatively, if it was felt that they needed to display the marks of any recent punishments they'd endured, as a warning to the other children about the consequences of 'misbehaviour', they would sometimes be forced to remain in just their display pants, or even entirely without clothes!

Hastily getting to his feet, Skylar rushed over to help as Peter staggered into the room, half supporting Noah, who seemed almost unconscious. Peter was dressed in his jeans, but Noah was still naked. His slight body clearly showing the marks of a particularly savage beating, that had left deep reddish and blue welts; some of which had made cuts to his skin, creating blood smears. The mixture of bruises and blood smears covering an area from his lower back down to his thighs.

"Did Vittorio do that to him?" Cooper whispered, as he helped Peter and Skylar gently lay Noah face down on one of the mattresses, before covering him with a blanket to give him a little modesty. "Like, did he do something wrong?" Given that Vittorio had been rather lenient with punishments, of late, resorting mainly to use of a paddle through not wanting to have his saleable 'merchandise' too badly marked, it seemed a little strange for him to have suddenly treated Noah so brutally. More especially when he was still being regarded as a possible 'innocent'. Peter shook his head quite vigorously.

"No. It was an effin' client!" he half snarled. "We were both booked to be entertainment for Lester McKinney, the movie producer. If you've seen any of his films, you'd know that he's into nasty horror themes. You know... the sort where people get trapped in an old house and are stalked by some deranged killer. Anyway, it was just supposed to be a bit of photography session... like, with me and Noah bound and gagged in various ways; sort of weird kinky stuff, along with a bit of light punishment. At first, Lester just took photos of us tied up and then spanked us with his some small paddle thing that certainly stung a fair bit. Which was what Vittorio had said was as far as they could go. But he had some other friend with him who decided to get real nasty with Noah."

"Do you know who he was?" Skylar queried. Peter gave a quick shake of his head.

"I think, from the way he and McKinney were talking, he was someone else in the film industry. When Vittorio realised that things were going wrong and was trying to get us out of there, the man even kept offering Vittorio money to buy Noah, straight out," he continued. "Simply because he liked the way he screams. And I don't think that being whipped was everything that happened. Not by a long shot! Boy, was Vittorio really pissed off when he realised what had been done to Noah. Not only because Noah's screaming had forced him cut the session short, but because he'd clearly stressed to McKinney beforehand, that it was to be nothing more than photographs and a bit of light spanking. Like, that there was to be nothing done to mark us, Noah in particular, because he might still be needed for that special function thing that Vittorio's been on about for the last few weeks."

"So he also..." Skylar asked. The incomplete question did, however, not really require an answer. While he, Cooper, Riley and Luka were still 'innocents' — the 'vestal virgins' as Vittorio tauntingly described them — they were all very well aware of the abuses to which some of the older boys, including Peter, were subjected; the older girls, likewise. Abuses he knew he'd also be eventually forced to endure, if he didn't find some way to escape before then. Peter nodded.

"It was pretty horrific," he added in almost a whisper. Technically, they'd both been on the 'assignment, but Skylar knew that Peter was actually referring to the very brutal and savage manner in which Noah had been assaulted.

"So it was really bad?" Cooper whispered, looking down at Noah. Peter nodded.

"Very bad," he murmured. "Hopefully, he won't end up bleeding too much. Or for too long."

"So where are his clothes?" Skylar asked, wondering if Noah was also going to be subjected to more brutality from their 'captors' for some minor indiscretion.

"They're upstairs," Peter said with almost a sigh. "It was just too difficult to get him properly dressed after what he'd been through, and the fact that we also had to leave the place in a bit of a hurry. Mainly 'cause Vittorio got a bit spooked, when some other people turned up, unannounced. He didn't want to hang around, in case anyone upstairs had heard Noah screaming and got suspicious about what had actually been going on, downstairs. Angelo had us sneak out a back way. With Noah still naked and gagged to keep him quiet, so we wouldn't be seen and..." He lapsed into silence for a few moments; simply looking to where Noah was lying without moving and seemingly only semi-conscious.

"What are the blue lines around his wrists and ankles?" Cooper asked, looking at where Noah's feet and one hand were visible beyond the covering of the blanket.

"That's from his being tied up," muttered Peter angrily. He showed Skylar similar marks on his own wrists. "We both had our feet and hands tied so that we were spread-eagled. Like, so that we couldn't move! It was okay for the photographs, because we weren't even touched all that much. McKinney just adjusted the way we were tied up. But after the photos, it suddenly got really nasty... and creepy."

"How? Skylar quickly asked. 'Nasty' he could understand. 'Creepy' sounded weird.

"Because they suddenly turned off all the lights so that it was pitch black," Peter murmured.

"So all the really bad stuff happened in the dark?" Skylar queried. Peter gave a quick nod of his head.

"Yeah. After the lights were turned off, all we heard at first, were some weird noises and then, all of a sudden, they started hitting us again. What made it worse was that they didn't say anything. You could just hear the sound of breathing; like them and us… at least, until Noah started screaming. It turned out that they were wearing night-vision goggles, which meant that they had no trouble in hitting us in the right places. It took me a few minutes, however, to realise that it was only Noah who was getting really hurt… because, all of a sudden, he really started screaming. Anyway, after a few minutes of Noah's screams, the lights were suddenly turned back on, which pissed-off McKinney and his friend, because they were almost blinded by the sudden light. That's when I realised that they had the goggles."

"So that's what made it creepy?" Cooper queried. Peter nodded as he moved the blanket a little to ensure Noah was properly covered.

"So McKinney's friend was trying to make it a bit like that creepy scene in the 'Silence of the Lambs'?" Skylar suggested. Peter quickly nodded.

"Sort of!" he murmured. "At least until Vittorio and Angelo came in and..." He left the rest of his comment incomplete as the noise of a lock being pulled back suddenly took their attention. As Angelo came through the door and threw a bundle of clothing onto one of the spare mattresses, he glanced down at Noah.

"He's not awake yet?" he almost demanded, giving a leg that Noah still had exposed, a slight nudge with the toe of his boot. Peter gave a fairly emphatic shake of his head.

"He's hurt pretty bad," he murmured. "I doubt he'll want to move for a while." For a moment Angelo was silent, giving just a small shake of his head. Then, appearing to think better of thrashing Noah into wakefulness, he gave an irritated sigh.

"Well, just do your best to get him properly dressed. Even if he isn't awake!" he snapped. "Not unless you want him to travel naked!" He reached down, grabbed the bundle of clothing and shoved it into Peter's hands. "And be quick about it! We need to move, right now! Vittorio wants us to head to one of the other houses... like, out of state. He's still just a little spooked by the actions of one of the unexpected guests. According to Miguel, she started asking McKinney some awkward questions, so Vittorio feels that she might have figured that something illegal was going on downstairs and might call the cops. So we might just need to stay hidden for a few days, just in case there's some unexpected police action that's a bit difficult for us to have our FBI friends shut down."

***

Rylan listened carefully. He could hear the scrunch of shoes on the track ballast coming closer. He kept his torchlight focussed on the ground, hoping to be able to quickly work out whether whoever was approaching was some form of danger. In some ways, he hoped for a bit of company. A solitary life, underground, could be a little unnerving, especially when you spent so much time on your own and in the dark. It just seemed necessary to have a little normality, at times; particularly, in being able to get enough to eat and drink, and being able to find toilet facilities well away from where you slept.

Not that food was now any sort of problem. After having made a successful attempt to visualise and then 'jump' to the dumpsters behind the café that often threw out its stale food, he'd quickly realised that by simply looking through the front windows of the café when they were closed, and visualising himself inside the place, he could easily help himself to fresh food directly from their fridges. The only problem being that he had to do so late at night, and that tended to set off the shop's alarms; an event that had totally startled him when it had first happened, scaring him into simply returning to his hideout as quickly as he could. Now, he realised that, as long as he immediately grabbed what he wanted and jumped to safety, he could be well away from the place before any police or security personnel were likely to turn up to investigate. And if he didn't take too much, he figured that it might be that his nightly 'meal stops' would go virtually unnoticed. Especially if the owners of the café simply decided that, with there being no clear sign of a break-in, the alarms must just be malfunctioning.

With a sense of relief, he'd also managed to find a bathroom that, while temporarily closed to the public, still worked in a rudimentary fashion. He also preferred to only visit there at night, because the facility was in the process of being renovated, and during the day there were sometimes workmen there. His sudden, brief appearance one morning, just before lunch, had evidently caused quite a stir amongst the small group of workmen, judging from the conversations he'd overheard later in the day on the platforms. He had wondered, afterwards, if news of that small 'faux pas' had filtered back to Mama Hattie. Or, more worryingly, to his mother, or TakerZ, or to whoever the military group was who were also trying to track him down.

"It's the kid with the torch! Get him!"

The sound of a voice, which he immediately recognised as being from one of the nastier gang members, suddenly brought him out of his mental meanderings and back to his present circumstances. He quickly realised that he still had the torch turned on. As the rapid sound of the gang's shoes on the ballast, showed that they were hurrying towards them, he flashed the torch briefly in their direction. Its illumination showing that there were four older teenage boys hurrying towards him.

"Spread out so that he can't dodge away! But be carefully of the third rail," one of them yelled.

Rylan forced himself to keep the torch focussed on them until they seemed about ten feet from the alcove he was in. Watching, almost with a sense of amusement, as they tried to fan out to block his scurrying away. Then, quickly switching it off, he visualised his new hideout and 'jumped'.

CHAPTER FOURTEEN

Underground....

Arriving on a platform at the station that the woman had mentioned, Andrew stood still for a moment, trying to concentrate in the hope of immediately sensing Rylan's angelic signature. Tris kept close beside him, while all around them the pedestrian commuter traffic surged back and forth as people entered or exited the waiting subway trains. Unfortunately, the late morning rush was still in full swing.

"It's a bit hard to be all that accurate with so much happening around us, but I get the feeling that he's somewhere quite near to us," Andrew finally said. He closed his eyes and blocked his ears for a moment, as if trying to shut out the sound of the platform noise. "I'm getting the hint of a signature that could be him. I can also sense that it's somewhere that's dark, but is perhaps close enough for him to see what's happening on one of the platforms," he murmured, almost to himself. Tris gave a slight shrug, glanced towards the dark maw of the tunnel to his left and rolled his eyes. That particular detail seemed rather obvious.

"At this level or above us?" he asked, suddenly sensing that, perhaps Rylan had returned to street level and, therefore, was not where he was expected to be. Andrew was quiet for a moment and then gave a slow shake of his head.

"Below," he murmured. "It's as if he's somewhere further under the ground."

"Below the subway?" Tris queried.

"Hiding somewhere down there," Andrew replied, pointing downwards. He shrugged and gave a slow shake of his head, as if imagining the difficulty of their quest. "There's at least one more level of tracks that are in use, according to the diagram in the foyer and very likely some of the old disused subway lines close by, that we'll also need to check out. The old tunnels would be the perfect hiding place, if you really wanted to totally disappear for a while."

"If you like living like a mole," Tris retorted just a little sarcastically. At the same time not too keen on the idea of them having to explore pitch-black tunnels, even if they were no longer in use.

"Come on," Andrew said with some enthusiasm. "Lets go down one more level."

Joining in with the surge of travellers exiting from the platform as another of the trains departed, they made their way along a corridor and then turned sharply left. Heading down a flight of stairs that appeared to lead to a platform below where they had just been. Emerging onto the new platform, Tris was pleased to note that it was not too crowded, certainly not when compared with the platform they'd just been on.

"Should be easier to spot him if he's here, somewhere," he murmured. Andrew nodded.

"Keep your eyes sharp," he suddenly whispered, as he looked towards the tunnel entrance to their left. "I'm starting to recognise a distinct angel signature, that seems very close."

"That could be him," Tris whispered, as he suddenly saw a small, hunched figure emerge from the darkness of the tunnel beyond the barriers and cautiously clamber up onto the platform.

Trying not to make his actions too obvious, Tris tugged at Andrew's sleeve and surreptitiously indicated towards their left. Andrew nodded.

"It's him," he whispered and then was quiet for a moment. "His individual signature is very similar to Lara's," he eventually continued. "Now, let's just let him get well away from the tunnel, before we try to grab him. We don't want to end up having to chase him back up the line. Not if a train is due." They moved cautiously in their efforts to get into a position to block Rylan from fleeing back into the tunnel. Trying to make it appear as if they were just a father and son waiting for a train, and perhaps wanted to get into a carriage at the far end of the next train

For a moment, they watched as the boy moved across to where there was a clear plastic rubbish disposal bag and dropped something into it. No one else on the platform seemed to pay all that much attention to him, even as he fumbled around the top of the bin.

"He's masking," Andrew whispered. "Even if he doesn't realise that he's doing so."

"How can you tell?" Tris murmured, as Rylan hastily perused a newspaper that he'd got out of the bin; seeming to examine a few of its pages before dropping it back into the bin.

"Because the people near him don't move," Andrew said quietly. "If they actually realised that he was there, they'd tend to move away a little, just in case he might be a pickpocket, or even just because he doesn't look all that clean. Now," he whispered, as he put out an arm and directed Tris to move to his left, "let's just spread out a bit to try to box him in." As they did so and moved closer, a couple of people seemed to take note of what they were doing, and began to watch them with idle curiosity.

"Okay," Andrew whispered. "You call his name, to distract his attention, while I try to grab him." Tris moved a few step closer to the boy as Andrew circled behind him.

Before Tris could say a word, however, Rylan suddenly looked at him and then, perhaps sensing movement behind him, turned to see Andrew moving closer. An instant later, he vanished! His unexpected disappearance creating some loud gasps of astonishment from the people who'd been watching the interaction.

"Well, we did know he was likely to do that, even if he doesn't fully understand how he's doing it." Andrew murmured, as he and Tris resisted the impulse to do likewise.

"So where is he going?" Tris asked, as they slowly moved towards an exit from the platform. There seemed no sense in hurrying, given that, for the moment, they'd lost track of the boy.

"Most likely to some little hidey hole where he feels safe," Andrew muttered. "Just as I mentioned earlier."

"So how do we work out where that is?" Tris queried. "If he can 'be', it could be anywhere in New York."

"It'll probably be somewhere underground, given that's where he's been spending most of his time, lately," Andrew said, as they began to work their way up the stairs. Keeping well to the left to avoid travellers who were in more of a hurry.

"So how do we track him down?" Tris queried.

"The same way we just did," Andrew said with a smile. "Given that we managed to get reasonably close to him, it'll be easier for me to be able to sense where he is. What I'm getting at the moment, however, doesn't make too much sense, because all I can see is total blackness. If we wait until he makes a move, then, once I work out where he is and I can get a better visualisation of where he goes, we can simply lay a trap for him.

But for the moment, let's just give him time to settle. Then I can work on getting a clearer visualisation. Maybe one that we can also jump to."

***

"Okay," Andrew murmured as he downed the last of his coffee and indicated for Tris to finish off his hot chocolate. "I have a clearer visualisation, but it's still just a little puzzling and quite hard to figure out."

"Why?" Tris immediately queried. Half wondering why Andrew would be having trouble in picking up on a simple visualisation, now that he'd been close enough to get a proper feel of Rylan's aura.

"Because all I'm still getting is almost complete blackness," Andrew muttered with a slight shake of his head. "Or as near to total blackness as makes any sense. It's as if he's hiding inside some sort of box… or a place with no windows."

"If he's underground, that would probably be logical," Tris muttered a little sarcastically. Andrew rolled his eyes a little in response to the comment, as he continued to concentrate.

"And yet, at the same time I can not only sense the confines of a small room, but also a sense of power. Thankfully, it doesn't appear to have any train tracks. It's almost seems as if he's hiding inside some sort of small room… or, maybe…."

"What sort of power?" Tris nervously interrupted, keeping his voice low and perhaps hoping that it wasn't an indication of the presence of a turned angel. From what he now understood of his past, he knew that a powerful turned angel by the name of Ahaitan had once caused him, and those around him, considerable trouble.

"Electricity," Andrew replied, seeming to immediately sense Tris's slight worries. "I get the impression that he's in a confined area that contains equipment that serves as some form of switching for the power needed for some of the tunnels. It seems that it's just normal power for the signal lights, nothing like the really high voltages that are required to power the trains." He paused a moment and shook his head. "The biggest problem is that it's hard to figure out where exactly it is."

"You think it's likely to be in one of the tunnels?"

That would certainly seem to be..." Andrew was suddenly quiet, his face almost instantly becoming a mask of intense concentration. "Hang on a minute," he suddenly said. "It seems like our little tunnel-mouse is on the move again." Reaching out, he grabbed Tris by the hand.

An instant later, after some surreptitious use of 'be'ing, they were on a platform below the Port Authority Bus Terminal. To their surprise, Rylan was standing just a few metres from them, looking cautiously around. The moment he spotted them, he disappeared. Once again, causing gasps from quite a few of the travellers waiting on the platform.

"Wait here, while I track him," Andrew hastily exclaimed, as he ducked out of sight behind a pillar and promptly disappeared.

Once on his own, Tris looked around at the people near to him. Some of them seemed to be watching him with more than just idle curiosity, even as they still discussed what they'd just seen with quite some degree of animation. Especially given that his and Andrew's arrival had seemed to be one of the factors that had caused the other boy's sudden disappearance.

Immediately retreating back down the entry corridor to one of the few bathrooms that seemed to still be open on the subway platforms, Tris hurried inside, and after a hasty look around to ensure that there was no one about to observe his actions, made himself invisible. Almost as he did so, however, the door to the bathroom was flung open and two of the men who'd been out on the platform, hurried in.

"Start checking the cubicles at the far end," the first man exclaimed, as having given a quick glance towards the vacant urinals, he then began shoving open the doors of the cubicles nearest to main door. "He might not be the one TakerZ sent us out to grab, but, given his age and looks, he'd still be worth good money if we can grab him and hand him on to that Network group TakerZ's been dealing with."

"TakerZ will still expect us to get the other kid!" his companion retorted.

"I know, but we may as well grab this one while we're at it," the first man responded, a little irritatedly. "It'll keep us in his good books, in case one of the others find that other kid."

Rather than returning to the platform, and having quickly remembered Mama Hattie's reference to TakerZ, Tris waited and listened, hoping that his eavesdropping would give him some sort of clue as to where TakerZ lived and where these men would take Rylan… presuming they could ever catch him.

With their having eventually investigated all the cubicles and found nothing, apart from a drunk sleeping off his stupor, Tris followed after the two men as they puzzled over his disappearance. While they'd made several more references to TakerZ and the 'kid' they were supposed to be finding, there was also an interesting comment made about a building due for demolition somewhere near Bryant Park, and some homeless old 'bag-man' called George, whom some of TakerZ's other crew were going to 'shakedown' for information about a homeless kid called 'Rebel'. Whether Rebel and Rylan were one and the same was moot, but somehow it did seem rather likely.

***

Rylan leant back against the wall of the alcove, breathing heavily and wondering whether he should have simply stayed in his bolthole for the rest of the day. Still, from a little further along the tunnel, he could hear the noise of passengers waiting on the platform. In an almost automatic action, he quickly drew his feet back as a train rattled by. Its brakes squealing as it slowed for the platform. At the same time he felt a little puzzled; trying to figure out how the man and boy, who'd tried to waylay him on the Lexington and 59th platform a little earlier, had been able to know where he was going and get to the Bus Terminal underground platform so quickly. Not that it was the first time he'd had to dodge people who seemed keen on getting close to him. He was dead certain that he'd seen TakerZ several times in the past few days on the Grand Central, 51st Street and Times Square platforms, and always in the company of two or three other dark-skinned teenagers. Maybe it was just his imagination, but something about the way they'd been perusing the crowds on the platform had immediately given him the impression that he was the target of their searching.

Still, while he could teleport himself, he could always get away from being captured, even if his doing so while on the platforms was starting to create some unnecessary attention. It was better when he could do his escape visualisations when he was in one of the safety alcoves just beyond a tunnel entrance. As the train began to depart from the far end of the station, he reached into his coat pocket, grabbed his torch and began to give it a shake, so that he wouldn't be in complete darkness.

An instant later he stopped his actions as, almost abruptly, the man from the platform was suddenly beside him. Rylan quickly scrambled to his feet and visualised his bolthole. As he reached his dark hideaway, it seemed the man was with him less than a second later.

"Wait!" the man started to exclaim, as he also seemed to stumble slightly for his footing in the dim light cast by Rylan's torch. Rylan didn't! Flicking off the torch, he quickly visualised a scene just inside a tunnel on yet another subway route... the Broadway Line. A moment or two later, the man was once again beside him. His next jump took him to the abandoned City Hall station, and once again, his pursuer only seemed a second behind him in appearing. Now anxious to get away from the whole subway system, and get more distance between himself and his pursuer, Rylan quickly thought of his old bolthole on the sixth floor of the derelict building.

The instant he arrived in the old hideout, he realised that there was further danger. Someone else, it appeared, had taken over his secret place and was now asleep on the old leather couch that had once been his bed. Covered over with the same blankets that he'd found during his search of the upper floors. The fact that the man was not dressed as a derelict, and was of a youthful, dark-skinned appearance — which certainly didn't match with most of George's cohorts — had Rylan immediately aware that it was likely that the man was waiting for him to appear and was somehow connected to TakerZ.

He turned, flung open the door leading into the corridor and hurried from the room. Still worried that the man who kept appearing might somehow be tracking his visualisations, but also not wanting to wait, in case the man on the couch might awaken at the sound of his intrusion, or his pursuer suddenly arrived, Rylan raced down the stairs. Taking them two and three at a time, as he headed down to the foyer. All the while hopeful that he'd possibly find that George had not yet left on his usual ramble uptown.

Just as he hurried into the room where all the old men usually slept, and saw George on the far side of the room, he was suddenly grabbed in a bear-hug and a cloth was pressed over his mouth; the unexpectedness of the attack, combined with the bitter smelling, sleep-inducing chemical on the cloth, quickly fogged his thoughts. Before he could react properly, and visualise a new hiding place, he simply collapsed into blackness.

***

Andrew stood still, keeping close to the stairway in the abandoned station, and trying to catch a further visualisation. Hoping that the boy would settle somewhere, instead of simply 'be'ing to a whole range of new visualisations. For an instant, he'd had a glimpse of a room with a couch on which someone was sleeping. Then, a few moments later, after jumbled scenes of a stairway and then a brief image of an old man, all mental trace of Rylan had suddenly winked out. Almost as if it seemed that he was no longer in New York.

With a sigh, he sent a thought out to Tris and arranged for them to meet outside the main entrance to the subway at Lexington and 59th.

"There's are some more people out there trying to grab Rylan," Tris quickly exclaimed, as soon as Andrew arrived. "They also tried to grab me. Like, they even followed me into one of the bathrooms, when I needed somewhere to go to become invisible. That's when I heard what they were planning."

"And they were definitely after Rylan?" Andrew queried. Tris gave a nod.

"I'm pretty sure that's who they were after, even though they called him Rebel, or something like that, because they mentioned TakerZ. You know, that man that Mama Hattie had had to rescue Rylan from. They also mentioned something about TakerZ hoping to get good money for him from something called the Network. That's why they also wanted me." Andrew was silent for a moment, deep in thought.

"I think we might need to get Mykael and Ithuriel in on this situation," he eventually murmured, giving a nod of his head. "With a spooked kid who's able to 'be' so easily, we need to be able to cover a number of his most likely hiding places and hope that Mykael or Ithuriel can take away his abilities quicker than I can. In the hope that we can get him incapacitated for long enough for us to explain why we want to help him."

"Can't you do that?" Tris immediately questioned. Andrew gave a slight shrug.

"If I have time to do so," he replied. "But with Rylan seeming to have become pretty adept at jumping from place to place, and extremely wary of anything unexpected, it's hard for me to get to work on him. We really need to have someone far more powerful helping us. Someone who can slow time and totally immobilise him as quick as blink."

***

"We got him, finally," Jakes exclaimed as he hefted the comatose boy from his shoulder and dumped him onto the couch at TakerZ's flat. He leant forward and quickly drew back the hood on Rylan's jacket to show his face, as TakerZ sauntered over to take a closer look.

"And he's also a boy, 'cause we checked," Jakes added with a nasty smirk. "You know, like, down there!" TakerZ seemed to nod, almost knowingly.

"Now that's much better than I'd hoped," he muttered, as he took a careful look at Rylan. "A boy with his good looks... well, I can certainly press Vittorio for quite a bit more for him."

"Why not keep him and put him out on the streets yourself?" Jakes questioned. "You know, make him drug dependent and then put him to work for his fix? Like you do with some of the young women?" TakerZ shrugged.

"Too much hassle," he murmured. "With a kid like this, I'd probably have to end up having to keep him locked up twenty-four seven. And then supervise all his clients. The moment I put him out on the street, no matter how much I might make him drug dependent, or frighten him into being obedient, the first pig that sees him will have him off the street and into care before you can say 'I told you so!'. Vittorio has all the right contacts to keep that sort of situation well under control. If any of his kids ever manage to get away, he just contacts a few special clients with political clout, and before the street pigs can do anything, a couple of his 'friends' in the FBI arrive to take care of everything. After all, if some of his kids ever got a chance to do some talking, there'd be some pretty big names going under, you mark my words! People with shit-loads of money and important positions in government, congress and the judiciary and such!"

"So what do we do now?" Jakes asked eagerly. Perhaps having expected some chance of having a little 'fun' with their captive. TakerZ shrugged.

"You could go and help Rogz and Fat-boy. It seems they've spotted another likely kid that we could grab, hanging around on the subway. Somewhere down near Lexington and 59th, they said, when they last rang in."

"Well, what about him?" Jakes asked, indicating towards Rylan. "Like, for when he wakes up?"

"I'll take care of that now," TakerZ replied, giving a nonchalant shrug. He wandered off to the bathroom and, after rummaging around in the bathroom cabinet, returned a few moments later with a syringe and a small vial of fluid.

"A shot of this will have him out for a fair while. Which means no chance of him trying to scarper," he laughed, as he prepped the syringe and squirted off a little excess of the drug. He wandered over to where Rylan lay, and rolled the boy onto his stomach. Roughly wrenching the back of Rylan's coat out of the way, he pulled down the back of the boy's jeans a tad and injected the drug into the top of his partially-exposed right butt cheek. "By the time he comes to from the effects of that little dose, it'll all be done," he laughed. "He'll be Vittorio's little problem, and I'll have my money." Having finished with the injection, he tossed the empty syringe onto the low coffee table, alongside the empty vial, and pulled Rylan's coat back down to cover him up.

"So we're not going to have a bit of fun?" Jakes queried. TakerZ gave a quick shake of his head.

"Not this time," he replied a little sullenly. "It seems Vittorio's dead keen to have a bunch of innocent kids for some special event he's got going down. I was told outright, that if the kid was touched in any way he wasn't going to pay us a dime." He paused and looked across at Rylan. Appearing to be deep in thought, before turning back to Jakes and Runner. "Anyway, as I just said, how about you two get out to help Rogz and Fat-boy track down this other kid they've spotted. While you're doing that, I ring through to Vittorio and make arrangements for this one to be picked up. They evidently need him fairly urgently."

***

All the captive children began to head back upstairs with a real sense of trepidation. According to Vittorio, their next engagement was to be 'the' event… the special entertainment that had been in the planning for quite a few months. The time when all the 'vestal virgins' would come to understand the true reality of what was planned for them, instead of wasting time in various basements 'sitting on their assets', as he, and his helpers, so bluntly put it.

They'd been dressed in the Native-American costumes once again, which was how they'd first be presented as a group, before they'd end up being stripped down to their display wear for individual appraisal, and then paraded for possible purchase at an auction.

"Did you hear something up here earlier?" Noah suddenly asked as he eventually followed Skylar down the hallway to where Vittorio and Angelo were waiting to fit them with their special, travelling necklaces. The 'keepers', as Vittorio called them, given that they were designed to keep them from absconding. "'Cause when I went to the toilet earlier, like when Vittorio was checking me over for bleeding, I thought I heard someone crying. Like, possibly a little kid." He stopped still for a moment. Luckily being last in line, that didn't cause any hold up, or result in anyone bumping into him. "Listen!" Both boys stopped still. Carefully trying to listen for anything untoward. Neither of them hearing anything at all, except for the noisc of the other captives being fitted with their keepers.

"What was it?" Skylar asked. Noah shrugged.

"Probably nothing," he murmured, still seeming to be listening intently. "There!" he suddenly said. "Can you hear it?" Almost as he spoke, there was a sharp slap, followed by a yelp from somewhere in front of them, followed by Vittorio bellowing for whoever it was who'd been disobedient, to stand perfectly still. Skylar gave a shake of his head, even as he tried to adjust his Native-American costume to give him a little more cover at the back.

"Like earlier, I just thought I heard a kid, crying," Noah murmured as they hurried to catch up to the end of the queue. "It sounded just..." He left the sentence incomplete and shrugged.

"Probably just that flippin' cat mewling," Skylar offered, with a shake of his head. A cat that they'd already seen hanging around the house while they'd been there, was always raucously complaining that it needed to be fed.

"Come on, you two," Angelo suddenly shouted from the doorway. "Get in here, before I have to give you a little incentive!" He slapped the small strap that he was holding in his right hand against the palm of his left, as an unsubtle reminder to them of its purpose. Not that he had any intention of using it too brutally at this time. Vittorio had stressed that the 'merchandise' for this special occasion had to be completely 'mark-free'. After all, there was no point in letting potential buyers at what was essentially a 'slave auction' get the idea that any particular 'item' might prove to be 'difficult', behaviour wise.

Skylar and Noah hurried through the doorway, anxious to not suffer extra discipline. Vittorio stood waiting with their 'keepers'.

"We don't need any unnecessary delays," he muttered a little angrily, as he stepped forward and fastened Skylar's explosive accessory into place. "We've already got to make a fair bit of a detour back towards New York in order to rendezvous with Gregor some time tomorrow. He's bringing us the final 'vestal virgin' for tomorrow night's little showpiece." He slapped Skylar lightly on the behind to move him on, as Angelo pushed Noah forward and then indicated for Skylar to head out to where the truck was waiting.

"I just hope you're healed enough to be able to pass off as 'innocent', if Gregor fails to meet up with us," he murmured, almost as if to himself, knowing the unfortunate damage that had been inflicted on the boy, a few days earlier.

Noah shuddered, now fully aware of the likely extent of the brutality that would eventually be wreaked upon him. At the same time, in the silence that followed, he once again, thought he heard crying.

"Get a move on," Vittorio suddenly said, as having fastened the 'keeper' into place, he lightly slapped Noah on the behind to send him on his way. "Don't keep the truck waiting."

***

"So what's the situation?" Mykael asked, as he and Ithuriel sat opposite Andrew and Tris in the small coffee shop just off Broadway.

"Well, the boy is definitely developing much as we thought," replied Andrew with tempered enthusiasm. "He can 'be' almost at will and also seems to be able to mask to some degree. Although he may not realise that that's what he's doing, or even how he's doing it. He also gives the appearance that he's probably got wings, and is trying to hide them, judging by the way he's dressed. The woman who'd been looking after him, Big Hattie, also confirmed that fact, because she could see that Tris had wings and mentioned that Rylan also had them."

"So what's the complication?" Mykael asked. Andrew gave a slightly weary sigh.

"Well, not only is he difficult to nail down, because he seems to have got 'be'ing down to a fine art, but he now seems to have simply disappeared off the radar, so to speak," he said casually. "One minute he was there in my senses, as I was tracking his leaps, for want of a better description, the next, nothing. Almost as if he'd been totally shut down, somehow." Mykael gave a knowing nod of his head.

"That's happened before," he murmured. "A good many years ago, as I remember correctly. When Alexei was about the age Tris is now, some idiots working for a mad bird photographer by the name of Henry Pearson kidnapped him from right outside of his school. They bundled him into the back of a car outside his school and then, before Alexei could simply disappear, he was made comatose with some chemical, and kept in a state of sedation. Because the drugs also dampened his aura, it made it almost impossible to track down where he was being held. At least, not until he woke up. And then, as it turned out, he was simply able to make his own way to safety."

"So you think that's what's happened here," Andrew queried.

"There were some other people after him," Tris interjected. "Like, besides his mother and that military lot. They also tried to grab me, as well, from one of the subway bathrooms. Only I'd made myself invisible before they could corner me."

"And why do you think they were after you?" Ithuriel asked. Tris gave a slight shrug.

"From what I heard them say, they were working for a man called TakerZ, who Mama Hattie told me was really nasty, and was something she called a pimp. They also mentioned something about a group called the Network. I think the idea was that TakerZ was planning to sell Rylan to them."

"Which is very likely to be why they also wanted you," Mykael muttered, reaching out to affectionately tousle Tris's hair. "They'd probably be getting paid pretty good money to deliver good-looking children to this Network group, whoever they are. More especially runaways; children who may already be classified as missing."

"So what do we do?" Tris quickly asked almost a little impatiently. "You know, to get Rylan back?"

"There's not much we can do, until he resurfaces," replied Mykael, with almost a sense of resignation. He glanced towards Ithuriel and they seemed to exchange some silent thoughts.

"Should be safe enough, if we're all there," Ithuriel murmured, as he looked towards Tris. "And if we can read their thoughts, it might just help us get some idea of where Rylan has gone."

"What are you planning?" Tris asked rather suspiciously. Half-wondering if, once again, he'd end up in the little yellow dress.

"While we wait for some connection to Rylan, we're going to set up a situation to take down TakerZ and his nasty little group of friends," Mykael quickly explained. "To see if they can give us a link to the Network. And you, my little angel-mouse, are going to be the bait in the trap!"

"The what?" Tris almost squeaked. He quickly looked around to see if his sudden exclamation had attracted any unexpected attention. It hadn't.

"You will go back to where those two men tried to grab you and let them take you," Mykael quickly explained. He quickly indicated towards Ithuriel and Andrew. "Don't worry. We three will be with you at all times, so you'll be quite safe."

"And then?" queried Tris rather nervously.

"When they take you to TakerZ, we'll take over and take them all to some place that they deserve to be. As I said, if I can read their thoughts, it might just give us a chance to get a heads up on this Network organisation and a better idea of where they've taken Rylan."

"But we'd better hurry with it," Ithuriel added. "We don't want to still be occupied with this TakerZ fellow and his cronies, if Rylan suddenly resurfaces.

***

Tris wandered back along the Lexington Uptown platform and then slouched into a seat. Trying to look nonchalant, or even rather bored. A feeling in direct contrast to the tension he felt inside. So far he'd spent almost two hours just wandering back and forth between the two levels of platforms, without seeing either of the men who'd been so keen to trap him, earlier.

While having three invisible angel guardians with him, did make him feel less nervous, it still didn't entirely take away the sense of trepidation. At the same time, it was nowhere near as bad as how he'd felt when he'd been out in the cold, nighttime wastes of rural Wichita, wearing just a flimsy yellow dress, awaiting the arrival of Pastor Isaac and his friends; fully knowing that he was in for some very severe punishment when they captured him. This time, he figured that the men who were after him would probably just force him to go with them to wherever it was that TakerZ hung out. They might even be quite nice about it, in trying to coerce his co-operation.

"Not too bored," A voice suddenly said from right beside him. Tris gave a small shake of his head, as he looked up to see the shadowy outline of Andrew seated to his left. He could also see the vague outlines of Ithuriel and Mykael about ten yards to his right.

Immediately behind them, however, he suddenly saw the two men who tried to capture him earlier, emerge from the stairs onto the platform. Now accompanied by another man whom he hadn't seen before.

"That's them," he whispered. "Over there! Just behind Mykael and Ithuriel. Only there's now three of them." Andrew nodded and quickly pointed out the men for Mykael and Ithuriel. The guardians moved closer and followed after the three men; keeping almost within touching distance.

For their part, the three men seemed to quickly spot Tris and after a quick verbal exchange amongst themselves, the two who'd tried to grab him earlier moved nonchalantly closer.

"Hi, kid," said the first man to get close to Tris, rather casually. "You look lost. You needing some help?" Tris nodded and tried to look a little despondent.

"You needing a place to stay, 'cause you's a runaway?" the second man asked. Once again, Tris nodded.

"Then we knows just the place," the first man said with a beaming smile. "No worries about the pigs, or truancy officers, or child welfare, or any of that official shit. Just a safe place to sleep and as much food as you can eat. If that's what you want?" Yet again, Tris nodded and got to his feet. In his head, the whole scenario seemed so much like a situation in a book he'd just finished reading… when a young runaway called Oliver Twist met up with some character called the Artful Dodger.

My name's Jakes," the first man said with a warm smile, as he took a hold of Tris's wrist. "And these are my friends, NineR and Rogz." He indicated for the third man to come a little closer. "Anyway, we'll take you to meet TakerZ. He's a close friend of ours who likes helping young kids. 'Specially those that be runaways."

Keeping close on either side of Tris, they began hurrying him towards the exit from the platform. If anyone else on the platform thought it strange to see one small white boy in the company of three obvious gangsta types, they didn't show it. Or at least, no one tried to intervene in any way to check that if there was anything untoward in what they were seeing. Everyone seeming intent in concentrating on their phones, iPads, or whatever else took their attention. As the group of three men and one boy headed up the stairs to street level, the vague, shadowy forms of three adult angels followed closely behind.

Once at street level, Jakes hurriedly directed Tris towards a waiting van. As two of the men clambered into the back seat, with Tris between them, Jakes climbed into the front passenger seat.

"Okay, Fat-boy. Move it," he announced to the driver with almost a laugh. "Don't want to keep TakerZ waiting with such precious cargo!" As the van moved away from the curb, the three guardians went airborne to track its progress more easily.

In the back seat, Tris was suddenly surprised to find that he was quickly gagged and bound. His hands tied behind his back, his feet bound together at the ankles, with a rope joining the two so that he was unable to stand. As further ignominy, a black cloth bag was placed over his head.

"This is just so you don't see where you're going," Rogz laughed, as he straightened the bag. "And the ropes are just so you don't try to do a runner on us." Tris remained silent. Not that he could do much else. At least, not without the risk of giving away what he really was. Nevertheless, he remained hopeful that Mykael, Ithuriel and Andrew would still be tracking his progress. Almost as he wondered about that, Mykael's voice was suddenly in his head, telling him 'not to be worried', and that 'everything is under control'.

As much as was possible, given the uncomfortable way that he was now tucked up across part of the back seat, Tris tried to keep calm and not create too much of a fuss. A little wary of the fact that becoming difficult to control might result in him being rendered comatose, either through drugs or being struck about the head.

The ride in the van seemed to last quite a while, with several stops and starts that were obviously caused by traffic delays, to go by Fat-boy's constant cursing of other motorists and snail-paced traffic light sequences. Eventually, they seemed to pull off whatever main thoroughfare they'd been on, into a much quieter place. Perhaps, Tris mused, some sort of alleyway. Very quickly the van stopped and then, after a brief delay, accompanied by the grating noise of a metal door being raised it moved forward a little. The door was then quickly lowered. By the sudden absence of street sounds, Tris realised that they'd parked inside a garage, or a warehouse of some type.

Still bound, gagged and hooded, Tris was then unceremoniously slung over a shoulder of one of the men and after a short journey in a lift, followed by a bouncing march along a couple of cold corridors, they entered a much warmer room.

"We've brought you a little present," said Rogz with a slight laugh, as TakerZ looked up from where he was checking through the money he'd been given for Rylan. Payments in cash meant that such illegal dealings as the buying and selling of children were far less easily traced. He seemed, however, just a little startled at the unexpected intrusion, as he hastily shoved the cash back into an open briefcase, perhaps not wanting his underlings to know exactly how much he'd been paid for Rylan, in case they demanded a bigger cut of the money.

"He needs a place to stay," added NineR, with a smirk, as he dumped Tris, still hooded, gagged and hog-tied, onto the couch. The same couch that Rylan had been placed on a few hours earlier.

"Ta-Dah," Rogz announced, as he quickly removed the hood from Tris's head. "Another little cutie for Vittorio's harem."

"Pity you didn't arrive with him sooner," TakerZ muttered, giving Tris a quick perusal and liking what he saw. "I just got rid of that other brat, a little over half an hour ago. Gregor seemed really keen to get him to Vittorio as quickly as possible. There's evidently some special event the Network's got scheduled. Didn't even bother to undress him and check him over, like usual. Just decided he looked cute enough and carried the kid straight out to the van. Seems he's got to catch up to some precious shipment that's already on the way to be 'evaluated', as it were." He laughed a little at the slight joke, and was then quickly serious once again.

"At the same time, he obviously won't be too keen to have to come back here, straight away. Gregor don't like to be too visible, if you catch my drift. And especially not in the Big Apple, given the warrants out for him." He gave Tris a further, more careful, perusal. "Still, another pretty little boy will be just what Vittorio wants, if we can keep the kid under wraps and out of sight for a few days." He moved closer to Tris and grabbed at his clothes. "Let's just have a look at the rest of…"

Whatever scrutiny he was going to make of Tris was quickly abandoned, as there seemed to be a flash of bright light as dazzling as lightning. Almost in the instant that the three angel guardians appeared, the five men in the room suddenly found themselves in restraints; their hands secured behind their backs in cuffs and their feet shackled.

"What the..." TakerZ exclaimed. His utterance immediately cut short as a gag was roughly thrust into his mouth. Similar gags appeared, almost instantaneously, in the mouths of the other four men.

"Amazing what a little time-slowing can allow you to do," Mykael said with a wry smile, as Tris quickly visualised himself as standing on the other side of the room and out of his restraints.

"So what happens now?" he queried. Mykael gave a shrug, seeming to concentrate on TakerZ for a moment or two.

"You stay here for a moment," he eventually replied. "Now that I've garnered enough of their thoughts to know what they've done with Rylan, we're just going to take these five to somewhere they won't find all that enjoyable." He indicated for Tris to grab the briefcase with the money. "And if you just keep an eye on that for the moment, you can probably arrange to drop it off to Mama Hattie, a little later on," he added. "She appears to be someone who could, no doubt, find a good use for it."

The three adult angels disappeared clutching their captives, only to reappear a moment or two later without them.

Where did you take them?" Tris questioned, seeming just a little surprised at how quick the disposal of his captors had been. Mykael replied with a semi-casual shrug, even as Ithuriel and Andrew seemed to grin a little.

They're now lying on the floor of a vacant cell in Attica," Mykael quietly explained. "It's a maximum security prison, so, not only will it take some time for them to get out of their restraints, once they come to, it'll also take them some time to explain how they got there and why," he added. "Trying to convince the prison authorities that they're not meant to be there will probably take some doing, given the glacial manner in which the American judicial system usually seems to work in rectifying mistakes, and how unlikely it is that they'll be believed if they start trying to explain about being kidnapped by angels."

"And it's also highly likely that there are already warrants out for most of them, anyway," Andrew added. "Given the type of activities they're involved in."

"So what happens now?" Tris queried. Feeling a real sense of relief that his 'bait' ordeal was now properly over.

"Well, once you've dropped off that money to Mama Hattie, we can start making plans for capturing Rylan," Mykael replied rather matter-of-factly. "Then, as soon as Andrew gets some hint of where he is, we'll be ready to spring into action. Now, while you go and see Mama Hattie, we three will use the time to explore where he's been visualising, so that we can cover the most likely places he'll go to, whenever he decides to reappear."

***

Tris made a visualisation of the bathroom he'd used at the St. Joseph's shelter. An instant later, having been pleased to find that the room was unoccupied, he made himself visible and wandered off in search of Mama Hattie. A quick glance revealed that she wasn't in the female dormitory. With a sigh, Tris followed the sound of voices. He had hoped that she'd be where he'd first found her, and not somewhere out on the street. Eventually reaching an area that was obviously some sort of large kitchen, he was pleased to see that Mama Hattie was seated at a bench beside a table at the far end of the room, busily peeling potatoes. As Tris hurried across to her, one of the other two women present gave him a smile.

"Looks like you got yourself another little visitor, Hattie," she said with a slight laugh. "This be another one in need of your protection?" Mama Hattie shook her head.

"No," she rumbled. "He's just here to help find a safe place for Rylan." She beckoned for Tris to come close. "Have you found him?" she asked in almost a whisper. Tris responded with a slight shrug.

"We think so," he replied. "We just have to get a final visualisation." He paused and looked around. "Can we talk, somewhere?" he asked. He glanced down at the briefcase he was holding in his right hand. "Like, in private?" Mama Hattie gave a nod, and then, getting slowly to her feet, indicated for him to follow her back towards the female dormitory.

Once in the room, she carefully sat on the same bed as she had been on when Tris had last visited.

"We've managed to make some contact," Tris quietly explained as he took a seat opposite her and put the briefcase in front of himself. "But it seems that he's a bit scared, because he doesn't realise that we're trying to help him," he continued. "He keeps escaping from us."

"Us?" Mama Hattie quickly queried. Tris gave a slight shrug.

"Me and my guardian angels," said very softly. "That's what we are. Angels." With a quickly glance towards the door he quickly made his wings visible for few seconds. Strange as it seemed, Mama Hattie didn't seem to find anything all that surprising in his doing so.

"So Rylan's supposed to be with you?" she murmured, giving him a warm smile. Tris nodded.

"His sister's with us already," he quickly explained. "As I told you last time. Her name's Lara, and she and Rylan are actually twins. Unfortunately, they got separated and adopted by different families when they were little. When Lara started to grow her wings her parents took her to a hospital to try to find out what was wrong with her, and that's when the U.S. military stepped in and took her from them. Which is also why they've been asking after Rylan. When I rescued Lara, a few weeks ago, the U.S. military went back to see her parents and that's when they realised that she also had a twin brother. Rylan had already taken off, however, because of…"

"I know why," Mama Hattie suddenly interrupted. "Rylan told me all about what had happened to him. Like, with his father and some Pastor something or other." She gave a slow shake of her head, as if to express her disapproval of what had happened. "I also know that he had wings just like yours," she eventually continued. "That's why I realised that he was something special, and needed protecting."

"That's why we need to rescue him," Tris murmured. "Only, at the moment, he's a little spooked and then, he disappeared, sort of. Mykael thinks…"

"Michael?" Mama Hattie gasped and hurriedly crossed herself. You don't mean…?" Tris gave a hurried shake of his head. Immediately realising to whom the woman would be referring.

"He's a different Mykael," he hastily replied. "Even spells his name a bit different. He's still powerful and important, but obviously not as much as… as you know."

"And he's your guardian?" Mama Hattie quietly queried. Tris nodded.

He'll also act as a guardian for Rylan, when we find him," he added, as he picked up the briefcase, leant across and laid it on the bed beside her. "Anyway, I have something for you." He flicked open the catch to show her its contents. Mama Hattie gasped as she saw the bundles of notes, and then waved her hands in a slightly flustered manner.

"I don't need your money, Honey," she exclaimed, giving a slight laugh at the way the words rhymed. "I'm just happy to help out any kids who need a bit of extra looking after." Tris gave a slight shrug.

"Well, this will help," he said nonchalantly. "You can do with it what you wish."

"But I can't take your money," Mama Hattie rumbled. "That wouldn't be right."

"It's not mine," Tris replied with the hint of a laugh. "It's actually TakerZ's. It's the money he got paid for capturing Rylan and selling him on to some group called the Network. But don't you worry, we've already got plans underway to rescue Rylan from them.

"The Network?" Mama Hattie queried. "And they paid TakerZ all this, just for my little 'Milky Bar Kid'? All this for…?" She left the question incomplete.

"They're a secret group who kidnap kids for rich people who like hurting children," Tris replied, again half wondering what a 'Milky Bar Kid' might be. "But as I just said, my guardians have it all under control. The moment Rylan surfaces, they'll simply grab him from them."

"So he'll be safe?" Mama Hattie earnestly asked. Tris nodded.

"My two senior guardians, Mykael and Ithuriel will ensure that he doesn't get hurt in any way," he explained.

"Well, what about TakerZ?" asked Mama Hattie rather cautiously. "Won't he be angry about losing all this money?" Inwardly, she felt a little worried that TakerZ might get a hint of where his money had gone and cause trouble for her and the shelter. Tris gave an almost amused shake of his head.

"I doubt it," he replied with a further hint of a laugh. "At the moment, he and his nasty little friends will be too busy trying to talk their way out of Attica. That's where my guardians left them, after we let them try to capture me as well. And, Mykael feels sure that with the likelihood of them having arrest warrants already out for them, this little stash will be the last thing on any of their minds."

"It doesn't look that little," Mama Hattie rumbled, lightly fingering at the bundles of money in the brief case with some interest. Tris shrugged and pushed the briefcase closer to her.

"Just use it as you wish," he said. "Maybe some of it could help Cee-Cee go to college. We angels certainly won't be needing it." Mama Hattie reached over and shut the briefcase; not making any attempt to count the money.

"Will you let me know when Rylan is safe?" she asked, as she then slid the briefcase into her bedside cabinet. Tris hastily nodded. A little wary of wanting to make a firm commitment until he knew that Rylan had been rescued from wherever it was that the Network had him hidden.

CHAPTER FIFTEEN

An Awful Fate....

Skylar awoke and eased himself into a sitting position, quickly aware that the truck in which they were being transported had stopped. Given that they'd already been on the road for almost a full day, with only a brief lunch and toilet stop at some factory, where the truck had been driven inside a warehouse, he wondered whether they had finally reached their destination, or were still en-route and stopping for some other reason. Not that he was looking forward in any way to what they'd been told about tonight's special 'entertainment' session.

Before they had embarked on this current stage of their journey, Vittorio had made considerable mention of the fact that, now that he had acquired the last boy he needed for his 'special event', there was no sense on delaying their introduction to the realities of what he'd always had planned for them, and that he was already in the process of making arrangements to pick up the new boy from some contact who'd be coming from New York.

According to Vittorio, it was also likely that most of them would be permanently auctioned off tonight, after their part in the 'entertainment' was over; especially if a particular client was prepared to pay enough to compensate the Network for not having their ongoing earning capacity. For that reason, their numbers not only included the twelve 'innocent' boys and girls destined to be the main aspect of the entertainment, but also Peter and Noah, who had been brought along as 'back-ups', but might now both be deemed as being 'surplus to requirements'. Noah having been included as a possible alternative to the new acquisition, if it had ended up that it was not possible for Gregor to meet up with them in time.

Earlier in the day, before they'd left the basement and been secured in the back of the truck, each of them had been taken upstairs to be checked over by Vittorio once again and then videoed while dressed in a Native-American costume. The last aspect being so that the people whom they were destined to 'entertain' could start to check them over beforehand, with regard to not only making a choice for tonight, but also the possibility of purchasing them as personal playthings. The new videos would be added to the material already posted on-line — via the dark web — so that any other people wanting a 'slave' for their personal use could also start to make bids. Vittorio seemed certain that this would surely increase their worth; although he could still veto any bid, if he felt that any particular child would be worth more to him by remaining as a part of his touring 'harem'. For some strange reason, this mode of thought seemed to apply to the boys in particular.

Skylar, like most of the others, felt some small relief in that he hadn't been videoed totally naked, although it hadn't lessened his fear of what he knew was scheduled to happen, later tonight.

Having seen, over the past few weeks, the way in which Peter had been regularly taken out for sessions of serious abuse, and the aftermath of the abuse that Noah had unfortunately suffered, he was, like all the 'innocent' boys and girls, well aware of what would eventually be his fate. Whether he'd be auctioned off tonight, or retained by Vittorio for future entertainments, was something over which he knew he had no control, although

Cooper was already sure that he'd be destined to be auctioned, given that Vittorio had already made several nasty comments about being keen to recoup his losses, given what he'd paid out to Cooper's stepfather.

"I wonder if we're there yet?" he whispered nervously. Cooper gave a slight shrug, and wiped at his reddened eyes.

"Does it really matter?" he murmured resignedly. "There's no 'effin' way we can escape!" He fingered his keeper and then reached out and rattled the chains that secured each of them, by an ankle, to a bar running down the centre of the floor of the truck. "Not when we're chained up, and also have these!" He again carefully fingered the necklace that was padlocked around his neck. Noting, as he did so, that the green light was glowing on each of the other necklaces around the room to show that they were all 'armed'. Vittorio had told them that they would be removed when they reached their destination, but had also reminded them that they could all be set to explode if there was any hint of trouble.

Like all the children in the hidden compartment, Cooper and Skylar grew tense as they suddenly heard the sound of the rear doors of the truck being unbolted and opened. For a moment there was simply silence, with none of them even daring to speak.

"Maybe it's a police check," Cooper eventually suggested, as he nervously fingered at his collar. "You know, like when they check that a truck's properly loaded." They listened for the sound of voices. Hoping against hope that it might signify some official police action and that the necklaces might be deactivated. Instead, they heard scraping as the fake barrels were moved to one side and the disguised door was eventually unlocked. Vittorio suddenly stepped into the dimly lit compartment.

"Don't panic," he sneered. "We've still got a fair way to go. In fact, a good three to four hours or more, so just relax. I'm sure that none of you is really in all that much of a hurry to be 'initiated', as they say." He paused as a slight smirk reached to the corners of his mouth. "By the way," he then continued, "that particular part of tonight's entertainment I'll also be capturing on video; so you'd better make it worth my while. After that, well, for some of you, it'll all depend on what the bidding is like and how you've responded to losing your innocence."

He turned and gestured behind him as Angelo entered with a blanket-wrapped bundle slung over his left shoulder, which was then carefully dumped onto the mattress shared by Cooper and Skylar, who were nearest to the door. As the blanket was pulled aside, they immediately realised that the 'bundle' contained a boy.

"This is the last of the 'innocents' for tonight's entertainment," Vittorio announced with a smirk. "I managed to have a friend acquire him in New York yesterday, so he's certainly in for a real surprise, when the drugs finally wear off and he wakes up." He stooped, quickly fastened a chain around the boy's ankles and then locked it onto the central bar. Getting to his feet, he pointed to Skylar and Cooper and dropped a plastic bag containing another Native-American costume at their feet. "In the meantime, you two will get him suitably attired. Strip him completely out of what he's wearing and then get him properly kitted out. I'll check on how you've managed with him when we arrive at the venue."

"But how do we get his jeans and underwear off if he's shackled?" Skylar nervously asked. "They'll get stuck on his feet and… and the chains." Vittorio eyed him for a moment. From the expression on his face, Skylar almost expected him to lash out with the back of his hand. Instead he turned to Angelo and nodded. Angelo quickly handed him a short flick knife.

Vittorio, in turn, reached down and hauled Skylar to his feet, before handing him the knife.

"Use this to cut them off," he barked. "He won't be needing them for tonight, and there'll be plenty of other clothing in storage that he can use afterwards, if I decide not to auction him off." He reached forward and grabbed Skylar by the throat, almost lifting the boy off his feet. "Any funny business and I'll be using this very same knife to cut your 'effin' throat… slowly and painfully. Understand?" he snarled, hardly waiting for Skylar to nod a nervous reply. "Now get to work!"

Having finished with his instructions to Skylar and Cooper, Vittorio ushered Angelo before him out the secret door. He stopped in the doorway and looked back at the captive children.

"Tonight is going to be a real special night," he said, leering around the back of the van. "Tonight, all bets are off. Once the auction is finished, the customers will be able to do whatever they like to you, short of outright killing you." He turned to follow after Angelo. "When you've got the back doors securely bolted, tell Sergio to get moving," he muttered as he began to close the door. "After the delay of having to wait for Gregor to catch up to us with sleeping beauty, we'll have to make up a fair bit of time if we want to get to the venue on schedule."

With the doors closed and the truck beginning to move, Cooper and Skylar set to work to get the new arrival ready. As they rolled him onto his back, Skylar suddenly started.

"I know him," he exclaimed. "He's a kid who used to go to my old school in Oakton, only he used to have really long hair then. His name's Rylan Daniels, and he went missing about the same time as Mum and I left for Texas. About a week or so earlier, I think."

"Was he a friend of yours?" Cooper asked. Skylar gave a quick shake of his head.

"Not really. Like, we weren't in the same class or anything," he murmured, half-wondering whether he should mention about

Rylan being rather effeminate. Instead, he quickly concentrated on the task in hand, carefully using Angelo's flick knife to cut down either side of Rylan's jeans, so that they could be easily removed.

Feeling a little embarrassed, but wary of what Vittorio had threatened, Skylar then quickly cut the sides of Rylan's underpants and removed them, so that he and Cooper could quickly fit the breechcloth into place and secure it with the thin belt of leather cord. Knowing that to not do so correctly, would most likely result in all of them being severely punished. Perhaps even as an impromptu part of the evening's special entertainment.

The other children watched them with an casual air of indifference as, with Cooper having also removed Rylan's shoes and socks and fastened the small leather anklets with feathers attached just above the newcomer's ankles — they were all wearing similar adornments — the two boys quickly focussed their efforts on removing Rylan's coat, and T-shirt in order to fit a ceremonial breastplate over his upper body. An item, made of fake bone beading, similar to what all of the boys were wearing. The girls having, instead, a type of binding around their chests that could only have been described as an attempt to create an ancient Native-American styled bikini top. Not that any of the girls was far enough into puberty to actually require anything more than a training bra. Surprisingly, the skimpy attire didn't seem to bother any of them all that much, given that several times in the last few weeks, as the special 'innocents', they'd all been housed together, almost naked... except for their display pants; the whole twelve of them, both boys and girls.

"Holy shit," Cooper suddenly exclaimed as, with them having turned Rylan over so that he was face down, and removed the grubby coat he was wearing, Skylar carefully cut away the last remnants of his T-shirt. "He's got wings!"

The other children hurriedly crowded closer, as much as their ankle restraints would allow, to get a look as Skylar quickly cut away the remains of Rylan's singlet.

"He must be an angel," Natasha exclaimed in a whisper. Skylar just continued to stare. Knowing Rylan from school and Phys. Ed. classes, what he was now seeing did not make any sense whatsoever.

"I thought you said that you went to school together?" Riley muttered. Skylar shook his head a little, as if trying to fully understand what he was seeing. He'd seen Rylan in a state of undress often enough when they'd been changing for Phys. Ed. classes, but there had never been any thought that he might be an angel.

"I did," he quietly retorted. "He used to go to my school and, at one stage, we were even in the same class. He also went to the church I used to go to. He even got sent to the same boot camp as me."

"Did he have wings, then?" Jessamine asked. Skylar gave a quick shake of his head.

"No. Well, not that I ever saw," he replied. "We used to have to do P.E. classes together, so I'd quite often see him when we got changed. Most of the class used to steer well clear of him because they thought that he was a bit of a gay perv, but he certainly didn't have wings then."

"Do you think he's still gay?" Cooper tentatively asked. Skylar gave a slight shrug.

"It won't matter, given what we're all in for," Peter muttered just a little cynically. "Although I doubt Vittorio will want to auction him off, when he realises what he is."

"We should try to wake him," Jessamine suddenly suggested. The others looked at her for a moment in some surprise.

"Maybe he can help, or something," Jessamine continued. "Like, maybe he can get other angels to come, or something."

Noah moved closer with one of the water bottles and began to splash a small amount onto Rylan's face. For a few moments there was no reaction, but then, rather groggily, the boy opened his eyes and looked about. Instantly seeming rather surprised at where he was, how he was dressed and that there were other children who were similarly dressed surrounded him.

"Skylar?" he softly queried, as he recognised his old classmate. "Skylar Jefferies?" Skylar quickly nodded a reply.

"It's good to see you're awake," Skylar replied, as he helped Rylan into seated position.

"Where are we?" Rylan asked, looking around at the other children and the interior of the compartment.

"Sealed in a secret compartment in the back of a truck and on our way to become slaves," Peter replied rather bluntly. "We're the property of some nasty group called the Network who transport children around the country for rich effin' perverts!"

"Can we get out of here?" Rylan asked. Peter pointed to the chain attached around his ankles and how it was attached to the bar in the centre of the truck.

"Not unless you've got some bolt cutters in your back pocket," he replied a tad cynically. Rylan looked down at the chain and then, remembering the incident with the handcuffs, immediately visualised himself on the other side of the compartment without it.

"How did you do that?" Cooper excitedly exclaimed, as he tugged rather futilely at his own chain.

"It's just something that I know how to do," Rylan replied. He looked at the other children for a moment. "How much time have we got?" he asked, instantly rather alert. "Like before they come to get us?"

"Vittorio said that we'd be travelling for at least three or four more hours, maybe a little more," Noah murmured. "Then we'll be taken out to be the 'entertainment'." Rylan seemed deep in thought for a moment.

"Okay," he eventually said. "I think I can get you all out of here. I'll just need to get a good visualisation of this room." He moved over to stand by the doorway and made a mental image of exactly how the room looked, hoping that, even with it moving, he'd be able to return to take each of the children to safety. Having done so, he returned to where all the children were now standing.

"I'll probably have to do this one at a time," he said tentatively. "Cause I'm not sure how many I can take with me at a time." He reached out and grabbed Skylar around the waist. "Just trust me," he whispered. "Where we'll be going will be quite dark, but safe."

"Wait!" Skylar hastily interrupted. He quickly fingered the necklace. "I've still got my keeper. It's a necklace thing that Vittorio puts on us while we're travelling so we won't try to escape. If I get too far away from the truck, it'll explode and blow my head off."

"That's easily fixed," Rylan replied, after a moment's hesitation, during which time he glanced around the room to see that all the children were wearing similar devices. An instant later, they were both standing on the far side of the truck, with the necklace and the ankle chains clattering harmlessly to the floor where Skylar had previously been standing. As Rylan also realised that, just as had occurred with Xavier J. Hernandez, Skylar was beginning to slump into a semi-comatose state, he quickly visualised his secret bolthole in the underground. An instant later, they both disappeared, leaving the remaining children open-mouthed in astonishment.

***

"I'm getting something," Andrew suddenly announced. "It's very faint, but it's definite." He was silent, for a moment or two. "He's still a little fuzzy-headed and it seems to be taking him a little time to work out things, but I get the impression that he's in something that's moving. It feels like... like it's a room somewhere. It could be inside a caravan, or something of similar size. And he's not alone. I sense that there are other children with him, but they're all really scared of something nasty that's about to happen."

"I think we should take up positions," Mykael murmured. He turned to Andrew. "Where do you think it's most likely that he'll go?" Andrew was quiet for a moment and then nodded.

"I'm starting to get an image of the bolthole," he suddenly announced. "That room that we found in one of the subway tunnels. It's most probably where he'll be going. From what I'm getting of his thoughts, I think he's going to try to take the other children there, one at a time."

"Okay, we'll deal with it," Mykael replied, indicating towards Ithuriel almost in the instant that he vanished. Ithuriel immediately followed after him.

***

Arriving in his bolthole — albeit immediately staggering just a little under the comatose weight of Skylar Jefferies — Rylan suddenly realised that the small concrete room he had been using as a hideout was no longer in darkness. It seemed lit by a slightly strange glow; its source appearing to come from the two men who were already there. As he went to teleport elsewhere with Skylar, however, he suddenly found that he was unable to move.

Having slowed time momentarily to deprive Rylan of his angelic abilities, Mykael quickly summed up the situation, and moved close to the boy, effectively blocking the small doorway, to prevent him from simply taking off into the darkness of the tunnel.

"We're here to help you," he said, indicating for Ithuriel to take Skylar from Rylan's grasp. "But, firstly, let's go somewhere far more comfortable," he added, taking a hold of Rylan by the wrist. With a visualisation to Andrew and Tris, as well as to Ithuriel, he grabbed Rylan's hand and disappeared.

An instant later, they were all standing on the porch of the Robertson's farm. Even as Rylan looked around in astonishment at the unexpectedly tranquil surroundings, and the fact that it was now fully nighttime, Mykael was already leading him through the door and into the warmth of a dining room, with Ithuriel close behind with Skylar in his arms.

There was immediate chaos as Grandma Betty, Granddad Roger, Mischa and Zhenya looked up in surprise and then, having quickly assessed the situation, sprung into action. After all, it wasn't the first time they'd been asked to look after comatose youngsters at short notice.

"Sorry to intrude but it's a bit of an emergency," Mykael quickly explained. "We seem to have quite a few children involved in a rather nasty situation."

"I'll start getting beds ready," said Grandma Betty, getting quickly to her feet. She indicated to where Ithuriel was still holding Skylar. "Mischa, if you could help, please."

As Mischa took Skylar from Ithuriel and hurried down the hallway with him, following after Grandma Betty, Mykael quickly indicated for Rylan to be seated.

"But, I've got to go back," Rylan almost pleaded, even as he, just a little reluctantly, obeyed Mykael's directive. "I… I promised them that I would..." He suddenly stopped talking, as it seemed to dawn on him that, without his ability to teleport, he couldn't do as he'd promised. Tears began to slip down his cheeks.

"Just tell me what's going on and we'll take care of it," responded Mykael rather comfortingly. "I can have many more angels here in an instant to complete the rescue." Rylan looked at him in puzzlement for a few seconds.

"I... I'm... I'm an angel?" he finally squeaked, accompanying his question with a befuddled shake of his head. "But... but, I... I'm not dead! Am I?"

"No. But you are very special," Mykael replied. "And you are an angel, even if you don't understand why it has all come about. Now, while Andrew gets his brothers here to help, how about you tell me what we're looking for. Like, who is this other boy, the one Grandma Betty is currently putting to bed, and where did you find him?"

"That's Skylar Jefferies," Rylan quickly replied. "I used to know him from school. We weren't really friends or anything." He dropped his head a little, to look down at his feet. Suddenly seeming rather embarrassed. "No one really liked me all that much, back then."

"We can talk about all that sort of thing a bit later," Mykael said consolingly. "After all, there are problems in your life that do need to be worked through. But what I need to know now, is what's going on with the place you were in, and how did you get there?" Rylan gave a slight shrug and sighed.

"I don't know what's really going on," he murmured, before looking around at the other angels, who now all had their wings showing. "It started when I was trying to get away from him." He pointed to Andrew. "Only I didn't know that he was an angel, then; or that I was one as well. I just thought I was some sort of freak, and that he was just another of the people trying to capture me; like my mom, and TakerZ and some military guys."

"So how did you end up with Skylar?" Mykael asked. Rylan gave another slight shrug.

"I don't really know," he murmured. 'One minute I was trying to find George, this homeless guy who'd helped me after I left the Fulchers, and then the next thing, I woke up in the back of a truck, chained up by my ankles and dressed like this. And there were a whole lot of other children there, the same; you know, like, dressed like me and Skylar."

"Do you know why they were there?" Mykael continued. Rylan once looked at his feet.

"I think that they're all going to get hurt," he murmured, blushing just a little as he continued. "You know, like, by being forced to do bad things."

"So you decided to rescue Skylar, and made a visualisation of the interior of the van so that you could go back and get more of them?" Mykael suggested. It was a purely rhetorical question but Rylan nodded, nevertheless.

"I promised them I would," he almost pleaded. "As I said, I think they're all being taken somewhere where they're going to be sold off as slaves."

"How many of them are there?" Mykael quickly asked. Rylan seemed to take a moment or two to count in his head.

About twelve... or maybe fourteen," he replied. "There's six girls, I think, and all the rest are boys. All of them also seemed to be about my age. And... and they're all chained to some metal bar in the centre of the room. And… they're also wearing some necklace things, which Skylar said would explode if they get too far away from the truck. He said that someone called Vittorio had put the necklaces on them to stop them from trying to escape. Only as I said, it's like they're all in a truck, and… and it's moving."

Mykael nodded, and then turned to Andrew.

"You got it clearly, as well?" he queried. Andrew quickly nodded. As Rylan looked at him in some surprise, Mykael suddenly reached forward to put a hand on the boy's forehead, and then hurriedly scooped the boy into his arms, as he seemed to almost instantly fall asleep where he was seated.

"I think it would be easier for us to do this rescue without him, given that he doesn't fully understand the extent of his abilities, as yet," he said as if to explain his actions. He looked around and quickly handed Rylan off to Zhenya, who immediately headed off down the hallway after Mischa and Grandma Betty.

"He won't wake for quite a while," murmured Mykael, as Alexei, Tristan, Gofraidh and Aerynn arrived in the dining room almost simultaneously, followed, a few seconds later, by Taylor and Conlaodh.

"We've got a rescue to do," Mykael hastily explained, as Gabriel also arrived. "And the only visualisation we have is for the inside of a moving vehicle. It seems that our destination is a hidden compartment inside a truck. From what I've managed to glean from the mind of our newest little angel, it seems that there are at least a dozen children, maybe more, who are currently chained to a bar inside the truck, and who are destined to be the special entertainment at some private function later tonight. And by 'entertainment', I'm meaning various depravities. Rylan says that they're also wearing some sort of necklaces that are designed to explode if they get too far away from the truck that's transporting them, so we'll need to very clear in how we make our visualisations, so that nothing unnecessary comes with them, when we bring them back here. It'll mean that they're well away from whatever was planned for them and also give them a safe place to sleep off their transportation. Besides the necklace things and the ankle chains, Rylan also gave me the impression that we could be working to a fairly tight schedule, so, pick up on my visualisation and meet me there." He turned to Tris and grabbed his hand. "You'd better come as well, just in case there are more children than we expect," he added. "But keep close to me, just in case we get unexpected trouble."

Tris nodded eagerly. Feeling excited that Mykael felt he was responsible enough to be included. Mykael quickly turned to address all the angels.

"Be sure to be invisible and intangible when you first arrive, because we don't know how much room we'll have," he hastily suggested. "And have your wings showing when you do make yourselves visible. I think that will help keep the children calm. After all, it's odds-on they've already seen Rylan with his wings and, given what he promised them, they'll be expecting some form of angelic help. If there's more than we anticipate, then Ithuriel, Gabriel and I will bring back the extras."

Granddad Roger watched. Shaking his head a little, as the eleven angels simply disappeared.

"I suppose I'd better warn Betty to expect quite few more," he murmured. "We might even have to put a few of them two to a bed."

***

An instant later, the group of eleven angels slowly made themselves visible inside the back of the truck. The children looked at them in astonishment.

"Did Rylan…" Luka began, then paused, not quite sure how to continue as he watched Tris kneel beside him.

"Rylan and Skylar are safe," Mykael quickly replied. "Fast asleep at a very safe place. However, he made it clear that he'd made you all a promise, so that is why we're here." He indicated towards Tristan. Stepping forward, and into a slight crouch, Tristan easily scooped up Jessamine, visualised himself on the far side of the room, so that the ankle chains and the 'keeper' clattered harmlessly to the floor, and then simply disappeared.

"And she'll be safe?" Persia queried, looking to where Tristan and Jessamine had been a moment earlier.

"You all will be," Mykael said softly, stepping towards Cooper. "When you wake, you will be a long way from here and totally safe. After that, those of you who have homes to go to, will be returned to your families' He glanced down at Cooper as he stooped to cradle the boy into his arms; already understanding from what he could read of the boy's mind that there were no thoughts of a happy family reunion. "For those that don't... well, we'll just have to find other safe places for you to live," he murmured.

***

In less than fifteen minutes, all eleven angels had returned to the farm. Each of them holding a, now comatose, child in their arms. Although Gabriel had brought both Martyn and Maia, while Ithuriel had brought Peter and Riley. Almost immediately, Grandma Betty began directing them down the hallway to the rooms in which there were beds all turned back and waiting. In Tris's case however, he had arrived still kneeling, so that he didn't need to fully support even Luka's slight weight.

"This way," Granddad Roger announced, taking Peter from Ithuriel, Zhenya doing likewise, in taking Maia from Gabriel, as Mischa quickly knelt to take Luka from Tris's grasp. "Betty's already got beds set up for them all; although we'll have to double-up a few more of them. We've already doubled-up Rylan and Skylar, and Jessamine and Persia, just in case we needed more room." The angels, in turn, quietly filed down the hallway to put the children to bed. Given how far they'd been transported, it was unlikely that any of them would wake for at least a full day, or perhaps even longer.

A few minutes later, when all the angels were back in the dining room, Mykael looked around at them all.

"Well done," he murmured. "That will at least save a few children from a rather horrible fate, and, perhaps more importantly, help keep a promise that our newest boy-angel had made." He turned to Tris. "You, will now go home," he announced rather brusquely. "Before Amanda and Joshua start to think that you've forgotten where your home actually is," he added with a slight laugh. Tris immediately looked a little embarrassed. At the same time, he did realise that he could have been there a lot more often than he had over the last week or so.

"But, I want to..." he protested rather weakly.

"No 'wants' or 'buts'," Mykael interjected in a tone that, while not appearing to contain any great sense of rebuke, still brooked no contradiction. "You can come back tomorrow, after lunch. And bring Lara with you when you do, so that she can get reacquainted with her brother." He waved his hands on a dismissal motion. "Now, scoot," he added. "Go on. Go home. Straight away!" With a slightly cheeky look, Tris immediately disappeared. He was already looking forward to bringing Lara back with him the next day. Mykael then turned to the other angels.

"Now, before we settle down to any home-baking and hot drinks, given Betty's penchant for such entertaining, I have an extra little mission I'd like some of you to help me undertake. From what I managed to get from Rylan's thoughts, and what I've been able to glean from some of the other children of exactly what the owners of that truck had planned for them, I think we should arrange an extra special surprise for our nasty group of traffickers; something that will turn out to be a rather rude shock for them. Especially when they open that secret compartment expecting to find fourteen timid and very frightened children." He gave them a quite conspiratorial smile. "It will, however, require a quick trip to the Everglades and the use of time-slowing to do some careful wrangling."

***

"We found him!" Tris enthused, as he arrived back in his bedroom and hurried out to the family room. "And he's got wings and he can 'be'."

"I take it you're talking about Rylan," Joshua retorted with a slightly wry grin.

"Of course," Tris replied. Not picking up on the slight sarcasm and half-wondering why they would think it could be anyone else, considering that finding Lara's twin was the whole reason he and Andrew had been away in the Big Apple.

"So where is he?" Lara asked.

"Up at the farm," Tris quickly explained. "Mykael put him into sleep mode because there were a whole lot of other children to be rescued as well. It was ever so smashing how we did it, 'cause they were all trapped in the back of a big truck. So after Rylan had rescued this kid called Skylar, and we'd found out where the truck was, Mykael and Ithuriel got Andrew and all his brothers to help go to rescue them. I helped bring back one of them, too… a boy called Luka. The children were all chained up, and started crying when we suddenly appeared. So…"

"Why?" Lara quickly interjected. Tris gave a slight shrug.

"I think it was because they were pleased to see us," he replied. "'Cause when Rylan took Skylar to safety, he'd promised that he'd come back to help them all get away."

“So where are they now?” Amanda asked.

“As I said, up at the farm, with Rylan,” Tris replied. “They all ended up fast asleep from being transported, so Grandma Betty and Zhenya were busy organising sleeping arrangements.”

“What about Rylan?” Amanda queried, looking just a little puzzled. “If he’s an angel, he wouldn’t have been asleep.” Tris gave a quick flex of his shoulders.

“He wasn’t when he arrived with the boy called Skylar. But, after Mykael had worked out just what was going on, he put Rylan to sleep as well. I’m not sure why, but I think it’s because he wants to keep a close eye on him for a while. Like, so that he knows to come here and can properly learn what his abilities are, and not just take off somewhere.”

“So there’s now about a dozen kids up at the farm, fast asleep?” Joshua queried. Tris quickly nodded.

“And more,” Tris explained. “In fact, six girls and eight boys. Although, one of them is Lara’s brother, so he’s an angel. It was a bit of a crush with so many, so Grandma and Granddad ended up having to bunk a few of them together... like, you know, in the double beds. Like Persia ended up with Maia, and even before we got back with most of them, Grandma Betty already had Rylan sharing a bed with Skylar. So then, it was...

“That should make him rather happy,” Lara interrupted with a teasing laugh, causing Amanda to give her a quietly scathing look.

“If they’re both asleep and sharing a bed, then that’s all there is to it,” she said softly. “Anyway, I think matters regarding his sexuality might change somewhat, now that he’s an angel,” she added, glancing across at Tris, who, despite the problems that had occurred when he’d been taken over by Ahaitan, still seemed to be very innocent, for want of a better word, in all that regard. To be sure, he understood the mechanics of sexual reproduction and sexual preferences in relation to human biology lessons, but it didn't seem to be anything in which he seemed to have even the slightest interest on a personal level, beyond the fact that Lara was a sister to him and a 'friend'. In the same way that Melanie, Rachael and Victoria were also just 'friends who were girls'.

"Will we adopt him as well?" Tris quickly asked. "Like, you know, Rylan?" Amanda briefly dropped her head to the side and exhaled softly. In a way, it was something that she and Joshua hadn't really thought about all that seriously; although it did seem to be the logical solution for where the boy should eventually live.

"Well, if he's Lara twin, I supposed that would be the correct thing to do," she replied. "But we'll need to talk to Mykael about all such developments, I'm sure." In a way, while she felt it unlikely that Rylan would pose any threat to Tris, she hoped that Mykael would be able to clarify the situation for all of them.

"Mykael wants me to take Lara up there tomorrow. After lunch sometime," Tris continued. "So that she can get reacquainted with Rylan." Joshua seemed quietly thoughtful for a moment or two.

"With that many children to sort out, it might be handy if we all go," he suddenly suggested. "I'll pop over and see if I can arrange for Steve Robertson to order a helicopter to take us up there tomorrow."

"Can we come too?" asked Tris eagerly. "Like, in the helicopter?"

"If you want to," Joshua replied. "I thought you'd both just..."

"But it'll be fun being in a helicopter," Tris replied. "And, different."

"I wonder if there's anything we should take?" Amanda mused. "Like maybe food or..."

"They could probably do with a stack of clothes,"Tris quickly interjected. "Cause they're all just dressed in these weird Native-American costumes, that leave half their backsides showing. You know, like with just a piece of cloth that sort of goes under their legs and is held in place by a belt." He hastily grabbed a tea towel from the bench and awkwardly tried to demonstrate what he was describing. "And none of them had any proper underwear," he added. "Like, nothing at all underneath the cloth."

"I'm sure Steve Robertson can sort out something in that regard," Amanda quietly suggested. "Maybe by getting a stack of jeans in various sizes and an assortment of new tops and underwear for both boys and girls."

"What about footwear?" Tris queried.

"Let's just concentrate on getting them properly covered first," Joshua suggested. "I'm sure the need for socks and shoes can wait just a bit. If necessary, we'll just have to arrange for an extra trip to the shops, afterwards. And anyway, Mykael may have other plans for what will happen to them. I doubt he'll want to have them all end up on the island. After all, it's very likely most of them will have parents who'll still be looking for them."

Joshua suddenly glanced down at his watch.

"It's getting quite late," he murmured, getting up from his seat. "I'd better head up to the big house and talk to Steve, before he and Evelyn head off to bed." He glanced towards Tris and Lara. "You two want to come?" Nothing more than an eager nod was necessary, as the two angel-children hurried to grab coats. Eager to impart the news of what had happened, and the prospect of there being a further new angel, and possibly some other children, coming to the island.

CHAPTER SIXTEEN

Safety….

"None of them are awake yet," Granddad Roger rumbled rather matter-of-factly, as the blades of the helicopter finally idled to a halt. "Not unless the sound of the helicopter has roused them." He waited just beyond the range of the blades as Tris, in a slightly crouched position, hurried over to him for a hug, followed at a slightly more leisurely pace by Steve and Evelyn Robertson, Joshua, Amanda and Lara, as well as Peter McCormack and Kate Ferris. The latter two present just in case there proved to be a need for medical assistance for any of the children, especially given the dire circumstances of the life in which they'd been involved.

"Mykael's been checking in about every half an hour, or so, but he doesn't expect any of them to wake until quite late this afternoon; most likely, right in time for tea," Granddad Roger continued, once greetings had been exchanged.

"I'd better hurry in and give Betty and Zhenya a hand getting things ready," Amanda quickly said. "With so many extra mouths requiring feeding before the day is out, even if we're just dealing with children's appetites, there'll be a lot to prepare.

"Just don't trip over all the boxes," Granddad Roger called as she hurried towards the porch. "There's a swag of stuff dumped there. A truckload that arrived by special delivery, just before lunch, courtesy of some local clothing retailer."

"I told them that there'd be a considerable bonus if they managed to get it all here before lunchtime," Steve said with a slight laugh. "They seemed very keen to help, although, with us not being too sure of how big the children were, I think we've probably cleaned out half their stock. At least, what they had in sizes suitable for ten to thirteen year olds."

"Well, it'll be good for the children to all have fresh underwear and a choice of new clothes," Granddad Roger mused as they followed rather more slowly after Amanda. "I doubt that they'd feel all that comfortable remaining in what they're currently wearing. More especially with the connotations it held for what was going to happen to them."

"Conna... what?" Lara queried, as they all stepped up on the porch.

"I think Granddad's referring to the fact that it was what they would likely have been wearing when they sold," Joshua quickly explained, not bothering to mention the more sordid aspects of that process. "I doubt they'll really want to be reminded of that fact." They hurried inside, taking care to dodge around the stacked boxes of clothing.

"Tris," Grandma Betty called from the kitchen, immediately that they were inside. "Perhaps you and Lara could give Mischa and Zhenya a hand with sorting out some of the clothing? We'll need to have the boys' clothes and girls' clothes in separate boxes, so that they can be put into the bedrooms where the children are sleeping. Once you've done the sorting, you can probably help decide which of the rooms would best for them to get changed in, later on.

Tris and Lara hurried to comply with her directive, anxious to not only get the clothes sorted, but to see the children for whom they were meant... even if they were not yet awake.

***

"I think it's time I woke up your brother," Mykael said, looking across at Lara, as he drained the last of his coffee. "And before you two get reacquainted, I'd like the chance to talk to him alone and discuss his future. I also think that it would be nice for him to be fully awake for when the other children come to. After all, they owe their rescue to him, even if other angels brought them here." He beckoned for Tris to come with him, but indicated for Lara to wait.

Moments later, they were in the Blue room, as Grandma Betty called it. Both Skylar and Rylan were still fast asleep, cuddled into a position where they were actually facing each other and looking very much at peace with the world; a very far cry from the horrific situation they'd been in a day earlier.

Going over to the boxes of boys' clothing that had been left in the room, Mykael quickly sorted out a couple of, still wrapped, sets of new underwear. Singlets and pants along with a couple of pairs of jeans and a selection of T-shirts and jumpers, which he placed on a chair beside the bed. A large selection of shoes and socks, for all the children, was still out on the porch. They'd be sorted out at some later stage.

With that done, Mykael moved closer to the bed and gently placed a hand onto Rylan's head. Almost instantly, the boy seemed to wake. For a moment or two, appearing totally confused by the whole situation. Such as who the two people with wings, who were standing beside the bed that he was in, were? And where he now was? He certainly didn't recognise anything about the room, or why he was dressed as weirdly as he was. And more particularly, why he was sharing a bed with Skylar Jefferies. A boy whom he'd once wished might be his best friend. As he looked at the two angels, and noted his own wings, various thoughts started to come flooding back, mainly about the truck and all the children being held captive. That was where he'd found Skylar Jeffries.

"I would like you to be awake and properly dressed before the others," Mykael said quietly, interrupting his scattered thought meanderings. "They will want to thank you."

"Why?" Rylan asked rather tentatively.

"Because, by your actions, we were able save all of them," Mykael softly replied. "If you hadn't tried make the best use of what you knew of your abilities to rescue Skylar and made a promise to the other children, we might not have been able to help them." Rylan turned and looked down at Skylar.

"So where are... where are the others?" he whispered, realising that Skylar was still fast asleep.

"In other rooms," Mykael replied. "This house is a safe place for angels and other children who have difficulties."

"So why were you all trying to capture me?" Rylan asked, looking firstly at Tris and then at Mykael.

"Because we had to get you away from the military," Mykael gently replied. "They'll only want to keep you locked up in a cage, until they work out how they can make use of you; just the same as they were trying to do to your sister. At least, until Tris, here, rescued her."

"My sister?" replied Rylan, hastily wiping at the tears that were suddenly in his eyes. "You know where she is?"

"Of course," Tris replied. "She's out in the dining room with my mum and dad. We've all come here from the island."

"What island?" Rylan asked a little bewilderedly.

"It's where we all live," Tris replied brightly. "And you'll be coming to live with us. Like with Lara and me and my mum and dad."

"They won't want me," Rylan whispered softly. "Not when they know what I am."

"If you're worried about issues of sexuality, don't," said Mykael, with a smile. "We already know those details, and we'll simply sort out all those difficulties when we have everyone safe."

"Well what about what's happening to me?" Rylan asked nervously. "I... I mean..." He indicated his wings.

"It's the start of your angel abilities," Mykael replied. "You'll end up just like Tris." At a subtle signal from Mykael, Tris spread his wings to their fullest extent, before folding them down tightly. Rylan's eyes grew slightly wider at the sight.

"Is that what mine will eventually be like?" he asked rather cautiously.

"Probably," Tris quickly answered. "Lara's are growing pretty quickly now, too. She's even started learning to fly, which you will also be able to do."

"Fly?" Rylan echoed.

"Because that's what we can do," Tris replied.

"But why?" Rylan asked. "Like, why has this happened to me? It's not as if I'm particularly good, or… or I spend a lot of time reading the Bible, or something, so… why?" In the back of his mind was also the thought of how he always felt that he'd been attracted to other boys, rather than girls. Figuring that that must surely count against him being 'special' in any way. That was certainly what his father and Pastor Isaac had constantly drummed into him.

"That, we cannot always know," Mykael calmly replied. "Suffice to say that sometimes what is planned for the future has to reveal itself in its own time. In the meantime, it's my task to keep you safe. Now, I know you've been through some very difficult times, but you'll need to put that all behind you. This will be a totally fresh start. A safe start, where you will be able to learn the proper use of your abilities, in a place well away from any people who will want to hurt or exploit you. When your sister, who's anxiously waiting to meet you, started growing her wings, she also went through some difficult times. The people who'd adopted her sold her to a military hospital research facility. She ended up being locked up in a cage, as if she was some sort of strange animal to be studied."

"That's why I had to rescue her," Tris added. "And teach her how to do all the proper angel things, like tele..."

"So if I'm an angel," Rylan suddenly interrupted, as if having only just put all the facts into a proper perspective, "how has that happened? I thought you said I wasn't dead?"

"And you're not," Mykael countered with a warm smile. "You're just a child-angel. A boy with wings, along with some other abilities, which I will restore to you when you can promise me that you won't just vanish."

"So... I'm... I'm like the mutants in the X-men films?" Rylan cautiously queried.

"Well, they're just made up stories," Mykael replied, with a small shake of his head. "But that's sort of the right idea. Humans are changing. You know, evolving... but certainly not at that rate." He pointed to the pile of clothes on the chair. "Now, I've put some fresh clothes out for you, so how about you get yourself dressed into something a bit more normal and then come out to get reacquainted with your sister and meet your new parents." The issue of his staying with Joshua and Amanda had already been discussed and decided upon. Rylan glanced at the pile of clothing and then at Skylar.

"We'll just leave him to sleep a little longer," Mykael murmured, appearing to understand his thoughts. "Humans take a little longer to get over being teleported. And, by the way, we call it 'be'ing, because you can just be where you want to be. Now, get yourself dressed and then come out to the dining room. I'm sure Grandma Betty will have something nice to eat and drink waiting for you."

Tris and Mykael left the room. For a moment Rylan just stared at the clothes and then at Skylar. Like most of the boys at school in Oakton, Skylar had always been wary of being seen to be friendly with him, and vice versa. Perhaps, now that they were somewhere else, things might be a bit different.

Eventually he clambered out of bed, and quickly removed his costume. Feeling just a little self-conscious about being totally naked, he hastily began trying on the new clothes. Hopping awkwardly around on one foot for a few moments, as he tried to get fresh underwear on, as quickly as possible, before Skylar awoke and saw him undressed.

Eventually dressed in new underwear and jeans, he selected a large T-shirt to give his wings more freedom. Wondering, as he did so, how it was that the other angels seemed to be able to wear normal clothes and somehow still have their wings showing. After a moment or two of thought, he tried to visualise himself on the other side of the room. Nothing happened. He was obviously still without his abilities.

Realising that they'd all be waiting for him, he took a last look at Skylar and then, just a little nervously, headed out into the hallway. Not only would Lara be there — he wondered how different she'd look, given that he hadn't seen her in quite a while — but he would also now have new parents waiting for him. The same people, it seemed, who looked after Lara and the boy-angel called Tris. He opened the door, and then quietly closed it behind him before heading down the hallway to where he could hear the sound of voices.

Emerging into the brightness of what was obviously a dining room, he immediately looked a little nervously at the people seated around a large table. Mykael got quickly to his feet and came over to usher him into the room.

"Everyone," he quietly announced, "I'd like you to meet Rylan. Our newest boy-angel and already a hero for helping instigate the rescue of over a dozen children from a very dangerous situation."

He turned to Rylan. "You will already recognise some of these people, because they were here when you first arrived. And Tris and your sister you will already know. More importantly..." he directed Rylan around the table to Amanda and Joshua, "... these two people will now be your parents, given that they already look after Tris and have recently adopted your sister."

Rylan turned and beckoned for Mykael to lean closer.

"But what if they don't want me?" he whispered, his eyes suddenly welling with tears. "You know, because of what… of what I am?" he added belatedly, to make it clear that he wasn't referring to his developing angel status. Tris hurried over and quickly put an arm around his shoulders.

"Don't worry about it," he said brightly. "Mum and Dad already know all about that and it doesn't matter to any of us. Anyway, you need to be with Lara, so we will easily have room for you. And Mykael thinks it would be good to have all us angels together; not that we'll be the only angels on the island."

"You mean there are more of us?" Rylan queried, wiping at his eyes. Tris pointed across the room to where some of the other angels were gathered and watching the interaction.

"Andrew, Taylor and Conlaodh are all brothers, and there are four more of them," Tris quickly continued. "And they're also my uncles. Andrew still lives on the island, but they all grew up there."

"But they'll be adults," Rylan almost whispered.

"Not always," Andrew said with a teasing smile. He, Taylor and Conlaodh quickly morphed into young boys of about eleven or twelve. Rylan was immediately amazed to realise that two of them were identical twins.

"W... we ca... can do that?" Rylan stammered, totally astounded by what had just occurred.

"When you're older," Tris replied. "When you're an adult. Of course there are lots of other things you'll have to learn first," he continued. "Like being able to make your wings invisible and being able to 'be'... which is like teleporting. "Although, it seems that you already know how to do that, which was what made it difficult to save you."

"I called it 'jumping'," Rylan murmured with a touch of embarrassment. Tris gave a nonchalant shrug.

"That's probably as good a name as any for it," he said with a smile. "But there are still other abilities you will have to learn Most of them are fun... like, with flying."

"So who teaches us all those things?" Rylan asked rather eagerly.

"The special older angels who act as our guardians," Tris quickly explained. He turned towards Mykael and Ithuriel. "Mykael's the main one for us. But there's also Ithuriel and Gabriel and Raphael and a whole lot of others who help. Mykael and Ithuriel seem to be the ones who do the most teaching. They also reprimand us if we do something wrong." Rylan immediately looked a little dejected. He leaned closer to Tris.

"Will they be annoyed that I'm probably gay?" he whispered.

"I doubt it'll make any difference to anybody on the island," Tris reassured him. "Let alone any of the angels. Just like it won't make any difference to Mum and Dad. They're already used to Matthew Ryan coming over to see me."

"Matthew Ryan?" Rylan queried a little bemusedly. "You mean... like, Mattie Ryan from Oakton?" Tris nodded.

"He also lives on the island. After he'd also been sent to the special boot camp, he didn't want to go back to Oakton, afterwards. Not after what had been said about him by Pastor Isaac and knowing that everyone had found out about what had happened to him. Anyway, his stepdad's now in prison, along with your dad and Pastor Isaac, so he and his mum now live on the island. Same as where you'll be living."

"And the first two lessons you will need to learn are, firstly, how to think your wings through clothing," Mykael said, with a warm smile. "And, secondly, how to make your wings invisible when you don't want people to see them." He looked towards Tris and Lara. "I'm sure your sister and Tris will be quite keen to show you how. But all that can at least wait until after you've had something to eat."

***

Skylar awoke and immediately looked around, trying to work out where he was. Knowing that his sleep had been partly disturbed by the sound of a door closing. He didn't recognise the bed he was in, or the room. Although, by the subdued light seeping through the curtains he guessed that it was daytime. Wondering how long he'd been asleep, and curious about the way the blankets seemed rucked back a little, he felt beside himself. The sheets to the side of where he lay still contained some residual warmth, making it obvious that he'd been sharing a bed... but with whom?

He gave a shake of his head. The last thing that he could remember was being in the back of a truck, shackled by his ankles to a bar in the centre of the floor, and on his way to be sold as a slave. He shuddered at the thought. Had that already happened, and was this just the aftermath? Somehow, he didn't think so.

In fact, the more he thought about it, his last recollection was simply of being grabbed by a boy that he knew from school, from back in the time when he'd been living in Oakton. Had that been whom he'd shared the bed with? Rylan Daniels?

At the same time, it had all seemed strange in some weird way. Especially as it seemed as if Rylan had had wings and had been able to, somehow, move from one side of the room to the other in an instant. The thought suddenly came to him. Rylan was an angel! And yet, that very idea didn't make sense.

He looked at the floor beside the bed, seeing the crumpled costume that the person who'd been with him must have been wearing. Obviously, they'd been able to dress in other clothes. He looked at the assortment of clothes stacked on the far side of the room for a moment and then decided that it might be best to ask permission before getting dressed in anything new.

Easing himself out of bed, Skylar tiptoed over to the door and opened it. He could hear the sound of voices from further down the hallway. Quickly checking that his costume still managed to cover him properly, he cautiously made his way to the source of the conversations and found that he was standing in the doorway to a good-sized room, where people were seated around a large table. To his amazement, some of them had wings.

"Well, you're the first one to wake," a tall man with wings said, as he then beckoned for Skylar to come closer. He turned to others at the table. "That means they should all be waking up fairly soon." Skylar simply stared, until an elderly woman came over and took his hand and directed him to a seat at the table. Just moments later, it seemed, she'd placed a bowl of hot soup and a plate with some large hunks of buttered bread in front of him and encouraged him to eat up.

As he took a few tentative mouthfuls, he glanced nervously around the room, realising that there was only one other person whom he recognised... Rylan Daniels. And like he now somehow thought he'd imagined while in the truck, Rylan obviously also had wings, from the way his T-shirt was bunched out at the back.

"A... am I dead?" he queried. The tall angel shook his head.

"You might have been, if Rylan hadn't rescued you," he said rather calmly. "Or at the least, have ended up being very badly hurt." Mykael then turned and indicated for Rylan to follow Tris out onto the porch in order to select some new shoes. As Rylan went to head outside, Skylar quickly got up from his seat, hurried over to him and gave him a hug. Not showing any sign of reticence or embarrassment in cuddling a boy that everyone at school in Oakton had once been at pains to avoid, or had tried hard to not be seen to befriend.

"Thank you for rescuing me," he whispered. Rylan nodded and looked away for a moment.

"I didn't touch you," he whispered in return. Skylar looked puzzled for a moment. Trying to figure out what he meant. "Like, while we were in bed together," Rylan quickly continued, by way of explanation. "I didn't touch you in any way. I didn't even know that would happen. Like, that we'd end up in the same bed. I just woke up and you were there, beside me. I think it was because of how many children there were to rescue."

"We can still be friends," Skylar whispered, giving him a further hug. Their attention, however, was immediately taken by the sight of Cooper emerging rather cautiously from the hallway; his face also reflecting a great degree of bewilderment at the strange scene confronting him; most particularly, the gathering of unknown people that included both adults and children with wings. He tugged at the sides of the back of the loincloth, as if trying to spread it a little wider to cover more of his behind. Then, still a little embarrassed at how he was dressed, but recognising Skylar and Rylan, he hurried over to them.

"Where are we?" he quickly whispered. His last memory was of being of being in the back of the truck, a boy with wings disappearing with Skylar and then more people with wings suddenly appearing out of thin air.

"Somewhere safe, it seems," Skylar replied equally softly as he, with just a slight blush of embarrassment, hastily released his grip on Rylan. "They've got food for us and it looks as if we're in a farmhouse of some type, but I have absolutely no idea of where it is… or how we really got here."

As Jessamine also came cautiously into the room, quickly followed by Persia, and then Noah, Mykael came over to the doorway and put a hand on Rylan's shoulder.

"I had also planned to have the doctor check you over, but I think it might be best if we just get all these other children sorted out first," he murmured. "I'll also need to explain to them where they are and how that came about."

***

Over the next hour, as the children awoke, they were fed, and then directed to separate rooms to be dressed in the new clothes that had been provided. This was also accompanied by discreet medical checks that soon uncovered the fact that most of them were still 'undamaged', for want of a better description, apart from some residual bruising from recent punishments on a couple of them. Peter and Noah being the exceptions. They had unfortunately suffered rather more severe abuse. Although Rylan had also been abused, given that it had obviously been quite a while ago, he seemed quite healed. Nevertheless, if it proved necessary, Peter McCormack would be scheduling him for ongoing discreet medical checks over the next few weeks.

When they were eventually all assembled together in the dining room, Mykael quickly introduced everyone and explained that they were now in a safe place well away from any danger, how they arrived there, and that arrangements would be made to get them returned to their families as soon as possible. For a start, it would simply be a matter of each of them providing him with a phone number for contacting their parents, and then his arranging a suitable time and place for the exchange to take place. Steve Robertson had already made an offer of the use of his Lear jet for their transportation back to the U.S. of A.

"Now that you have some rough idea of how you came to be here, and what will happen over the next day or so, you might also like to watch this," he eventually announced, turning on the television set in the room, selecting an input mode, and then connecting a USB drive into the side panel. "I recorded it off the news while you were all asleep." Using the remote, he scrolled to the appropriate device image on the screen, opened a folder labelled Fox News Broadcast, and pressed play.

The screen flickered for a moment and then showed two of the regular Fox News front persons. The children listened, with casual interest, as the announcers explained that there had been an emergency at the residence of a high-ranking government employee with tenuous connections to the Pentagon.

They immediately showed more interest as the view switched to a reporter on site. Behind him was a night view of a rather palatial-looking, three-story building, set back from the road and surrounded by quite spacious grounds so that there seemed to be no close neighbours. On the current view, the looping driveway, the front of the building and one side were illuminated by the flashing lights of numerous police cars, emergency response vans, a couple of medical vehicles, two large trucks with cages and the spotlights of a good number of on-site television broadcast vehicles. They appeared to be haphazardly gathered around what appeared to be the entrance to an underground car park.

"From what we've been able to ascertain," the on-site reporter announced, "Just prior to a private celebration taking place, the basement level of the building had to be entirely evacuated after about a dozen live alligators were discovered inside the trailer section of a truck parked in the underground car park. The ground floor was also evacuated as a precaution." He glanced towards the building. "Now, according to what we have been informed by the local police… and at this stage some details are still rather sketchy, due to internal security requirements… the trailer was supposed to be bringing the staging for a special musical performance that was to take place this evening for a quite select audience. Further details of who that audience was to be, are at present not available, owing to security and privacy concerns. From the little we've been able to learn about the incident, however, it seems that, when the supervisor and two stagehands entered the back of the truck to start sorting out the items associated with the evening's entertainment, they ended up being trapped in what appears to have been a strangely divided-off compartment in the vehicle and were attacked by a number of rather large alligators. Two of those persons have now been confirmed as fatalities, having bled to death before they could be rescued, while a third is in the process of being rushed to an intensive care unit. From what we've been able to ascertain, it seems he may possibly have lost both of his legs in the attack. Police have also arrested the driver of the vehicle, Reginald Vargas, on a charge of transporting wild animals without a proper license. Amongst those dead, we can report, was a Mr Vittorio Colaris. It appears, according to various unconfirmed sources, that he was an entrepreneur well known for providing specialist entertainment services at selected high-status private functions. A number of senior FBI investigators are presently on the scene and will soon be conducting further investigations to uncover the mystery of how the alligators came to be loose inside the back of the vehicle and what part the animals were supposed to be playing as a part of the entertainment. There is also a mystery as to why there were numerous pairs of handcuffs and some strange necklaces strewn about the floor of the hidden compartment. The FBI has assured us that there is no other threat to this area, now that the alligators have been tranquillised and are being readied for a return to their natural habitat."

"Like having senior FBI officials there will lead anywhere!" snorted Cooper angrily, as Mykael paused the DVD. "They were probably already there for the effin' entertainment! Which meant having their fun with us! Doing whatever they liked with us! And as for the local police, they'll be no help, whatsoever, because, whenever any of us got away, Vittorio knew people in authority who just got us returned to him. As me and Skylar soon found out."

"I told them that's what would happen," Peter added with a knowing nod of his head. "'Cause me and Noah had had the same thing happen to us, the one time we tried to get away. It's like you get to the police station and they're all caring and promising to get you back to your parents as soon as possible, and that sort of thing. And you think you're going to be safe until, next thing, a couple of special FBI officials arrive and take over. Then, before you know it, you're in the back of a limo being taken back to the Vittorio for punishment."

"What I don't understand is… how did the alligators get in there?" Skylar asked.

"The same way as you were got out of there, I guess," Rylan answered, looking towards Mykael.

"I just hope it was 'effin' painful," Peter muttered with some vehemence. Having been on the receiving end of Vittorio and Angelo's brutality on quite a number of occasions, sometimes it seemed just because they wanted a bit of 'fun', he had no sympathy whatsoever for any of their captors. Mykael quickly switched off the television and disconnected the USB drive.

"There will probably be more about it all on upcoming news broadcasts," he murmured, "But it's most unlikely that the real truth will ever come out."

"You mean about how the alligators got there?" Riley queried.

"Well that too," Mykael said with a smile. "But I was actually meaning more along the lines of what the 'special entertainment' was ever supposed to be. Given the scandal that would erupt, if the truth was ever revealed, you can be sure that there will be people with money making sure that those details never see the light of day. It's amazing how often various senior politicians will claim that there is no evidence to consider. Especially if any of it would reflect on their status in society and their political careers, not to mention any likely criminal repercussions. The issue of the handcuffs and explosive necklaces will just get quietly swept under the rug, as they say."

"And become fodder for various conspiracy theorists, no doubt," Andrew murmured. "Most probably trying to prove that the alligators were really aliens."

"But can't you do something about that?" Rochelle quietly asked, turning towards Mykael. "I mean, you have all sorts of powers and... and kidnapping children is illegal. Especially for what they intended to do to us!" Mykael looked down at her and shrugged.

"We shouldn't have really been involved at all," he replied, almost a little wearily. Perhaps knowing that what he was about to say, and where it was leading, would be hard for any of the children to understand. "It was only because Rylan had promised to help you all get away and pleaded with me to rescue you, that we thought we should help."

"So we were supposed to just get brutalised and whatever?" questioned Rochelle rather bluntly. Again, Mykael shrugged his shoulders and sighed softly.

"Sometimes things are meant to happen in a certain way because it's just the way things are supposed to be," he replied. "It's simply a part of whatever is planned for your life while you are here," he continued, before glancing across to where Tris, Rylan and Lara stood with Amanda and Joshua. "As Tris's Uncle Alexei would tell you, upsetting the plans for some events can sometimes lead to rather unexpected consequences. Even if you still think that you are helping."

"You mean that sort of weird infallibility clause thing that he sometimes mentions?" Tris quickly queried. Mykael cocked his head briefly to one side and nodded.

"Let's just say that, sometimes, an action that might seem quite small and innocent, can trigger a whole series of events that have rather more serious consequences," he murmured.

"So what happens now? Like, now that we have all been rescued?" Jessamine cautiously asked, before he could explain his reply to Tris's query a little more fully. "Do we stay here? Or do we go home? Or, what?"

"As I said a little earlier, over today and tomorrow I will be making contact with your parents to arrange for your immediate return home," Mykael quickly continued, pleased to have got away from having to explain anything more about the infallibility clause and how it was supposed to operate. "Most of you, of course, will have parents desperately waiting for you to be found. Parents who will have been praying for your safe return, so..."

"Mine won't," Cooper gruffly interjected. "My 'effin' step-dad sold me to those bastards! And I'm sure he knew exactly what they would do to me." He spread his hands, palms upwards, in a gesture of futility, as tears suddenly welled in his eyes. "That's what Vittorio told me, anyway. So… so where do I go?" Mykael seemed thoughtful for a moment or two. Perhaps being caught a little off-guard by the mere fact that perhaps more of the children, beyond Cooper, might not have welcoming homes to go to.

"Other arrangements will be made for those who have difficulties with going home, or who would be likely to end up in the care of Social Welfare," he eventually explained. "Just as Rylan will be coming to live with his sister and new stepbrother, places will be also found for you to be with a loving family."

"Can it be on the same island that Rylan is going to?" Cooper quietly asked.

"That may be possible," Mykael replied with a smile at the earnest expression on the boy's face. "Especially if there is no one else to take care of you. There are a number of families there who would probably be more than willing to take on an extra child. In the meantime, those without families to go to, will simply remain here at the farm, while we get everyone else sorted. What I'll get you all to do now, however, is to give Grandma Betty your parents' contact details. After which, Mr Robertson will take photographs of all of you for the purposes of providing you with new passports. I will then arrange to get the passports sorted, overnight, and make contact with your parents to arrange your safe return. Wherever that is still possible."

"How can you possibly get passports done overnight?" Jessamine quickly asked, her face reflecting some puzzlement at that idea. "It usually takes weeks for them to do all the special checks required. Even if you do them on-line." Mykael responded with a subtle raise of one eyebrow.

"Let's just say that, as angels, there are ways in which we can speed up the procedure. Mainly by bypassing some of the bureaucratic validating processes that tend to waste so much time, unnecessarily. Now that might not seem to be completely legal, in the true sense of the word, but don't worry, they will certainly be quite legitimate, and good enough to pass muster at any airport, without anyone realising how they were created."

"So they're fakes?" Jessamine countered.

"No, they are quite real and authentic," replied Mykael rather casually. "It's just that if anyone ever bothered to check, which they won't, they'd find that the usual trail of time-wasting 'cross-checking'… for want of a better word, that's been enacted since nine-eleven, will seem to be 'lost' somewhere in the system, as it were. After all, it's highly unlikely that any of you have links to any major terrorist organisations."

"So we won't have problems?" Jessamine queried, at the same time exhibiting a sense of relief at being able to go home so quickly.

"Not in the slightest," Mykael replied, giving her a warm smile. "If everything goes as planned, most of you will be reunited with your parents by a little after lunchtime the day after tomorrow."

Having explained what would happen, Mykael then turned to Rylan and beckoned for him, Lara and Tris, to follow him out onto the porch. Once outside, he indicated for them to be seated.

"Okay," he said, looking directly at Rylan. "Now that you know what is going to happen for most of the children, and know that they will be safe, I want you to understand a couple of things. Before I return your abilities to you, I need you to promise me that you will do as I ask, at all times, with no just taking off on your own whenever you feel like it. As one of the senior guardians for Tris, Lara and yourself, I have to ensure that you are all kept safe. As Tris can tell you, there are some very nasty people out there, both angelic and human, who can cause you very serious problems, if you're not careful; problems far worse than anything that you might have already experienced; perhaps that you could possibly even imagine. The island, where you will mainly be living, is your safe place. No one can hurt you while you are there. Nor will anyone who lives there ever want to hurt you. Do you understand?" Rylan hastily nodded a reply, even as he tried to think of what could be worse than what he'd suffered at the camp.

"Okay," Mykael said, also giving a nod of his head. "Now, just as I have previously asked of your sister, when you go home, you are to remain on the island, unless chaperoned by a senior angel. Andrew, Conlaodh, or Taylor will usually be available, if not myself or Ithuriel. You may return here, to the farm, if you are also with Tris, but I forbid you to go anywhere near to any place where you may have previously lived. Understand?"

"But there are some people I would like to thank for helping me," Rylan queried. "Can I go…?" Mykael cocked his head briefly, to one side.

"If you're referring to the Fulchers, Old George, and Mama Hattie, I will arrange for you to go with Andrew, and maybe Ithuriel, to pay them a visit. I suggest that you also take your sister, and Tris, with you. After all, Tris has already meet Mama Hattie a couple of times." Rylan nodded eagerly, then looked a little tentative.

"Do I get my abilities back?" he queried. "Like, being able to 'jump'?" Instantly, he felt a sense of lightness in his body.

"You will also need to learn other new skills," Mykael added. "Like, how to be invisible, to fly, to make just your wings invisible and to also make it so that you can wear normal clothes by having your wings pass through whatever you are wearing." He glanced towards Tris and Lara. "Perhaps that's something you two could help him with over the next couple of days, while you're all here at the farm and once you get back home. I suggest starting with wings invisibility and being able to make Rylan's wings appear through his clothes," he added. "Especially if he wants to go and visit people to say thank you." He indicated for them to all head back inside. As they did so, he moved close to Rylan.

"This is the start of a new life for you," he whispered. "A chance to forget all of your past problems and look forward to a happy future. But, as I said a moment ago, for you to be properly safe, you must be prepared to accept my guardianship, in all matters. To do as I say when I ask, even if you may not always agree with my decisions. Any restrictions I may impose are as much for your own safety, as for any other reason. And don't feel that you're being singled out. I have also placed Lara under similar restrictions, and to a lesser degree, even given his greater experience, Tris. Those restrictions will gradually be relaxed as you develop more control of your abilities. You will also be obedient to Amanda and Joshua, Tris's parents, at all times given that they are now to be your parents. Understand?" Rylan hastily nodded a reply.

***

Gathering the children around him on the porch at the farm, Mykael casually indicated for them to be seated. It was early in the morning of the day after their first meeting, and in the meantime, he'd done his best to contact all the parents that the children had listed. With, of course, the exception of Cooper, who had, rather understandably, simply refused to give up any details whatsoever of where he'd been living prior to his abduction.

"Well," he said casually. "I have good news and bad news. The good news is that, having made contact with your parents, it seems that, in general, most of you will be welcomed home with open arms. So for…"

"Mine wouldn't have," Cooper quietly interrupted. Mykael looked around at him a little sternly, and then smiled to show he wasn't too annoyed by the interjection. Fully understanding the boy's reticence to ever be returned to caregivers who had, it seemed, simply sold him into slavery. In some ways, it beggared belief that even stepparents would stoop to such callous behaviour, but as they say, the proof was in the details. Cooper's abductors had known the secret password and could have only got it from his parents.

"There are one or two exceptions," Mykael explained, looking directly at Cooper. "Given that, when I was making contact, I did meet with… let's just say, some 'unexpectedly negative reactions' from a couple of parents. In which case, alternative arrangements will be made for those children to live away from their families, if they so wish. In the interim, however, they will simply remain at the farm until further arrangements can be made and finalised." He watched as the children looked firstly at Cooper, and then around amongst themselves. All of them perhaps a little curious as to whom of them had parents who had, inexplicably, reacted without enthusiasm to the news of their being rescued.

"To continue with the good news," Mykael quickly continued. "For the following nine of you… Luka, Riley, Maia, Natasha, Jessamine, Rochelle, Camille, Martyn and Peter, arrangements have already been made for you to be reunited with your parents in Hartford, Connecticut, early tomorrow morning. I have avoided using the more major cities, in order for there to be less chance of you being totally swamped by media coverage. The true circumstances of your rescue, however, will need to be kept entirely secret, because details of that will only lead to more media scrutiny and intrusion into your lives, and perhaps even bring unwelcome forces into the mix." He looked around the group. "In particular, there is to be no mention whatsoever of your being rescued by angels. Nor of the fact that you were in any way involved in what was on the news about the alligators in the truck. Not unless you want to end up with various reporters and conspiracy theory activists, as well as the usual intrusive religious groups, badgering you and your families about angels, for years to come. Understand?" The children all quickly nodded, almost simultaneously. "All you need to say is that you'd been kidnapped and that the truck you were in broke down, and your shouts for help were heard by a private investigator who was trying to track down…" he looked around the group. "Let's say… Rylan, given that, as far as we know, there are still people looking for him in New York. His mother, for one."

"So how do we get there?" Natasha eagerly asked. "Like, to Hartford?"

"After a helicopter flight from the farm to a nearby airfield, you will travel to Hartford by Lear jet… courtesy of Steve Robertson," Mykael quickly explained. "He has also supplied you with the proper clothes you are now wearing, and is the owner of the island where the child-angels live. He is also covering all the extra transport and accommodation costs for your parents to get to Hartford… where he feels that your parents may have some hardship. As I mentioned would happen, yesterday, you all now have new passports which you will receive once you are in the air so there'll be no hassles with American immigration officials. After landing, you will then meet with your parents in a conference room at Bradley International airport. After which, arrangements will be made, by Ithuriel, Gabriel and Mr Robertson, to help you and your families, return home."

There was a general buzz of excitement as the children discussed those details; some of it being simple curiosity as to how Mykael could've arranged everything, including passports for them all, so quickly.

"Now before you all head in for lunch, for the children I haven't yet mentioned…" Mykael eventually continued with a slightly raised voice. All eyes immediately turned to Cooper, Noah, Skylar and Persia. "…I will discuss your circumstances in a few moments, if you care to wait. This being because, apart from Cooper, who has no wish to return home, I either met with a decidedly negative response from the caregivers with whom I spoke, or because I have not yet been able to make contact with anyone at the phone number or address that was provided."

He then waited until most of the children had headed back inside to start lunch, before indicating for the four remaining children to come in a little closer.

"Now, as Cooper has already intimated, there isn't a viable happy family for him to return to, so an alternative accommodation arrangement will be made for him." He turned his attention directly towards Cooper. "So, as I said earlier, until that is all decided, you will simply remain here at the farm. Understand?" Cooper responded with an eager nod of his head.

"That suits me just fine," he said softly. "I like being here." The farm was certainly a major step up on his previous home life, even if it was to be only temporary. Mykael then shifted his gaze to Noah and Persia, and then sighed as he drew them in a little closer.

"For you two, the situation however, is a little more awkward. In both cases, I sensed a quite negative undercurrent in the way your parents responded to the news of your being rescued and as to why you'd been kidnapped. In both cases, there seemed to be an attitude, and some sort of assumption, that you were now 'damaged goods', to put it politely." He turned to direct his next comment directly to Noah. "Although I didn't mention it, apart from informing them that you'd been kidnapped by child slave traffickers, given the greater extent of abuse that you suffered, in your case, that sort of attitude might have been vaguely understandable. They seemed to take an inference, however, from that fact that you'd probably been very badly abused." He shook his head a little. "To be honest, I would've expected loving parents to overlook matters over which you had had no control and not be so willing to jump to conclusions about what had happened to you. Nevertheless, I think that, for the moment, it would be best for you to also remain at the farm until an alternative accommodation can also be arranged." Not wanting to mention the fact that Noah's mother had assumed that he'd been forced into 'hustling', and had mentioned, several times, that she'd be constantly worried about him being a bad influence on his two younger brothers, he then turned towards Persia.

"The situation, with regard to your parents is even more puzzling," he quietly continued. "Given that you did not suffer any major abuse, beyond a couple of paddlings, and some awkward touching, I would have expected your parents to have been more accepting of your return. However, it seems that your father, in particular, has taken the stance that, since you were raised in a closed-off Christian commune, any activity outside of their jurisdiction and influence has somehow marked you as 'unclean'. So I feel that…"

"I think I'd rather remain outside their influence," Persia quickly interrupted. "The elders had already planned a marriage for me for when I turned fourteen. I think it would have been to one of the older men. Like, somebody already old enough to be my father. 'Cause that's what usually happens when the elders make the marriages arrangements. Some of them even have more than one wife. They just choose a new girl every few years."

"Well, as I said, earlier," Mykael said softly, not appearing to be put out by her interruption, "you will also remain here at the farm until an alternative family is found to look after you."

"I know my mother would definitely want me back," Skylar hastily interjected, as he immediately realised that he must be the one where no contact had been possible. "Even if we are just living in an effin' trailer-park."

"That's what puzzles me a little," Mykael quickly replied, turning towards him. "I've tried the cellphone number you gave me, but it now seems to be disconnected. I also visited your home, but, while everything about the place still seems to indicate recent occupation of some kind, no one seems to be living there at the moment."

"She wouldn't have just gone off and left me," Skylar said, as his eyes seemed to well a little with tears. "I just know she wouldn't. She must just be trying to find me."

"Well, that might just be the case, but the best way for us to work that out will be for you and me to go to where you live, and see if anyone in the trailer park knows where she might be," Mykael suggested. "We can even do that later tomorrow, after the other children have been dropped off in Hartford, given the time difference between Connecticut and Texas."

"Can Rylan come with us?" Skylar quickly asked. Mykael seemed to consider the request for a moment.

"I think, for the moment, I'd prefer for him to remain here," he eventually decided. "He still hasn't mastered keeping his wings invisible and we may end up in situations where that would be necessary."

"But I want to let my mom know how he saved me," Skylar pleaded. Mykael gave a nod of his head.

"I understand that," he said calmly. "But let's just get things sorted with finding out why there was nobody at home when I called in to where you live, and why no one is answering the phone." He paused for a moment. "We can, however, take Tris with us, as proof of your angel rescue, if you like. We can then arrange for your mother to meet Rylan when he has greater control of his abilities."

He turned and looked towards the sky for moment before returning his attention to the four children.

"Now, how about you head off and join the others for lunch," he then continued. "Tell Grandma Betty that, as much as I would like to stay for a bite to eat, I have an important meeting, elsewhere, to get a few accommodation matters sorted."

"Can I just ask you something?" Noah quickly interjected. Mykael cocked his head a little to one side and then nodded.

"Fire away," he said with a smile.

"Rylan told us that you were able to take a visualisation from him of the back of the truck. Like, you know, when you and the other angels rescued us."

"That's correct," Mykael replied, just a little intrigued as to where the conversation was headed.

"So, does it have to be an angel, or can you take a visualisation from anyone? Maybe someone like me?" Noah tentatively asked. Mykael gave a nod, still not quite sure where the questions were headed.

"It's possible," he replied. "Especially if you can visualise a place very clearly in your mind. Why do you ask?" Noah sighed softly and then shrugged.

"Well, I may be wrong, but at the last place we were kept at, just before we were taken out to the truck to head off, I was sure that there was another kid somewhere upstairs," he explained. "Like, not down in the basement rooms where us older boys and girls were kept, but in one of the rooms upstairs."

"And what makes you think that whoever it was, was younger than you?" Mykael asked with some curiosity, quickly picking up on the fact that Noah had described himself and the others as the 'older' children.

"Because I heard them crying and it, sort of, sounded that way. Like, just like a real little kid," he murmured a little uncertainly.

"And when did you hear this?" Mykael quickly asked. After all, it was quite likely that people like Vittorio and his cohorts might have had other children that they had 'acquired' in some way. Noah cocked his head briefly to one side. Feeling pleased that what he was suggesting was not just being dismissed out of hand.

"It was when we were all upstairs being prepared to head off for the special entertainment. You know, all us kids that were rescued," he quickly continued. "While Vittorio was inspecting us and getting us dressed, I had to make a last minute trip to the toilet. When I was in there, I could hear this other kid crying. Only it was quite faint. Sort of sounding like they were locked in a different room, somewhere; but not, like, anywhere in the basement. Then, when we waiting to get fitted with our 'keepers', I asked Skylar if he'd heard anything. He hadn't and we tried listening again, but it was a bit too noisy and he suggested it might've just been the cat mewling. But I think Peter also heard it, because he mentioned something about it when we were in the truck."

"And you think that the kid might still be there?" Mykael quickly asked. Noah hastily nodded.

"If Vittorio and the others weren't able to go back for him, because of what happened with the alligators, and nobody else turned up at the house, I think that might be the case."

"So, what visualisation can you give me?" Mykael asked, knowing that it wouldn't take more than a few minutes to check out the situation, even if it eventually turned out to be a false alarm of some type. Noah gave a shrug.

"We spent quite a bit of time in the basement room," he suggested. " I certainly know what 'that' place looked like!" Mykael exhaled softly.

"Can you give me something upstairs?" he quickly countered. "Going to a locked basement, would take a bit of extra time, if I needed to visualise a way out of it."

"How about the room where Vittorio got us dressed?" Noah suggested. "Or... or the toilet?"

"I think the first of those would be best," Mykael replied with a wry smile. "Just try to remember exactly what the room looked like." Noah quickly shut his eyes. Trying to visualise the upstairs room where he'd also been subjected to a quite humiliating inspection to check for bleeding, before being forced to dress in the skimpy Native-American outfit. An instant later, Mykael vanished.

***

Mykael looked around for signs of life, before making himself visible. The room was deserted; the whole house as silent as a tomb. To one side were racks and shelves of clothing. Clearly the 'costumes' the children had been forced to wear for various 'entertainments'. Not that they took up too much space, given how scant most of them were. Remaining invisible, in case there was anyone elsewhere in the house, he moved quickly into the next room and noted, from the view out the window, that, as Noah and some of the other children had mentioned, the house was quite isolated; sited well away from any neighbours who might find activities at the house a little suspicious. So much so, that no other buildings could even be seen beyond vast fields of grass... at least not from that particular window.

Moving further into the house, he quickly checked each room, easily finding a room that looked as if it was used for punishment, and perhaps other nefarious abuse activities, the bathrooms the children had mentioned, a kitchen area with the remnants of meals stacked on plates, that were now swarming with ants, beside the sink, a dining room, as well as stairs leading down to what would obviously be the basement rooms. Now feeling relatively confident that no one else was in the house, he made himself visible and continued down a hallway leading towards the back of the house. A little as he had expected, three of the rooms were simply empty bedrooms; the beds unmade and rumpled from use, in a manner that somehow suggested that the house was always just a temporary stopover. The last door off the hallway, however, was locked. Rather than visualise himself into an unknown space, he simply kicked it open. It eventually took two or three heavy thumps before the doorframe splintered and the door swung open.

The sight that greeted Mykael was almost horrific, as was the smell of the room. Handcuffed, by ankles and wrists to a stained mattress on the single bed in the room was a small boy, who looked to be only seven or eight years of age, dressed in just a pair of white underpants. For a moment, the boy was so still that Mykael wondered if he was still alive. The noise of the door being broken open, however, seemed to create a small, delayed response, as he slowly turned his head to look towards the door; the fear of what might be about to happen to him clearly evident in his eyes.

By the smell of the room, and the state of the boy's solitary item of clothing, it was obvious that the boy had recently soiled himself, a factor that was inevitable given his being unable to move from the bed. Hurrying over to him, Mykael put his arms under the boy's shoulders and legs and immediately visualised himself and the boy — sans underwear — into one of the spare bedrooms; the one that had two beds.

Placing the boy onto one of the beds in the room, he rushed back to the bathroom, soaked a couple of flannels in warm water and grabbed a couple of clean towels. Once back in the bedroom, he grabbed the boy's legs and lifted them, before hastily cleaning most of the mess from his behind, much as you might do with a much younger child, as the boy simply watched him in silence. That task completed, he flung the flannels and towels to one side, before grabbing a fresh blanket from the other bed and bundling the boy up in it. An instant later he was back at the farm, with the boy now comatose in his arms.

"This one's going to require a bit of special treatment," he called to Grandma Betty. "It looks as if he's been chained to a bed for two, possibly three, days, so he's probably been without food or water for all that time. He also needs a darn good wash." There was instant activity as Amanda hurried over to grab the boy from Mykael's arms. Grandma Betty hastily instructed Mischa to start running a bath, as she rushed off to prepare a bed for the boy. Peter McCormack hurried after her, medical bag in hand.

"So I was right?" Noah quietly asked as he came over to Mykael. "There definitely was someone upstairs?" Mykael nodded.

"You did good," he replied, reaching out to tousle the boy's hair. "Given that Vittorio and his Network crew are no longer in operation, it's quite likely he would have died before anyone ended up going to the house."

"Any idea who he is?" Tris asked, as he also came over to Mykael. The guardian shook his head.

"We probably won't know any details until he wakes," he replied. "And that's not likely to be until tomorrow, unless I purposely wake him."

"If he hasn't had any food for a couple of days, it might be good to do that," Granddad Roger quietly suggested. "You could always put him back to sleep, afterwards. Like you did with Rylan, the other day."

***

Everyone watched as the boy slowly worked his way through the last of his soup and two slices of toast and then looked around the room a little warily, obviously a little taken aback when he realised that some of the people in the room had wings. He tugged, for a moment, at the jacket of the brand new pyjamas he was wearing, Mykael having made a speedy trip to Erinsmuir to get some new underwear and sleepwear while the boy had been having a nice warm bath. Any other clothing he might need could wait a couple of days.

"Now," Mykael said softly as he picked up a chair and then sat on it, facing the boy, "you're safe and well away from anyone trying to hurt you. All the bad men have gone. We have seen to that. So can you tell us your name, how old you are, and how you came to be at the house where I found you?"

The boy remained silent for a moment, as he continued to look a little nervously around the room, perhaps trying to reassure himself that what the man with wings was saying was true, and that it wasn't all just a trick. At the same time, the care with which he'd been bathed and dressed had him feeling that he really was in a safe place and with people who would care for him. And that Vittorio and Angelo would no longer be able to hurt him.

"My name's Oliver Nathan Steeden, and… and I'm seven… almost eight," he eventually whispered. "Only my grandma always just used to call me Ollie."

"That's good," Mykael said encouragingly. "So were you living with your grandma?" Oliver nodded.

"But she died," he whispered, his eyes welling with tears. "So…so I ended up at the police station, after one of the neighbours called for an ambulance. One of the ambulance men told me that she'd had a heart attack."

"Do you still have your parents?" Mykael asked. "Like a mum or a dad who could look after you?" The boy exhaled softly, wiped at his eyes, and then gave a slow shake of his head.

"They're both drug addicts," he replied rather resignedly. "So most of the time, if they were not out looking for drugs, they just stayed in bed. I usually had to feed myself with whatever I could find, and then my school started to notice that I was truant too often. That's why I got sent to live with my grandma."

"So is there anyone else who could look after you?" Mykael quietly queried. "Like uncles, or aunties, or more grandparents?" Oliver simply shrugged and looked down at his bare feet, which didn't even reach to the floor from where he was seated.

"Not really," he eventually whispered. "We didn't see all that much of the family, because of the drug problems. I think they all shifted away, so that my mum and dad wouldn't keep begging them for money.. or... or stealing from them. I don't... I don't even know where any of them live, now, or... or even remember what they were called." Mykael nodded and decided not to press the boy for more details of possible relatives. Such details could be researched at a later stage, if it was decided as being the best course of action.

"So what happened after you ended up with the police?" he then asked. "You know, after the ambulance had taken away your grandma?" Now more curious as to how the boy had managed to end up at the isolated house and in captivity. Oliver seemed to shrink into himself a little, almost as if a little scared of what to say.

"One of the ambulance men took me to the police station, and at first they were really nice to me," he finally said. "They promised me that, because they couldn't return me to my parents, they'd contact Social Welfare and see if they could contact my other grandparents. And that, if they couldn't, they would still find me a nice place to live." He paused and gave a small shake of his head. "But then, after I was there for most of the day, some FBI men turned up and, after talking with some of the police officers, said that they would take over. Then they took me to this other man… I think he was called Victor, or… or something like that. Anyway, once I was in his car, he took me to that house where you found me and locked me up in one of the rooms. He said that he knew of people who would really love a little boy like me, but he had to keep me locked up so that other people wouldn't find me and hurt me."

"And what about the handcuffs?" Mykael asked. "If the door was locked, why did they need to handcuff you?" Oliver gave a slight shrug.

"I don't really know," he whispered. "The man just said that he would be away until the next day, and that he'd be back late that night, so he just wanted to make sure that I didn't go anywhere. Then he made me take off most of my clothes and lay on the bed. He took all my clothes with him and then came back and put the handcuffs on me. I couldn't even get up to go to the toilet. I tried not to mess myself, but…" He once again, looked towards his feet with a sense of embarrassment.

"Well, you'll be safe here for a few days," Mykael murmured, figuring that he'd heard enough of the situation; at least as much as he really needed to know for now. The boy clearly did not have acceptable parents, or relatives to which he could return. Otherwise they would have already looked to take care of him, the moment they'd heard of the grandmother's death, rather than leaving his future in the hands of Social Welfare; a lack of action that had simply allowed the chance for him to get snatched up by Vittorio's Network. He then reached out and touched the boy's forehead, catching him as he immediately fell asleep. Amanda, once again, hurried over and scooped up the boy; quickly hurrying away to put him in the bed Grandma Betty had prepared for him. Mykael exhaled softly.

"Looks like I might have to find accommodation for yet another child. I just hope…" he murmured.

"He'll be staying with us," Grandma Betty interjected, glancing towards Granddad Roger. "I'm sure Mischa and Zhenya can help us look after him."

"Are you sure?" Mykael asked with some surprise. Grandma Betty nodded her head rather vigorously.

"That's one little boy who needs a lot of TLC to help get him over a nightmare," she replied, with a further look towards Granddad Roger. "He'll certainly get that here!"

"Well, I suppose that's one accommodation problem easily solved," Mykael replied, rolling his eyes a little at the elderly woman's forthrightness. "Now I just have to sort out a few others. So, if you'll excuse me, I have a meeting back on the island that I need to attend. I'm already running a little late, as it is." He instantly vanished.

"If it becomes a problem, he can always come to the island for a while," Joshua quietly suggested. Grandma Betty turned towards him and scowled slightly.

"If you're thinking that your granddad and I are too old to look after one little boy…" she testily replied, leaving the statement unfinished, but its message clearly understood. As far as she was concerned, she and Roger, along with Mischa and Zhenya, would be quite capable of raising Oliver and she was determined that they would be doing so.

***

Mykael looked around the gathering in the schoolroom, which included Steve and Evelyn Robertson, 'Fangs' and Amy Davies, Ethan and Rowanne Dunn, Jamie Ryan, and Raymond and Kate Ferris. Although they were still helping out up at the farm, Joshua and Amanda would also be kept up to date with circumstances, as it proved necessary; not that they would be entirely out of the adoption processes. With it having already been decided that they would eventually end up with Rylan as well as Lara, given that they were twins. Given the importance of the situation, however, and the awkwardness of a few of the matters that might need to be discussed, all the island's children had been asked to remain in the pool complex under the supervision of James Martin.

"I called you all here, because our finding of Lara's brother seems to have unearthed another small problem," Mykael eventually began. Hoping that by making it a 'small problem', it might convey the understanding that the 'small problem', whatever it was, would be easily solved. Most of those present seemed to nod, or give various indications that they already knew a fair bit of what to expect. After all, when Tris had arrived home from taking part in the rescue, it hadn't taken all that long for the bush telegraph to inform the whole island that there were now fourteen children fast asleep up at the Robertson Farm, including the missing boy-angel, and that they had been rescued from an extremely dangerous situation.

"As Tris has no doubt let you know, our finding of Rylan also resulted in the rescue of a further thirteen children from a rather nasty fate," he quickly continued. "And earlier today, I also rescued yet another young child who'd been left tied up at the house the other children were last at. But where he'll now be living has already been resolved. He's likely to remain at the farm for the time being. Betty Robertson was quite adamant on that little matter." He sighed and rolled his eyes a little as if to express how bluntly the elderly woman had put forward her point of view.

"Anyway, to explain the main situation a little more thoroughly," he then continued. "Over the past few months, the first children we ended up rescuing, after Rylan had started the ball rolling, as it were, had been kidnapped from their homes by a paedophile trafficking organisation that supplies children as slaves to rich clients. When we rescued them, they were on their way to be auctioned off at a secret location." He didn't feel it was necessary to mention the other nasty fate that was actually awaiting the children. "As you will, of course, already understand, Rylan will eventually be coming to the island to live, given that he is Lara's twin and also an angel. As for the other children, early tomorrow, nine of them will be returned to loving, anxious families, who have had the authorities trying to locate them ever since they first went missing. That, as you will quickly realise, leaves four children still unaccounted for. Three boys and one girl." He glanced around the room and then exhaled softly.

"In the case of Skylar, who is eleven, it is simply that, as yet, I have been unable to make any contact with his mother. A mother whom he repeatedly assures me will welcome him back home with open arms. I sense, however, that that particular issue might not turn out to be quite as straightforward as he seems to think, so I'll return to that matter in due course. Regarding the other three children, Cooper, who is twelve, appears to have simply been sold into slavery by his stepfather, now that his mother is dead, and the stepfather has remarried and, as such, has no desire to ever return home; or perhaps it would be better put that he simply has no welcoming home to go to." He paused a moment, as small gasps of shock exemplified the way the island's parents viewed such a situation.

"As for the remaining two," he eventually continued, "unlikely as it may seem to caring parents such as yourselves, when I spoke to their parents, I sensed a strong sense of rejection. A negative response clearly based on the supposition of them now being 'damaged goods', so to speak."

"Have they actually been hurt that way," Rowanne quietly asked, not wanting to put full voice to what was in her thoughts. Mykael responded with a casual sigh and a small shrug of his shoulders.

"In the case of Persia, nothing too serious, beyond some quite inappropriate touching, a couple of spankings and having to pose for photographs that weren't always very nice. Well, certainly not for a girl of only eleven years of age. Her family, however, are involved with some quite reclusive church order, and reacted very negatively to the idea of her return. Mainly, I sense, because with her having spent time living outside their control, they feel that she would know far too much of the outside world than they would wish. In talking with her parents, I quickly intuited that she would have some difficulty fitting back into their extremely authoritarian ways. Perhaps as a consequence of her being away from such a restrictive lifestyle and meeting other children outside their church, even if it was while being held captive, she also has no desire to return to them. Especially with the prospect of eventually being forced into a very early 'arranged' marriage to a very much older church member. Someone, so she tells me, who would most certainly be old enough to be her father."

"I'm sure we could take her on," Kate Ferris quickly announced, looking to her husband for mutual approval. "After all, we do have Sophie's room spare, and it would be nice to have another little girl to look after. Especially one with such a beautiful name." Raymond Ferris nodded his agreement.

"We could take on… who was it? Cooper?" Amy hastily suggested. "I'm sure that Finn would appreciate having a brother. Even if it was just to somehow even up the numbers. You know, two brothers and two sisters."

"That would be good," Mykael said, giving a nod of his head. "Again, with Cooper, it's mainly just a case of some inappropriate touching and photographs, although he did suffer a few quite nasty beatings, so he informs me. Mainly for trying to escape."

"What about the other boy?" Ethan cautiously asked.

"If you mean Noah," Mykael replied. "I'm hoping to put him with Colin and Alice Watters. Unfortunately, he has suffered some more serious abuse, and, while he will probably end up doing his schooling on the island, for a little while at least, I feel it would be good for him to have easy access to Peter McCormack, just in case he has ongoing problems. Like Cooper, he is only just turned twelve, but has been in captivity a little longer than most of the others."

"We could still take him on if the Colin and Alice find it a bit awkward," Ethan hastily continued. "But you did also mention another boy…"

"You mean… Skylar," Mykael interjected.

"Yes," Ethan continued. "You intimated that you might have a bit of a problem finding his mother. If that turns out to be the case, I'm sure we could take him on. Both him and Noah, if that proved necessary. After all, there's plenty of room in this place."

"Well, that's likely to be the case, to some degree, even if Noah does end up with Colin and Alice. After all, he will still need to go to school, and I'm sure Steve would rather not be doing a school boat run every morning and evening; nor would it be reasonable to expect Noah to take the bus to and from

Erinsmuir every day of the week, while his other new friends are homeschooled on the island. If he was able to stay over here during the week, with you and Rowanne, or Steve and Evelyn, for his schooling, he could then just spend the weekends back with the Watters. As for Skylar, we'll just need to wait and see how things go when I take him to where he was living."

"So when is this all likely to happen?" Rowanne asked. Mykael seemed to give a casual shrug of his shoulders.

"I'll be hoping to reunite most of the children with their families, tomorrow," he replied. "If we leave quite early, and given the time differences between here and the States, it'll probably still be not quite lunchtime when that happens. After that, I hope to spend some time with Skylar, trying to track down his mother, so it's likely that anything to do with sorting out the remaining children will not be until later on tomorrow, or, more than likely, even the day after that. Which will give you a bit of time to get accommodation set up."

"So what's the situation with the other boy you mentioned?" Evelyn quietly asked. "The one that you rescued earlier today? You said that he would be remaining at the farm for the time being."

"Grandma Betty took quite a shine to him," Mykael said with a slight laugh. "Well, he is quite a little cutie, and she was quite adamant that he should remain at the farm to be raised by herself and Roger… with help from Mischa and Zhenya. It seems that he'd been sent to live with his grandmother because his parents were drug addicts, but she died, unexpectedly. After that, with Social Welfare not being able to contact any other of his relatives, someone with a link to the FBI's darker side had a hand in letting the same paedophile network as had abducted the other children get a hold of him. If Noah hadn't alerted me to his likely presence, he might have died. When I found him, he'd been handcuffed to a bed, in a house miles from anywhere, for almost three full days." For a moment, there was silence, as everyone seemed to be shocked by what they'd heard.

"So you think my mum and dad will want to adopt him, fully?" Steve eventually queried. Mykael shrugged.

"I guess so," he replied. "Although Joshua did mention that he could also come here if needed."

"So why do you think he wasn't with the others that you rescued?" Evelyn asked.

"Well, given that he's only seven, going on eight," Mykael explained, "it seems that Vittorio was evidently lining up an extra special adoption deal for him, if you get my drift. Obviously, to someone willing to pay a very substantial amount for him."

"Those bastard's should swing for what they've been doing," Ethan muttered. "Especially to kids that young!"

"Or any age!" Amy added angrily.

"Well, they won't be doing it anymore," Mykael replied with a slight smirk. "When they opened the hidden compartment in the truck, where'd they'd put all the children, they had an unfortunate altercation with some very hungry alligators. Let's just say that it didn't turn out all that well for any of them."

CHAPTER SEVENTEEN

An Unexpected Setback....

Having waved goodbye to Steve Robertson, who would be heading to George Bush International Airport, in Houston, where it would be easier to organise a refueling, Skylar quickly hurried through the terminal of the Orange County Regional Airport towards the main exit. All his main customs details and passport checks had already been dealt with during the stopover in Hartford to reunite the other children with their parents, so his arrival at Orange County's small strip was just to get him, Tris, and Mykael a little closer to his home in Pinehurst. In some ways he felt a little nervous; hoping that the reunion with his mother would turn out to be just as joyful as those he'd witnessed in Hartford. Particularly, the almost excessive displays of affection shown to Riley, Maia, Natasha, Martyn, Luka and Camillé... their families almost awash with tears at their safe return. For Peter, Jessamine and Rochelle, the welcomes had been a little more subdued, but no less thankful.

While his being on his own, as he traversed through the building that served as some sort of terminal, appeared to elicit a few mildly curious looks from some of the airport officials, he didn't feel too worried. Not with knowing that Mykael and Tris were both beside him. Albeit, still in a state of invisibility to avoid most of the CCTV cameras.

"Wait here," he suddenly heard Mykael whisper. "We'll just make use of one of the bathrooms to become visible again.

A minute or two later, the angel guardian and the boy-angel hurried back over to where he was waiting.

“Now, we need to get out of here before they notice that Tris might be glitching any of the remaining cameras in their CCTV system, find the taxi Steve has arranged for us, and check out where your mother might be,” Mykael instructed, as he hurriedly ushered the two boys through the main doors towards where a couple of taxis waited for likely passengers. Looking across, they noticed that one of the drivers had a small cardboard notice displaying the name Mr Jefferies. They hurried to his cab and got in. If the driver thought that the adult was a Mr Skylar Jefferies, then that perhaps suited their purpose. If he was also under the impression that Mr Jefferies was wealthy enough to be able to pay him, in advance, for a full twenty-four hours hire, along with a very sizeable tip, then that might just mean that he'd not be too put out by having to just wait around at various places, as required.

“We don't live anywhere flash,” Skylar suddenly murmured, having given the driver directions to his home. In some ways, suddenly feeling just a little embarrassed at the fact that he lived in a very basic trailer park. In an area of town where the streets were simply designated by letters ‘Avenue A’, ‘Avenue B’, ‘Avenue C’, and so on. “It's just, like, a big caravan that doesn't go anywhere. You know, in a trailer park. Not a proper house or anything, ‘cause we couldn't afford that.”

“All that really matters is finding out where your mother might be,” Mykael quietly assured him, looking at their surroundings, as the cab driver hurriedly turned left onto Edgar Brown drive and began heading towards Orange; Pinehurst being a suburb on the western outskirts of the main city.

***

Skylar stepped up to the door of the trailer and cautiously tried the handle. Much as he'd expected, it was locked. He also quickly realised that the spare key that he'd been given when he and his mother had first moved in, was now lost. Having been taken from him by Vittorio when he'd first been abducted. He sighed in mild exasperation, and then glanced towards where Mykael and Tris were waiting, before stepping down off the small porch area and looking at his watch.

"I haven't got my key," he murmured. "But it's not a day when she'd normally be working afternoons, so she should be home." He sighed softly and looked towards where his mother's car would normally be parked. "Her morning shift at Lucy's doesn't usually go this late." Mykael made a slight moue expression of his mouth and cocked his head briefly to one side, already sensing that things might not turn out too well.

"But things would've hardly have been normal with you missing," he murmured softly. Skylar nodded a nervous understanding of that fact.

"But where would she be?" he queried. "I can't get in otherwise. I lost my key when..." He left the statement incomplete. Perhaps somehow wanting to put everything of the nightmare of the last few months well behind him. Knowing full well, just how lucky he'd been that Vittorio had had a special entertainment planned and that he'd escaped a nightmare situation of a parade of clients having full reign to abuse him in any way they liked, right from when he'd first been abducted. The sort of abuses he'd seen the results of with some other of the Network boys, including Peter and Noah.

"How about we go and have a talk with the owner of this place?" Mykael suggested, nodding towards the rather palatial house to one side of the trailer park; its grandeur making for a rather sharp contrast when compared to the ramshackle condition of most of the trailers. While he could have simply opened the trailer unit himself, he felt it might be best to do things legally, so to speak.

"He's not that nice," Skylar softly replied. "Or at least, he didn't like me all that much... or any of the trailer park kids, for that matter. He seems to think that we'll all end up in trouble with the police."

"People who willingly exploit others less fortunate than themselves quite often have those sort of attitudes," Mykael murmured as they began making their way towards the trailer park owner's residence.

A few moments later, they stepped up onto the porch of the house. Mykael and Tris stood back a little as Skylar cautiously knocked on the door. It took a few moments for there to be any response. Eventually, however, the door opened to reveal a squat, slightly over-weight man clutching a glass of some liquor in his right hand.

"So you're back, are you?" he sneered, seeming to focus on Skylar and ignoring the presence of Mykael and Tris. "Didn't like life on the road, I take it?"

"I was kidnapped!" Skylar snapped angrily. "If you'd bothered to read the papers. I only escaped a couple of days ago. Now, I just want to know where my mother is!" The man shrugged and wearily slouched against the doorframe. Almost as if the effort of standing unsupported for any length of time was too much for him.

"Ain't seen her in more 'n three weeks," he muttered rather bluntly. "Must owe me at least a month's rent already. Probably gone off looking for you, no doubt, 'cause I ain't seen her down at Lucy's lately, either."

"Can I get a key to get inside?" Skylar asked. The man eyed him more than a little suspiciously.

"Not until I get the back-rent that's owing," he muttered, glancing towards Mykael and Tris. "I don't need you lot clearing the place out and doing a runner, with money still owing. You pay me what's due and you get a temporary key." Skylar sighed and turned towards Mykael in the hope of him being able to intervene. Mykael seemed to give a casual shrug, and then, after what seemed to Skylar a strange instant of shimmering, withdrew a billfold from his pocket and extracted a large number of one hundred dollar bills.

"That should cover any back rent, and also the next month or two to come," he said with some officiousness, stepping forward to quickly hand over the notes. "Now, if you don't mind, could you please be quick about providing the boy with that spare key." With a sigh, the man grabbed the money, and without bothering to count it, stuffed it into his pocket and stepped back into the side room that was obviously his office. Appearing somewhat pleased that, even at a glance, the money he'd been given was certainly far more than enough to cover any back-rent that was owed, as well as close to at least three more months.

"My mom won't be able to pay you back," whispered Skylar rather guardedly, looking up at Mykael. "Not if she's not working."

"Don't worry about it," Mykael murmured with a smile. "I don't expect it to be paid back. It wasn't my money in the first place."

"So, who's is it?" Skylar queried in some surprise, half wondering if Mykael, being an angel, had some strange access to unlimited finances.

"His," Mykael replied with a wry smile, pointing a finger in the direction the man had gone. "It's from a stash he's got hidden away in the back of a filing cabinet in his office. I could read from his thoughts that, at first, he was a little wary that I might be some sort of undercover police officer who could be onto his drug deals. He's been selling a bit of 'ice' to get extra income. Not that that's any of our concern, at the moment. Anyway, by the time he gets around to counting it again, he'll very likely have forgotten just how much he had hidden away in the first place. And even if he does work out that there's money missing, he won't be able to connect any of it to you. So don't worry about it."

"But how did you do all that so...?" Skylar began, shaking his head in puzzlement.

"Angels can slow time, to some degree," Tris whispered. "They also know and see things other people don't know, which is why I always have to be on my best behaviour." He turned and gave Mykael a disarmingly teasing smile. His guardian simply responded with an amused slow shake of his head.

A moment or two later, the man reappeared and casually tossed a key in Skylar's direction. Caught a little off-guard by the man's actions, Skylar juggled it a couple of times before catching it properly.

"Don't mess the place up," the man growled. "And you'd better sort out what's happening with your mother. I certainly won't have you living there on your own." Skylar looked up at Mykael. "Or let you have any other brats staying over!" the man added, glancing towards Tris.

"Let's just check out your stuff," Mykael muttered to Skylar, ignoring the man's complaints as they stepped down off the porch and the man wandered back inside. "It's possible that there may be some indication inside your trailer of where your mother might be."

"What if we can't find her?" Skylar asked. Tears began to well in his eyes. Mykael placed a hand on the boy's shoulder and a finger under his chin so that he forced Skylar to look at him.

"If we can't find your mother, then we'll simply go back to the farm for the night, when Mr Robertson arrives to collect us. You certainly won't be left on your own."

"Will Rylan still be there?" Skylar asked. Mykael gave him a slightly curious look.

"Is that important to you?" he asked. Skylar gave a slight shrug.

"I know he's a bit, you know..." He made a slightly limp-wristed gesture. "And at school all the other boys avoided being anywhere too near to him because of that. But, he did rescue me, so I should at least try to be his friend."

"That's the proper way to think of it," Mykael murmured, with a nod of his head. "After all, it's not as if he's contagious, or anything. If it's not the way you are, then you just tell him that you just want to be a friend."

"He'll probably be sharing my room when we go home," Tris added brightly. "At least until Mum, Dad and Granddad Robertson sort out an extra room for him."

"If... if we can't find my mom, like ever," Skylar asked a little hesitantly, as he again looked up at Mykael. "Could I live on the island, too? Like, where Tris lives?"

"That might become necessary," Mykael replied, with a nod of his head. "But let's not put the cart before the horse. Let's just check out your trailer and see if there's anything there that might help us to locate your mother." He began ushering them back in the direction of Skylar's trailer home.

As Skylar eventually stepped up to put the key into the lock, the door to the trailer directly opposite opened and a woman looked out at them. From somewhere inside, her TV was blaring the opening spiel and theme music for American Idol.

"That's Mrs Rogers," Skylar whispered, as the woman seemed to look them over a little cautiously, peering a little shortsightedly over the top of her glasses.

"Oh," she suddenly exclaimed, in a sudden burst of recognition. "It's you, Skylar. Your mother will be so pleased that you're back.

She was absolutely frantic when you first disappeared. She was putting up posters of you all over the place and kept going on about how your father must have grabbed you. At least, that's what she told the police, when they were here."

"I wouldn't go with him even if he flippin' paid me," Skylar snorted, as he inserted the key he'd been given into the lock. "His taking off was the flippin' reason we had to leave Oakton, in the first place."

"So what happened to you?" Mrs Rogers asked, waddling a little closer in her fluffy-duck slippers.

"I got kidnapped while doing my paper route," Skylar replied, turning to face her with the door slightly open. "By some really nasty people." He then quickly indicated towards Tris and Mykael. "Luckily, these people helped me to escape before I got too badly hurt. Now I'm just trying to figure out where my mom is."

"Your mother's in hospital," Mrs Rogers said softly, and almost a little apologetically. "I thought Williams would have at least have had the manners to tell you that."

"She… she's in hospital?" Skylar echoed, ignoring the slightly cynical reference to the trailer park owner. Mrs Rogers nodded.

"Been there for a good couple of weeks, at least," she continued. "More 'n likely, three or four. Took rather sick at work, evidently. About a week or so after you went missing. That's where her car is, I'd guess."

"Why?" Skylar asked. "Was she in an accident or something?" Mrs Rogers shook her head.

"Way I last heard it, she's got major medical problems," she murmured. "Although, you'd best go and see her yourself to find out what's really going on. I'm only going by hearsay, but it don't sound all that good."

"Like what?" Skylar asked just a little abruptly

"Some form of cancer!" Maybelle Rogers murmured, dropping her voice to almost a whisper as she ended the sentence, as if not wanting to say the word too loudly. "A real aggressive type from what I've heard! Her liver, or pancreas, or something... at least that's what someone down at Lucy's said. But, look, you'd best find out the rest from your mom. As I said, I'm only going by what gossip tells me."

"Do you know where she is?" Skylar quickly asked. "Like, which hospital they would have taken her to?"

"I think it was somewhere on the west side of Orange," Mrs Rogers muttered. "Most probably Baptist Orange. But you might need to check in at the local medical centre to find out. If it's pancreatic cancer, then it's quite likely she may have already been shifted to a hospice." Skylar looked up at Mykael.

"Can we go, now?" he asked rather impatiently. Mykael gave a slight nod and glanced towards the waiting taxi.

"Let's just sort out a few things here, first," he replied softly, directing Skylar and Tris to enter the trailer. "We can head to the medical centre, afterwards." Once inside, he watched through the window, as Mrs Rogers seemed to continue looking at Skylar's trailer for a moment, before ambling back inside her trailer to continue watching the repeat of American Idol.

"Okay," he quickly continued. "Firstly, let's get everything you need, or want to take with you, together," he suggested. "If your mother's in hospital, you may need to stay at the farm for a quite few more days." He quickly directed Skylar towards his bedroom. "You just go and get everything you want to take with you. Clothes, books, computers and stuff, while I grab a sheet to put it all into."

By the time Skylar had returned with a third armload of his property, and then his bike, Mykael had a bed sheet spread out on the kitchen table and was carefully stacking the items into its centre.

"So how do we get all that to the farm?" Skylar asked. "We won't be able to fit it all in the taxi. Certainly not if we're also taking the bike." Mykael gave him a wink and then, having grabbed the top corners of the bed sheet, with one hand and the bike with the other, seemed to shimmer slightly. As he did so, the bundle disappeared from the table, and also the bike.

"Where did it all go?" Skylar asked, looking about in astonishment. Mykael gave a slight shrug.

"It's on the porch up at the farm," he said, with a wry smile. "Where you'll be staying for a couple of days, with Cooper, Noah, Rylan, Persia, Tris, Lara and Oliver for company. Mischa will get it all sorted out into one of the bedrooms for you."

"But how?" Skylar exclaimed. "How did it all disappear?"

"The same way as Rylan got you from the back of the truck," Mykael quickly exclaimed. "We can be anywhere in an instant." He glanced at Tris and then took Skylar's hand. "Now, let's go and find out what the situation is with your mother."

***

Angela Jefferies looked at her son with tear-filled eyes. She held out her hands and beckoned him into her embrace. Skylar hurried to her, and for a few minutes, remained in her grasp as they both quietly cried.

"I thought you must be dead," she eventually sobbed softly as, having been released from her grasp, Skylar sat on the edge of the bed. Taking extra care, as he did so, to avoid disturbing the various tubes and wires that connected his mother to various monitoring devices. "Especially when the police couldn't find any sign of you, apart from your bike and your papers. They eventually tracked down your dad, somewhere west of Chicago on another long-haul run, but he denied any knowledge of where you might be. In fact, according to the police, he didn't even know that we'd left Oakton."

"I got kidnapped by some group called the Network," replied Skylar equally softly, as he placed his right hand on her right; carefully avoiding the cannula on the top of her hand. "These men just grabbed me and bundled me into their car. The next thing, I woke up and I was tied up and in the basement of a house, where a man called Vittorio told me that he now owned me. He even put a tattoo on my shoulder as proof." He pulled the left sleeve of his T-shirt up to reveal the image of a letter 'N' inside a circle. As Angela Jeffries looked in shock at what she was seeing, and the implications behind it, Mykael quietly reminded himself to remove all marks of tattoos from the children, at some time in the future.

"So it wasn't your dad, or someone working for him?" Angela Jeffries half-croaked. She turned her head and grabbed for a tissue. Trying, at the same time, to stifle a sudden bout of coughing and then wincing, as even the effort to do that seemed to hurt.

"No. But it may as well have been, considering what they were planning for me," Skylar muttered angrily. He quickly explained to his mother that, because of his similarity in looks to Finn Wolfhard from 'Stranger Things', a paedophile group who specialised in trafficking children around to rich clients had targeted him, based on what they'd seen of some video that had been made of him at Pastor Isaac's boot camp. Making sure to include the detail that, while he'd suffered a fair few beatings, and some unwanted touching, he'd managed to avoid suffering any other major indignities.

"So how did you get away from them?" Angela Jeffries asked, when he seemed to have finished relating his experiences.

"I was rescued by angels," Skylar said proudly. "And the funniest thing was… although it didn't seem funny at the time, what with me being shackled to an iron bar in the back of a truck and on the way to be sold for…" He paused a moment, deciding not to mention more about what might have happened if he hadn't been rescued, then continued. "You know, that really gay boy… the one who everyone used to make fun of at school in Oakton? Well, he got thrown in with us at the last minute. Because he was unconscious, me and Cooper… like, one of the other boys who'd been kidnapped, had to get him properly dressed for where we were going and when we did, we found that he had wings. It turns out that he's an angel. So he was able to rescue me. And then he got other angels to rescue everyone else."

"You mean Rylan Daniels?" Angela Jeffries exclaimed disbelievingly. "The boy… the boy who used to be at your school? He's… he's an angel?" From her time on the PTA, back in Oakton, she knew that the 'situation' regarding Rylan Daniels' sexuality had quite often been mentioned. Usually, whenever there was some new instance of bullying to be worked through and resolved. Rylan Daniels being, in a good many instances, the unfortunate 'victim'.

"Well, he wasn't when he was at school," Skylar hastily explained. "But it seems that he's somehow turned into one. Just like Tris, here." He indicated towards Tris.

"You're an angel?" Angela Jeffries whispered a little bemusedly, and perhaps a touch disbelievingly, as she turned to look at Tris. In response, Tris nodded, and after a quick look around to see that he wasn't likely to be seen by anyone outside of the curtains around the bed, made his wings visible for a few seconds.

"They're going to look after me until you get better," Skylar softly announced. "So that you don't have to worry about me being on my own, and being safe and all that." Angela Jeffries slowly wiped at her eyes.

"I won't be getting better," she murmured. "The doctors have given me just a few weeks."

"But why?" Skylar exclaimed, as tears immediately began flooding down his cheeks. He wiped at them, rather futilely, with his hands. "That's not fair," he sobbed, before quickly turning to Mykael. "Can't you change things? Like, to make her better again? You know, like, make the cancer go away?" Mykael gave a shake of his head and reached out to put a hand on his shoulder.

"As I explained up at the farm, some things are just meant to be," he said softly. "It's just a part of the way a person's life has been planned."

"But that's not fair," Skylar sobbed. "If Mom dies, I've got nobody!" He shrugged off Mykael's hands. "I'm certainly not going back to my dad! Not for any reason!"

"That won't be necessary," Mykael said softly, placing a hand upon the boy's head. An action that seemed to have an immediate calming effect. "While your mother is alive, I will arrange for you to have frequent visits to see her. Hopefully, every day, if that can possibly be arranged. In the meantime, for the next couple days, you will live at the farm while I finalise arrangements for you to be adopted by one of the families on the island. And don't you worry. They already have children about your age so I'm sure you'll have no trouble fitting in. And don't forget, Tris, Lara and Rylan will also be there."

"So I'll be living with the angel children?" Skylar murmured just a little more brightly. Mykael nodded.

"Not in the same house, obviously," he replied. "But you will see them every day, especially when you are at school, because Tris's parents will be your teachers."

"Are they angels too?" Skylar quickly asked. The mere idea of being taught by angels, or of anyone having angels as parents, seemed almost beyond belief. Again, Mykael shook his head.

"No, but they've all been helping protect child angels for quite a while. For some of them, ever since they were at school themselves, in fact. Of your likely foster-parents, the father also helped protect some of the child angels, and the mother is actually a step-sister to several of the angel children."

"So how many angel children are there?" Skylar immediately queried. Mykael gave him a wry smile.

"You've actually met quite a few of them already, because they were the ones that helped with the rescue," he hastily explained. "While they've now grown, the newest ones… Tris, Lara, and Rylan, are still just children." He turned to where Angela Jeffries was sitting open-mouthed with amazement at what she was hearing.

"There is an island that has child angels? And the world knows nothing about it?" she eventually murmured, giving a slow, almost disbelieving, shake of her head. Mykael nodded.

"And Skylar will live with them?" she continued croakily, as she seemed to gasp a little for breath and wince against some inner pain. Mykael quickly reached out and placed a hand on her forehead. The action seemed to immediately take away her distress.

"Skylar will be living with a family on the island who love children," he quietly explained. "It is also a place to which his father will never have access. In fact, as far as he's concerned, Skylar will have simply vanished off the face of the Earth."

"So what will happen when...?" Angela Jeffries whispered, leaving the question incomplete. Mykael seemed to understand what she did not want to say. At the same time, he seemed to be making new plans in his head.

"I will arrange to take care of everything," he said softly. "Your assets, in particular those items that Skylar may not wish to keep, or need, will be sold and put into trust for his future education. The family he will be with, however, will have no problems in looking after him. Money is certainly not an issue for them. Not in any way at all. So…"

"Mr Robertson even has his own Lear jet," Skylar quickly interrupted, with some renewed enthusiasm. "That's how we got here." Mykael nodded in agreement.

"As for yourself," he then continued, "I might look into the possibility of arranging for you to come to the island as well. To enable you to spend as much time as is possible with your son."

"But, what about being here, and all the medication that I need?"

"The island has its own medical facilities, as well as a doctor on call, and a nurse."

"But I can't afford to pay for private care," Angela Jeffries whispered. She gestured towards the facilities around her. "It's using all my health insurance as it is just to pay for..."

"All costs will be covered," Mykael interjected. "The main priority will be for Skylar to be able to spend time with you. I'll be back in a couple of days. Just give me time to get everything sorted on the island." He gestured for Skylar to give his mother a further hug, before indicating for them to leave. "We need to let her have her rest," he explained. Skylar reached out for his mother, gave her a quick cuddle and then hurried after Tris and Mykael.

"Now, is there anything else you need to collect, while we're here in Orange?" Mykael eventually asked, putting an arm around Skylar's shoulders to comfort him as they walked down the steps of the hospital towards the waiting taxi. The boy wiped at his tears. Perhaps just starting to come to terms with the fact that he would soon be motherless, at least until an adoption was arranged.

"There's a bit of stuff in my locker at school," Skylar half-whispered. "Just some books and... and also some clothes that I liked. You know, like a jacket that Mum got me for when I started school. I was at Pinehurst North Middle School."

"Well, we may as well get them while we're here," Mykael suggested, ushering them into the back of the taxi, and then asking the driver to take them to the school.

***

"Now, give me a visualisation of somewhere safe within the school we can go to and we'll clear out your locker," Mykael said, placing a hand onto the boy's head. "Somewhere away from the main offices, so we don't have to waste time trying to explain your sudden return and being out of class."

An instant later, they were standing in a boys' bathroom. To their surprise, a small boy was curled up on the floor and being kicked at by two very much larger boys; boys whom Tris quickly realised were, in some ways, much too old to be at a junior high school. Almost instantly, before the two bullies realised that anyone else was present, the scene was frozen. The assault suddenly held in check.

What did you do?" Skylar asked, his face a mask of astonishment.

"Just slowed time to some significant degree," Mykael replied. "Or, in essence, allowed us to move at a much faster speed than normal."

"Can I do that?" Tris excitedly questioned, this being the first time when he had been properly included in such an action. "Will you teach me?"

"In time," Mykael replied. "When you're quite a bit older." Ignoring Tris's sudden slight look of disappointment, he quickly turned to Skylar. "Is this a regular occurrence in this place?" Skylar nodded, even as he continued to look, with some bewilderment, at the static tableau in front of him.

"It is, if you're small and white and from the trailer park," he added resignedly. "Those two are TJ and Riggs," he continued, pointing towards the two older boys. "The special stars of the football and basketball teams. They're supposedly 'role models' for the whole school... as the Head of Sport reminds us at every flippin' pep rally," he continued a little cynically. "But everyone knows that they're in remedial classes and were held back a year 'cause they failed Year Nine. The trouble is, as long as the sports teams win, the Principal thinks that the sun shines out of their..." He left the statement incomplete, perhaps unsure of whether to voice a rude word in the presence of a senior angel.

"And their victim?" Mykael asked, looking towards the small, obviously Year Six boy curled up on the floor for self-protection; a boot from one bully about to hit where boy's hands covered his face; a boot from the other about to leave an imprint on the small of his back.

That's Timothy Fleetwood," Skylar murmured. "He's one of the 'baby nerds', as all the 'jocks' call us 'first years' who're in the top class," he continued. "TJ and Riggs always pick on him, because they know he's too scared to fight back... or to even report them. This," he continued, pointing to the debased scenario in front of them, "will simply be because he didn't have any money for them, today." He shrugged. "TJ and Riggs are always demanding protection money from some of us small kids," he added; the use of 'us' a clear indication that he'd also been on the receiving end of such threats.

Mykael was silent for a few moments as he continued to survey the scene. He seemed to shimmer for a moment and then, with a casual sweep of his hand, Timothy Fleetwood was suddenly gone.

"Where did he go?" Skylar asked, looking about in astonishment.

"He's on the floor outside the nurse's office," Mykael quietly replied. "Given that he's already got a bloody nose and some nasty bruises, before we leave I'll plant a suggestion into her head to fully investigate the cause of his injuries."

"And what about these two?" Tris asked, looking to where each of the two bullies were still frozen in time and were both poised with a foot in the process of delivering a hefty kick to a boy they regularly tormented. "Can't we teach them a lesson?"

"We shouldn't really interfere," Mykael replied.

"But you've already changed things by moving Timothy Fleetwood elsewhere," Tris countered. "So we could do something."

"Well, what you suggest?" Mykael asked, the slight smile on his face seeming to indicate that he'd perhaps already guessed what Tris wanted to do. Tris glanced at the two bullies, still frozen in their action of kicking, and then at the concrete block wall to one side of where they were standing.

"Uncle Andrew told me that Uncle Alexei once did this to teach a bully a lesson. Like, when he tried to punch Uncle Tristan," he said with a small laugh. A moment later, with Skylar's assistance, he'd removed the bullies shoes and socks and manoeuvred each of them so that, instead of their vicious kicks hitting the body of a small boy, their now bare feet would collide with solid concrete.

"I suppose it will be rather hard for them to explain how they both managed to break a foot by having it collide with a wall," Mykael mused. "But it's likely to mean that they won't be lauding it on the sports field for quite a while. Perhaps even long enough for some of the children they've been bullying to get the courage to speak up about it." He turned to Skylar. "Now, instead of hanging around here to see the results of our mischief, let's just find your locker, get what you need, and get out of here."

They hurried out into the corridor; a moment or two later hearing the strident cries of pain that suddenly emanated from the bathroom as Mykael immediately undid his slowing of time. As they began making their way towards the lockers, a bell sounded. Within a minute, it seemed, the corridor became a seething mass of pupils, all of them intent on hurrying to their next class. A good many of them seemed to look at Skylar with some sense of surprise; perhaps keen to say something, but not sure whether to do so simply because he was accompanied by an adult… and a boy they did not recognise. Nevertheless, Tris and Mykael could not fail to hear the whispered comments of 'frog face' and 'he's back' that seemed to quickly distill their way through the bustling crowd of pupils.

Arriving at the Year Six lockers, Tris immediately noticed the name 'frog face' was also crudely scrawled across the front of Skylar's locker. Seeing Tris's reaction, and knowing what they'd all heard whispered, Skylar simply shrugged.

"That's what they all call me," he murmured. "TJ and Riggs started it. It's the same as what the bullies call the kid in Stranger Things… the one that I look a bit like." He sighed and gave a slow shake of his head. "At least it's better than 'piss-pants'," he continued softly. "That's what they call Timothy, 'cause one time, when they were having their fun by giving him a wedgie in one of the bathrooms, he wet himself." He began fumbling in his pockets, and then shrugged, resignedly. "I haven't got my flippin' key," he sighed, exasperatedly banging his fist on the locker door.

An action that immediately caused a number of other pupils at the other lockers to glance in their direction; perhaps thinking that it might be the start of some altercation. In response, simply Tris leant forward and grabbed the lock in his right hand. It immediately seemed to make some soft clicking noises before suddenly opening of its own accord. Having removed the lock from the door and handed it to Skylar, Tris then stepped back and indicated for him to open the locker.

"Just grab what you need," Mykael instructed, before turning to Tris. "Once he's got everything he wants, go out to the taxi and tell the driver to take you straight back to the trailer park. I'll meet you there, when I'm finished with a few things here." Noting Tris's look of puzzlement, he leant forward a little. "I'm just going to assist the nurse in reporting the ongoing abuse of Timothy Fleetwood to the head of this institution," he whispered. "Hopefully, by intimating that I'm a welfare official in the process of investigating some allegations of bullying, I can do something to make his life a little better." He then hurried off in the direction of the main offices.

As Skylar reached in to grab his jacket, pencil case and a few books from the locker, in the process dislodging a few posters of himself that had been disfigured and scrawled on in a variety of ways and then shoved through the gaps around the door of the locker, Tris noticed a large man in a tracksuit hurrying by in the direction of the bathrooms.

"That's the Head of Sport, Mr Osgood," Skylar quickly explained, with almost some perverse sense of amusement. "Looks like the word's already got to him about his two 'favourites' being injured." Tris watched as the man disappeared around a bend in the corridor.

"Does he know that they're bullies?" he queried. Skylar nodded.

"Of course," he murmured. "But, as far as he's concerned, it doesn't matter what the sports jocks do around the school just as long as the sports teams win. That's why Timothy, or any of us, never bothered to report kids like TJ and Riggs. Mr Osgood just makes it difficult for any of us normal kids to take action against the 'jocks'. Like, if you say anything, he just turns it all around to make it seem that you've disrespected the sports teams in some way, so you've probably deserved whatever happened. And then takes it out on you during Phys. Ed. Periods. Usually by finding some weak excuse to have all the nerds just run laps for the whole period. Like, if he suddenly decides one of us has taken too long to get changed. He just sends us running, even if the jocks are still faffing around in the change rooms, getting ready."

***

"You'll be in here again," Grandma Betty said, as Skylar paused in the doorway to the blue room. "Noah and Cooper are sharing the two bed room further down. I can put Rylan elsewhere, if you'd prefer not to share the double bed."

"It's okay," Skylar quickly replied, quickly looking to where Rylan was seated on the edge of the bed and then across the room to where all his personal items were still wrapped up in the tablecloth. As he'd already noticed when they'd arrived back, his bike was now out on the porch. "I don't mind if he shares with me. It'll be just like when all the rest were here," he added. Rylan immediately looked up in some surprise.

"You don't mind if we share?" he quietly queried, seeming to show some sense of surprise at Skylar's comment.

"Well, we are friends," Skylar replied. "And I trust you. Come on. Let's get ready for bed. I want to get a good night's sleep 'cause Mykael's said that we're all going to the island tomorrow.

I think he's trying to work it so that I'll be living with one of the families there, as well. At least until I know what's happening with my mom."

In less than ten minutes, having quickly changed into shorts and T-shirts, without any embarrassment about being seen in just their underwear, they were tucked up in bed, side-by-side.

"Why don't you mind about what everyone used to say about me, anymore?" Rylan suddenly asked as Skylar reached out to switch off the bedside lamp. "You know, what changed your mind?"

"Because, out of all the children in the back of the truck, you chose me as the first rescue," Skylar replied, as the room was enveloped in semi-darkness. "Even though you knew that I would be the one who would know all about your past. You know, like, what everyone used to say about you."

"I wanted to rescue all of you," Rylan countered. "You just happened to be closest, I suppose."

"Well, at least you saved me from being… you know, Skylar replied."

"I know what you mean," Rylan whispered. "I've had it happen to me, and it's horrible. Not that I ever wanted any of it. And when we were at school, even 'though I thought certain boys were quite cute, I never ever thought about doing bad things with them. Like, you know, when we were getting changed for P.E. and stuff, despite what all the others used to go on about me being a perv. If they hated me, I hated myself even more for not being normal! And then my dad just decided…" He stopped and wiped at tears that had suddenly flooded onto his cheeks. Skylar quickly turned on his side, reached over and put an arm across his chest.

"Well, I'll always be your friend," he said, giving Rylan a quick kiss on the cheek. "I promise. But let's just say, a friend who's a boy, rather than a boyfriend, just to avoid confusion," he quickly added as Rylan put a hand up to touch his cheek where he'd been kissed.

"That's the first time any boy has ever said that he'd be my friend," Rylan murmured. "Apart from the Fulchers… James and Henry. And of course they didn't know about me being… you know."

"Well, maybe things will be different when we're all on the island," Skylar whispered. "After all, it's not as if you're contagious or anything." Rylan was quiet for a while.

"The funny thing is, I suppose, for a while, I wanted to be a girl, like Lara. That was when I was much younger, of course. And then it was like I was just sure that I was gay, so I thought that I was supposed to have a boyfriend so that we could…" Perhaps out of a sense of embarrassment, he didn't finish the sentence. "Well, that's what my dad always said was supposed to happen. Which is why he and Pastor Isaac started treating me so badly. And of course, when I was at Oakton Middle School, it was also really difficult. You know, what with what everyone was saying about me. At first, I didn't really care, 'cause at that time I actually think I had a bit of a crush on you."

"You had a bit of a crush on me?" Skylar quickly queried.

"Well, I thought you were quite cute and I'd have liked for us to be friends," Rylan replied somewhat defensively. "But I soon realised that, with all of what everyone was saying, it was probably better not to make things too obvious. Anyway, after you, it was Christopher Makin that I sort of liked for a while, and then Mattie Ryan. Especially with him being so quiet and a bit reserved. For a while, I even thought that he might be a bit like me, although, maybe that was just wishful thinking. In the end, I just didn't want to make it difficult for everyone, so I just tried to keep it all to myself, in the hope that people might stop being so nasty."

"So is there anyone on your radar at the moment?" Skylar asked a little tentatively. Rylan gave a slight shake of his head, and then exhaled softly.

"The funny thing is that, since I've had my wings, I don't know what I feel," he murmured. "Like, whether I even want a have a boyfriend… or a girlfriend. At least not in… not in that sort of way?" He sighed softly once again, and seemed to take a few minutes to think things through. "In a way, it's like those sort of thoughts are just not there anymore. I just want to have friends… and that's it. It's not as if I don't like boys anymore, or that now I like girls or something. It's more like, those sort of feelings are just not there anymore, either way."

"Maybe that's because of what you've become," Skylar whispered. "Like, now that you're an angel." He reached out under the blankets and touched Rylan's hand. "Just friends. Okay?"

"Just friends," Rylan murmured in reply as he shut his eyes. Hopefully, all the children on the island would look at him the same way as Skylar… as 'just friends'.

CHAPTER EIGHTEEN

Solutions....

"So that makes you sure that it was all planned?" Mykael said, as Cooper completed relating, in some greater detail, the circumstances of how he'd ended up being abducted and how he was also certain that he had, in truth, been sold to the network by his stepfather. "The fact that the man who grabbed you knew the exact password that your stepfather had said that you must always use?"

"Well, I certainly hadn't told anyone about it," Cooper replied a little bluntly. "And Angelo didn't seem at all surprised that I asked for one. He just said, straight away... 'Saskatchewan. Which was where your grandmother on your mother's side was born'. Now, there was absolutely no way he could ever have known all of that, unless someone had told him."

"And his name was Angelo?" Mykael queried, recognising the name from what had been on the later news reports about the alligator attack. Cooper gave a casual shrug.

"Yeah. Only I didn't know that when I was abducted, 'cause he used some other name. I didn't find out his real name until after I was locked up in one of the holding houses and found out that he was one of Vittorio's helpers," he replied rather quietly. "He was also the one who kept saying that he just waiting until he'd be able to... to... you know," he whispered. Immediately dropping his gaze to the floor with some sense of embarrassment.

"Only Vittorio kept saying that he would have to wait until after the night of our special performance… if I wasn't sold at auction. But luckily, that's when you and the other angels rescued us. Like, before anything really nasty had happened."

"So what happened up until that night?" Mykael queried. Cooper cocked his head briefly to one side for a moment.

"Well, most of the time, we just got photographed," he said quietly. "Like, while we had to do a strip tease, or while we were wrestling with each other and stuff like that. Sometimes we also had to act as… as… like waiters. You know, taking small trays of food around so that the clients, as Vittorio called them, could look at us more closely and touch us… which wasn't very nice. But if we didn't do exactly as we were told, we were likely to get paddled in front of whoever it was we were supposed to be 'entertaining'."

"And that was as far as it had got?" Mykael queried. Cooper nodded.

"Yeah, because, as I said earlier, Vittorio wanted about a dozen of us to be, as he put it, 'innocents' for some special secret party that was being arranged. It was where some of us were even going to be auctioned off to people who would want to keep us. Like, as their personal slave. So we'd eventually end up with them doing anything they wanted to us.

"And there wasn't any chance to escape?" Mykael asked. Cooper shook his head.

"Not really," he murmured. "We were usually kept locked up in the basement of houses a long way from any other houses. Like where you found Oliver. And when we travelled anywhere, it was always in the back of trucks and for that we were usually chained up and also gagged, so that we couldn't call out. The onc time Skylar and I managed to get away and find some policemen, we thought we'd be safe. But then some FBI guys turned up at the station and said that they were involved in investigating the case, and that they would take us back to our parents. Instead, when they took us out to their car, Vittorio was already waiting for us. That night, when we were taken back to the basement of the house we were staying in at that time, we got really done over. I think we each got about thirty strokes of the strap while hanging by our arms from hooks on the wall. And it was in front of all the other kids, which made it really embarrassing because we were just wearing these little cotton display pants, that were like the bottom part of a girl's bikini. Vittorio said that our punishment was to serve as a warning to us, and everyone else, not to think that the police would ever be able to help. I couldn't even walk properly for days, afterwards, let alone sit down. Mind you, it wasn't the only time we got strapped. And then for our last few trips we always had to wear those necklace things that would blow our heads off if we tried to escape."

Mykael was quiet for a few moments. Well aware that what had happened to Cooper, and all the others, would not be the only such case of acts of depravity being enacted on innocent children. Even now, other organisations would be indulging in similar criminal trafficking behaviour; moving in to take the place of the Network in exploiting vulnerable children for profit. He was also acutely aware that having changed the fate of this one small group might inevitably lead to awkward questions being asked; particularly of those who had now been returned to their parents. The children who would end up on the island would be in enough isolation to avoid any such problems. And as far as the rest of the world was concerned, in some ways, they would simply cease to exist. Children whose disappearance would always have them listed as unsolved cases. For those who were not, however, there would always be the inevitable curiosity as to exactly how they had escaped. Questions that the media and other curious people would ask about… who had rescued them? And how? Who had abducted them? And where they'd been held for the past few weeks or months? And, inevitably, where they'd been in the time between their rescue and their eventual return to their parents? The timing of the rescue and their return home still left more than two full days to be accounted for, and questions were already being asked, in the media, about the strange necklaces and ankle chains that had been found in the truck at the centre of the 'alligator incident'. It wouldn't take too much scrutiny for the two events to be linked, even if just tentatively. Then, given the importance of the people involved in the 'incident' at the entertainment venue, a whole political storm could possibly erupt, keeping the events in public focus for months.

He sighed softly. It was just to be hoped that the children would keep their promise not to mention angels; that they would continue to say that they didn't really know how it had all happened. To repeat the fabrication that they had simply fallen asleep while chained up in the back of a truck and on a long journey, and then awakened, at some later stage, to find that some undercover police action group, acting on the advice of a private investigator looking for Rylan Daniels, had rescued them.

"Well, given that it seems you're still not all that keen to ever go home, I've arranged for you to be adopted by one of the families on the island," he eventually said.

"Like, I'll be with Tris and Rylan and Lara?" Cooper eagerly asked. Mykael gave a quick shake of his head.

"Well, not in their house. That won't be possible. But one of the other families on the island, the Davies, have said that they will be happy to take you on," he casually explained. "They already have three children, all about your age, or a little younger… two girls and a boy. Their names are called Rachael, Victoria and Finn, so I'm sure you'll fit in very nicely. There will also be two other children living in the same house and you'll be able go to school where you live."

"What about Tris and Rylan and… and Lara? Cooper quickly asked. "Will I still see them?" Mykael gave a quick nod of his head.

"Of course," he replied. "They'll be living in one of the other cottages on the island and their parents will be your teachers."

***

Mykael took Noah quietly to one side. While most of the children, who'd been held by the Network, obviously knew of the nasty instance of abuse he'd suffered, it seemed best not embarrass him unnecessarily.

"Given that your parent's seem quite reluctant to have you back, it has been arranged that you will be adopted by Mr and Mrs Watters and will live in the village…"

"So I won't be with the others? Like, on the island?" Noah quickly interrupted, his eyes quickly beginning to well just a little with tears. Perhaps wondering if the extra abuse he'd suffered might be responsible for his isolation." Mykael quickly put an arm around his shoulders to draw him in close.

"Of course you will," he hastily reassured him. "But, because you will possibly need a few discreet medical checkups for a few weeks, I feel that your being in the village, at least for weekends, will enable you to be seen by Peter McCormack, without it being too obvious to the rest of the village that it is for anything other than just a friendly visit."

"So what happens during the week?" Noah quietly asked, feeling just a little unsure of exactly what was being offered.

"For most of each week, you will be on the island, with the other children," Mykael explained. "Each Sunday night, Steve Robertson will pick you up in his boat and take you over to the island; or if the weather's too rough to risk taking out the boat, then either myself or Andrew will arrange to get you to the island, so that you will be able to go to school, just as would be expected, on Monday morning. During the week, you will stay overnight in the big house with all the other children, which will also include Persia, Cooper and Skylar. That means you will remain on the island until after school finishes on Friday, when you will return to Mr and Mrs Watters for the weekend, unless of course, there are some other special events happening on the island that you might like to attend. That way, while you are in the village, you'll be able to have any medical checks that you might require and it will all be quite discreet. Understand?" Noah nodded a cautious reply.

"So, is there something really wrong with me?" he quietly asked. "You know, as a result of..." He didn't continue, somehow sensing that Mykael would be already well aware of the likely extent of the abuse he'd suffered.

"Probably not," Mykael replied. "But it wouldn't hurt for that whole situation to be kept an eye on for a few weeks, just in case you may have picked up some small infection." He felt reluctant to mention the possibility of more serious problems such as hepatitis C, herpes, or even an HIV infection. "There is also the added protection in that, with Mr Watters having being a police officer of quite high rank, he would have some serious clout, for want of a better word, if your family ever decided to try to create problems for you. That is, presuming that you might wish for them to know where you are?"

"No! No way," Noah hastily replied. "If Mom and Dad were going to be stupid enough to try to blame me for being abducted, then I doubt that anything would change if I was living at home. Now knowing what they think, no matter what I said, it would still just end up being all my own fault."

"Okay," Mykael said, giving a knowing nod of his head. "Now, how about I take you to meet your new parents?" He reached out to grasp Noah's hand, and then paused. "Oh, and before I forget…" He quickly pushed up the left sleeve of Noah's T-shirt and placed a hand over the Network branding. For an instant, Noah felt a slight tingling. Then, as Mykael removed his hand, he looked down in astonishment. There was no sign of the N inside a circle.

"We certainly don't need that mark reminding you of things you'd be best to forget," Mykael murmured. "Now let's go and meet a few people."

An instant later, Noah found himself in an upstairs room of another building; a room that was obviously some form of family area. For a moment he felt quite disorientated and a little weak at the knees. Mykael quickly put out an arm to steady him; the touch seemed to immediately give him a small surge of energy.

Noah gave a slow shake of his head. Instantaneous teleportation was still something that he was not yet able to fully comprehend; particularly how, on the first occasion it had occurred, when he'd been rescued from being chained up in the back of the truck, he'd awakened to find he was in a nice comfortable bed and that almost a full day had elapsed. And yet, on this occasion, it seemed no time at all had passed and that, apart from a slight dizziness, he didn't even feel all that tired.

"You will be more fatigued later on," Mykael whispered, appearing to understand his puzzlement. "Let's just say that I wanted you to be fully awake to meet you new caregivers, rather than having you wake up, once again, in a strange bed, not knowing where you were."

"The farm and Tris's grandparents were okay," Noah quietly replied as he looked around the room. "And certainly much better than when I was abducted and woke up on a dirty mattress on a concrete floor in the basement of a house; wearing just my soccer shorts, and with my hands and feet tied behind my back."

"Okay, let's go through to the next room and meet your new caregivers," Mykael continued, directing Noah down the hallway towards what appeared to be bedrooms. Turning into the first room, Noah found two people waiting with welcoming smiles. It appeared they'd obviously been expecting his imminent arrival, given the way the woman was still carefully straightening a few items on the dresser; although to be honest, Noah wasn't quite sure whether that was truly the case, or not.

"Well Noah, we've set this room up as your bedroom," the man said, indicating towards the bunk level bed, a work-desk with a brand new computer and other equipment. "There's also an extra bed that folds down over your work-desk, for if you want to have any of the children from the island staying over at any time. There's also a further pullout bed that slides out of the way under your own bed, if you want more than one friend staying over. And as for anything thing else you feel you might need, you only have to ask." He turned to indicate the woman standing next to him.

"And to get the introductions out of the way, this is my wife, Alice, and I'm Colin. It would be nice if you could see us as being Mum and Dad, but if you feel more comfortable with just Uncle and Auntie we'll understand." Noah hesitated for a moment, and then looked around the room. At home, he'd always had to share a room with a much older brother, with his two younger brothers sharing the next room. A bossy sibling who'd usually relegated him to just a single bed in the corner, seemed to always resent his presence, and certainly never allowed him any serious time on their 'shared' computer.

"I think I will like being here very much," he quietly replied. "And I'll try to remember to make it Mum and Dad, if that's what you would prefer." He glanced towards Mykael, as if for approval, and then, a little tentatively, moved close enough for Alice Watters to gather him into an embrace.

"We'll also be arranging for the doctor to visit you here, if needed," she whispered. "Just so that you don't feel too awkward about people seeing you having to go up to him for checkups. Most of the people in the village will then just think he's calling in for a drink, or to see us."

"And tomorrow, we'll do a special shopping expedition into Erinsmuir to buy you some more clothes," Colin Watters added. "We've already got pyjamas that will fit you and a good stack of fresh underwear, but I'm sure you'd like to choose your own jumpers, jackets, trousers, and such."

"That would be really nice," Noah murmured shyly. "I didn't usually get too much choice in buying clothes. It was usually just 'hand-me-downs' from my brother... or my parents just bought stuff and made me wear it."

***

Skylar watched as the helicopter landed. Nervously waiting to see how his mother had coped with the trip across most of the USA as well as the Atlantic, but well aware that it would be best to let the medical personnel do what they needed to do, without interference. His interest heightened as the side doors slid open, two of the crew jumped to the ground and then began to manoeuvre the gurney on which his mother lay, held in place by soft leather straps, out onto the helipad. Skylar felt slightly relieved, and wiped at the tears that had welled in his eyes, as his mother eventually seemed to spot him and gave him a tentative wave.

Mykael had made arrangements for his mother to spend her last few weeks on the island, quickly realising that having to transport Skylar to Orange, Texas, every couple of days to visit with her, would not only be inconvenient, but would also raise too many questions as to how he was getting to and from the hospital and whereabouts in Orange he was staying. More especially if there was obviously no one else at the trailer park to look after him.

Given that all the medical equipment that had once been brought to the island for Taylor, after his hang-gliding accident and for Tris, after his exorcism, had simply been put into careful storage when it had no longer been required, it had simply been a matter of re-setting it up in Taylor's old bedroom and then checking that everything still functioned properly.

The choice of using the Houseman's cottage, where Jamie and Mattie Ryan now lived, had been decided on, because it would also allow room for Skylar to stay overnight with his mother, if he so desired. It also meant that Jamie Ryan would also be available to keep an eye on matters. Kate Ferris would obviously still be 'on-call' if needed and Peter McCormick had been asked to make daily visits, and even stay on the island, if and when required.

Following after the medics, as they wheeled the gurney from the helipad in the direction of the cottage, Skylar moved a little closer. A part of him just wanted to run over and put arms around her, but he realised that he should still wait until everything was set up properly and his mother was comfortable. He suddenly started as a hand was gently placed on his shoulder.

"Just let them get her settled," Mykael murmured. "You'll soon be able to spend as much time as you want with her." Skylar nodded. "At least, until..." Mykael added, leaving the statement unfinished.

"I know," Skylar whispered, as tears again welled in his eyes.

"And much as you'll want to spend time with her, over these next few weeks, it will also be good to let her have some time to rest," Mykael quietly advised. "And for you to realise that you still have a life to live."

"So how long has she got?" Skylar asked as he turned and cuddled himself against the guardian angel. Mykael carefully enfolded the boy within his arms.

"The hospice suggested maybe a month," he replied. "When it does happen, and tough as it may be to be without her at first, you will still have plenty of people to support you, and Rowanne to act as the mother you may need."

"And what will happen with everything back in Orange?" Skylar murmured. "You know… like, afterwards?"

That's already being taken care of," Mykael replied. "Everything that won't be needed, like furniture, your mother's car and so on, has already been sold or donated to charity. The more personal items of your mother's are also on their way here and her bank accounts have been transferred into accounts in your name, with all of it to be overseen by Steve Robertson, until you turn eighteen. That has been done to ensure that your father can make no claims whatsoever on your mother's estate; such as the money your mother still had set aside from the sale of your house in Oakton and the money from the sale of personal items from the trailer. As far as he will ever know, you and your mother no longer exist."

"What about payment for her being here?" Skylar asked. Mykael gave his shoulders a slight squeeze.

"It's all covered," he replied. "All medical costs… everything. So don't you worry your pretty little head about it." He paused a moment, and then put a hand under Skylar's chin to ensure he had the boy's complete attention by meeting his gaze. "When your mother does pass over, we will also arrange for her to be buried on the island. Most probably, next to the old church where there is already a graveyard. When that happens, just remember that you will have lots of support to help you get through it." He looked towards the Houseman's cottage and then took Skylar's hand. "Now, how about you and I go and see how your mother is settling in?"

"Can I take Rylan to see her later?" Skylar quietly asked. Mykael gave a small nod of his head.

"I'm sure that will be possible," he said as they approached the front door to the cottage, which was still open. "But let's just take things slowly… one thing at a time."

CHAPTER NINETEEN

Finalities....

"Well, you are still around," the woman at the door to the St Joseph's Homeless Shelter softly commented, with some hint of surprise, as Rylan, followed by Tris and Lara, wandered in from the street. Andrew, still in a state of invisibility, followed after them. Content to let them deal with the situation, given that there was now little chance of any threat to their wellbeing. "Big Hattie will be pleased to know you are safe. She's been more than a mite worried about you, ever since Dumper told her that you'd disappeared off the radar, so to speak."

"Is she in?" Rylan quickly asked. The woman nodded.

"Try the kitchens," she suggested. "They'll probably still be clearing away all the breakfast leftovers and starting to get lunch sorted. Rylan gestured for Tris and Lara to follow him, as he quickly headed for the kitchens.

Mama Hattie was sitting at the large table in the centre of the room, busily peeling potatoes. She looked up at the sound of them entering.

"Oh my goodness," she exclaimed, "you're all here." She got up and, as fast as her generous bulk would allow, hurried over to where they were standing and then ushered them towards the privacy of the female sleeping quarters. Once out of sight of anyone other than her three visitors, she grasped Rylan and hugged him.

"I was so worried when Dumper first told me that he couldn't find any trace of you in the tunnels," she murmured. "Especially after old George mentioned that a couple of TakerZ's lot had grabbed you. And they obviously haven't got out of Attica, as yet, because, according to old George, nobody's seen hide nor hair of any of them, all that recently."

"It was a bit nerve wracking being the bait for that," Tris commented. "Like, letting them come after me, not realising it was a trap." Mama Hattie nodded and then turned to Rylan.

"So how did you get away from the people who TakerZ sold you to?" she asked. Rylan smiled.

"They drugged me, at first, but once I came to, I was able to get away quite easily," he eagerly replied.

"And he also helped us rescue a whole lot of other kids who'd been kidnapped," Tris quickly added. "Once he got Skylar to safety, Mykael was able to…"

"Michael?" Mama Hattie interjected, her eyes suddenly wide with astonishment. "You don't mean Archangel Michael?"

"No, no," Tris hastily replied. "As I mentioned last time, this is another Mykael... one not quite so high up. He acts as our guardian." Mama Hattie seemed to nod her head slowly in understanding; perhaps remembering back to that earlier time.

"And you are?" she then asked, turning her attention to the one angel who had not yet spoken.

"I'm Lara," the girl answered. "Rylan's sister."

"Twin sister," Rylan quietly corrected. "That's why the military were after me. Lara got away from them and they thought that if they found me, they could use me as bait to lure her back. They didn't know that I'd also grown wings."

"They were keeping me in a cage," Lara added. "Like, ever since my wings had started growing. Once I was able to 'jump'…"

“Jump?” Mama Hattie queried, perhaps thinking of normal human behaviour.

“It’s sort of a bit like teleporting,” Tris hastily explained. “Only we normally call it ‘be’ing. Like, you can just be where you want to be. He then quickly demonstrated the process by disappearing and then immediately reappearing on the far side of the room, leaving Mama Hattie quite wide-eyed in astonishment. Lara nodded, and then, as Tris wandered back to join them, continued her explanation.

“Anyway, once I managed to get away from them by doing that, I then met up with Tris, who took me to a safe place. After that, we found out that Rylan was somewhere in New York, so that was why Tris came to see you.”

“So how did you two end up getting separated in the first place?” Mama Hattie queried, looking from Lara to Rylan. “Like, if you were twins?”

“We got adopted out to different families, when we were about six,” Rylan said rather softly. “Mainly, because I was going through a bit of a strange phase at the time, and the people who adopted Lara thought I’d probably end up being a bit of problem as I…” The rest of his comment faded to nothing. Nevertheless, Mama Hattie nodded an understanding of what he was reluctant to say.

“And do you still feel that way?” she queried, perhaps remembering how a frightened young boy had shyly confessed his secret to her, after she’d rescued him from the clutches of a well-known pimp; and how she’d realised, even at that time, that he was no ordinary child. Rylan shook his head and then shrugged.

“Not really,” he murmured with some embarrassment. “Now that I’m like this, it’s a bit weird because I’m not sure if I think that way anymore.”

"Well, that's probably for the best," Mama Hattie said, reaching out to draw him in close; one arm around his slender waist. "I'm just glad that you're safe and..." Whatever else she was about to say, was left mute as Cee-Cee entered the room and squealed with delight at seeing Rylan.

"You're safe!" she exclaimed rushing over to give him a quick hug.

"These other two are his twin sister and step-brother, I think," Mama Hattie said. "And like I once told you, they're really special. The three child-angels exchanged a quick glance and then made their wings visible for a few seconds.

"You're angels?" Cee-Cee exclaimed in astonishment. She quickly turned to Rylan. "No wonder you had nothing to confess that time when I hid you in one of the church confessionals, next door."

Rylan gave her a shy smile in return. Knowing that, at that time, he did have things to he could've confessed, not that he was necessarily to blame for any of them, and perhaps not now wanting to revisit the past, and all the things that had gone wrong in his life over the past year or so.

"There's someone else here who'd probably also like to see you, now that you're safe," Mama Hattie murmured. She quickly indicated for Cee-Cee to head to the men's dormitory.

Less than a minute later, Cee-Cee returned, followed at a slower pace by George.

"Well, Rebel, it's good to see that you're safe," he said, as Rylan hurried over to give him a hug. "We were all rather worried for you; even old Alf. Especially after TakerZ's crew turned up and grabbed you. They didn't give me a chance to warn you."

"They're angels," Cee-Cee exclaimed. With a quick look around, Tris, Lara and Rylan again made their wings visible for a few seconds.

"And I've got a safe place to live," Rylan quickly added. "With my twin sister."

"Well, I'm just pleased that you managed to get away from TakerZ," George murmured. "That dude's nasty. Although I ain't seen him around much lately and from what Hattie tells me, you got him and his lot set up in Attica."

"Our guardians decided that they needed to be taught a lesson," Tris explained. "So I had to be the bait for TakerZ's cronies, so that they'd capture me and take me to his hideout. Then the guardians put them in handcuffs and transported them to Attica."

"How do you know Mama Hattie, and why are you living here?" Rylan asked, as soon as Tris had finished. A little curious as to why George had moved to the shelter from his old haunt.

"Because I came looking for you," George replied. "I was worried for you, after that first time that TakerZ had tried to grab you. It didn't take too long for the grapevine to let me know that you'd been seen with Hattie."

"So why didn't you come to find me straight away?"

"Because I knew you'd be safer with Hattie. Then, after TakerZ and his crew started causing problems at the building, I moved in here. Leastwise, until Jakes and NineR grabbed me and took me back there. Which, strangely enough, was when you suddenly reappeared, and they knocked you out with some drug."

"Would you all like to stay for lunch?" Hattie suddenly queried, getting to her feet. "That way you can tell us the whole story while we eat. Ain't going to be almost nobody else in today for lunch, so I can set us up a table a little away from anybody else that does turn up." Tris, Rylan and Lara immediately looked towards the shadowy outline of Andrew, who nodded.

***

Rylan stepped cautiously up to the front door of the house that he'd once broken into, pushed the doorbell, and then took a hurried step back. From inside, he could hear the sound of voices in earnest conversation. He had hoped that, by arriving later in the afternoon, he'd ensured that Marlow, Henry and Thomas would be home from school. Hearing footsteps, he stepped back a little further to be with Tris and Lara. Andrew stayed one step behind them, as if corralling them into one place.

As Marlow opened the door, Rylan quickly stepped forward once again.

"Hi," he said softly, before gesturing a little nervously towards Tris, Lara and Andrew. "Um… may we come in?"

"Of course," Marlow exclaimed. She hastily ushered them inside, and shut the door. At the same time, calling out to let the rest of the family know that Rylan had returned.

"Have you still got…" she whispered leaning in close so as not to be overheard. Rylan nodded and made his wings visible. Marlow glanced at Tris, Lara and Andrew. Perhaps wondering why the other two children didn't seem all that fazed by the sight of Rylan's wings. Having looked towards Andrew for permission, once he gave a slight nod of approval, Tris and Lara also made their wings visible.

"You're all angels?" Marlow gasped, taking a hurried step back. Rylan nodded as Henry and Thomas came hurrying in, followed a moment later by Margaret Fulcher. Almost as one, they all stopped and stared in amazement at the sight of the three winged children.

"There are others like you?" Margaret Fulcher asked, in a statement of the obvious. Nevertheless Rylan quickly nodded.

This is my twin sister, Lara," he said, indicating towards her. "And this is my new stepbrother, Tris," he added, quickly indicated for Tris to step forward. "And this is our Uncle Andrew," he added. "He acts as our guardian when we go visiting."

"And you are all…?" Margaret began, leaving the question incomplete. While Andrew had not bothered to make his wings visible, the answer still seemed obvious.

"Rylan and Lara have been adopted by Tris's parents," Andrew quickly explained, watching as Thomas and Henry seemed to be giving the children's wings some close scrutiny; perhaps curious as to how they could make them simply appear, and disappear, through their clothes. "So they now have a safe place to live, where they can be what they are without any problems. It's a rather secret place," he added before putting a hand on Rylan's shoulder and pulling him in a little closer. "Rylan has been through some difficult times, as you may already know, but will now be able to grow up in a proper, caring environment. He wanted to come and thank you, however, for helping him when he was out on the streets."

"I'm sorry I ran away," Rylan murmured. "It's just that, I didn't know who I could trust. Like, with people connected to churches, 'cause one church man did some very bad things to me."

"I understand," Margaret Fulcher hastily replied. "But please, all of you, come in and sit down… make yourselves comfortable. James should be home soon and I'm sure he'd also like to know that Rylan now has a safe place to live."

"Can we take them through to the family room?" Thomas quickly asked, looking towards his mother and then to Andrew. "Like, to play games and stuff?" Tris, Rylan and Lara immediately also looked rather earnestly towards Andrew, who responded with a nod.

"If your mother doesn't mind, I'm sure that would be okay," he said with a smile. "I'm sure I can explain everything of what has happened with Rylan to your mother."

"Would you like to stay for tea?" Margaret Fulcher tentatively asked, perhaps not quite sure if angels would eat normal food. Andrew cocked an ear to the happy noises emanating from children as they hurried away; Lara already trailing off after Marlow; Rylan and Tris hurrying after Henry and Thomas.

"If that would not be imposing on you, I'm sure the children would be delighted. It will also give them a little more time to get reacquainted."

"Is… is there anything special that you need?" Margaret Fulcher queried, suddenly feeling just a little flustered. Andrew smiled and shook his head.

"At the age those three are, they still have the normal appetites of most children," he replied. "Including the usual dislike of necessary vegetables, apart from Tris who's a bit of a vegetarian, and a love of too many sweet things. To be honest, given the situation, I'm sure they'll be more than happy with anything you decide on."

***

Rylan leant in close to Skylar for a moment, and then gave him a slight nudge with an elbow.

"It's a good thing I'm not seriously gay, anymore, and desperately in love with you," he jokingly murmured, looking around at the other children seated at the various tables in the swimming pool complex or splashing about in the water.

"Why?" Skylar quietly queried, giving him a rather puzzled look. Rylan glanced around the tables once again and grinned.

"Because, if I was, you'd have some serious competition," he whispered half-jokingly. "What with Mattie Ryan being here, and Tris. And Carwyn and Cooper are quite cute as well. Especially in their speedos."

"You'd have to prise Mattie away from Melanie with a crowbar, first, by the look of things," Skylar murmured. "And Tris would probably be totally off-limits; what with being your step-brother. Anyway, he seems quite taken with Lara. So that would just leave me, Cooper and Carwyn. And Noah, of course… And we're just friends. Right?"

"So you mean that I would have to go after Cooper, Noah or Carwyn?" Rylan teased, grinning broadly.

"However, you don't have those sort of feelings anymore. Remember?" Skylar replied, playfully slapping the back of Rylan's hand in mock admonishment… the sound a little louder than they'd expected within the confines of the pool complex. An action that, firstly, caused the other children nearby to look around in their direction and, secondly, for Skylar and Rylan to suddenly burst into a fit of giggles.

"It's good to see you both so happy," a voice from behind them suddenly said, startling them both just a little. Immediately feeling just a little embarrassed that their amusing conversation may have been overheard, they turned to see Mykael with a hand on the back of each of their chairs. They'd not noticed him arriving.

"We… we were just joking about, who Rylan would want out of Cooper, Noah and Carwyn. Like, if he still wanted a boyfriend," Skylar laughed. "Not that he really has those sort of feelings anymore."

Mykael quickly glanced down towards Rylan.

"So you feel it was just a phase you went through?" he quietly queried. Rylan gave a casual shrug of his shoulders.

"I don't really know," he murmured a little embarrassedly. "It's more that I don't have any… any… any of those thoughts anymore. Not about boys, or girls. I mean, we were just joking about which boys I thought looked cute, but I don't want to do anything with them. Well, not like that, at any rate. I just want them to be my friends."

Well, you should just treat them that way yourself," Mykael suggested. "Be friendly, and be a boy who can be trusted." He quickly turned to Skylar. "Now, I have good news for you. As Mr and Mrs Davies had already volunteered to adopt Cooper, you will be staying permanently with Mr and Mrs Dunn, who are Carwyn and Melanie's parents.

"Well, what about Persia and Noah?" Skylar asked, looking across to where they were sitting, side by side.

"Persia will still be living with Mr and Mrs Ferris and Noah will continue to stay with Mr and Mrs Watters, over in the village. Like now, however, he will only be there for weekends. For most of the week, including nights, he will be staying in the big house with you, Carwyn and Melanie. That's so he can be here for school."

***

Tris stood watching as James Martin carefully tried to help Rylan get over his fear of floating, unaided, in water. It was a slow process, simply because Rylan seemed to have an almost irrational fear of his head going under, and would, even after a few seconds, reach out in desperation for the safety of his tutor, or whoever, or whatever else was at hand to support him.

While, it had turned out that Lara had had quite a bit of swimming tuition when she was younger, so was quite adept at swimming a number of strokes, Rylan's parents, by contrast, had made no such efforts. His mother often writing notes to have him excused from the school pool on some slight pretext or another; usually because she felt he desperately wanted to avoid being bullied in the changing rooms; or in the pool, itself. Having endured numerous instances, during the few times when he had got into the pool, of being pushed under or dunked, in a semi-playful, yet quite callous, bullying game of 'drown the homo', Rylan had been equally pleased for any excuse to avoid being in the pool; a situation that simply resulted in even more teasing. Not that his mother had bothered to take his side against his father when the abuse had got really bad!

"I don't know why he's so scared?" Lara sighed, as Rylan again splashed out desperately for the safety of the pool surround; his eyes wet with what was clearly not pool water. "It's not as though Mr Martin would ever let him drown."

"Sometimes there are things happening inside our heads that, for some reason, we can't fully understand," Tris replied thoughtfully. They continued watching as James Martin carefully hoisted Rylan up out of the water so that he could sit on the pool surround.

"I think that's enough for one day," he murmured. "We can try again, tomorrow." He looked towards Tris, who hurried over to drape a towel around Rylan's shoulders.

"Come on," Tris murmured, urging Rylan to his feet and in the direction of the boys' changing room. "You may as well get out of your speedos and into something warmer. Then we can shoot home and see if Mum's got some hot chocolate, or something."

"How can I get over being so scared?" Rylan queried as they began to enter the boys' changing rooms. "I don't know why, but I just feel…" He left the comment unfinished. Still unsure what particular fear it was that made it impossible for him to relax in the water and just float.

Maybe Mykael can help," Tris replied. "We could ask him tonight. Like, after tea. He might know if there's some reason why you're be so scared. And then maybe you and I could also do some extra sessions to help you gain confidence."

"You won't get angry if I grab out at you? You know, like I tend to do with Mr Martin?" Rylan cautiously asked as he began to remove his speedos. Using his wings for a bit of extra modesty, even 'though he was in a cubicle with the doors closed. Feeling a little worried that the possibility of his grabbing at his stepbrother, even in the pool, might be taken the wrong way.

"We're brothers," Tris casually replied. "And friends who are boys. Why should that be a problem? I'll just be helping you learn to swim!"

***

"I hear Noah's invited Cooper to stay over in the village, this weekend," Rylan said quietly, glancing over towards the village's watering hole, as he and Skylar wandered through the village, clutching their new guitar cases. They were heading back down towards where the boat was moored, having made the trip to Erinsmuir on the bus, under the chaperoning of Andrew, to choose their new instruments. Skylar's new instrument was, in fact, actually a bass guitar.

An idea they'd formed over the last few days of being on the island was that, if they made some good progress together and then included Tris on keyboards and someone like Finn, Noah or Cooper on drums, they could start their own rock band. Eventually adding Carwyn on alto saxophone, Victoria on flute, and Persia or Melanie as a lead vocalist. They both had good voices... although Persia's had more of a rock feel about it. Matthew had also already indicated that he might be interested in taking on a brass or woodwind instrument, as well as continuing with his piano lessons. Whether it was to be a woodwind or brass, he wasn't too fussed... just as long as it wasn't the trombone! Or a euphonium! ...even if he could possibly use the latter to imitate ships' foghorns of foggy days. His current preference seemed to be for soprano saxophone to compliment Carwyn's alto. Skylar nodded in response.

"He also invited me," he murmured. "He said that his new mum and dad… like Mr and Mrs Watters, said that he could have two or three friends over from Friday night until Sunday evening. In fact, any weekend that he wants to have a sleepover. I think it's so that Noah doesn't feel too isolated on weekends. You know, with him having to come home to the village while all the rest of us stay on the island."

"Do you want to go?" Rylan asked just a tad tentatively. Skylar pursed his lips a little and shrugged his shoulders. Actions that seemed to imply that somehow he thought the sleepover idea might be a bit of fun.

"You could always come too," he eventually suggested. "If your mum and dad, and your guardians, don't mind. I'm sure the Watters would have room for you. After all, Noah sort of said, when he asked me… 'the more the merrier'. And if there wasn't a spare bed… well you and me could always share." He leant over and gave Rylan a slight nudge with his shoulder. "After all, it's not as if that hasn't happened before."

EPILOGUE

"We really need to have a talk about your future," said Mykael rather quietly. He indicated for Rylan to have a seat, beside him, on the front pews of the church.

"I want to stay with Lara," replied Rylan a little tentatively. Feeling that, despite Amanda and Joshua's repeated assurances that his orientation did not matter to them, like the Holts, they might prefer to not have to deal with a boy who might still turn out to be of 'different' orientation eventually going through adolescence.

"That won't change," Mykael quickly reassured him. "Tris's parents have clearly stipulated that they are more than happy to have you staying with them. And you certainly won't have been the first boy to arrive on this island in the wake of rumours of being gay. And, for that matter, I'm not just talking about Matthew Ryan. There have been others. Even Tris went through a period of rather strange behaviour. Although that was more the temporary influence of a turned angel who tried to take him over."

"Turned angel?" Rylan hastily queried.

"An angel who is working for the 'dark side'... to use a modern film reference," Mykael quickly explained. "A deviant angel who likes to coerce people into doing bad things to hurt other people. Very much as was enacted upon you by Pastor Isaac and your father. And for all the other children we rescued, by Vittorio and his ilk. It's highly likely that a turned angel was controlling those people in some way."

"So they can make us do bad things?" Rylan asked a little nervously.

"Sometimes," Mykael replied. "And sometimes they act on the people around you. Much as your father did to you, and Matthew's stepfather did to him by constantly impressing on him the idea that he wasn't normal. Thankfully, after some awkward times when he was still a bit unsure of himself, Matthew Ryan now seems to have found companionship with Melanie. Likewise, Tris now seems to have taken quite a shine to Lara. Perhaps more than as just an adopted sister, if you catch my drift. He did, at some time in the past have issues similar to you. Not that he ever thought of himself as being 'gay'. It was simply the deviant actions that Ahaitan forced on him."

"Ahaitan?" Rylan queried. Mykael nodded.

"He was a particularly nasty turned angel who tried to take over Tris's mind, by suggesting all sorts of nasty things that he should do with the other children."

"Such as…?"

"Well, we needn't to go into the details of all that, because it wasn't Tris's true behaviour. In fact, for most of the time, he didn't even realise what he was doing… or saying. But, nevertheless, it did cause him major acceptance problems, for a while. That's how he became involved with rescuing Matthew."

"So, you think that a turned angel may be what's made me…?" Rylan quietly asked, leaving the complete question unsaid.

"Possibly. Although, as happened with Matthew, I feel that the bad influences on you, the actions of your father and Pastor Isaac and, in particular, what happened to you at the boot camp, have not helped you to properly understand your own feelings," Mykael replied, thinking back to the uneasy feeling both he and Tris had noticed in the 'containment' room at the church camp. "It's more than possible that that is where the 'turned-angel' influence has been. But getting back to matters in hand, I know you feel that, as we spoke about the other day, you don't really have feelings either way, anymore. But that doesn't mean that the situation might change. If it does, it might be best for you to come and talk with me about it. Understand?" Rylan nodded.

"Like, if I suddenly had feelings for one of the other boys… like, Cooper or Carwyn or Noah or… or Skylar, that was possibly more than just us being friends?" he whispered. "Or maybe even Tris?" He dropped his eyes to the floor in embarrassment as his voice almost tailed off to nothing.

"It doesn't really matter who it might be; it's just important for you to be able to recognise the signs," Mykael replied. Watching as Rylan looked down at his hands. Something in the boy's manner seeming to indicate that he might just have some vague feelings for his new angel brother. Although, perhaps it was just that he was feeling a little wary of doing something, or making a comment, that might just be taken the wrong way.

"I think I used to have a bit of crush on Matthew," he eventually sighed. "At that time, I used to think… maybe I hoped, that Mattie also, sort of, liked me a bit. Not that he ever made it all that obvious. He was just very quiet and shy. I suppose, it was bad enough that I was so obviously mixed up. More especially with the way I ended up being treated by most of the other kids. They would've given him hell if they'd ever thought that we were an item… like, that he was my boyfriend." He gave a slightly resigned shrug. "But he seems to have changed, now. He and Melanie seem rather close." Mykael gave a slight nod of his head.

"He does seem to have made his choice,' he said, softly. "As for you, it really all depends on what you want to be?"

"Like, whether I'm an angel or not?" Rylan queried, almost with a sense of... 'of course I want to stay as an angel'. Mykael quickly shook his head.

"That's not going to change," he replied. "I was actually thinking more along the lines of you as a person." Rylan suddenly looked rather puzzled.

"I don't get it," he said softly. Mykael turned to the side and took the boy's hands in his own, forcing Rylan to also turn to look directly at him.

"What you may not realise is that, the confusion you've felt about yourself, these last few years, is not uncommon for boys," he said with a knowing nod of his head. "Unfortunately, as I said a moment ago, with having been fostered by William Daniels, you ended up with someone who decided to take a very nasty advantage of that possible confusion. Now that you're here, on the island, you can start your life in a totally new way. Whatever you want it to be."

"And you can help me with that?" Rylan cautiously queried. Mykael gave a quick nod of his head.

"It still has to be entirely your decision," he said, reassuringly. "You can even stay exactly as you are... if that's what you'd really prefer."

"The difficulty is that, since I've got my wings, I don't really seem to think about that sort of thing all that much," Rylan murmured. "Like, whether I like girls or boys. I mean, I really like having Skylar as a close friend, and all the other children are pretty friendly towards me. It's just that, even if I feel that Carwyn, Finn, Noah and Cooper are cute, I also tend to think Rachael and Persia are pretty cute as well. And Lara, even 'though she's my sister. But, beyond that, I just don't know."

Mykael smiled and nodded his head rather knowingly. It was likely that Rylan's continued development as an angel would eventually result in him not having strong sexual feelings either way; the same as would also eventually happen with Tris and Lara. Friendships would certainly develop, but like with the seven previous child-angels, they were all most probably destined for a celibate life.

"Well, there's no need to rush things," he said almost casually. "Just don't ever be afraid to come to me, if you start to feel unsure about things. I can help sort things out for you, you know."

***

Tris alighted and wandered around to the side of the church, to where Andrew was busy weeding the flowerbeds. For once he was on his own. Rylan was having extra swimming lessons and Lara was off with Persia, doing some baking under the watchful guidance of Grandma Evelyn.

"Problems?" Andrew said as he tossed a few weeds into the bucket sitting on the grass close to where he was kneeling. Tris gave a quick shake of his head.

"Not really," he murmured. "I just wanted ask you something."

"Like what?" Andrew asked, rocking back onto his haunches, expectantly. Perhaps expecting some question of extreme importance.

"The first time I met Momma Hattie, she called Rylan her little 'Milky Bar Kid'. I just wondered what a Milky Bar was?" Tris asked. Andrew laughed a little in response to the query.

"It's a bar of white chocolate," he replied with a smile. "And I haven't had once since I was little. They used be on sale in New Zealand and Australia and the promotion always featured a picture of a very blonde-headed kid dressed as a cowboy. Probably still does. Hence the name."

"Really?" Tris queried.

"Really," Andrew replied, getting to his feet. Having peeled off his garden gloves, and dropped the trowel he'd been using into the bucket, he put an arm around Tris's shoulder.

"How about you and I make a little trip to New Zealand to get some?" he suggested. "If we bring back a couple of dozen, everyone can try one. I doubt even Rylan knows what they really taste like."

TRIS GENEALOGY #3

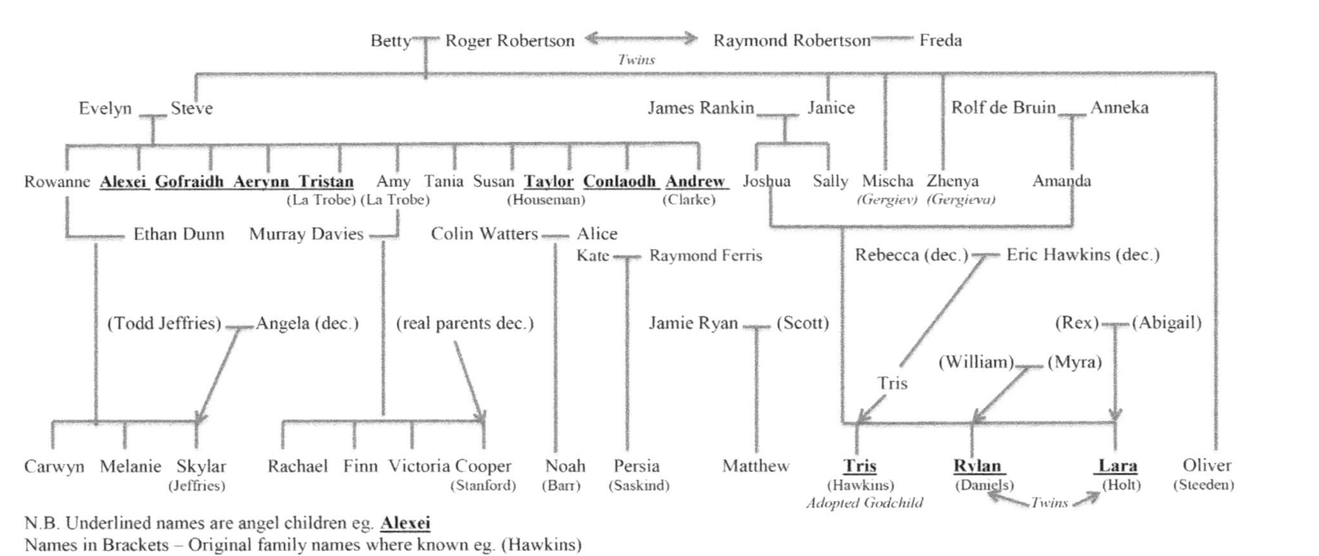

N.B. Underlined names are angel children eg. **Alexei**
Names in Brackets – Original family names where known eg. (Hawkins)
dec. = deceased
Sets of Twins = Roger + Raymond, Alexei + Gofraidh, Aerynn +Tristan, Taylor + Conlaodh, Rylan + Lara

Tris 4 – 'Hidden Dangers'

by Morgan Bruce

The fourth installment of the intriguing new sequel to the 'Alexei' series... aka 'The Angel heptalogy'

Having survived the clutches of Ahaitan, brought down the evil-doing of his manipulative uncle and found two new angel-children – twins Lara and Rylan – Tris and all the new children on the island set off on an extended holiday to the USA.

Anxious to avoid the intrusive paparazzi, who immediately start to follow such a wealthy family as the Robertsons, becoming intrigued as to why some of the children cannot be photographed, Mykael reluctantly allows Tris, Lara and Rylan to do their own sightseeing, away from the rest of the family. At first, while in New York, they simply visit the people who'd helped Rylan when he was on the run, but eventually visit a few places that would be best avoided. This includes Pastor Isaac's church camp, where they unwittingly attract the attention of a turned angel, who then decides to cause them problems. When Rylan is attacked while on a sleepover away from the island, Mykael then puts into operation a plan to eliminate this threat to their future. Unfortunately, it also involves the considerable risk of using the three angel children as 'bait' to lure in their antagonist.

A SKIP IN TIME

by Morgan Bruce

When Martyn Brooks awakes one morning to find himself in a totally unfamiliar world, it's just the start of a nightmare day. Admittedly, he is still in the same bedroom, in the same house that he's always lived in, but, somehow, it's all changed.

The immediate sense of bemusement he feels at the change in his surroundings then escalates, when a strange woman opens the door and demands that he get out of bed, in order for him to not miss the bus for school… along with the threat that, his failure to do so will result in his having to deal with his father, later, over being disobedient.

Even the fact that he should have to go to school immediately has him puzzled because, as far as he understands, it's 2012 and a teacher-only day before the start of the April school holidays. As he dresses for school the puzzlement increases. For some reason, even his uniform is different. He now has a black shirt instead of white? And since when did he have to wear a cap?

A short while later, after coming to realise that the rest of his house is also strangely changed, and he now has a younger sister, he finds himself wandering across the road to a bus stop. Another boy is waiting there who, it seems, is his new younger brother.

The trip to school through changed streets, and a glance at a morning newspaper, however, soon brings further startling revelations. It's Friday, April 13th, 1962. In some totally unfathomable way, he has managed to jump back fifty years in time.

With no clue as to how he can return to his proper time, Martyn is about to realise that he has awakened into a nightmare existence; a day of tribulations and sufferings that will, however, eventually lead to the solving of a fifty-year-old mystery.

Review Requested:

We'd like to know if you enjoyed the book.
Please consider leaving a review on the platform from which you purchased the book.

Lightning Source UK Ltd.
Milton Keynes UK
UKHW012308290721
388013UK00001B/103